TALBOTT STREET

By

Hutton Hayes

Cover art courtesy of Indiana Historical Society

ISBN: 0-75961-884-4

This book is printed on acid free paper.

1stBooks - rev. 03/23/01

For Raul, with love

through what
uncharted galaxy
do we venture
eyes closed
hearts open
arced as we are
in the great ellipse
of love?

Jonathan Randolph Thayer

PROLOGUE

Indianapolis, December 1991

That we are periodically impelled to the outermost extremity of our emotional limits is a commonplace recognition of our fragile humanity. And grief defies the rules of logic, shrouding reason with visceral debris and other such offerings from the metaphorical heart. Such are the messages delivered by this mad mad month of December following the death of my dearest friend from complications associated with AIDS.

Not long after having arrived in this city for a second time an inner voice began to take on harder tones, to employ harsher tactics, in its quest to force my exit - to boot my ass out, you might say, out and far away - suggesting that only more grief might lie in wait around the blind corner. I soon became victim to its relentless power - a knotted stomach, a quickening pulse and a tight-throated chord linking both to other forms of wordless fears. If I'd taken heed of this voice I would have left immediately following his death, wildly grabbing my flight bag as I blindly ran away. That has been my method, my always predictable ploy. Run, run, run, run, run. Yet, another voice, more soothing and passively calm, only today has begun to suggest otherwise. So I wait for the battle to end.

Odd, witnessing the dissolution of the tiny weak transient thing we call mortality. My bereavement has given me a slow learner's glimpse of an extraordinary man's solitary end: the pure neutral truth of the dreadfully infinite thing - death. I'm haunted by nothingness, the vacuum of his absence from tomorrow. Yes, he's dead and gone now, untouchably displaced from our cozy continuum of space and time, but oh how easily I'm able to recall the sweet fading tenor of his soft sick voice. It's been a week now, and that voice still resonates within as his memory reconnoiters about these cold, gray December days.

We've parted for the third and final time, and the presently unbearable thought of his absence moves me to begin to fix in mind's eye his face and manner and voice and thought. His history. Ah! He would've laughed at that one. He ridiculed, always with significant humor, my need to summarize, encapsulate, derive meaning from given physical facts. That marks the continual point of contention, the tense cold place of our invariable difference. It is the exquisitely crafted rift which erupted between us throughout the many years of our friendship, and as I reflect upon that friendship I find that the sometimes great distances cast between us (geographically, emotionally) were the product of a single temperamental difference. While I habitually soared upon a flimsy carpet of abstractions he happily anchored his feet below. As a result I remain intrigued by the possibilities of lives lived differently. In our case there was between us, always, a remoteness, yet the inarticulate closeness of comparable hearts.

Without question, each successive departure became tougher to take, our farewells harder to bear. We met at college, Princeton, then parted after graduation in nineteen seventy-seven. He returned to his hometown, Indianapolis. I found a job in D.C. We communicated intermittently, a phone call here, a letter or card there, an occasional telegram. Five years after leaving Princeton, in late nineteen eighty-two, he caught up with me in London, by phone, and invited me to Indianapolis. I accepted, stayed a year and then left under brutally difficult circumstances. I returned to Princeton to teach, and there followed eight years of absence, silence but for a silly annual Christmas card and a telegram announcing the birth of his son. I vividly remember finding the telegram in my mailbox on a bright spring Princeton afternoon. It read: *Nick. I'm a father. A boy. 8 lbs. Charly's well. Love. J.R.*

And then came that awful call just a few weeks back when he asked me to return to help him die. Christ, I couldn't deny him! True, eight years earlier I'd scurried away from Indianapolis leaving a trail scented by anger and heartache and ruin. I'd moved east and left him for dead. Figuratively. He was anything but that, of course, the most animated man I've ever known. Yet I both hated and loved him, and the easiest, most comfortable, tact was to kill his memory. Strangely, I thought of him as dead, yet always presently possible. But now he *is* dead, and my challenge is to disentangle the emotions and assuage the pain while seeking the meaning of the years which were our lives together and apart.

Yet, impregnable walls of anger and fear now separate him from me, and me from you - quite a testament to the powers of this syndrome, perhaps the late-twentieth century's most potent death-stalking metaphor. That's why I'm frightened of meeting it head on, openly. I find it easier to begin with the fact of my friend's death and then to reverse to earlier times, much earlier, before working my way back to the present. True, this method is much easier - yet less noble, cowardly. Still, with death there are no simple narratives. Just memories. And the memories, just now, are pregnant with comparisons, particularly the similarity of my first visit to Indianapolis in December of nineteen eighty-two and this perhaps final return spanning the holiday season of nineteen ninety-one. In fact, when I arrived in Indianapolis just a few weeks ago, just after Thanksgiving, I couldn't help but slide into a gradual sense of *deja vu*. Nine years earlier I'd arrived as winter crept through the Midwest, but I'd come under far different circumstances. In both instances the weather toyed with dull grays and intermittent flurries, yet the funereal atmosphere which surrounds me now in no way mirrors the hope of my first arrival.

While boarding the plane for my recent return flight to Indianapolis, the phone conversation of a week earlier continued to play in my mind, particularly the weakened tenor of his fragile voice and the quivering heaves between his carefully chosen words as he wept. This frightened animal was not the man I'd known and loved, and as the plane swept up into the thinning air I found myself recalling Hamlet's ruminations on the slippery tricks of death:

> *If it be now, 'tis not to come; if it be not to come, it will be*
> *now; if it be not now, yet it will come; the readiness is all.*

Yes, the readiness is all, but neither of us was prepared for what was about to occur. *No more lessons on the meaning of mortality,* I thought. So I spent most of the flight watching the clouds form their eery silhouettes and finished a strong scotch on the rocks only moments before the wheels slid onto the silky tarmac. Unlike my first visit to Indianapolis back in eighty-two, no one met me at the airport. I grabbed a cab as rain fell over the silent city and eventually was delivered to the Indiana University Medical Center. There followed moments of anxious loitering about the hospital halls, interminable moments spent planning an entry of bright smiles and good cheer and a showering of false promises. Then I remembered his sharp sense of observation, penetrating and intense, and knew that he'd spot my obvious trepidation at once.

I circled the exterior of the hospice unit for fifteen minutes as I prepared for the pain, eventually making my way through the the wing housing those fighting through the final stages of disease. Persons with AIDS - PWAs in modern parlance. I hadn't thought to check in for a pass at the guest lobby, nor was I stopped for lack of a pass after I'd entered the unit and had walked past the brightly-lit nerve center of the nurses' station. There, all was chaos. Nurses, orderlies, physicians and administrative staff apparently were scrambling through another run-of-the-mill day, and I seemed to be invisible as I walked past the anarchy of this ghastly three ring circus. Onward, and my eyes played with the vivid scenes of various stages of AIDS-dying while walking past each new room with its inevitably emaciated body - rooms stale and repugnant and reeking of a melange of medicinal efforts, vile fluids, human waste, the odors of death. Room upon room upon room. I can still see the tiled floors, hear vague intercom voices, sense the rush of anxiety and the coming of fear. I was numbed by the possibility of witnessing this slow wicked death beyond the human abstractions which filled the rooms leading to his. I wasn't prepared for him, nor his family, nor the fear, never the death, and when I finally found his room number and slipped beyond the door I don't know which saddened me more - the fact that his violated and shrunken body lay silently alone, or the sight of the monstrous technological contraptions, wires and tubes and plugs and pumps, which were instrumental in adding a few more precious moments to his newly artificial life.

I was stung by the odd mixture of odors in the room, a blend consisting of women's perfume, canned oxygen, musty quarters and the mildly rank odor emanating from the skin of my dying friend. The perfume I recognized at once as the preferred fragrance of his former wife, though nearly every thing else about him and the room remained unrecognizable Walking toward his bed, I began to feel nauseous as the putrid air jabbed hard at me. Shit, perspiration, piss and perfume. Near the window he lay asleep in the room's single bed, tossing fitfully, and I tip-toed closer until my thigh touched the side of the bed as I leaned over him. From that overarching position I took note of the inexorable power of his illness and indisputable fact that he'd prematurely aged, frighteningly so. His once-thick hair was thin and damp, clumps of it matted to his pale forehead. Beads of perspiration surfaced on his face, collected in small pools and then streamed down his creased cheeks and into the linen. His eyes, though closed, signaled pain and discomfort with heavy dark bags and layers of crust, just as the gaunt face gave testament to an incredible loss of weight, creating a sharper jaw line, narrow and weak. His always firm chin jutted outward and up toward me, as if pointing. There were also cracked lips, chapped nose and purplish splotches of Kaposi's sarcoma scarring the balance of his once-fine face. But most frightening of all was the dissonant wheezing sound erupting each time he inhaled, a macabre two-step of mucous and flesh known to the doctors as *Pneumocystis carinii* pneumonia. Living tissue gone awry. There he lay, wasted and worn nearly beyond recognition as his life slipped slowly away, but oh how very different he had appeared when I'd last seen him, and by God oh how differently it had all begun! I walked to the window, thinking of absolutely nothing at all, though at the edge of consciousness I was aware of other sounds creeping into the room as the tiled halls echoed with other frightened voices from otherworldly rooms. Moments later I pulled a chair up to his bed and watched his labored breathing for a long silent stretch of time before I placed my face in my hands and wept.

When I pulled myself together moments later, I leaned back in the steely chair, wiping my eyes, and pulled from a table beside his bed a thick, worn ledger book which upon closer inspection I found to be a journal he'd been keeping. Curiosity trumped guilt as I trespassed into that rarefied land of his private thoughts, casually skimming, reading at length here and there, noting the dates. He'd apparently been keeping the journal for years, though the entries had grown more frequent during the previous few months. And they were eclectic. Part daily diary, part miscellaneous observation, part reminder, part prayer. Scattered throughout were isolated thoughts, a few diatribes, a series of poems. Yes, poems. Christ! He was a banker by trade, anything, frankly, but a poet, and yet, a poet he'd become as death neared. So as I waited for him to stir awake, I read through a portion of the journal written just a week earlier. He'd entitled the section, *Talbott Street: A Gothic Tale*:

You get there, if you wish, from Monument Circle in downtown Indianapolis, that ambiguous mandala of uncertain significance containing, among other urban features, mulch, mortar, memory and modern dreams. Yeah, you begin there and travel north along a path they call Meridian Street, a modest midwestern city's gallant corridor bound, in the beginning, by the riches of the chosen and the few - architects, bankers, developers, lawyers - and there find forbidding doors concealing unknown pleasures within (and beyond which it is said the only sounds which may be heard are meager palpitations of Republican hearts).

With the handful of early blocks which stretch from the Circle northward there evolves a stodgy cleanliness, an odorless neutrality of conservative fibers fusing limestone foundations to the very street. To the west are extravagant hotels, business towers, small jewelers, large restaurateurs, social clubs, insurance companies - American capitalism and its gray drab unharnessable energy stifling the passersby with the infamously uncaring and invisible hand. To the east lies a sullen midwestern irony, a mall and a memorial to remind a forgetful populace of the prices paid in the name of freedom. You find there green grass and green shrubbery and large hardwood trees to soothe the eye and to caress the modern soul. There is, first, University Park and its fin de siecle lamps, slumbering fountain and bronze statues of Abraham Lincoln and Benjamin Harrison. Further north you find the war memorial, a hulking limestone skeleton entombing memories of the anonymous dead. Further still, there is Obelisk Park with its miniature monument `a la Washington and a faceless fountain and perfect walks. The American Legion mall follows with its wide-arced open spaces ending at the public library.

Traveling further north, the once-great Corridor undergoes transition. The street worsens at Tenth where the interstate intersects the downtown arteries. Here, the circulation is poorer, the asphalt cracked, the buildings in the embryonic stages of disrepair. Glancing casually over your shoulder at the Greek revival and neoclassical structures, you now merely note a mass of forgotten plans, nearly chaotic, without focus. The clientele is questionable by the standards of the first Meridian mile, the semi-vacant buildings anonymous in listless stances. Forgotten. There are no great secrets to be found beyond their dour doors, and if there were you'd take little heed, for the powerful secrets lie ahead as the Corridor grows quickly poorer beyond Fourteenth Street and where the pervading sense is uneasy, hard and hateful. Architectural resplendence metastasizes into unforgiving chaos. The broken windows, the abandoned buildings, the rusting cars, the filthy alleys, the porno stores and the girlie houses coalesce into an eclectic menagerie of torn shutters and anxious hearts squealing impenetrable voices into the dark. You see, Meridian loses itself and its past once beyond Sixteenth Street, is fused into blind duration of presence, amnesiac time, and the only glimpse of the former avenue is had by way of imaginative

CAT scans as the skeletons of the doomed structures attest to the heyday of greatness gone by. The past is parodied by ghostly voices from windowless worlds within. Gone, lost, buried. Glancing from side to side you take note of the slow poverty, the shiftless stances and the dubious milieu by now in the full swing of bubbling chaos, and then, as if the embryo of filth and decay had begot what the first Meridian mile would not have - the prodigal urban son - there slides onto the very street the alluring tendrils of a modern netherworld. This is purpose again. Its home is its filth, its need, its anonymity. It is, in its singular manner, as powerful and enticing as that from which you have just come. For, what is power if not the manipulation of need, and what difference exists in the various forms of need if at bottom they fill the coffers of desire?

*In the end, these are matters of taste only. No morality questions here. Meridian north of Tenth and south of Thirty-eighth is merely that which has come before without the designer label. Glancing again from side to side you witness all of the signs. Once beyond Sixteenth on either side of the street you catch sight of whores warming up to their strolls, hustlers strutting their tumescent wares, pimps Cadillac-cruising their changing turf and the lost and the dying peeping from windows to find their patrons in the slit of an eye. It is, this part of Meridian, that which history forgot. While a private and conservative populace turns its face in shame, the shameless do their needed work through the weakened crevices of human guilt. This chapter is torn from the memory book and is swept into the ghetto gutter and down into a sewer's precipitous void. Yes, and further north are the adult communities of carnal responsibility: ingenious pornography, ambiguous perversion, slight filth of the heart and dirt of the street. Foulness is everywhere, and as you come closer to it, not the filth, but **IT**, you sense that this world is defined by a nexus unknown to old-and-near North Meridian - cheap restaurants, dirty lofts, adult bookstores, titty bars, easy pussy, hustler cock, hungry pimps, crazy nymphs, lost souls without hyacinth ... ah, ghouls on a Saturday night!*

When you finally turn east onto Twenty-second, you know you are nearly there. The smell of the neighborhood, the swell of the human eye, the secret flutter of nastiness in the heaving, heavy heart. In the back rooms bordering the area alleys, the real work is done. Pay up front, receive in the rear. East on Twenty-second and past Pennsylvania Street and then you are there. It is so simple, so unpretentious, nearly unnoticeable during the daylight hours when the lifeless marquee isn't lit, yet as with the prophet's inner eye or the poet's silent breath, meaning lies within. The facade is the constant lie, though the heart yet pumps the dreams within. You stand before it, before both the building and the avenue, and you think nothing of the view. They are, both the avenue and the building, named Talbott. Talbott Avenue and Talbott Street. The one as ordinary an avenue as one may find in any slum in America: vacant, anemic, torn, undone. And the bar just another club in another ghetto in another town.

And opaque cosmetics can't quite hide a mid-life crisis visible from unministered roof to stinking sewer. You stand amidst the trash on the walks, glancing north and then south along the avenue. Nothing changes it. No definitions can soothe your uneasiness, your need to make it respectable. So you turn and leave and return only at night.

After placing the journal back on the table, I didn't know whether to laugh or cry, immersed as I was in a wildly emotional passing of *deja vu`*. Those images were, after all, the very images which had emerged during the early days of my first visit back in eighty-two when he'd driven me north on Meridian Street, that highly visible corridor which provides a kaleidoscope of the city's changing face from the civilized attempts of downtown to its seedier, less calculated, underside further north. That's how it once appeared, how it once *could* have been described, Gothic contrivances and all. But like my dying friend, all of that has changed now - the bar, the avenue, the city, its inhabitants. Only memories remain, reminders of the disintegration which I experienced during my first visit to Indianapolis. They are what I seek now. Memories, such as those which might give meaning to time spent in Indianapolis during two visits eight years apart. Memories, such as those which might give meaning to the love I found and lost there. Memories, such as those which might give meaning to this disease which stalks the final two decades of the twentieth century. If such not be the case, what do we make of the vast structure of personal recollection? What shall we do with the essence of the act of retrieving from memory former patterns of thought? If we think and act, must we not also remember? Is memory the bedrock of consciousness?

Ah, but these vague statements compel little sense of feeling in the abstract, and perhaps there is no better way of fleshing out *feeling* than by beginning with that first, titillating image of Talbott Street. Oh sure, I'm still running from his death, and from AIDS. I'm confronting this mess peripherally, aware that the virus attains victory in the very same manner, but my reasons for doing so aren't altogether selfish. I do this for his sake as well, since I prefer not to wrap his memory, just now, in the shroud of death. After all, with him there was always great vibrancy, wit, beauty, and he was a genuinely beautiful man. He who at times I so admired, so deeply loved. So, I'll roam the spectrum of time, running backward and then forward and then backward again. After all, I've spent these last few weeks more nearly in the grip of the confined past than within the soft boundlessness of the ever-moving present. And although this method of the grieving mind tacking from present to past to present again entertains the disadvantage of confusion, I suppose, in the end, that is always the method of our making of meaning. Besides, there's always T.S. Eliot's words to ponder:

Time present and time past

xiii

Are both perhaps present in time future,
And time future contained in time past.
If all time is eternally present
All time is unredeemable.

That is why I'll leave my friend temporarily sleeping toward his anonymous death in an anonymous hospital bed while I settle in to describe what once was. Hold on to that image of *Talbott Street*, on Talbott Avenue. Lest you forget, we arrived there by way of the Circle in downtown Indianapolis. Of course, in order to make that trek you must first travel to Indianapolis. That is your choice, your affair. You get there as you like, but I'll tell you how I arrived.

1

Mobile to Princeton

I came to the whitened midwestern landscape in December of nineteen eighty-two when the roads to the world of insuperable meanings seemed to be leading westerly with the glorification of Ronald Reagan and valley girls and sometimes hip California neuroses. The American world was to some only a film then, and a bad one at that. And how could I have been certain, really, that the alluring cinematic montage and the voluptuous westering cliches were misleading, indeed wrong, and that the loosened trends were not the all and all of the matter? Amid those easy undissected certitudes how was I to know it wouldn't be the West but Indianapolis which would teach me what the remainder of the world could not?

My route to the city they endearingly call, Indy, however, was somewhat circuitous. I came from the sweltering marsh lands of Alabama, Mobile to be precise, where my mother concluded the damp erotic act with the bloody clarity of the febrile womb as she pushed me into the world, a kicking crying stubborn son who killed her with feet and hands and swollen thoughts. Simply, she died while bringing me into the world. With my pink body came an unplugged artery, and the blood we shared was of a consecrated cycle, life to death to life. Our breaths met but for a moment, and then she was gone. So the fates had it in for me; of that for a long while I remained convinced.

I still haven't a clue as to who my father was, nor it seems was my mother certain, and there being no family left to raise me my fate was cast with foster care. I suppose that's why to this day I detest Charles Dickens, not to mention the phrase *cute as the dickens* which was the manner in which many a potential foster parent described me. Still, the foster families were kind enough (no sexual abuse, no physical violence), and my sensitivity to my orphaned status was more or less self-imposed (a couple of bullies notwithstanding). Still, if sadness intervenes before its proper time, before one can rightly assimilate its powerful negative message, one lives reflectively, or so I did. To feel outcast and forlorn in the void of childhood and adolescence, during the critical years where bravado meets discontent, one sometimes is forced into a life of reflection. And in the end I endured the echoes of emotional silence by wrapping myself between the leaves of books, except for those of Dickens. I grew bookishly arrogant, quietly reflective. Then, toward my later teens, I took to planning my escape, since the ambition instilled by the lashings of guilt, along with those damnable books, imparted a need to accomplish something in the name of loving memory. I came to believe that I owed an ambiguous, indeterminable debt to my mother, having

1

willingly accepted my role in successfully purging a human life. So I charted my course, and hoping to find my niche I decided to wander far from Mobile to escape the shadows cast from the morose corners of my mind. And wandering seemed natural by the time I was to leave since I'd traveled from home to home all my life. It was a natural act for a young man finger printed for the death of his mother at every turn, on every page of unredeemable memory which spoke of her. How could I remain to absorb the blame and echoing silence?

So it was that during my senior year of high school I found the time was ripe for separation. I was a brainy, bookish kid heeding the easterly call and prepared to leave Mobile with a scholarship, grant money and meager savings from part-time jobs which would allow me to eke out a poor undergraduate's existence at Princeton. Princeton, you ask? Is that not an odd choice for one not properly pedigreed? Were my Ivy League expectations not a sign of arrogance (an orphan boy from the deep South with patrician aspirations and monied dreams and that sort of thing)? I was warned by counselors that Princeton was elitist and clubby. Perhaps Vanderbilt was a better choice since a family legacy in a club was required if you were to happily succeed at Princeton. Of course, I knew all about the clubs. After all, I'd read all of F. Scott Fitzgerald by the age of seventeen; I knew the club profiles through his protagonist, Armory Blaine - aristocratic Ivy, philandering Cottage, athletic Tiger Inn, literary Quadrangle, prim and proper Cap and Gown. Yes, I knew all about them and the snobbery associated with them just as I'd come to understand the monied, Waspish element which was the cornerstone of the university. But that was all beside the point since clubs were no longer the sort of popular thing they used to be. Besides, I answered, freshmen and sophomores eat in residential dining rooms. So it was that my guilt and I prepared for the prodigal exeunt. And leave I did. In August of nineteen seventy-three I left for Princeton in a flurry of fear and hope, a concoction of duty and desire fused with the congenital dispensation of despair.

*   *   *

Ah yes, Princeton. The university sported a storied past involving the Quakers, the British army, General Washington and the Continental Congress. What better cast might you desire? Washington defeated the British at Princeton and Trenton in 1777, and the little burg served briefly as the nation's capital for five months in 1783. Home of the Continental Congress. Site of a famous Revolutionary War battle. Fertile field of the budding democratic mind.

These facts offered a peculiarly romantic luster to my choice of Princeton, peculiar in that until then I'd remained devoutly nonromantic about such things as place and time. Oh sure, the romance had more than just a bit to do with the curiosities of social maneuvering and the power of money, but the more potent influence was the aforementioned work of F. Scott Fitzgerald. Oh, I agree it was a silly phase, but I was an impressionable kid who'd been caught up in the romantic fervor of *This Side of Paradise* and *The Great Gatsby*. For a short while I identified with *Gatsby's* narrator, a man whose name I shared, and it mattered not at all that the geography was all wrong. I emigrated from the South while Fitzgerald's Nick rolled in off the midwestern prairies, but we shared twin obsessions with the past. Picture it and laugh, but I cried more than once while reading those magnificent lines from *Gatsby: we beat on, boats against the current, borne back ceaselessly into the past.* So, Fitzgerald and his slippery allusive romantic green light pushed me out of the South and into New Jersey, and New Jersey is where I came of age.

My reading had prepared me for what I was about to find, since I'd memorized the University's storied history from the granting of its charter in 1746 to the latest available information on the costs of enrollment. Already, I'd imagined myself studying within the confines of the Woodrow Wilson School, strolling into Whig and Clio Halls to hone my debating skills, romping inside the Charles Caldwell Memorial Field House, drinking wildly on the bleachers in Palmer Stadium, rowing cavalierly over the calm glistening waters of Lake Carnegie and sleeping (if ever the occasion should arise) in one of the Gothic dormitories of the Oxonian-like towered quadrangles. Most importantly, however, I fantasized my arrival at the Fitz Randolph Gateway, that entrance of drab stone and coarse wrought-iron and robust mounted eagles, and eventually ended these reveries before the famous Nassau Hall and its giant phallic cupola. At the time I didn't reflect long enough upon the fact that Fitzgerald's paradise was Jazz Age education, pomp and fluff and circumstance belonging to a long lost period, but that fact was in itself an education to be reckoned with. Yes, much had changed since the days of Fitzgerald, and although Princeton still catered to the rich and a whiff of clubbiness could still be had with any deep breath, in the end I was happy with my dormitory accommodations and non-club food and studious undergraduate life. True, I never found the radiating warmth of the twenties, but I happily settled instead for esoteric poetic secrets, the words of Adam Smith and the long passionate friendship with my buddy, Johnnie R.

And simply stated, it's a continuing wonder to me that we were able to become such fast friends following our inauspicious beginning. You see, I supplemented my meager personal resources and scholarship money with nightly swings in one of the dormitory dining rooms pouring soup into bowls for the rosy-cheeked boys like Johnnie R. who worried not about tuition fees and economic survival. I clearly remember the look of money on his handsome face when, during my first week behind the serving line, he sauntered through with his usual self-assurance while demanding from me an extra piece of perhaps New Jersey's worst fried chicken. Frazzled and short of temper after a day full of such gallantly rude requests I countered by telling him that he could, instead, take the piece I'd just placed on his plate and conveniently, strategically, insert it in such a

3

position within his body so as to make it difficult, if not impossible, to walk erect. He stood back, tense with anger, but soon enough he regained his composure and walked on by, managing a smile. He later came through the line a second time, and before I could make an equally outrageous demand he offered to buy me a beer. Surprised, I accepted. And so began the most extraordinary friendship of my life.

Okay, the guy had it made. His father (Ivy, '39) had sent him off to Princeton with a liberal allowance, a legacy, a corvette and a slightly patrician Hoosier air. The money came from his father's wholly-owned bank in Indy, and the plan was to slowly groom Johnnie R. for the chairmanship of the bank. He willingly obliged. Ah, Johnnie R.: demanding, spunky, energetic, good-humored, self-assured. Intelligent, witty and charming, he was an enigma from the beginning. An only child, he also had lost his mother when he was quite young, but he made little time for grieving and remorse. Perhaps that's why I so easily came to love him, to care for him as a brother might care, the scintillating riddle of his passion and poise teasing me with the fact that he was all I could never be, temperamentally. In the beginning I was infatuated with him, perhaps idolized him; he was the perfect alter ego. The melancholy streak so prominent in my own makeup remained undetectable in him. He was also a man in charge.

"I've got to get back to the dorm right after the game," I said to him one lazy Friday afternoon, months after we'd first met as he and I and some mutual friends walked across campus on the way to a basketball game. "I need to study. I should have studied longer last night."

"Nick, Nick, Nick," he answered. "Such regret in your life. Lighten up. Live for the day. Life's too damned short to entertain such enfeebling emotions."

"No, I mean it," I said. "I need to ace this exam."

"Me too," someone else piped in.

"And me," said yet another.

Johnnie R., leading the pack, stopped abruptly, turned to face us and held his arms out and up so as to block us from passing. We'd had a few beers and laughed at him as he played his game.

"Gentlemen, are you boys or men?" he asked.

"Men!"

"Cool or nerds?"

"Cool!" we played along.

"Sober or drunk?"

"Drunk!"

"Thennnnnnn," he said, leaning ever-so-slightly forward, "Carpe diem!"

"Carpe diem!" we agreed, and Johnnie R. turned to lead us to our destiny, a pack of wild boy-men hunting for adult meaning within the safe confines of the academic world.

4

This guy who had little time for regret, exuded a steady charisma; even had I tried it would've been difficult to dislike him. I was thrown off balance by the combination of his singular good looks and the controlled swash-buckling personality. Like the *raison d'etre* informing the initial in his name he seemed a larger than usual picture of life to a lonely bookish southern kid. His given name was Jonathan Randolph Thayer, but early on in our careers as students he was forced to accept the new appellation, Johnnie R. Several of our dorm buddies went by the common name of John, and Johnnie, and in order to alleviate confusion they agreed to simple adaptations. Initials were added to names for convenience. However, the R. only ostensibly represented Randolph. To those of us who had seen him naked in the showers, there existed an infinitely more interesting reality enumerating the abbreviation. Johnnie R. was one of those overly fortunate fellows who, with unabashed pride, fell heir not only to a large bank account but was genetically blessed with an unusually large cock as well. Oh sure, we all know that *really* doesn't matter, right? Ridiculously trite? Helplessly feeble-minded? Decidedly chauvinistic? Well, no, not to a hopeful and horny throng of eighteen-year-olds, and since he was want to walk around naked in the halls of the dorm his particularly fleshy attachment was seen and noted by all. As time passed and it was further rumored that he remained quite active with his sizable tool, fortunate beyond our envious dreams, the R. began to absorb a broader meaning. He became quite the celebrity, at least in the dorm, and later in his club, for the chronicles relating to his none-too-delicate member. His quite healthy cock eventually was dubbed *The Ramrod*, and from that day forward Johnnie R. was so called.

Yes, Johnnie R. was larger than life to many of us, since Lady luck had intervened on his behalf. A good-looking guy, he sported a pair fine blue eyes, wide-set and questioning though simultaneously assured that the answers he had were correct. I noted that gift that first evening as we talked over several beers. One was never quite prepared for his next onslaught. The eyes deceived any intent. The thick sandy hair, those thin sleek brows, that strong straight jaw, all hid the next clue. He was a step ahead. Still, for all of his gifts, and his luck, he did sport his demons. They were a function of appetite, both sexual and fiscal. One could understand a man of money desiring to keep that which he had and adding to the coffers in moderation that which he had yet to receive. But Johnnie R. was ruthless, blinding in his passion to be the best, and the best in a banker's world is the wealthiest, the most financially secure. Even he would agree that he was never quite able to rid himself of the mighty pleasures of money. It was the second great passion of his mind. Yet, demons exist to conflict with greater demons, stronger desires, a Heraclitian tension on the not-quite-grand scale of human needs. If it's true that love is a creature born of the metaphorical heart, a creature which feeds upon the very core of its existence, then too can it be said that lust enters where the weakened and shrunken heart can feed no more, a

5

distant child, a prodigal. What I'm trying to say is that his fiscal demon presented a much smaller bugaboo in comparison with his astounding sexual appetite. And perhaps, just perhaps, such a twist as this wouldn't have been so tragic if he hadn't found Charly during the years following graduation.

How appropriate her name seemed; how right it was. I was jolted when I received that crumpled and damp telegram in my cramped and drab London flat a few years later. It said, simply: *Nick: To be married. Name - Charly! Age -24. Sex - female. Date - 5/1. I miss you buddy. J.R.* The catch was personal. The joke wasn't a joke at all. He was serious alright, but he was serious about the probabilities of his humorous end. You see, it does matter that her name was Charly, or her nickname, rather, for the starchy and solid calling for Charlene. Yes, it mattered deeply, just as it mattered that there were, for me, numerous Talbott Streets, two Meridian Streets, a mass of amorphous definitions for every conceivable word or phrase or thought. The importance lay in the very simple fact that Johnnie R. shared his lusts among women and men. From that first day together I knew of his sexual preferences, and throughout the years which followed our first meeting I noted that depending upon his very fickle needs he might find sex with either a man or a woman on a given day. He wasn't averse to finding them together, or, as it were, back to back.

Johnnie R., for all that he had to lose, was quite open about this fact with me, though not, of course, with his fellow Ivy cronies or his dormitory friends. Still, whether you adhered to Kinsey's ten percent or some lesser contemporary percentage, more than a few of our fellow students were homosexual, and Johnnie R. undoubtedly carried on sexual relations with some of them. He occasionally let slip a comment implicating a friend or anonymous passerby, but he never publicized his bisexuality to friends other than me. And Johnnie R. was hardly the type to join the Gay Alliance of Princeton. He desired a low profile on the gay front, and was it due to the need to protect his closeted sexual secrets that he remained active with women throughout his storied Princeton career? This tactic provided a show for the boys who dreamt of having the women he was rumored to have laid. He fanned the fires of hearsay, knowing it was good fodder for the cannon in the event of later war. I'm certain that most, if not all, of his straight friends wouldn't have believed such a rumor: "Of all people, not Ramrod. Anyone but him." No, Johnnie R., on that topic, was silent with everyone but me, and on that early autumn evening when we drank those beers in a pub just off campus, he was forthright and daring. We'd put away four a piece, and already we'd found common ground in that we'd both lost our mothers. We finished with our introductions, divulged our favorite Princeton alum (Fitzgerald for me, of course, but hometown Hoosier Booth Tarkington for Johnnie R.), traded our mundane freshmen philosophies and felt the strength each in the mind of the other before he allowed this simple observation: "You'll want to know

now, because it would be unfair to tell you later should we become friends, that I'm bisexual. You know, ac/dc, fence-rider, switch hitter."

This, the second of three elements in that inauspicious beginning (the chicken fiasco being the first) would have ended most budding friendships, particularly when an unworldly straight southern kid without the daring of Johnnie R. was involved. Of course I was stunned, though not merely due to my naivete and inexperience in sexual matters, but he was so open about it, so damned casual in telling me. Homosexuality had remained totally underground in my neck of the southern woods. One simply didn't TALK about such things in the sunny South. But he'd captured me prior to these statements for reasons already mentioned - the disarming manner, the promise of intrigue, his magical erotic spell. He fascinated me, and he realized his power over me from the beginning. I wanted badly to match his aplomb, this master of surprise. So I continued sitting there watching his expression of complete self-assurance as he gulped his beer. At that moment it was Nick and not Johnnie R. who was put on the defensive. We'd spouted off our liberal leanings all evening long in that smokey dingy noisy bar, and by then it was time, we both knew, to put words to the test. As the bar took on that dark and lively character of naughtiness which one can see and smell and hear and touch after four beers and a long day, and as his eyes met mine - questioningly, wonderingly - I countered with what little power I could muster by saying, with a slur, "If that's all you have to offer in the way of shocking revelations you'll have to do much better to beat mine." He took a drink, raised his brows. "Listen," I continued, leaning across the table, drunk, talking softly, barely audible above the drone of the bar, "I've got a better one. And this will knock your pants off. This will do the shock trick. Ready? Ready? Now hear this. My mother didn't simply die. I killed her!"

Well, he gave me one of those disbelieving *c'mon* looks, and we spent the remainder of the evening elaborating on our mutual confessions. I, of course, wasn't a killer, and he, in the nineteen seventies, wasn't an outcast. We were merely young and needy punks, drunk, waiting, uncertain. Perhaps in another environment he never would've broached the subject. If we hadn't been drunk such news most probably would've been kept under his hat, and perhaps, on another evening, I simply would've walked away. But he did openly discuss the fact, announcing that knowledge of his sexual preferences came as part of the package deal which was Johnnie R.'s friendship. And I didn't walk away, knowing full well that I desired a friend like Johnnie R. to introduce me to his world of sexual awakening and intrigue. Homoerotica? Well, that soon enough, but I'm convinced there was more than simple sexual curiosity working here. Johnnie R. was a rare bird, a diminishing species of combined beauty and beast, and I awaited the odd melange resulting from this particular combo.

As we left the pub and sauntered drunkenly up Nassau Street toward campus, high on equal parts of alcohol and mystery, I experienced a never-yet-perceived hopefulness to the early autumn air, easy and cool. I'd gained a very special friend indeed. We snickered and joked and laughed our way back toward our rooms, a growing bond between us, secrets and phobias shared, and as we later passed the Randolph Gateway Johnnie R. pointed out the distinction of the name he shared with the great entrance to the university. Rather than return immediately to the dorm, I insisted that we take a quiet spin around campus in order to stretch that magical evening. Plus, Fitzgerald was on my mind. I remembered, then, a snippet from *This Side of Paradise* where the campus is described in a warm, romantic light: *The great tapestries of trees had darkened to ghosts back at the edge of twilight. The early moon had drenched the arches with pale blue.* It was true, absolutely so. And as we walked further along we found, as Fitzgerald had years before, the mystery of those *shadowy scented lanes, where Witherspoon brooded like a dark mother over Whig and Clio, her Attic children* (I particularly liked that one) *these in turn flinging the mystery out over the placid slope rolling to the lake.* In fact, we did end up at Carnegie, wrestling in the leaves beneath the light of that romantic moon, and it wasn't until perhaps midnight that we ambled back to the dorm. As we neared it our shoulders brushed once, twice, three times, and Johnnie R. remained close, our shoulders continuing to touch in silence. An exciting uncertainty painted the evening, not so much sexual as philosophic. There I was, an introverted, basically diffident, kid with little to show in the way of successful high school romances, and I suppose I was ripe for the picking. Again, emotionally, if not sexually. Already I'd fallen captive to the charm of this strutting, cock-sure, full-of-life kid from Indy.

He knew it. Perhaps fifty feet from the dorm entrance, no one in sight, he placed his arm around my shoulder, pulling me close. And then the most extraordinary thing happened. He brought his face close to my cheek as if to whisper something, and was I simply incoherently drunk or did he actually, well, kiss me? Just a brush stroke, quick and easy. If not a kiss, ever so slight, what was it? I was stunned. Inarticulate. Uneasy. Thus was born the third element of our young and inauspicious beginning. What to do? What to say? How properly to react? I only know that I simply walked on with him, drunk, snickering nervously, avoiding the obvious and imminent confrontation. With a faint hint of seduction in his voice (of which he was a master) he asked me to come up to his room for one last beer from the mini-fridge, and I hemmed and hawed and nervously accepted.

With his roommate out of town for the weekend, we sipped beers alone. We chatted somewhat anxiously as our continuing bull session quickly developed into a silent stupor. Eventually, my body began to rebel. I began to doze off as I lay back on one of the beds. Not to be outdone, always a step ahead even when drunk, Johnnie R. took action. In a few quick movements which I could hear but not see, Johnnie R. had stripped, and when I finally mustered the sleepy energy to turn my head toward him I saw him standing in wait by the bed. He was efficient. Practical. All perfectly-tuned method. His gaze was strong. His eyes momentarily questioned.

"This isn't a good idea," I mumbled. True, I'd dated few girls, but I knew I wasn't gay. Horny, yes, but sex with Johnnie R. wasn't on my list of things to do before semester break.

"You sure?"

"Just friends and a beer."

"You ever tried it?" he countered, leaning over me and loosening my belt.

Though I could've stopped him my hands remained by my sides, and not least on my mind was the thought that to receive a blow job wasn't technically gay. Or was it? Uncertain, I slurred, "No. Just assumed. I need a friend, not a fuck."

"You'll never know until..."

"I assume. That's enough," I cut him off.

Perhaps more words were traded; I'm not sure. I only remember the stifled sense of anticipation in his eyes and the stiff salute of his healthy cock cutting the air before my blurred eyes. Then he leaned over me once again to unfasten my jeans. A few more of his quick and efficient movements and I was naked too. By then, both desire and mystery taking hold beyond my ability to control, I was hard. As those late adolescent hormones pumped double time through my body I jumped as Johnnie R. slowly slid his lips over my waiting cock. I remember, strangely, grabbing his thigh tightly, not to move him closer, not to hug, but to help push back the inevitable powerful screaming orgasm raging just below the surface. Not five minutes passed before I popped a young lifetime's worth of physical and emotional need down his eager and hungry throat. Then it was done, and I passed out.

Funny. In the morning I awoke still naked and sweating with Johnnie R.'s legs wrapped around mine and an arm across my chest. His face was buried in my neck, and I lay there for several minutes without moving thinking about what I felt. There were no other experiences with which to compare it. I was a complete sexual novice, and I sought internally for a sign, though primarily I felt ambivalence. The unusual closeness of another human being, flesh upon flesh, was exhilarating, but the source of the excitement was not. His damp hair in my face, the taut skin of his muscular body rubbing mine, the strong aroma of body dampness, sweat and musk, all of these served to form a masculine image that was difficult for me to absorb. Further, this montage left me unconvinced. Ironically, for one so accustomed to assume guilt I felt no remorse as I lay there naked with Johnnie R. I suppose I sensed a feeling of relief that I'd finally cast away that virginal shield and joined the wonderful and mysterious physical world. Yet, there was no fit for me, my heterosexual temperament far beyond the midpoint of Kinsey's scale to desire more fun from Johnnie R. I simply realized that though the aching sexual need had been adequately fulfilled I wasn't enamored with the source of fulfillment. Emotionally, yes. Physically, no. And I perhaps would have dwelt on this thought for untold minutes more had Johnnie R. not begun to respond to the waking sun with the beginnings of a huge erection climbing slowly up my hip and side. I quickly jumped from the bed and began to dress as he rolled casually over onto his back, hands behind his head, a hard-on raging with a "top o' the mornin'" perkiness, and sleepily smiled.

"Ah, oh! Homosexual panic! I'd recognize it anywhere," he said disarmingly.

"This is unusual," I stammered. "I'm somewhat of a novice."

"So I gathered."

"So?" I blurted out as I tripped while slipping on my jeans.

"So," he said, leaning on an elbow. "You've got two choices as I see it. We become friends. Or you panic. You feel guilty. You leave. You ignore me. We never talk again. And the beginnings of a great friendship are laid to waste."

He said this matter-of-factly, with a cocky manner which suggested either outcome would've been satisfactory.

"I'm not, uh..."

"Gay is the word you're searching for," he offered.

"Yes, gay."

"Fine," he said, sitting up. "But if you refuse to remain friends I'll be forced to report to the authorities the fact that you've admitted killing your mother!"

I laughed. He smiled. And moments later I walked out of the christening room. Friends indeed. A week passed before we met again, time enough to analyze and toss off the yoke of doubt, and when he walked up to the carrel where I sat studying in the Firestone Library and suggested we get a Coke, no sex involved, I agreed to join him. We casually reacquainted ourselves, tiptoeing around the hungry sex of a week before, and soon the ease of our first conversation returned. Later we grabbed a bite to eat, Johnnie R.'s treat on my day off from the dining room, and afterward we strolled through campus and eventually sat before the Princeton Battle Monument, chatting endlessly.

How odd, this friendship of unlikely companions. How unusual the dynamics creating it, sustaining it. If the sexual issue wasn't reason enough to thwart it, there was always the issue of temperament. Gloom and doom and despair versus the effervescent cardiac kid. Our backgrounds held no common link. Our pockets clanged with unequal change. Our interests dramatically differed. Johnnie R. preferred to hang out in the Commons or grab a beer or lift weights at the field house. I habitually scampered over to the library following classes and immersed myself within the sweet soft lost moments of bookish reflection. While I studied and read, Johnnie R. played touch football somewhere out on the quad.

It was there in the Firestone that I first encountered a transcendence, a spirit - something Johnnie R. never acknowledged, or cared to entertain. This began only after I'd picked up from a dusty shelf one afternoon a small book of poems by the poet Rilke, until then unknown to me. I returned to the dorm, mesmerized, and with a Coke in one hand and the *Duino Elegies* in the other I read and re-read the poems beyond midnight. As the fragile mental air met the wee hours of the evening the world changed for me, and the cause was the poet's lyrical explication of uncertain, yet possible, hope. In the *Elegies* Rilke betrayed no bitterness in his isolation, no lasting remorse. No self-pity. He spoke of courage and possibility in the face of despair. In one short elegy I was won over. He had me. And why should he not? Why should I allow the past to carry me away? The emptiness became a challenge, and as the master says, if I may paraphrase, in the first, yes, the first and the greatest of his elegies: Throw the emptiness out into the very void of space, into the vacant and scolding night, air of life and darkness, contradictory powers, flux of ages past, throw it out and watch the world lighten in the shallow and thinning air.

Suddenly, meaning seemed to be offered from a far different quarter. From that moment onward I understood that we'd been gathered into something much loftier, much more complex, than the mere stuff of this febrile physical world. I took note of the creative act, acknowledged that there was a secret psychological code at work. The solution to deciphering it seemed closer when the very folds of the brain would spread to allow in the mystical vibrations which might enter. Something was indeed happening. A mental click, an idea, a word. Language.

Steeped in the utterly magnificent power of those elegies of Rilke or the fantasies of overcoming of the wild and uncontrolled Rimbaud, I embraced the power of the poets to say the word. The Word. True, I held communion with Idea and was dumbfounded, becoming entangled in the silky and tenuous web of metaphysical hope. Truer still, my own meager attempts with the printed word weren't memorable. But I believed in them, completely. Like the fragment from the flow of a poem written during our waning months at Princeton (and dedicated to Johnnie R.):

We lay stretched over laments
Of lost causes. The ancient physic
Slowly embalmed us with yearning -
A yearning molded timeless,
Its power yellowing our souls
With fragmentary releases.
And so you ask, 'Who has seen
the Maskless One?' And so I say,
'It is the whimpering, shadowed face
Of time, disguising itself in traces
Of tortured light ...

They represented a shared knowledge of the frailties enveloping the human mind. They begged to differ with the hard cold material world, embracing the more nearly ethereal, the otherworldly. The Word.

I held these thoughts closely to the heart, keeping them hidden from all but Johnnie R. who indulged me during those searching years. As I've said, Johnnie R. understood my need, though only by analogy. We were both moved by forces seemingly beyond our control. He may not have understood my passion for the Word, but he did understand a driving aching need. Yes, we each possessed that aforementioned need, war with uncommon demons, and somewhere between the polar opposites lay a soft inviting common ground of youthful understanding. That is why he was good for me. Whenever I began to float up, up and away, Johnnie R. came to the rescue by anchoring me to the firm earth below. I learned from his great daring mighty ravishing love for life, and I was better for it.

And if his exuberance was contagious, he was also nearly always in control. Whether at a dance, a ball game, the library or in the Commons, Johnnie R. seemed to be in command, always a step ahead. "Ramrod! Ramrod! Ramrod!" his friends would shout for him to perform. At the football games it was Johnnie R. who organized our group into a shirtless row where each guy painted a letter on his chest to spell out **PRINCETON** in dark thin dripping paint. Johnnie R. was always **P**, the first man out of the block. He was also the guy who would demand to be passed up and down the bleachers over the outspread arms of the other anonymous students. With his arms pushed to his sides and a tummy full of beer he would yelp with approval as he was pushed up to the top and then passed down to the bottom in a roller coaster ride of simple unadulterated mirth.

Yes, we got on splendidly, made mutual friends, studied together, attended parties side by side, and ironically, double-dated together - female dates only. Even after Johnnie R. followed through with his father's wishes and joined Ivy (the oldest, most prestigious, all-male club) as a legacy following our sophomore year, we remained close. This doesn't mean, certainly, that his homosexuality didn't stir tension between us. His needs were hard to follow, his motives harder yet to understand. After a time I put no great energy into attempting to understand, and yet a peculiar element of curiosity remained long after the surprise had lost its power over me. After all, it was he who had casually tossed off my virginity. Sexually, I was indebted to him, though my debt was of the non-recourse variety, no personal guaranties; nonpayment couldn't result in foreclosure. I was, I suppose, a simple debtor to Johnnie R.'s unsecured creditor. The topic of homosexuality eventually passed into limbo, surfacing only infrequently, and on those few occasions when it did surface I ignored his innuendoes and went about my business. He might see a guy while walking with me and simply hum his approval. A few times, when we were drunk and festive and alone, his hand or touch would linger longer than normal. Or he would occasionally pop off some comment, usually when my love life was faring poorly, suggesting that I'd made the wrong decision in not reciprocating his desire.

And then came that uncommonly warm February day during our senior year when Johnnie R. and I strolled after class, mid-afternoon. We'd unwittingly taken one of those sentimental walks around campus (sitting before the art museum as Johnnie R. poked fun at Picasso's *Tete de Femme*, buying a soda near Palmer Square, hiking over to Cleveland Tower, taking a spin around Nassau Hall, chastising under our breaths the geeks exiting the hard and serious Fine Hall) and eventually reached a bench outside the Woodrow Wilson School. By then the sun had poked through to pamper us with a breezy unheard of seventy degrees. Lazily, I glanced toward the School and then tilted my head back as we both looked up at the fickle blue.

"I'll return, Johnnie R.," I said matter-of-factly, pointing toward the facade. "Eventually I'll return."

"Why?" he asked. We'd been over this more than once, and each time it elicited the same response. I shuffled my feet without answering, forcing him to pursue it.

"I've never understood why you'd consider staying any longer. Hell, Nick, there's no money in it. A Ph.D. isn't a good monetary investment in this day and age. Same pay. You're just delaying the monetary goods, buddy." I snickered to myself, still silent. He paused for a moment before continuing. "Dreams, that's all. Damn, they're all monks in there, holed away from civilization. Musty eggheads. Irrelevant as the old codgers at the Institute for Advanced Study across town. The century's leaving them behind, and if you stay you'll be as antiquated as them."

"I don't care about the money."

"Ah, yes. Ideas. Glorious but worthless ideas!"

"They lack the caliber of hard return you seek, Johnnie R."

"But you have no means of support, Nick."

"That's why I'll come back. I'll work and then return."

"And put off the failure till later?" he asked cruelly. He always knew how to make the dig at the right time. I looked at him with what he called an arrogant smirk, my head shaking side to side.

"Your priorities are so fucked, Johnnie R.," I said, the smirk a full smile by then. "You've got your focus on extra narrow today. Keep that up and you won't even be able to see the aura from the dollar sign at the end of your candy-colored kaleidoscope."

"Okay, sport, if money has no importance and books are the living end, why are you so damned unhappy?" he asked, ready to take me on. To his surprise I made no response. I just looked down at the brown grass, playing with a stick.

"He's speechless! I can't believe it!" he shouted, nudging me as he stood up with hands over his head. I looked over at him with a half-smile.

13

"No great love," I said weakly, simply.

"What?"

"No lover, Johnnie R. No female companion. Nothing," I answered truthfully.

"Then love me, lover!" he blurted out exuberantly, without an ounce of pretense or cunning. He remained standing before me, stunned as I was stunned, his hands slowly falling to his sides, helplessly. It was as if Johnnie R. had finally surrendered as he uttered those few choppy words without irony, without humor, without hope. He couldn't even smile. I understood immediately that he'd wanted it to come out oh so very differently - perhaps casually, half-joke, half-truth, carelessly spoken - but his voice wouldn't cooperate in this crucial instance, a temporary breakdown in his fine front-line defenses, and we could both hear the tinny sound of terrified desire in his voice. He was as vulnerable as I'd ever seen him. We both knew he could've said a hundred other things just then. For four years he'd done so. He could've invited me to Indy for the umpteenth time since his dad had agreed to make room for me at the bank, or he could've laughed or joked or sighed or just sat in silence shaking his head. But instead he shouted out four little words and gave it all away. The reserve was gone, the bucket dry. During those few minutes following his outburst neither of us took his eyes off the other. I just looked at him in silence for a long, long time, eyes squinting, and behind those handsome blue question marks I knew he watched me reviewing - in auto reverse, fast forward, pause, frame advance and finally, play - four years of friendship from a slightly different angle. Not until then did I realize I had him hooked, as foreign a feeling for me as Johnnie R.'s vulnerability was to him, and yet we both knew I was an unwilling and unwitting angler. Like the crying child who begs the father to throw the squirming terrified suffocating thing back, I felt for him just then. Not because I knew the score, but because of the way the game had ended. For Johnnie R. it was all in the play, and he'd turned the ball over just a few seconds before the buzzer. Poor Johnnie R. We tried to save the moment by changing the topic to who knows what, and we chatted a little longer before leaving the bench outside the School and the strange, out-of-season, blue sky.

So, you see, Johnnie R. never quite gave up on me, nor did he give up his many men. He openly defined himself to me as a thinking *machismo* - a man's man, a woman's man. One could reach such conclusions by simply catching a glimpse of the men with whom he might be found, typically sleekly masculine types with a rarified beauty similar to those found in magazine ads and packaged TV. I watched him during those four years in school as he tried one and then another partner, never seeming to find longevity with his mates, male or female. I didn't fault him for his fate, but I didn't care to share his dubious sexual destiny, though I often wondered how long it would take for the crash to occur. When and how would he be taken? And who would do it? I could only wonder at the depth of the relationship which might transpire should he fall in love since neither man nor woman seemed capable of sating his appetite. In his future banker's world, he would be expected to marry, but a world which didn't demand as an imperative, fidelity, would allow him to continue in his usual fashion. He would keep his men. The conflict was clear and unavoidable, and eventually his sexual destiny came in the shapely and intelligent form of Charly. Ah, Charly! She, the centerpiece of our later immensely tragic struggle in Indianapolis. Charly, the woman Johnnie R. married and the woman I loved. Dear, sweet Charly.

2

London to Indianapolis

Separating our departure from Princeton in nineteen seventy-seven and our later reunion in Indianapolis was a span of five years which began in Washington, D.C. and ended in London. I'd been accepted by the Foreign Service, an economic officer as it were, and my assignment, quite luckily, was London. Not only was London my home for four years, the city also presented my first sighting of Talbott Street. Meandering through a series of cramped quarters not far from Grosvenor Square and the American embassy was a narrow street named Talbott, and it was in a nondescript brownstone on Talbott Street that I chose to live for the tenure of my service stay. It was there, on Talbott, that I first learned of the mystery of urban isolation. Tucked away among faceless occupants and unrealized dreams, time seemed measured in neutered lives and sterilized schemes. All that hope and need for more came to nothing, and the children carried on the legacy after the blurred eye in the brownstone next door had closed forever. You might travel the high historical road to Trafalgar Square and Buckingham Palace and the Houses of Parliament, or you might find the dual sliver of personal and collective reflection in the mighty Thames, but no matter, you returned to your small home in the evening to be lost among the countless crowd and severed from any connection with meaning. You slept and worked and returned night after night, which is why Talbott Street became a simple vacancy for me, a soullessness, a cocoon which never blossomed into beauty, a process which never revealed hope. In fact, during bleaker moments I entertained the terrifying image that death was perhaps not unlike the nothingness I'd found there.

Of course London did have its times, the gray slumbering notwithstanding. High-culture moments, such as doing it tip-top at the Royal Opera House in Covent Garden, followed by equally highbrow food, drink and a tincture of reserved laughter at one of the diplomatic functions. Low-brow fun with the guys in my section as we not-so-secretly slummed in Soho where many whistled at the whores and played coyly along with nude dancing girls in strip joints. I particularly enjoyed my initiation to Jazz, British style, at a club on Frith Street where we slurped our draughts as we pounded out the chaotic rhythms of the music. Still, something was missing, a hint of warmth which might easily lay near the heart, and though there were moments of satisfactorily consummated lusts and efficient sexual gratifications, there was no great love. This fact occasionally caught me off balance during a random hour of any given workaday, sending me out of orbit for days. I remember walking through the great sprawling Rupert Street Market among stalls of flowers and fruit and breads and game, and above the bedlam of the blaring din I suddenly heard the hollow tinny echoing of my own aching heart. (Romantic weakness? Fitzgerald's timeless joke come roosting home?) Whether on Fleet Street at rush hour weaving in and out of the window-gazing crowd or in the ever-wandering tube at midday, that cardiac clang might be heard as if, within, a tiny toy marching soldier were beating out dead time with thin uncaring cymbals and unfeeling wooden hands.

That's why at the end of my four-year contract I opted to move on. Frankly, diplomacy might be fine, but I rarely witnessed its energetic movements. There was little romance in the Service, that sterling element being a concoction of my thwarted fantasies beyond the Princeton years. The problem was the stasis of an economist's duties within the mind of one who desired more. I was a man out of his element, a professional groper in numbers who loved his poetry more. While locked tight in the belly of the embassy with graphs, variance reports, forecasts, market analyses and the like, I had little exposure to the more nearly revealing political apparatus of the diplomatic world. There was no pomp and circumstance beyond the occasional embassy party where we middle-tiered staffers gulped our drinks and exchanged our farcical greetings while vainly awaiting something wildly memorable, wonderfully idealistic, infinitely dreamy. *(Bond ... James Bond)* And of course no such wild and wonderful and dreamy happening occurred. That's when I understood I needed to leave London, the embassy, the dream and Talbott Street.

It was a case of comparing the verities of change with the similitudes of stasis. The similitudes gave an education, I suppose, but in increments so small through spurts of time so long and drawn that I became bored and restless. I spurned them, leaving whenever the pain of boomer angst settled near the pacing heart. So I skipped out on the aged routines and found those not always sweet verities of change. Ah, sweet change. Though eventually I came to realize that the word, *change*, loses all relevance and meaning as it pushes us on like the scolding cranky voice of an old habit, in the beginning I was attuned to its power and lessons. It taught much more rapidly, although more chaotically, than the *Great Wait*. Besides, there remained from my Princeton days the unresolved issue concerning Rilke's *Others*. There had to be *Others* silently awaiting the perfect companion who would understand, who could feel the isolated pain, who would carry it in the same manner, who fought it in the same fashion, who would hope as I'd hoped, as Rilke had hoped. One must search them out physically, avoiding the temptation to sit and wait.

So Rilke again: Thrust away! Gather the strength and energy unused of the drawn arrow, yes, gather within the seed of strength and consequential form the power to release the promise into the world, and suddenly, with a rush too powerful and too comprehensive and too certain to describe, find the arrow no

17

longer drawn back, the string no longer taut, as the arrow liberates beyond its measure, seeking its target, hoping for peace in the respite of its deliverance. Momentum complete. Target found. Change.

And, finally, from Rilke's *First Elegy*: *Because to stay is to be nowhere*.

Yes, to stay is to never find. To go gave the appearance of hope. Change didn't guarantee success, but it seemed to me to argue in favor of it. Already, I'd discovered that the companion wasn't to be found in Mobile nor Princeton nor Washington nor London, so I suppose it was only logical that I should hook up again with Johnnie R. out in Indianapolis, perhaps learn from his example, his immunity to remorse or guilt or brooding silence. Perhaps there I'd find the *Other* whom Rilke had promised.

He'd returned home to Indianapolis upon graduation, and I'd laughed at him then for wanting so badly to return to his native Midwest, the Corn Belt, in order to begin the long torturous process of growing old and searching for answers to those indomitable questions which burned through our minds during those stimulating romantic Jersey days. He only laughed back with a knowing smile which informed me that he did, after all, have a home to return to. I came to envy good ole Johnnie R. after a time; whenever we corresponded after our departure from Princeton he seemed altogether content, almost relieved that the transient years had been left behind. So it was with excitement that I took his call in September of nineteen eighty-two while in my flat in London, and when I heard Johnnie R.'s echoing transcontinental voice finally ask the question, "Nick, I've got an opening at the bank. I need someone with your experience. Will you come?" I could only respond with a resounding, "Yes!"

* * *

I left London draped in its dreary gray sleep in early December and was off to Indy. I'd never entered that sweet midwestern center of Indiana - home of the farmer, basketball, corn and the Republican party. Oh yes, and the homespun secrecy of the innocent human heart. I found what I expected to find, and more. While touching down within the confines of the Indianapolis International Airport, a title of some exaggeration, that disquieting internal gnawing suddenly seemed to cease, and this I took as a good sign. The sun shone brightly through an intermittent cloud cover, and the warmth of a transient spring seemed to settle over the city. Home at last, I thought.

Johnnie R. immediately spotted me among the airport Christmas crowd. I'd taken only a few steps beyond the gate when I heard a shout, a roar of recognition, and as I turned I found him with arms high in the air, waving ecstatically as he motioned me toward him. His lithe frame nearly crashed through the crowd as he pushed his way forward, smiling widely, even wildly, as certain of his quest as he was undaunted by the mass of bodies separating us. He seemed not to have aged during our five-year separation, his thick brown hair askew, those narrow brows accenting the confidence of his blue eyes, the lips parted lightly for his bright toothy grin.

"Nick! Nick! Nick!" he yelled, fists clenched as if he'd won a race. He reached me just beyond the gate, broad smile and all, and gave me one of his huge emotional bear hugs. Oblivious of the crowd and the attention he'd attracted, without hesitation, he took me by the shoulders, facing me squarely.

"Nick, ole buddy! You daydreaming son-of-a-bitch! Welcome!" he said, hugging me again. His smile contained assurances that he'd been right about Indianapolis all along. To him I was had. And his comment concerning the daydreaming was apt. I'd stood gazing, only half aware of the surroundings, enjoying for a moment the serenity which the landing in Indianapolis had given. I could only be partially aware of my new home just then. Johnnie R. knew it.

We grabbed the luggage, and once outside I noted that the snow was melting into the softening brown soil, hidden riches beneath. It was a healthy sign, though I tried to appear coy to it all, silently skeptical that I might become excited over matters of melting snow and college pal reunions. I wanted to remain at a distance from its emotional effect, fearful that if I became overwhelmed early on I'd never wean myself from it should Indianapolis turn out badly.

Johnnie R. wasn't discouraged. He knew my tricks. We walked toward the car, and he laughed as he pulled me close with a muscular arm over my shoulder, gesturing in a frenzied fashion with his free hand as he chattered on. He chirped like a spring bird, hopeful. In fact, during those early days back with Johnnie R. I found a satisfaction not unlike the years spent at Princeton, an era when the crisp and robust exchange of ideas formed a highly charged ambience, a balanced sentimentality, a favorable progression in human events. In the car, driving back into the city, he remained enthusiastic.

"We're going to make this town over, buddy. It's never going to be the same!" he announced triumphantly. I grinned as he clenched a fist while swerving through the traffic. "I mean, we're right on time, revving the engine just as this city's being located on the map. If they're ready to stop ignoring us I'm ready to show them what we've got."

"I think you're right, Johnnie R."

"Of course I am."

"Though I'm at a bit of a disadvantage," I suggested. "You're set up here. It's your city, your family's bank, your fable. Christ, you can't go wrong."

"And neither can you, Nick. I'm bringing you in on this one. It's yours to have if you will." I smiled with a shrug. "And dammit, you can't let it slip away. Reflect on those lazy days at Princeton philosophizing over a six-pack of beer and you'll realize life's only beginning. Hell, we were punks then, kids, brats.

19

We abstracted everything. Emotions, pain, existence from day to day. It was a game. But this is the real thing, and we're knocking at the fucking door!"

While looking through the window I noted briefly that snow lay lightly on the ground after all, scattered intermittently, gray and dirty with holiday traffic wear. The dark ambience of London's gray environs somehow inviting me to note the similarity. The contradiction lay with the sun. It glared, nearly blinding me as I watched the city approach. I shielded my eyes with my hands as I said, "You believe it, don't you?"

"Of course I do. This is it. Right here. Those so-called insuperable meanings of yours all come down to us, right here, right now," he answered, tapping the steering wheel for emphasis. I smiled at his misunderstanding.

"No. I mean the bit about school. You really do think it was all shit, don't you?" I said, turning to face him.

"Let's say I've seen both sides, the real and the unreal, and the reality isn't the two-dimensional existence of Princeton. It's making a living, knocking the system dead. We'll take it by its balls and twist it into shape." He paused for my response, glancing at me. When I didn't respond he flashed his contagious smile again, nudging me on the shoulder while adding, "Hell, Nick, at Princeton we merely tore the system apart, shredded what was given. Now we can make it over rather than simply dream." Again, he paused briefly. I turned toward him and held his glance. Through the glare I could barely make out his lips as he added, "Dreamers are out, Nick."

He needn't have said more, touching as he did that hard cold place of disagreement between us. A temperamental and metaphysical difference. The failed introverted poet versus the successful gregarious capitalist. Sure, the Princeton years in one sense represented tried innocence, a series of false cohesions, crumbling cosmologies, tattered hopes. But there was more to it than that. They had been wonderful years for both of us, what he would later refer to as the best years of our lives. "Maybe," I said. True, parts of life at Princeton were an abstraction, a deed of the mind and an opening for the soul. It strikes me as funny even now thinking of Johnnie R.'s reference to a two-dimensional existence, stick figures in a cartoon, a Tuesday morning run of *Doonesbury*, three frames and out. Perhaps that's why I still hold so tightly to the memories of those early years; they alone denied the cartoon.

Those were my thoughts while sitting in the car with the gabbing Johnnie R. as we closed in on the skyline of downtown Indianapolis. In nineteen eighty-two the Indy skyline, like my return, was a modest attempt, the beginning of a focus, a proud challenge to that which lies just out of reach, and as I took in the view I glanced at him and wondered why he'd asked me back. Sure, he could indulge me. With his setup he had it made. But really, after five years apart, why the call? The reasons necessarily involved more than honor of pals and shared college secrets. He was holding back.

"You'll love her, Nick," he suddenly offered, referring to his wife, Charly, as he pulled me from the past. A wide smile came over his face as he looked straight ahead.

"I'm sure I will."

"There isn't another like her. She's frighteningly bright, cool, secure."

"And, and...." I played the game with my own smile.

"And beautiful."

"Of course. You always got the beautiful ones, Johnnie R.!" I said. This was absolutely true. Whether with men or women he'd had it made.

"Jealous, Nick?"

"Yeah. Yeah I am. I'm anxious to meet this mystery lady."

"Ah, not so fast," he teased. "The suspense is everything. First, a short tour. Then maybe some coffee."

"Then?"

"Then Charly."

I played along, pretending to surrender as I placed my hands in the air as Johnnie R. reached over and gave me a pat on the leg. As the car gobbled up the interstate we became quiet again, and I looked out the window, noticing the soot and smoke creeping into the December air. Cornering the interstate and moving through the southwest side of the city we passed the polluted industrial outposts, a dirty raw nerve, and this temporarily foul backdrop reminded me, for a moment, of Newark with its stale and acrid air. Filth seemed to pour in. The air carried a singular stench, rotten and chemical. Death in the lost and soiled city.

I tried to ignore the mood by seeking brighter signs of life as I leaned back in the seat and took in the slight changes in scenery. We scrambled off the interstate and onto the major thoroughfares of downtown where the caustic odors had been left behind as we approached the clean and manicured heart of the city. Indianapolis, as you enter from the east, is skirted with warehouses painted somber colors, but once on Market Street, as you drive toward the center of the city - the Circle - things brighten. Enterprises of the sole proprietor, the middle man, the tiny wholesaler come into view, but it's not until you're received a few blocks ahead by a large bank tower and the newer office buildings that you find a real city. Downtown is clean and well kept, modern, comely as brick and mortar not maltreated can be comely. You take Market Street west and find hovering over it a coliseum, and just beyond that landmark you spy the Circle ahead. Further up Market you travel until the paved street transforms into new red brick and a large circular pad, the heart of the city.

Johnnie R., still sporting his earlier smile, was pleased to show off his city. We drove around the large Circle once and then exited north off Meridian Street, driving past the family bank housed in a large tower north of the Circle. Johnnie R. slowed the car and nearly stopped traffic while pointing out the building where I'd be working. Then came that first drive up Meridian Street, the empty

21

spaces filled periodically by small chatter. I watched in fascination as the city's face changed, taking note of the street's facades which reflected back class distinctions made obvious by brick and mortar and ivy and trees. Further north, as we approached Thirty-eighth Street, the character of the neighborhoods transformed from the seedy to the genteel. The poverties of the inner city, the small ghettos of urban cycles, were purged from the rich sister known as North Meridian, or Meridian above Thirty-eighth. This was Easy Street.

As we continued north the homes slowly were recast into Tudor mansions of leaded glass and vine- covered brick resting on sprawling lawns. Conspicuously wealthy by the standards of Meridian south of Thirty-eighth, scores of prominent homes lined the city's most prosperous street. I grasped the connection. This was *his* home. Johnnie R. was of the north side, was heir to the fortunes which the wealthiest of Indianapolis could provide. So it came as no surprise to me when he slowed the car once again and pointed to an elegant shrubbery-lined drive bearing toward a sprawling Tudor. It was immaculate, all freshly painted stucco, fine red brick and spectacular leaded glass.

Johnnie R., undaunted by the traffic jam he was causing, came to a complete stop on Meridian as he pointed out some of the finer features of his home. He easily could have pulled up the drive, but he chose the course of inconvenience. It was vintage Johnnie R. Control. I glanced at the house, turned to look out the rear window, then looked back at him. The traffic was rapidly piling up, and we got a jolt from the guy behind us as he laid on the horn. Without concern, Johnnie R. continued talking of the house. When the same driver honked a second time Johnnie R. gave the finger, all certainty and nonchalance. This went on for an uncomfortably long time before the traffic began to pass us. When the guy behind us yelled obscenities as he went around, Johnnie R. ignored him, undaunted, resolute. Johnnie R. the Intrepid. He didn't move the car until the traffic had cleared.

"Nick, let's get some coffee before going in," he said with a smile, leaning toward me.

"C'mon, Johnnie R. Introduce me to your wife."

"She's cooking tonight, a real treat, believe me," he said, playing it to the hilt. "But it'll be an hour or so before she's ready for us. Let's go."

I reluctantly agreed as he slowly drove away from the house, continuing north on Meridian. The radio droned on, and we were quiet again as we took in the sights along the street. I watched as we darted east off of Meridian onto Westfield. A canal ran parallel to the road where small ducks had docked for the winter, a nice reprieve from the small mounds of drab gray metallic snow. Johnnie R. cursed the pot holes in the road, but he said nothing more. I looked ahead and then at Johnnie R. He occasionally looked back at me, gazing in some profoundly uncertain way, and I wondered if the confusion in his glance were the same which I offered him. Just as I'd wondered, really, why Johnnie R. had invited me to Indianapolis and had questioned his uncertain motives, he too must have wondered why I'd so easily and quickly accepted. (Ole Nick lost in the modern jungles of existential despair.) Perhaps that's why I remembered his allusion to power: grab the world by its aching balls and twist. The metaphor was crude and painfully simple. Survey the world by way of purely mental calculation and then take charge. Tally Ho! Tally Ho!

Moments later we reached Broad Ripple Village, an unincorporated burg in north central Indianapolis which had been swallowed up by the larger city years ago. The village seemed nothing more than a random collection of small restaurants, store fronts, boutiques, barber shops, book stores and hidden bars. The sidewalks contained students, businessmen, punkers, housewives, sixties holdovers, rednecks and yuppies. Quite unpretentious, physically unimpressive. Easy, laid back, calm. I entertained the notion that they all came to get away and share their midwestern dreams, their Corn Belt-fed whims and needs.

A few steps from the car we entered a dimly-lit coffee shop, an insomniac's warm paradise filled primarily with college students and a few odd hangers-on. Talk was of food, drink, sports, clothing and sex. A small fireplace which lay in the middle of the large room did its best to heat the space. To one side lay a large solid oak bar stacked with varieties of coffees, uncountable mugs and an espresso maker; beneath the glass-enclosed counter were the obligatory pastries. We ordered coffee from our table in the back of the shop near a group of spirited college students from Butler University.

"So tell me more about this perfect lady, Johnnie R.," I said after the waitress took our order.

"Well, she *is* great!" he beamed.

"Yeah?"

"It's not all peaches and cream, of course. Nothing ever is, Nick." He gave me a sidelong glance, reading my expression closely. He nearly added something more but apparently thought better of it. I tried to fish him out.

"I'm not sure how to phrase this, Johnnie R."

"Then don't," he said matter-of-factly, though with the hint of a smile.

I charged on nonetheless. "What about the guys?"

"You're really damn curious, aren't you?" he said, breaking into a full smile. The old bravado had returned. I shrugged my shoulders and tilted my head in silence. Then he added, "Sure, there are bad times, but we're making our way beyond them."

Evasive tactics. Vintage Johnnie R. Yet, what was it that pushed me on? Jet lag? Caffeine withdrawal? Envy? Why was I taking such liberties following five years of separation? This was, after all, a reunion. Still, at the risk of spoiling the moment I ventured on. "Johnnie R., the sex itch was always, shall we say, a prominent feature with you."

"We have an understanding."

"Christ! This isn't one of those imported marriages from the land of fruits and nuts?" I egged him on. Unfortunately I'd misread him. He answered with a distant tinny reply.

"I don't see other women. I'm on the line there, believe me. She satisfies my need for the feminine. She's all I desire."

"But the guys? The guys remain, and she goes along with it?" I pursued, deciding to throw caution to the wind. I was far too fascinated by the prospects of his marital arrangement to contain my curiosity.

"Let's say we don't discuss it, or rarely so. There are tense moments and then they're over. Back to normal."

I hesitated a moment, avoiding his eyes, before I added, "If she's so goddamned great...." Bad move. I'd hit the nerve. He looked at me coldly, his smile vanishing, yet he said not a word. He didn't need to. His expression conveyed a simple statement: If you're the friend I think you are, so subtle and sleek in your reserve, why don't you fucking leave that business alone? It's not your affair! And I did leave it there, looking away from him and around at the crowd. Strange, I thought during the silence, strange that I should have pursued it. I hadn't done so during the interim years. I'd left the sex bit in his hands, contraries and all. It wasn't like me, nor was it like him, to find anger over such obviously personal choices. Perhaps five minutes passed before he spoke again.

"Admittedly, it's not a good time for her, for us, but we'll be fine," he offered, looking away for the waitress. Once he caught her eye he turned to me and added, "Look, something came up this summer which you ought to know."

"Oh God, here we go."

"There's been a death in the family. Charly lost her brother this past summer."

"Christ, I'm sorry," I offered. "You never mentioned it."

"It was a lurid affair. Very difficult, Nick."

"Accident?"

"He was mugged and there was a struggle."

"He was murdered?" I nearly shouted, turning a few heads.

"Yes. They caught the guys a couple of days later. Punks, looking for drug money. He was in the wrong place at the wrong time."

"Where?"

"Well, not where you'll be staying," he said quietly. "Look, Nick, he was a good kid who got caught up in a bad crowd. You know, a rich kid who slummed once too often. Now, he's dead."

"How old?"

"Eighteen. He was only eighteen fucking years old. I still can't believe it," he said, his voice cracking. He looked down at the table, shaking his head.

"You should have told me, Johnnie R. Maybe I could've helped."

"It was a difficult time. There was so much going on."

"And Charly?"

"He was her only sibling, eight years younger. It hit her very hard, though she seems to be coping pretty well now."

"Can I do something?"

"Yeah, not worry," he said, smiling. "And please don't bring it up in conversation."

"Of course," I said, uneasy. The request wasn't unusual, but the tone was mysterious, edgy. "I'm coming at a bad time."

"No, no. Of course, not."

"Maybe she doesn't want me around until I find a place of my own."

"Nick, don't be silly."

"I'll stay at a hotel. I can line up an apartment in a couple of days."

"That's ridiculous," he said, patting my arm. "If there's a chill, it'll leave the air. She'll get to know you and like you. I'm sure of it."

"What do you mean, 'if there's a chill?'"

"Oh, it has nothing to do with the death," he said rather cavalierly. "In fact, having someone else in the house will be nice right now."

"Well, if not due to her brother's death, a chill due to what?"

"Look, Nick, it's nothing," he forced a smile. "Give her a chance. She'll love you like I do."

News of the death of Charly's brother made me uneasy enough, but the possibility that Johnnie R.'s wife disliked me, a man she didn't know, nearly took me under. It wasn't the fresh beginning we'd discussed just moments before. My anger began to rise. "Are you saying she's predisposed not to like me?"

"It's not that she doesn't like you. Hell, she doesn't even know you, Nick," he answered, signaling the waitress. "Look, the problem's the image. You're from the past, right? And in her mind the mysterious past and my bisexuality are intertwined."

"What?"

"Look, Nick, when she's confronted with this, someone she can pinpoint as representative of that period, she lets all her demons out."

"Oh, great."

"Wait."

"No, you wait, Johnnie R. She thinks I'm gay?"

"Maybe," he offered tentatively. "I mean I told her you were straight, right? And that should be enough. But I believe she thinks you might be."

"Oh, this is wonderful! Your wife's brother is murdered. Your wife, though she's never met me, dislikes me. And you tell me these things not while I'm still in London but after I've arrived."

Johnnie R. nearly spoke but hesitated when the waitress brought the coffee. We scanned the crowd as she placed the coffee on the table. Students, businessmen, flunkies. Talk ranged from poetry to pussy. After the waitress had left he said, "You make too much of it, Nick. Let's start over, okay?"

"Try me."

"There was a time when that was all I did with her. The lying, I mean. When the issue came squarely before us I had no choice but to tell the truth. Up to that point, and it was about a year, I lied about it. I mean I lied about where I was going and who I was with. At first she thought I was seeing another woman, and when I finally told her the truth she still thought I was lying. I couldn't win."

"So now you're suspect at every turn."

"Not as much now. In the beginning, yes."

"And now she feels I'm here to fuck things up."

"She thought you might be an old lover, if that's what you mean. And why shouldn't she. She knew my past, and I've talked about you a great deal. She merely made the mistake of a false association."

Uneasy with his casual reply, I said, "Look, Johnnie R., I don't like this inauspicious beginning. There's been a tragedy in the family and your wife thinks I came to town to sleep with her husband. You should have told me before hand."

"Come on, Nick. This will work out quickly, I promise."

I looked away in anger.

"I know her. She'll take to you quickly. It's going to be good."

Angry and implicated, I pushed him. "Why didn't she leave when she realized the truth?"

He hesitated, looking down at his cup. His hands surrounded the mug, taking the heat within his palms. "I don't know why she stayed, really."

"Hazard a guess."

"We were younger then, for one thing," he said. "Married less than a year, and we were in love. She was an unliberated romantic and I suppose she would've taken it as a personal failure had she walked away from it." He paused to sip. "Look, I loved her. She knew that I wanted to make it work. And Nick, I did want it to work."

"As easy as that?"

"It was hell in the beginning. She wouldn't let me touch her for weeks. It was three months before we made love again. She'll never again trust me completely."

It was getting to him. He continued with his hands on the mug, staring down at the table. Several moments passed as we sat in silence while listening to the young guys next to us discussing grades and fucking. The entire room suddenly seemed empty and trite. "She's seeing a shrink," he announced, a nearly inaudible whiff of air escaping his lips as if to laugh without trying. "Strange, you undoubtedly believe, that she should be the one to go. Why should it be her when I'm the one with the problem, right?"

"I'm not making a moral judgment, but their are practical problems."

"I don't approach it as a problem, simple as that."

"Whatever," I said, shrugging.

"Of course, the manner in which it affects our relationship is a problem, but the sexuality question itself, the question of sexual orientation, isn't a problem for me."

"That's a pretty big statement, Johnnie R."

"It's true."

"Maybe it's not a problem for you, but obviously it is for Charly."

"And she's coping with it."

"Okay, listen. Ethical questions aside, practically speaking, it's nothing but trouble. You're jeopardizing your marriage, perhaps your career. What about long term happiness? You can't say it's not a problem."

"I don't think of it in terms of good or bad or right or wrong. It simply is and that's all," he said, voice rising.

"I agree that your sexual preferences are your business. What a person does with his sex life is no one's affair. Unless that person's married. And then there are innumerable practical problems."

"Nick, she has the choice to leave. She doesn't choose to leave. That being the case, we go on with it day by day. That's all we can ask."

"Each time you go out without her the issue rises again doesn't it? It's endless, Johnnie R."

He looked at me angrily, fiery in the face, and he made a jerking motion with his hand, spilling his coffee on the table. Undaunted, he leaned over the table, his face inches from mine, and said sharply, in a harsh whisper, "What the fuck do you want to hear? Do you want the goddamned details? Okay, yeah, I dig guys. And you probably want to hear me say what kind of sex I like, right? And misgivings after its over, wondering if I've contracted syphilis or the clap or herpes? And you want to know how I feel when I come home late and she's crying because she's alone and wants me with her and at the same time despises me and our compromise? And you wonder if she wonders if I'll ever give her the same fucking diseases? Yeah, Nick, it's hell, it's a problem, and it's not solvable. We go on with it because we choose to do so. It all comes down to need, Nick, simple unadulterated need on the part of both of us. And we live with it. Do you like it now?"

He finished and quickly got to his feet. I thought for a short moment that he might leave me there, but he only walked to the counter to order another cup of coffee and to grab a rag to clean up the mess. Around us, the crowd was silent. Everyone in the place looked at me and then at Johnnie R. and back at me. Only when I brought my cup up to toast the curious faces did they slowly turn away. By the time Johnnie R. returned to the table the murmur of conversation picked up again. He sat and sipped his coffee and then spoke softly, without a trace of anger.

"Nick, she deals with this in her fashion, and the psychiatrist is her way. We never discuss the therapy, but it seems to have helped her. I deal with it in my fashion, and I don't feel the need for therapy. There are tough moments and some problems. We deal with it as best we can."

There was a strain in his voice, and the fatigue was visible in his face. He might attempt a cheerful posture, but he couldn't adequately conceal the pain. Those secular demons again. I wasn't surprised he'd been caught, only shocked that a reasonable man would allow himself to remain within the trap for so long. So we leaned back in our chairs as the conversations from other tables filtered between us. The murmur we'd met when entering had transformed by then into a shrill ring. Strangely, although quite loud, the noise was somehow comforting. Five minutes had passed when he spoke again.

"I know it all sounds bizarre to you, and as I step back I realize it myself, but beyond the strangeness you perceive there's love."

"We don't have to discuss it," I offered guiltily. He took a sip and waved me off.

"She's an artist. Very gifted. She draws and has had some of her work on the covers of smaller magazines. She writes a few stories now and then, too. She's had them published. Children's stories. It's good stuff."

"You'd never mentioned it."

"Yeah, it's a big thing with her to keep busy in that fashion. And she's her boss. Independent as hell about her work. You've got to see some of it tonight."

I nodded, indicating that I'd like to.

"She reminds me of you in that way, you know. That's why I think the two of you will get along so well. You both sport that artistic bent. Hers seems a bit more practical, I suppose, but it boils down to the same need."

"And I'm not, of course. Practical, that is. Thanks."

"Don't get worked up. I simply meant that you express yourself differently. She writes stories for children and does sketches and drawings for magazines. You write ethereal poetry . Too esoteric to publish. It's artistry in personal residence, so to speak. It's for you. In that sense it's not for the world, not practically applied."

"It takes the right kind of person."

"You're so damned smug at times, Nick."

"Forget it."

"No. I think it's important," he continued. "Come on, I saw you on the way over here. You still get lost in those god-forsaken reveries of yours. Why do you insist on locking yourself up and away from people? It's not healthy. You're totally morose at times. It's debilitating."

28

I knew he was right, and I had no desire to spend my first day in five years with Johnnie R. arguing about my temperament. Besides, I'd already decided to make a go of it. I very much wanted Indianapolis to work out. "I'm leaving it all behind, Johnnie R. You're right. I won't argue with you. Just don't give me a Norman Vincent Peale lecture."

"Good. The heavy philosophical days are over. I thought you'd never quit chasing ghosts."

"I used to call them companions."

"Oh, the perfect lover? Friend and confidante? Take it from me, pal, there are none."

"Perhaps not."

"Look, I'm sorry," he said. "I mean only to help. Hell, the letters from you all spoke of the same thing. Reading them was like going through the collected works of Schopenhauer."

"Okay, okay, okay," I surrendered, waving my arms in the air. I knew he meant well, attempting kindness.

"You know, in a way, a strange, nearly comic, black-humored manner, we all need each other just now," he continued. "It'll be good, all of us here together."

I toasted him and downed the coffee. He offered a wide smile. A truce. Minutes later we strolled back to the car. It was nearly dark, the sky a metallic gray, dead and cold. The air felt damp and of the gray, stretched thinly, with a chill. For a moment I remembered the gripping chill of London and then felt the cool, damp breeze of an Alabama February morning cover us in laconic waves. I thought then of the gaping wounds and the frail internal structures which our five years apart had revealed. We seemed so much weaker with time. And this emptiness would have won me over, promises to Johnnie R. notwithstanding, had what followed next not occurred. Just before arriving at the car Johnnie R. took his arm and placed it over my shoulder. Hurriedly, he hugged me. Then, loosening his grip, but with his arm still around my shoulder, he spoke softly, with emotion.

"We're going to be okay, buddy. We're going to be alright," he struggled to say with a tightness in his throat.

That's all it took. He had me. "I know," I said weakly. I couldn't fight both Johnnie R. and the dusk despair.

"We're going to take his goddamned city!" he announced triumphantly, his arms high in the air. He turned a full circle and let out a big guffaw which crashed through the wall of gray December air. When he turned back toward me he tilted his head slightly, a brightness to his eyes, and added, "But for now, supper!"

3

Indianapolis, 1991

Johnnie R.'s Journal

Entry, May 1991

*A retrovirus is a devious creation, a breed apart. This submicroscopic devil, deftly hidden by nature's hand, is the ultimate parasite. Either by way of quick genetic mutation or millions of years of plodding change, nature outdid herself. Enter, Technicolor. Supplemented with one of nature's quirky little surprises, reverse transcriptase, the virus can perform an elaborate, biologically poetic, feat on the grand molecular scale by creating a complementary strand of DNA from the viral chain of RNA. **Voile!!!** The necessary biological cycle is accomplished in the reverse. Now the synthetic strand of DNA can wreak havoc in a human cell. Oh yeah, and HIV is a retrovirus; HIV causes AIDS.*

*HIV is filled with the usual genetic stuff (an enzyme, some protein) but it also contains some custom-made, high-tech, state-of-the-art genetic machinery. A real tyrant, this fucker - a super-refined killer with an affinity for a particular kind of cell: T4-lymphocytes, the backbone of the immune system. It's modus operandi: knock and enter; transcribe; invade; mimic; hide; lie in wait. The viral DNA now induces the host T4 cell to reproduce **IT**, and with every cell division there is born a replicant surprise. So guess who's coming to dinner?*

But here's the clincher, the real rub, one of nature's horrible wonders. HIV offers an intriguing visual comparison for those who will take note. With the help of the electron microscope the sinister retrovirus reveals itself as a seemingly harmless spherical form. Filled with the mysteries, unseen by the eye, they look like fancy pin cushions with little round pin heads protruding from their surfaces. They are, in a word, mandalas.

Mandalas may take many forms, the most common being circular patterns representing psychic wholeness. You might say it belies the archetypal pattern marking the human goal of transcendence, wholeness, a uniting of opposites, a calculated closure, a significant end. The idea is beautiful, poetic, and many mandalas are themselves quite beautiful, striking in design, voluptuous in textures, perfect in symmetry. The comparison in structure between the human attempt at psychic wholeness, on the one hand, and the virus's insidious domination and destruction, its own peculiar story of integration, closure, and transcendence, on the other, is nearly too ironical to bear. Nature often dresses her most hideous creations in elegant attire. HIV is one such clad member of nature's very own. It appears fashionable in its mandalan circularity, a raiment of spherical wonder. By all appearances it seems quite harmless, yet it sports a heart of nothingness.

Ironically, HIV is a kamikaze virus.   Either nature has created a sophisticated pathogen somehow gone awry, a nearly perfect parasite just out of control, or the little fucking monster simply lives for the day, carpe diem, and before dying has a banging good time. Either way, on a molecular level it's insidious, covert, cloak-and-dagger - in a word, evil. It's here, apparently of this world, yet in a sense it's not. It's seemingly alive, yet it's not life as we know it. It's a natural mandala, physically a representation of nature's transcendent hope, and yet, in the end, it most certainly is not.

*   *   *

I read these words as I sat by Johnnie R.'s hospital bed waiting for him to stir. As he was to say later, "I'm stalking the virus, as the virus stalks me." Of course, he lost the battle, his smirky facade the sign of a man seeking courage while confronting that which will kill him. Sifting the facts while seeking the vital center. On a table beside his bed lay perhaps twenty books, all dealing with AIDS: personal memoirs, histories of the syndrome, a couple of novels, tomes on protocols, a dictionary of AIDS, lists of experimental drugs, black market guides. There was even an atlas with red ink markings on the city map of Tijuana, the great black market medicinal cornucopia for persons with AIDS. I thumbed through a couple of the books as I leaned forward, nearly touching Johnnie R.'s thin arm, and would have continued indefinitely if I hadn't heard her shriek.

"What in the hell are you doing in here?" a hefty, sanguine, white-clad nurse shouted from the door in a strange concoction of hoarse whisper and mini-roar. Stunned, I dropped the book on the floor, and Johnnie R. jerked awake. The nurse walked quickly forward. Standing, I didn't know whether to formally address Johnnie R. or to defend myself.

"I'm sorry. What've I done?" I asked, glancing down at Johnnie R. who was still coming to, his crusty eyes trying to focus on me.

"You could be transmitting anything to him right now. He's weak. You can't be in here like this," she answered sternly, coming close, motioning me to follow her to the door.

"I'm sorry. I didn't think."

"Obviously," she said, taking my arm like one would a child's. "And you didn't check in at the station. We have rules here."

"Nick!" Johnnie R. said softly, his voice weak but happy. I turned my head to see him trying to sit up. It was impossible. Not only was he too weak to manage that once-simple exercise, but the IVs, catheter, oxygen tubes, heart monitor and other contraptions had pinned him down. He couldn't maneuver.

31

"Hi, Johnnie R.," I said, loosening my arm from the nurse's grasp as I turned toward him. It was heartbreaking, watching him fail to manage something so elementary.

The smile continued as he said, "Listen -"

"John. I've told you, you must lie still," the white terror-of-a-nurse interrupted. "You'll loosen the IV and monitor." She walked past me and to the bed. She had an amazing touch. The cold and bold exterior temporarily gave way to a soft firmness, a maternal kindness witnessed not so much in the voice as in the movement of her hands, the tilt of her head, the slight, leaning twist of her body as she bent over him and adjusted his pillows. She placed his head carefully down on them, checking the tubes and the IV. Then, without a second thought, she slipped back on her doberman mask, turned and walked to me, grabbed my arm and began to lead me toward the door.

"This way," she said without emotion as I looked back helplessly at Johnnie R.

"Be easy on him, baby," Johnnie R. humored her. He was a mess, barely hanging on, yet his simple confident wit surfaced with apparent ease.

"John, there are rules!"

"What's the difference? I'm a dead man. We both know that. Now, c'mon," he said, the only vestiges of his former vitality being the soft, rhythmic play of his voice and that slight, cocky tilt of the head.

"Mr. Thayer! You promised!" she scolded him as she released my arm. She held her palms up, questioningly.

"Okay, okay, okay," he played with her, trying to lift his arms to mimic her gesture, showing retreat, but only able to roll his painful-looking eyes. "No more fatalism. But look, wrap him up and bring him back. This is the guy I've been waiting for, the one I told you about."

He uttered the words with such confidence, and playfulness, that she was unable to resist. I stood between them, the object of the battle. Badly as I wanted to be there I found it difficult to watch Johnnie R. as he endured obvious pain, grappled with his newfound weakness, faced his imminent defeat.

"You're a difficult man, Mr. Thayer," she said, holding off a smile as she took my arm once again and led me toward the door.

"And you're a tough taskmaster, lady," he came back, rolling his head on the pillow to follow our movement toward the door. "Go wrap him up now. Put him in one of those cute little gowns with cap and gloves and bring him back."

He followed those last few words with a wink that didn't quite make it. The spirit was still there; the body just wouldn't cooperate. Confused, I was led out of the room by the nurse, and just beyond the door we heard him say, "The pink one! Make him where the pink one!"

She lugged me down the hall, past the nurses' station and into a dressing area full of linens and gowns. As she tried to find the right size I attempted to make small talk, but she only grunted in response. All I could get out of her was the name Zelda.

"Ah, like Fitzgerald."

"No, as in Baker."

"Listen," I finally said as I began to slip into a bluish cotton gown thrown over my street clothes, "I'm going to be here as long as he needs me. We've got to get along."

"Just follow the rules," she said without humor, tough, efficient, unfriendly.

She plopped a cotton cap onto my head and ordered me to cram my hair beneath it. I tried to protest her attitude, still wanting to find a cordial middle ground, but she gagged me with a heavy white mask, placing the elastic band behind my head and allowing the mask to fall over my nose and mouth with a pop. Then she turned me around and pushed me forward and up the hall.

"You can stay fifteen minutes. Tops. He's very, very ill. We nearly lost him two nights ago. If you want him around for more than a day you'll play my game."

I nodded, numb with disbelief. Could it be so close, really so fucking close? I slowly walked back toward the room, at first unaware that she was placing on my hands the final touch, a pair of thin rubber gloves. She tugged at one of my hands and then gave both gloves to me with an order to put them on securely before returning to his room. I complied, and before entering I looked back at her, this no-nonsense lady, and knew, really, that I was as dependent on her as was Johnnie R. Wrapped up in gown and mask and cap and gloves I felt like a child being sent out in the dead of winter to wait for the bus. The gown was binding, the cap uncomfortable, the gloves cumbersome. The most prominent problem, however, was the raspy echo of my own breath within that onerous mask, a sheath of fibers that couldn't quite keep at bay the fetid odors as I re-entered his room. I braced myself against their sting, hoping I might come to feel awkwardly at home with them, but how do you escape the tumorous skin, the ulcerated sores, the perspiring torso, the foul breath from the wounded lungs, the close, darkening, stale air which supports life just before death?

I found Johnnie R. half-rolled onto his side facing the chair where I'd been sitting. He'd mapped out his territory and memorized the given boundaries of his movements. He'd apparently wiped his face a bit, somehow having juggled the tubes and wires to allow a quick swipe at his perspiring forehead. When he heard me coming I saw him shake himself from his drowsiness. He wanted it to be good, to act the part of a man in control, exude courage and humor during the moments he had left. He was, as always, a proud man.

"Johnnie R.," was all I could say as I leaned toward him with an outstretched hand. He couldn't reach so I simply lay my hand on his as I squeezed it softly, a grip that could never convey the simple, unformulated love I felt for him.

He shifted slightly and cocked his head. "Is that all after eight years? Hell, I can get that from Nurse Ratchett!"

I snickered, leaning over to hug him. But where and how? I worried about the IVs, the monitoring device, the oxygen tubes, the yellowed tube from the catheter inches from my thigh. Yet I somehow accomplished it, grabbing him securely by the shoulders and bringing him up just an inch or two from the mattress as I pressed my chest to him. Ah, the stinging selfish irrational fear which disease can instill. I knew enough about AIDS to realize that I wasn't in danger of contracting the virus, and likewise, I knew that bundled up in the sterile linens I wasn't in danger of infecting him. But the fear I experienced was the fear of *any* disease, any physiological step leading toward death, every little reminder of our fragile mortality. Combined with this obstinate wall of fear were the rank odors issuing from him, the same piercing odors at closer, intimate range. And, finally, there came the recognition, as I held him, of just how sick he was, how emaciated, bony, stiff, undone. He was just a thin reeking sheath of skin over an ossified frame. A delicate human wafer. Left were only the essentials, the organs that needed to do the primary work, the brain, the burdened pulmonary apparatus trying to gain the next breath, the damaged liver and kidneys attempting to cleanse the system, and the weakened heart as it slowly circulated the heated battleground which was his blood. As I began to pull away from him I felt his weak grip tighten for a moment longer before releasing me. Choked up, I turned away, pretending to shift the chair. I badly wanted it to come off well, to cut the crap and get on with it.

"Thanks so much for coming, Nick."

"I'm sorry I didn't know sooner. I would've come earlier," I answered, taking a seat, settling in.

"It means so much to me. I wanted you to be here with me. I mean it."

"We'll get you over the hump."

"Nick, no bullshit, okay?" he said, his breathing labored. "Let go of the positive outlook crap. It's nearly over, and that's okay too, because I want it to be over. I just don't want to do it alone, not here in this room, alone."

"Okay, Johnnie R."

"Look, I won't apologize for asking you to come. That's bullshit too. I needed you. I'd have done the same for you. You know that."

"Yes," I said. "It was easy getting away. I found someone to take my classes. Piece of cake."

"I just want to get the preliminaries out of the way."

"Okay, okay." I wasn't sure that he was up to talking, but he surprised me as he took up the slack, had the words ready to go. I could tell he'd been practicing them.

"You know, I almost didn't call. I didn't want you to see me like this, to remember me like this. You know? I mean, take Charly. I needed her but didn't want her to know, to see. Just pride, simple conceit, but Nick...." he hesitated, put a wired hand up to his sallow face and then let out a small cough of a cry as he added, "It's so damned humiliating. To go like this. So slowly....."

Johnnie R. began to cry, but softly, without force. He was too weak for more. I leaned forward and touched one of his hands, squeezed it hard. Burdened by the gown, stifled by the mask, I mumbled through the thick synthetic fibers, "It's alright, buddy. It's alright."

"Christ, I'm dying Nick. I'm really dying!"

"Okay, okay, okay," was all I could say, dumbly, with fear in my own voice, my own hot stale breath echoing back to me.

Johnnie R., between sobs, slowly uttered the words, "Nick, really, you've no fucking idea."

I shook my head, and simply held his hand. How odd it was feeling his thin flesh through the rubber foundation of the glove. How distant and helpless I felt as he continued crying, separated not only by the essential fact that he was to die, but by the stifling of intimacy due to the gaudy blue costume I wore. We were so many worlds apart.

Johnnie R. went at it for a few moments, barely audible whimpers and a few tears. I squeezed his hand again, waited for him to finish. It lasted but a moment longer, and then the tears disappeared as quickly as they had sprung. He let it pass, got it out quickly, and rubbed his eyes as he spoke. "No, none of this. I can't do the crying shit. We don't have a lot of time."

"I'm listening, Johnnie R."

"I've been sick for 18 months, very sick the last six. I worked full time until six months ago." He breathed deeply, closing his eyes. "When I knew I was getting close I called."

"I'm glad we've got this time, buddy," I said. He squeezed my hand. I looked at him squarely, this picture of Auschwitz, and waited for him to continue. We were both silent for a short time, listening to the sounds from the hall - footsteps, carts with rattling trays, intercom voices, a distant tinny rhythm of music. I helped him drink some water, fluffed his pillows, sponged his forehead. He catnapped for perhaps ten minutes before opening his eyes again to focus on me.

"Charly knows you're coming. She didn't resist," he offered, opening his eyes while cocking his head for a better view. "I can't tell you how much it meant to me to hear her say it was okay."

"I look forward to seeing her," I said, dissected by his sidelong glance. Was he seeking an emotional response?

"She's healthy. Seronegative. Christ, Nick, what if she'd gotten sick too. It's bad enough to die from this, but to know you've helped it kill. It would've been unbearable."

"Then you can stop kicking yourself."

"And the kid, Nick, he's adorable, a real card. A beautiful little boy. Healthy as can be. You received my telegram?"

"Yes," I answered, thinking back. "How long ago now?"

"He's four," he said, his voice suddenly livelier. The thought of his son connected with something quite vital within. Sporting a full smile he continued, "You know, I really wanted the kid. We both did. We thought we could make it work. But you know....."

"You don't have to go into it."

"No, I've got to talk. We divorced not longer after he was born. It had been good for a couple of years right after you left. I mean I didn't go out once in two years. Not one damned time. Sure, I wanted to do it, go out and get crazy, play the anonymous game. But I was good. Real good. And, Nick, we were happy ..."

"Time's up!" Zelda-the-Omnipresent yelled from the door. I nearly jumped from my chair. She was everywhere.

"Dear Zelda," Johnnie R. said over his shoulder, still on his side facing me. "Dear, dear lady, let's start over, okay?" He painfully rolled onto his back, turning his head toward the door. "Zelda, the best nurse and biggest pain in the ass in the whole wide world, please meet Nick, my oldest and best friend."

I stood; she remained at the door. I waved; she stared at Johnnie R. She was immovable.

"Now," he said, "if you want me to be a good boy you'll let him stay as long as he likes. Don't make me waste my energy arguing with you. Deal?"

She shook her head slowly, nearly spoke, then turned and walked away.

"She's a damned good nurse. But, really! If I were leaving the hospital in a week and this was my first time in it would be different. But now? C'mon!"

"I think you made your point with her."

"So, where was I?"

"Charly."

"Oh yeah." He shifted in the bed and looked up at the ceiling, saying nothing, as he sorted his thoughts. I watched as the catheter tube filled with his urine, an elementary biological fact well beyond his caring. A petty nuisance, nothing more. He was a proud man more interested by then in righting his life than hiding the piss and shit and sweat and vomit and tears. We sat in silence for a while longer, and eventually I helped to sit him up in the bed, several pillows beneath him and the head of the bed wound higher. "So, we had two great years without a hitch and then I started going out again. A little bit at first, then more frequently. I played it safe, very safe, but obviously she couldn't allow it. Not with the disease so widespread. She was scared for both of us. So we temporarily split up in early eighty-six, got back together six months later. I was tested. HIV negative. She got pregnant in August, and I guess it was in October that I started going out again. She cut off sexual relations. By then we were both angry, ready for a final break. And she divorced me."

"Let's don't go over it."

"I need to do this, Nick," he insisted, shifting yet again. He took more water and closed his eyes as he spoke. "She was right of course. She had to do it. For her own sake, the kid's. I was only in the house with the kid for five months before I moved out. And you know, that's what I regret most, time not spent with him. He needed a father. I needed a son ..." He opened his eyes and tried to breathe deeply, but his lungs, racked by pneumonia, drew breaths that were tentative, shallow, forced. I watched him move his lips, though words didn't follow. I poured more water, but he refused it. "She's still in the house, which is only fair. It was easier for me to grab an apartment downtown. And fortunately, it was an amicable split. You know Charly ... Besides, we'd been on and off for years. How many times did we start over? Four, five? We'd been practicing for the real thing for years. That she stayed as long as she did is still difficult to fathom ..." He paused to take more water, and I helped him to rearrange his pillows, being very careful not to disturb the wires and tubes. "Anyway, I wanted the best for her, for my boy. The settlement was very fair. She'll never need to work, though she continues her drawing and some writing. Children's stories mostly. And the kid's future's secure. That gives me comfort."

"Does she come by?" I asked, leaning closer.

"Every day, like clockwork. She's been damned good. In the room by nine. Stays till noon. Tries to get me to eat lunch. And sometimes she drops in during the late afternoon. A great help, all heart and soul," he said, before lowering his voice and adding, quite airily, "I know she still loves me. That's what makes it hard."

He shifted again, his eyes catching mine, seeking a response. I offered nothing as leaned forward to disentangle the oxygen tube from the IV. His hot breath smelled of something unutterably sour. He grimaced and I said, "I can go so that you can rest."

"No, Nick. Not yet. Please."

"Fine, just rest."

"Look, after the divorce I saw a great deal of both Charly and my boy. Odd, I know, particularly just after the divorce, but as I said it had been over for years. The adjustment was relatively easy. There were times when I came by every night of the week. I'd play with the kid, chat with Charly. He was too young to take away from Charly for any length of time, so we visited a lot over ice cream or a coke. It worked well."

"And has she brought him here?"

"The first few times in the hospital, yes. But this is my fifth hospitalization, Nick. I've been here for two weeks this time. I've gotten a lot worse. Even a month ago I didn't look this bad. We agreed that Ian shouldn't come by for any future visits."

"Ian?"

"Yeah, Ian Nicoli. Do you like it?" he asked, the excitement temporarily returning to his voice. He lifted his head from the pillow to find my response.

"Ian's a nice name."

"A partial tribute to you. I had to get you in there somewhere!"

"That's very thoughtful. I'm honored. Thank you," I answered uneasily.

"Anyway, once the Kaposi's spread he got scared. I lost all of this weight, these sores ulcerated and began to seep. The pneumonia left me speechless at one point. I started with the eye infections. It was one thing after another. Eventually, he didn't even recognize me. That hurt too much, realizing my kid didn't know me. Besides, he senses I'm dying. That's a funny thing, Nick. A kid doesn't understand death, yet he fears something about me right now. See's that I'm sick. Intuitively, I suppose, he senses the end. Part of the gene pool. We're programmed to know death, even if we can't articulate it."

"I want to see him."

"Maybe yet today. She might be back." Again, silence. His breathing was labored. I gave him more water, sponged the perspiration from his forehead, but he pushed to let it all out. Everything. "I never thought I'd get it, Nick. The great delusion, that feeling of immortality."

"Rest, huh?" I coaxed him.

"No, listen," he said softly, very distant by then, his mind apparently filtering through the memories of the last four years. "For awhile there, after the divorce, I was so damned lonely. I'd lost Charly, had naturally grown distant from my kid. My dad was offended by the divorce, said it looked bad for the bank. There was a lot of pressure, and I went off the deep end. I got a little crazy, self-absorbed. I started messing around at the baths. Took a couple of wild vacations to Mexico. I wasn't safe."

"Why are you doing this, Johnnie R.?"

"To fight the fear, Nick. You've no idea of the fear. The purely physical thing that's fear."

"I'm sorry."

"Realizing that I might well be HIV positive, for two years I was too frightened to get tested. Simple denial. It was somehow better not knowing. But then a few of the symptoms began to appear - swollen lymph nodes, malaise, night sweats, weight loss. My doctor asked me if I'd been tested. I almost shit my pants. Christ it was awful."

"I wish you'd called."

"You can't understand what it's like knowing a monster like that's inside you, an alien substance growing off your own vitality, waiting to weaken you enough to make the kill. Then it takes you slowly away. You know, the worst two weeks of my life, even after all of this," and he glanced at his scrawny legs and arms, looked at the monitor, wires and tubes, touched a Kaposi's lesion on his face, "yeah, the worst two weeks of my life were the two spent waiting for the test results. The anticipation was overwhelming ... And you know what, Nick? HIV's a lot like a borrower gone bad. There's always a long lag time between the first signs of weakness and getting notice of default. The whole time, for months, maybe a year, you knew he was going under. You knew from the beginning it was a bad risk but felt you'd overcome the odds. You entertained a fantasy that you were somehow safe. But once default occurred the dread disappeared. You got pissed. You planned. You acted ... Well, the same thing with HIV. I decided I'd beat the fear by acting, by understanding the virus. I'm stalking the virus as the virus stalks me. Thus, the books." Tilting his head, he glanced toward the full table beside the bed, then he briefly closed his eyes. "I read every new book on the subject. Christ, I know it by heart. The virus. Its life cycle. Its modus operandi. The opportunistic infections. I only want to be able to choose which one will kill me, to know how I'll die."

"This is taking too much out of you," I said, stung by the obvious truth, the overwhelming facts.

"Nick, I know it's over. I'm just waiting it out," he ignored me. "I mean, I need to die soon, before something more horrible occurs. I want to die of the pneumonia this time, because really waiting's the worst thing. Christ, my vision's already impaired. I see shadows more than bodies. I don't want to be blind. I don't want to die of toxoplasmosis or some such ghastly thing. Pneumonia's fine, even this brand. People die of pneumonia all the time."

"Take it easy, now," I said softly, taking his hand.

He turned toward me one more time, trying to rest on his side. I stood and leaned over him to help make the proper adjustments. He took my hand again, held it firmly. "Thanks for coming, Nick. I wanted to see you one more time. Make sure everything was okay between us. Make amends."

"Everything's okay between us."

"Somehow, having you close brings back all the innocence? You know? Youth and the bright, endless, always possible world of tomorrow."

I shook my head, remained speechless. I couldn't participate any longer. It hurt too much. But I held his hand for a long stretch of time while he rested, watching the monitor, listening for the nurses, hearing the oxygen through the tubes, observing the IV drip into the snake-like plastic tubing leading to the port in his chest. I remained for another hour, Johnnie R. dozing off and on, and when he told me that he needed to sleep he also handed me an envelope with a key to his apartment and directions to get there.

"I live there alone. There are two bedrooms. Take either one." He half-leaned forward on his elbows, barely stable. "And Nick, promise to call me later, before nine. I like to talk before I sleep. The nights are the worst. Promise?"

"I'll call."

"And tomorrow morning. Come by early?"

"I'll be here by eight."

I leaned over to hug him and then walked out of the room, waving behind me. I walked down the hall in a daze, a blue mummy, as my hot masked breath played like static on the radio.

*   *   *

Believing his fridge would be empty, I had the cabby stop at a fast-food drive-thru for some burgers and a shake on the way to Johnnie R.'s apartment. When I opened the door to his high-rise I found clean but sparsely decorated rooms, though I recognized a few pieces of furniture from his house on Meridian. Odd, the images and memories which returned from that earlier visit to Indy. Apparently he'd left Charly with a house full of new furniture and took with him a few older pieces, most of which seemed dated and worn. Still, this wasn't exactly the ghetto. His was an expensive corner apartment which overlooked the downtown skyline from one of the building's top floors, and if the spartan furnishings created a dismal air there was always the view from the window.

I plopped the suitcases down and placed the food on a table near a large corner window. I didn't bother to turn on the lights and ate in the near-dark before the skyline. The city had grown since I'd last seen it - several new high-rise business towers, the Hoosier Dome, some renovation along the old canal. It wasn't New York or Chicago, but like other cities dutifully strung across the vast belly of the Midwest, it could hold its own. The view was pleasing to the eye, and as I sat there I looked for landmarks. In particular, the Circle brought a smile to my face with its lighted monument - the world's largest artificial Christmas tree, as Hoosiers like to say. The lights on the Circle brought back memories of my first week in Indy nine years before, but I wasn't ready for them and chased them away by standing and turning on the lights to the apartment.

When I walked to the kitchen I was surprised to find that I'd been wrong. The place wasn't empty. The cupboards had been stocked. Canned goods, pasta, sauce, even my favorite junk food. The refrigerator was full - milk, eggs, juice, a sliced ham. In the freezer there was Haagen Daaz. It was all fresh, perhaps brought up that very day. I thought at first that Johnnie R. had had someone bring food up, perhaps the cleaning service, but on the counter, near a bottle of burgundy, was a note written in a script I recognized at once:

> *Nick, I knew you would be coming in late, and John was unable to stock the kitchen. I hope this will hold you for awhile. You'll never know how much John appreciates your coming. Welcome - Charly.*

The same artistic script, the soft assertion, the tentative conclusion. She seemed still to be in the room. That was Charly, somehow always present, always at the very edge of consciousness. I turned toward the windows and looked out through the gray dusk mist toward the monument. How complicated his death was becoming. Not only was I grappling with the first signs of fear and grief and loneliness, present too were the hard-hitting memories. Just as I'd begun to dig deep into my reserves for the power to remain steady as Johnnie R. went under, Charly was about to surface. It was nearly too much to bear. I'd come to town to help him die, but in the back of my mind I knew that Charly represented half the battle. The note sent me off. Nearly as hard as attempting to say goodbye to Johnnie R. was the preparation for the inevitable meeting with her, something I'd grappled with for a week. We'd have to get along, support each other, carry Johnnie R. through. It had to be handled in the right way, not too emotional, not too many tears. Yet the past invaded when it was least needed and most difficult to evade. I turned from the window and walked around the apartment before placing my clothes in one of the two bedrooms and unloading the toiletries in the bathroom. I walked to the kitchen, hesitated and then grabbed the Haagen Daaz. I sat in the living room and ate out of the container. Outside, it was too dark and wet to run it off, so I ate the ice cream guiltily while scanning several framed pictures on a side table nearby. A picture of his son was nearest me. I looked at the kid with amazement. He was Johnnie R. all over again. The thick dark hair, the sleek brows, those large blue eyes, the sensual mouth. He was grinning broadly, at Christmas, maybe three years old. He wore a Ninja Turtle outfit, wrapping paper and a Christmas tree in the background. He was a beautiful kid.

Near this photograph was one of Charly taken sometime since I'd left town. I looked for a long time at her eyes, saw them as I remembered them. They were a light brown with specks of green and gold, the golden specks holding your attention as if you were observing little question marks illuminating the soft uneasiness of her face. Her eyes contained a great depth which had always grabbed at me, a depth primarily negative, of sadness. The picture had been taken near a window, and the sunlight caught the auburn tones in her long hair. Her features were soft, somewhat vulnerable. Lips, cheeks, chin, brows. She was, in that particular light on that particular day, beautiful.

Next to the photo of Charly was a smaller framed picture of Randy, Charly's dead brother. A shot of adrenalin pushed through my guts. That odd expressionless face, those large, painful eyes, the dark, mysterious features. How many times had I seen that picture of a boy I never knew. And yet, how great was his impact on all of our lives. What further secrets could he divulge to add to those which surfaced nine years earlier? And could they change our new world as the earlier one's had changed the old? I placed the photo back on the table and reached for yet another.

It was one I remembered well, a photo which Johnnie R. had had enlarged. I brought it close and then laughed out loud. Johnnie R., Charly and me. It was the photograph taken on my first night in town. We had imbibed a great deal of wine and were slap-happy drunk. At some point Johnnie R. had managed to place the camera on a table at just the right level. He'd set the timer and then had run to Charly and me, plopping down on both of us just as the shutter clicked. Our faces were a mixture of laughter and surprise as Charly grabbed his torso and I grabbed his legs. On one side of the sofa a bottle of wine is falling to the floor. On the other side is an old photograph album we'd been thumbing through. Dishes and food are everywhere. Still, the photograph can't capture the Christmas music in the background, nor the wind against the window, nor the roaring fire to our side. It does easily capture the happiness.

I put the photo down and walked back to a window. At a certain angle I was able to catch a clear view of the Circle and its monument. Between the window and the lights of the Circle half a mile away there was only darkness. I watched the lights for a long while, and they brought back memories of that first night as well. It was useless to shake off the past, so as I slouched in the chair I surrendered to its pull.

4

Indianapolis, 1982

That first night in town back in nineteen eighty-two was so unlike the first evening of my return visit. The two had only the season in common. True, when Johnnie R. and I had left the empty coffee cups over in Broad Ripple in order to meet Charly at the house, I'd come to dread the thought of supper with her. Much as I'd wanted to meet her, Johnnie R. had dampened the prospect with his news that Charly wasn't particularly enamored of her husband's old college buddy. The fact that she might still be mourning her brother's death only made matters appear worse. If she had it in for me I wasn't prepared to fight her, thinking that I might go directly to my room, skipping supper completely. But our first meeting actually came off with a touch of humor. After we'd climbed from the car and had begun to walk toward the side entrance of their house, Charly peeped out of the doorway with a wide, wild, beautiful smile upon her face.

She said, with spatula cutting through the air, "You have time for a drink, possibly two, before the world's greatest ham is served. And I refer to the entree, not the server!"

Johnnie R. laughed; I was baffled. I'd expected the worst, perhaps abuse, but she came out not swinging at all. She was charming, good-humored.

"Of course we'll have a drink with the lovely lady," Johnnie R. said. He walked to her and gave her a kiss before turning to me with a snicker. "But she's about three ahead of us. We have some work to do!"

I could only laugh. Charly said, "I admit to having imbibed two rather strong scotch and sodas. But the ham will be impeccable."

Entering at the kitchen, Johnnie R. kissed her again lightly on the cheek before taking her free hand and holding it firmly in his. "Nick, my closest and dearest friend," he said, "meet my wife, Charly."

We shook hands, and that's when I noticed the power of her eyes, strengthened on that particular evening by the alcohol, a camouflage for the sadness. Light brown shades, the golden specks, the green questioning. When Johnnie R. left to prepare the drinks I continued to hold her gaze. I was making her uncomfortable, but with all the apparent incongruities I couldn't help myself. At times we're forced to merely stand and wait for signs or symbols of meaning. Eventually, she blushed, as I did, and the color made her, suddenly, beautiful.

One of the problems was that my imagination had conjured up a contrary image. I'd imagined that her beauty would be of a far different variety. I'd imagined a woman of great force and facial brawn, angular and stunning. I'd dreamt of a beauty of perfect proportion, large-breasted, square-jawed, short-haired, large-eyed, bold and, perhaps, terrifying. A woman comprising a daring, no-nonsense grace. But Charly was far from this. There was a softness to her, an unimposing, subtle beauty that subdued you by inviting you to seek out the contours of her desire. I couldn't get over, immediately, the breadth and depth of my error. She was very feminine, heightened with a particular refinement which I hadn't thought possible in a woman Johnnie R. might marry.

Charly eventually returned to the oven, taking care of a few last-minute items. That's when I took a closer look, discovered an instant attraction. She was tall and slender, about five-ten. Johnnie R. was only a couple of inches taller. She wore her hair long, loose, and the big sweater along with her jeans offered an unpretentious easy air. I watched her small movements as she prepared the dinner. Every move seemed calm and clean, steady.

Apparently realizing she was being observed, she picked up her glass and drank from it before turning to say, "He thinks highly of you."

"And I of him. Following these years of absence I still feel the bond, and I appreciate his call and the offer to bring me on at the bank. And I appreciate this," I said, gesturing with my arm to include the entire room.

"Ah, but you haven't tasted the ham yet," she said, taking another drink. She gingerly crossed her arms without spilling the drink. The alcohol had flushed her face.

"All the same, thanks."

"No need to thank me. Perhaps I should thank you. Though we've only met, I'm happy you've come. It's good."

"After talking with Johnnie R. I was under the impression that you might not feel that way. In fact, quite the opposite."

"I didn't know you then."

"And you do now?" Baffled, I tilted my head.

"Yes, I think so. And it's not the liquor, though I'll talk more freely I assure you," she answered, stirring the drink with a finger. "Frankly, I've thought a great deal about your coming the last few days and decided it would be good to have you, someone from the past."

"I won't get in the way."

"Oh, I'm sure you're right," she said. "I can already tell."

"Oh?"

"It's all in the eyes."

"Christ, a seer!" I laughed.

She smiled, nearly taking another sip and thinking better of it. She put down her drink and stepped forward slightly, though she was still some distance from me. She stretched her back, hands behind her, head tilted back, hair falling behind her. Again, with the light on her eyes she was extraordinarily attractive. She seemed much warmer, at ease.

"No, not a seer, Nick. I can call you Nick rather than Nicholas?"

"Yes."

"Not a seer, or rather seeress. I had imagined a hundred things about you before you arrived, not the least of which was trouble. But I see in your eyes that you aren't trouble. Searching, yes. But not trouble."

"It's a vote of confidence I could use."

"I gathered," she said quietly, turning to check the ham.

"I'm starting over, putting things in order, and this seems to be the right place to do that. II needed a change of pace from London."

"Believe me, it's not London!"

We both laughed, and a moment passed with neither of us talking, smiles still upon our faces. Then she said, "Welcome," and lifted her glass to me, emptying it. She was still smiling when Johnnie R. entered the room.

"Hurry, Nick, and catch her," he joked, placing the drink in my hand. I took a quick swallow. It was a strong scotch with little soda.

"I was telling Charly I appreciate the hospitality. A place to stay, good food, a stiff drink. Thanks for indulging me," I toasted them.

"Don't shame a friend. It's as if you wouldn't have expected it from me. Of course we want you, and besides, buddy, you're going to be the best economist the bank ever had. You'll contribute your share."

"Watch him, Nick. He's a genuine capitalist. The look of money is always in his eye. He's out to make a profit, friend or foe," Charly said, taking her fresh drink from Johnnie R.

"This isn't news to me, Charly. Remember, I saw the instincts blossom at school. The unseen hand was at work there early on."

"I'm immovable," he countered, drinking.

"And shameless," she said, smiling widely. The drinks had loosened her to such an extent that it was difficult to recognize her as the woman who once had feared my arrival. She wasn't volatile, or any more so than two drinks might induce. There was something at work there. She baffled me.

Johnnie R. said, "Think of my capitalistic greed as my version of the poetic instinct. You can both relate to that."

Charly, laughing again, "Ah, poetic license! Only in this case, Nick, he speaks of the document itself. With you, John, it's always the literal translation. No metaphor."

"I won't argue the merits of that. Besides, I'm outnumbered. Why not, instead, show Nick your etchings," he said spryly, with an expression of mischief.

"Drawings, you little fool. I only show my etchings to you!"

"Then so be it!"

"We have a bit of time. A quick review. Are you both ready?" she asked.

We were. She took each of us by the arm and escorted us up the stairs of that large Tudor home and into a room with a view of Meridian Street. She'd transformed a bedroom into her workroom. An architects drawing table was placed against one wall, and against the opposite wall she'd placed an old oaken desk upon which some of her stories lay. Drawings of all varieties lay about, but the common theme seemed to be homespun happiness, a family orientation. They were warm and casual and simple. Bright colors and light themes rendered them accessible to anyone.

Charly was in her element, and she took charge of us as she described her work, discussing present projects, future commitments. She seemed quite busy. I was impressed, not merely by her talent, which was certain, but by her sense of adventure. She seemed to control her world perfectly. She gestured endlessly with her hands, spilling at least half her drink on the immaculate parquet floor. She didn't stop talking while we were in the room, whether it was to answer questions or to elaborate on one piece or another. Johnnie R. winked at me at one point during her presentation, for it was just that, a lecture or symposium on Charly herself, and the wink seemed to say, "I told you so." He was proud. She was perfectly content to go in and out of that room every day of her life in order to place upon the great cartographical map of meaning her self-contained version. And why shouldn't she? Physically, the room was a beauty with the lovely floors and the antique rug. It was bright and airy and clean, a sanctuary for creation.

"And this is the latest drawing, part of a combination project involving a short story and a cover piece. What do you think?"

"I like it very much," I said, studying it closely. The drawing was of a small boy, perhaps five years old, looking directly at the viewer. His large eyes and shaggy hair combined with an expression of total resignation. The face conveyed sorrow, but sorrow of a child's depth. Nothing torturous. Nothing of the impending doom of adulthood. It was the countenance of a child without his toys only.

"It's based on an old photograph of John. Can you believe he was once an innocent? And what of the sorrowful expression? A thoughtful child, no?"

"Merely plotting. A latent Adam Smith awaiting his day."

She laughed lightly, quietly intoxicated. Johnnie R. bent over, holding his stomach, feigning hunger pains. "Feed me," he begged. It was back to the kitchen and then to the elaborate dining room where Charly unveiled a delightful meal. Ah, so much wine! Table talk was light and refreshing following the disastrous Broad Ripple conversation with Johnnie R. I spoke of London and the service, and eventually he and I reminisced about the days at Princeton while Charly sat back and listened. She was a picture of grace as a hostess, though I wondered how she accomplished this feat so successfully since she was quite happily drunk.

Later in the evening, after large quantities of coffee and brandy had been consumed, Johnnie R. took to comedy, imitations of old college cronies and mimicry of the well-known abounding. His impersonations were extraordinarily bad, making them all that more enjoyable. An evening which had begun tentatively quickly developed into near hysteria, and it was in the midst of this hilarity that we posed for the camera, catching Johnnie R. as he dove to the sofa while the shutter opened.

And later still, inconceivably, we found ourselves ice skating at the rink on Monument Circle in downtown Indianapolis. Charly, at some indeterminable point amid the raucous, had shouted, "Skating! We'll go skating! We simply must!" Johnnie R. thought it a great idea, and before I could convince them otherwise - "We've had too much to drink! I can't skate!" - we were in the car on Meridian Street traveling south toward the heart of the city and the daylight habitats of those who sleep north of Thirty-eighth.

"Ah, Nick! There's nothing like the Circle at Christmas," Johnnie R. informed me during the short drive south.

"They drape the monument with lights and call it the world's tallest Christmas tree," Charly chimed in.

"Yeah, and one of the fountains is converted to a rink during the winter. Lots of decorations."

"And music, gazebos, hot chocolate and people."

"It's the city all dressed up!"

So we skated, or tried to. They each hastily grabbed an arm and guided me over the ice as Charly shouted, "Hold on!" I did. In some manner still incomprehensible to me we skated slowly forward and then in circles over the small rink. The other skaters made was for us, the intoxicated threesome, as we cheered each passing minute that we managed to stay up. We weren't so much poised as we were contingently afloat. The ice remained as a cool and humorous fate, pushing us on in random circles.

How nice those moments following. While surfing the ice beneath the massive robe of glittering lights, the cold breeze caused our eyes to water and blur until everything in sight appeared as refracted, impressionistic light, a dripping montage of colors with no direction except away from the center of focus. The lingering effects of the wine and scotch warmed all but our pink noses against the chill. And far more quickly than any of us had expected we'd formed a comfortable bond. We joked and scrambled upon the ice beneath those dazzling lights as Christmas carols blurted out of the tinny speakers. I couldn't remember the last time I'd found such happiness or had felt such pleasure. With the bright skyscape as a backdrop we skated in circles for half an hour, and at the end of one of those seemingly endless dizzy loops we finally called it quits. We maneuvered our way back to the gazebo where we shook the skates from our feet and struggled to pull our shoes over thick wool socks.

"We should be getting back, guys."

"Good, I'm getting cold, and I'm very thirsty," Johnnie R. agreed, turning toward me. "A nightcap, Nick?"

"How about hot chocolate?"

"Hot chocolate it is," Charly chirped, taking us both by the arm.

Back at the house we were quieter. Johnnie R. built up the fire while Charly prepared the hot chocolate. He tuned in some jazz and Charly brought the drinks and the three of us watched the flames and coals build to a nice glow. We drank a couple of cups, but it wasn't long before the alcohol began to take its toll. Its lingering residue was as warming as the fire and carved out quiet spaces in the conversation.

Johnnie R. was the first to go. He seemed to have been putting wood on the fire one moment and sleeping the next. He lay on one of the two large Victorian sofas near the fireplace. At first he merely tilted to one side, and then he gave way and lay flat. Charly and I watched him make the descent into sleep. Once he was gone, she seemed to come alive once again. She covered Johnnie R. with an afghan, and then she took a seat in a small chair opposite me. She sat close, reclining, relaxed.

"He was out late last evening. I'm afraid he's done for."

"I'm sinking fast myself."

"Strangely, I'm not," she replied, smiling.

She was lovely, almost spry, as the fire's glow touched her soft face. I was amazed at her will, her ability to dig deeply into herself for more energy. It was she, after all, who had started drinking so early while Johnnie R. and I were sipping coffee and trading insults in Broad Ripple. Eventually, she leaned forward in her chair, her hands with the mug between them resting on her knees. With the fire and its glow at the periphery I couldn't see her eyes clearly, but she seemed rested and composed. And the warmth in the room was divided, by source, between the fire and Charly.

I reflected for a moment on her comment that Johnnie R. had been out late the night before. So he'd left her at home and had caroused and returned toward morning. How often now? And why did she remain, this woman, if her husband was wandering the streets and bars of the city seeking men? I couldn't put her face in juxtaposition with that of a trapped woman, her co-dependence painfully binding her to her husband's ambiguous needs. She was an enigma, perhaps more so than Johnnie R. I continued observing her closely as I thought of their compromised marriage, and she took her eyes away from the fire and met mine for a passing moment. I looked away, my eyes coming to rest on a photograph on a table near me. Again, those large, painful eyes and dark mysterious features. It was my first look at Randy, a good-looking but somehow other-directed kid.

"My brother," Charly offered, leaning past me and picking it up.

"A nice-looking kid."

"Yes, yes he was," she said softly. "He had my father's features."

I said nothing, felt I should offer nothing unless she continued.

"The distant look in this photo always attracted and repelled me at the same time. The eyes say something the voice never did, or perhaps could."

"Sometimes little brothers are like that. I know. I came with a package of three older sisters!"

"Something in the gaze is unfinished," she said, ignoring my attempt at humor. She placed the photo back on the table, sipped from her mug and added, "He died last summer."

"Johnnie R. told me. I'm very sorry."

"He was such a good boy. I mean, he was fun-loving, intelligent, industrious. He was to attend college this last autumn."

"I'm sorry."

"It was so tragic. The early death. The way it occurred. All that waste."

"I know," I said quietly.

"He idolized John. He wanted to go into banking, and John was excited about the prospect of grooming him."

"Well, he would've been with the best," I offered.

"But listen to me," she apologized, glancing at the fire. "I won't weigh you down with such things."

"It's not a burden."

"We're coping well now," she continued. "It was very difficult for us in the beginning. I think it hit John harder than it hit me. But we've accommodated it. We're moving on."

She was silent and I turned to face the fire, passing my mug slowly from hand to hand. How odd she should mention that Johnnie R. had grieved more. How odd that he had done so. But I decided not to pursue it. Instead, we both listened to the firewood popping with the heat. Perhaps a minute passed before Charly spoke.

"John said you needed a change."

"London was a bit dreary, a bit gray."

"And Alabama prior to that?"

"Not your typical childhood, foster care and such. But Charly I won't bore you with my past. That's why I'm here. To start over."

"You're angry with me."

"No, I'm only tired. A long long day."

"Of course. I understand," she said, leaning forward again. "But perhaps we can talk of such things in the future. I've a hunch ..." She hesitated as she peered at the fire, her mug now gripped steadily in one hand. She leaned back in her chair, her free hand playing with her long hair. A moment later she turned toward me and continued. "I've a hunch we're preoccupied in the same manner. The eyes, remember?"

"It sounds like mysticism," I said, playing coy. I too believed we shared a great deal in common, but the thought frightened me. It seemed dangerous.

"Perhaps. But those are the same eyes I saw in the mirror after John and I first became acquainted with our problems. Eyes never betray the pain of a soul."

I almost said, "Then it is mysticism," but decided against it. She'd made a second reference to Johnnie R.'s sexual habits, indirectly, and I wasn't prepared to discuss it with her. After all, it was he who was my close friend. He had invited me to his home. How could I allow her to confide in me? How could I open up to both of them? Instead I remained quiet as I watched the fire. The embers were hotter and darker but beginning to fade quickly. The flames were low, and the room darkened considerably. I could see only the outlines of her face as she spoke.

"I know you know. He told me, but I would've known without his having done so. He needs you now, just as you need the change you speak of. After this afternoon you undoubtedly know of our problems. If you're to stay you can't ignore it." Again, I was silent. She paused and then added, "My pain is of the soul as well. It's always an affair of the soul when love is concerned. In that sense we have a common bond."

"But my problems, whatever they may be, don't concern love," I said hastily.

"Perhaps lack of love."

"Why do you want to entrust me with your secrets?" I asked, leaning forward as well. I became angry that she would presume such a thing. I was angrier yet that she was probably right. She leaned back in her chair, pulling her knees up to her breasts, holding her ankles with her hands.

"Look, Nick, odd as it may sound, I do feel I can trust you. Admittedly, I was skeptical when I heard you were coming. I thought the worst in the beginning -"

"You believed I was a former lover."

"Yes, in the beginning. But after some thought I knew how ludicrous the assumption was. It would be extraordinarily stupid for him to do so. I knew he loved me and wanted to continue with the marriage. After some time I knew there were reasons altogether different for your coming."

"The comfort of old friends," I said, standing. I walked to the fireplace and stirred the coals. A small flame flared brightly and then died down. I sat back down as she continued.

"Yes, something like that. He needed you. The opening at the bank allowed his plan to fall into place. He felt, from your letters, that you could also use a change of scenery. He said to me before you came that you were undergoing a spiritual crisis. You intrigued me."

"And frightened you?"

"Yes."

"Though you knew I wasn't gay."

"Yes. The fear came from another quarter. I'd come across, in some of John's old school papers, some poems you'd written."

"Christ, that was years ago."

"He kept all of them. I read them, most of them very sad."

"Motherless childhood. Paternal clashes. Southern doom and gloom. But I'm changing all that."

"And along with his comments concerning your need for a change I feared what I might find."

She wasn't going to let go of it. "And?"

"And I saw your eyes. You were troubled, but not one to make trouble. Call it a mystical intuition if you wish. It's the hunch again. We share something, and I'm happy for it.

"Happy at the thought of pain?" I asked, bewildered.

"No, deliverance from it."

I was silent, indeed, silenced by her words. I liked her very much, but she puzzled me with her frankness, her ability to take one not at all close to her and compel him to feel confident of friendship. But just as I'd frightened her with an image which preceded my arrival, she frightened me. I feared her friendship, her intuition, and I was confused by the many changes we'd experienced face to face during the few hours of our acquaintance. Why was it that before her I felt naked, shaken? She sat silently. The embers were fast losing their heat, and the room was nearly dark but for the small lamp near the back of the room. We watched the coals for some time before she rose. She laid her hand on my knee lightly, carefully, and spoke.

"Welcome again, Nick. I'm glad you've come."

"Thank you."

She walked to the couch where Johnnie R. lay and shook him gently. She shook a second time when he didn't respond. He bolted upright, yelling, "What in the hell!"

"You fell asleep, John. Nick and I watched you sleep. Let's go to bed."

"I just dozed off," he offered with a yawn.

"Like hell," I said.

"What time is it?"

"Two," Charly answered.

"To bed, Nick. A long day tomorrow," he said, yawning again as he stretched.

"I want to stay by the fire, or what's left of it. For a moment. Do you mind?"

"Fine. Just turn out the lamp. Your room is the first on the left from the top of the stairs," Charly answered.

I stood as they stood, and as Johnnie R. walked by he put his arms about me. He hugged me tightly, patting my back. "I'm glad you're here, buddy. It's going to be good, I promise."

"I know it will be."

They left me standing there in the near-darkness. I walked over to the lamp and turned it off and then took my seat on the chair closest to the fireplace. I watched the coals continue to burn out, dark red to black. The embers popped and sizzled, hissed. I lay back in the chair and reflected on the day. It had been an unusual welcome, that first day in Indy. Mysterious, exhausting. Yet something warmed me to the prospect of this new home, this family. Running for so long, finding so little. I'd scratched and clawed my way from Mobile to London by way of Princeton and Washington, and for the first time since those prodigal Princeton years I felt close to something only previously imagined. Until then I'd tried to conceive such comforts without success. But the gyre had continued turning, and it was on to Indianapolis with its lure and promise. In the heavy warmth before the fire on that early morning, the day mysterious and ripe and full and promising, I leaned back and relaxed, drowsy and free. I dreamed of what good I might find in Indianapolis. I hoped, and it was pleasant to hope again.

5

Indianapolis, 1991

Those were the memories of my first day in Indy nine years earlier. Christ, how it had all changed. The idealism, the promise, the reprieve, the love. Temporarily, I'd found a family again, and it was as fine a moment as I'm able to remember. But by that evening of my return visit only the debris of memories remained. Death loomed around the corner; the promise was lost. A good life had been wasted. And the love? Well, the love had in the end tortured us all.

I walked back to the sofa and looked at the remaining photographs. It was touching to find that Johnnie R. had kept and framed a photo of the two of us standing outside the Firestone. There we were walking out of the library, books under our arms, standing shoulder to shoulder, grinning through the glare of the afternoon sun. All spunk and raw nerve and still more hope. Ah, we were immortal then! I held the photograph for a long while, touching its frayed edges, rubbing at a yellow spot upon the glass, turning it at different angles for effect. I returned it to the table only when the phone rang. It was Johnnie R.

"You forgot to call, Nick," he said, his voice soft, very weak.

"Shit," I said, looking at my watch. It was nearly nine.

"You have to call before nine or you can't get through. They close the switchboard."

"Sorry, Johnnie R."

I heard him sigh, then cough a bit. Then he wheezed through the receiver, "Everything okay there?"

"Yes. It's a beautiful view. And I found some old photos near the sofa. I'm looking at the old one of us standing outside the Firestone.

"Our junior year. October. The Friday before Homecoming."

"Christ, how do you remember such minutiae?"

"Because of you, silly! I remember every detail of my time spent with you."

I said nothing, could say nothing.

"So, did you eat?" he asked.

"Yeah. Charly bought food, left a note."

"She promised me she'd do it. She's great, Nick."

"Yeah, she is." He paused, coughed violently and was silent. I could hear him try to sip water, shift in the sheets. Then there was nothing.

"You okay, Johnnie R.?"

"Yeah," he answered. "I was just thinking about how, suddenly, every banal biological function takes on a significant meaning. For example, with a catheter you never take a piss but are always pissing. A transcendent piss. Christ it's ugly."

"Don't think about it."

"Those words from you?"

"Do you need me to bring you anything tomorrow."

"No. I just need to talk now," he said. "To hear your voice. It's the darkness. The frightening mysteries of childhood. It happens every night."

"I'm here as long as you need me," I said.

"It's like *Fanny and Alexander*," he continued. "Remember? The kids imagine things which adults can never see. Statues moving their arms. Paintings with big eyes that blink. Goblins in the dark?"

"Yeah."

"Well, that's what I see now. Faces in shadows. Voices in echoes. Signs of something beyond us right at my feet."

I was silent.

"I'm dying, Nick. That's why I know I'm close. I hear things I could never hear before."

"It's the medication. A side effect."

"Or dementia, right?" he countered, his anger temporarily beating back the tears. "I've seen guys fucking go crazy over night. Their brains just soft, mushy pears. They babble and they cry and they shit everywhere. Make hand paintings out of shit on the nice clean walls. Then they die, Nick!"

"It's okay, Johnnie R." It hurt to hear him talk of what we both knew was there.

"What do you believe, Nick? I mean metaphysically?"

"God?" I asked, caught by surprise.

"Or whatever. I mean, when you really let yourself go, really let go, what do you see? A nice pretty golden god? Sheer energy, maybe a current of godliness? Nothingness?" he coughed into the receiver, wheezing hard. Before I could answer he added, "Or just old *Green Acres* reruns?"

"Jesus, think of it," I played along. "*Mister Ed. Lucy. Dobie Gillis*."

"Or *Get Smart. Patty Duke. Donna Reed?*"

"How about *Star Trek*," I suggested. "That's apropos."

"Seriously, Nick," his tone hardened.

"It's been so long, Johnnie R. I haven't thought much about it."

"Of course. The great rift between the healthy and the living dead," he said, coughing again.

"Don't do this to yourself."

The tenor of his voice changed suddenly. Once again it was thin, tinny, on the edge. "I'm scared, Nick. I'm really scared."

"Tell me, buddy."

"Like I said earlier, it's not the physical aspect of death that frightens me. Not now. In the beginning, yes. That frightened me most. The pain, the wasting away, the fevers and chills. But that fear's under control. I'm used to being sick, a vegetable."

"C'mon, Johnnie R., don't do this."

"Hell, Nick. The only thing I fear now, physically, is blindness."

"Please, Johnnie R. Leave it."

"I mean, I'm fighting the pneumonia," he continued, "and I already have Kaposi's. Cancer with a purple hue. I might have Aseptic meningitis. I can take that. All of it. I just don't want to go blind."

"Quit, or I'll get Nurse Ratchett after you!"

"But you know what bothers me most? More than blindness? It's the other issue. The death of, what, the soul? The death of consciousness? Not seeing or hearing or feeling? I need something besides the gray, Nick, but that's all I see. Just haze. Nothing."

He sobbed into the phone, unable to cry, really, but letting loose with a wet, sobering, wheezing cadence. His lungs were too diseased to allow him to cry properly. And I was burning, shaking with his fear. I tried to console, but uselessly. "Take it easy, buddy."

"I always thought it would be different. Now I haven't a clue beyond the echo in my head. It scares me. I just need to hear your voice. That helps." He took more water, breathed deeply, regained control. I could hear the sheets move, a cup of water fall, his cursing. Then he was back. "I watched a program on the tube earlier. A holy roller from Montana saying the disease is God's revenge."

"Johnnie R., the virus is devious, but it has no has no moral code, no meaning of its own. You have to believe the universe is shaped differently than that."

"Some fucking universe!"

"It's neutral. Nature's unthinking way. That's all."

"To some, something consciously evil is better than nothing at all. Even sin is better than your neutral nothingness."

"It's just a fall guy, Johnnie R. It helps to make the metaphysical more nearly concrete. Stick with the energy, its' cleaner."

"Yeah, something like a current. Plug me in, watch me light your house," he said, trying to laugh.

"I see you in something more than a light bulb. Maybe a constellation," I said, trying to humor him.

"No, too cold and isolated. Too distant."

"Then, how about the monument lights. The Circle tree?"

"Hell, no. They're on only six weeks out of the year. Even in death I need steady work," he said, laughing again.

"Hmmmm, steady work, huh? How about static electricity?"

"Bingo! It's everywhere. You got it. I'll warm it up if you promise to join me."

"I promise."

"Good, I'll sleep better."

"We'll talk in the morning."

"Nick, don't hang up until I'm asleep, okay?"

"Okay."

"And Nick, do me a favor and bring that photo from the Firestone. Do that for me."

I agreed to do so, and he went on for awhile, bantering about nothing in particular. Hunting for a warm voice, a little love. Trying to find courage. Attempting to name and define his god. And within half an hour I could only hear his labored breathing, the faint echo of hospital static behind him and the slight shuffle of the sheets as his chest moved. Moments later a nurse picked up the receiver, told me he was sleeping and then hung up the phone.

* * *

Johnnie R.'s Journal

Armistice, 1991

What's the meaning of this disease which stalks the final two decades of the twentieth century? And what can we make of the emotional power it holds over us? How frightening are its possessory skills, dominating the wounded imagination of a sometimes hapless humanity, for instance, its ability to make us both love and hate in unequal measure. What is the meaning of the response to this virus which instills both fear and courage, which discharges a cacophony of reactions along the emotive pectrum from the compassionately humane to the vengefully wicked? What more abhorrent yet adept metaphor have we than this hideous concoction of nature which in turn has created a mentalscape representing a century's deposit of internal phobias projected on the contemporary canvas of the irrational? And what of the convenient scapegoats who must suffer and die in imposed disgrace in order to properly define this new death? And when the histories of these two decades are written, long after my imminent death, will there be a chapter entitled 'AIDS,' and will it be something more than a short synopsis concerning medicine and disease? Will it instead offer a critique of the social fabric of a century, its failures and its regrets? Perhaps this issue, rather than, say, the fall of communism or the advances in the sciences, will best give notice of the nature of our moral fiber to the future inhabitants of this lonely planet. Perhaps it shall attest to nothing less than the failures embedded in the human condition as the clock hands slowly turned and the century came winding down.

* * *

I read those words the following morning after reaching the hospital sometime after eight, but I couldn't go on with it and put the journal down. Wrapped in the same sanitary garb I'd worn the day before, now the required dress code, I passed time while waiting for Johnnie R. to wake and for Charly to show by looking out the window at the cold December morning. I seemed bent on pondering the finely delivered symmetry of my initial entrance and later return to the city while watching small snowflakes fall, and I instantly remembered a similar day nine years earlier. Those were the snowflakes from my second day in Indy back in eighty-two. They were the same snowflakes falling against an identical gray sky, two snowfalls nine years apart. Suddenly, I remembered Johnnie R. driving us down Meridian for my first day at the bank, and as I leaned against his bed it all came back.

6

Indianapolis, 1982

We'd left the house with a wave from Charly, and we'd met the cold morning in our dull wool pinstripes and starched shirts and awkward ties, our only armor against the windy cold and winter angst. The sun remained hidden by thick gray clouds, and only a few blocks from the house we found snow flurries, small soft flakes against a palette of gray swirled about by the nagging wind. In a few places where the current was strong the flakes whirled about in exquisite patterns on the asphalt. At the intersections, where the cross winds met, the flakes gathered into pockets where they were twirled about in small eddies of apparent steam escaping from beneath the street. The mirage continued at each intersection we crossed. In other places, nearer the curbs, the snow had collected into delicate mounds which reminded me of the fine white sand castles of Pensacola Beach where I'd visited many times as a child.

My first morning had begun inauspiciously enough with a shower as I tried to beat back the mild hangover from the wine I'd shared with Johnnie R. and Charly the night before, and while under the hot water I recounted the final conversation with Charly as the fire had burned out. Souls and common bonds? She'd made me uneasy, yet I couldn't be angry with her. Those wonderful eyes and her intuitive, nature had captured me. Plus, she had a knack for putting me at ease. When Johnnie R. and I entered the kitchen, Charly was already there dishing up breakfast. Wrapped in a thick red terry cloth robe, all smiles and gesticulation, she toasted us with her cup of coffee, saying, "The banking world will never know what hit it! Dashing!" Over coffee they each took turns goading me. I'd let on that I was suffering first-day jitters, and Charly in particular took her pleasure with me. With a sleepy smile and the cup nearly at her lips she said, sardonically, "A man of numbers and forecasts? Surely you're up to the challenge."

Career crisis? Transition questions? She was suggesting, of course, that this was the talk of those steeped too deeply in baby boom angst? Such terms pointed to a late-twentieth century dilemma which sounded too yuppy-fied to elicit a sympathetic response. Johnnie R., of course, had never felt such pangs; he'd nearly been born in the bank. His blood was there, literally. Likewise, Charly hadn't suffered such thoughts, but for far different reasons. Writing and drawing in her room on Meridian Street, seeking the help of the wealthy muse while waiting for Johnnie R., she seemed content. When she suggested that at times it was quite lonely up in her drawing room - "No one with whom to commune" - I quickly reminded her that she'd spoken only the evening before of communing with souls. The writers' secret muse. The voice of inspiration.

"But souls don't talk; they only listen," she responded between sips of coffee. "They move you through transformations of mood. That's all. Thus, the silence."

Her mystical intuition intrigued me, and those last few words remained with me as we entered the downtown financial district. Once there I was reminded again that being the bank president's son had its definite advantages. Johnnie R. rated a convenient parking space beneath the bank, the envy of any urban dweller. As we approached the bank off Market, just short of the Circle where we'd skated the evening before, the car nearly met the great circular brick pad when suddenly we began to descend. A huge door opened at the Market Street entrance of the bank, and the darkness took us in before I realized what was happening. We descended into the depths below the city and came to a stop within the large concrete parking garage beneath the bank. As we descended I nearly let loose with a wicked pun, a play on the idea that we were going down, going down on it, sharply and totally down, hobbing the knob of the gracious earth in the name of darker secrets. Ah yes, ascent and descent, the rhythm of a lovely suck job working through the depths of the dark groin. But I said nothing as the attendants at the bottom, sporting blank pale mole faces, gave a nice finishing touch to the tomb-like atmosphere, the sewer-world below the Circle and the city. Johnnie R. handed over the car keys and we hopped onto an elevator and shot upward into his family's bank.

Once within, Johnnie R. began in earnest a lengthy tour and my haphazard orientation. This began, most importantly, with an impromptu meeting with his father. We came out of the elevator on the uppermost floor, the *Executive Wing* as they call such corporate turf. There, the large windows of a magnificently paneled hall gave a panoramic view of the city which stretched thinly north and lingered on the pale horizon before disappearing into nothingness. Johnnie R. slipped beyond one of the hall's huge cherry doors as I took in the view. Moments later he returned with his father.

The old man obviously was in a hurry, an expression of slight impatience playing on his old face. He wasn't quite what I'd expected. Dressed immaculately in his gray pinstripe suit and white starched shirt, he was gaunt and pale, slight of build and stooped. His face was creased at the jaw and he had broad thin lips. The sum of these odd-fitting parts created an image of a man ten years older than his actual age. Immediately catching my imagination was the fact that his thinning white hair, along with these miscellaneous features, concocted an eery similarity to Laurence Olivier. Although in body and build there was no resemblance to Johnnie R., his crow's feet eyes were Johnnie R.'s a generation removed. They were blue and intelligent and serious. They were his strength.

"And here, Pop, is the new exec, the superman of economists. He's a genius, really," Johnnie R. announced with eager humor. He relished putting me on the spot, making it rough on me. The situation was awkward and embarrassing, and the circumstances weren't ameliorated by Johnnie R.'s dig. And I say awkward because the old man didn't bring me in at all. Johnnie R. did. There were no interviews, no evaluations of merit. It was cronyism, simply. I felt the old man would be sizing me up a bit more harshly than usual under these nepotistic circumstances. I squirmed with the heightened expectations which I knew I couldn't meet. Yet the old guy was no less cordial for it.

"Ah, young man, I apologize that we lack the time to properly sit and talk. I'm afraid I'm on a tight schedule," he said with a booming voice as he extended a slightly quivering hand. The contrast he presented was remarkable. An intimidating basso from a nearly broken frame.

"Thank you for having me," I answered, taking his hand. His grip was quite firm, much more unyielding than you'd expect from his frail appearance. After we withdrew I noticed he continued to shake, a mild palsy of some sort.

"We'll get to know each other soon enough," he continued as he stepped closer to me, so close, in fact, that I became uncomfortable. This, I knew at once, was a conscious ploy. He was well aware that his initial appearance before any newcomer would establish an image of weakness, frailty, even a hint of the Eighties **W** word: wimp. So he compensated for these professional drawbacks by concocting a few artificial tools which successfully insulated him. As with his voice, his ability to control social spaces was an easy tool for domination. He was utterly certain, in control, seemed to be relishing his power. I could tell immediately that he was a real ball buster, an ancient Hercules in a pinstripe suit.

"The important thing is that I've met you at last," he offered, touching my shoulder softly with his shaking hand. "Do you have any idea how long the mystery of your name has played in my mind? It's as if you are a part of the family."

"I'm gratified to have been asked to join the bank. I hope not to be a disappointment."

"Ah, never a disappointment," he quickly replied. "No, John has never disappointed me, nor have his friends. And he tells me you're the most highly regarded in that particular category."

"He's my closest friend."

"Yes," he answered, tilting his head slightly to one side, looking at me quizzically. "Now, I may become annoyed at your generation's flippancy on occasion" - and he looked me over carefully, still standing uncomfortably close to me as his warm breath wisped my face - "but never disappointed. I advocate independence in moderation. If you understand that we'll be fine."

"I'm sure we will." I was ill at ease and the old man knew it. In fact, his slight smile seemed to confirm that he was enjoying my discomfort. This was, perhaps, another shared family trait. Though stooped, with every new word he uttered he seemed to grow in stature. For a moment I forgot the palsy, the old face, the slight stoop of the shoulders, the fragile structure beneath the suit. He was by then, say, eight feet tall. I felt like a tiny boy before the principal. A touch of a quivering finger and he'd bowl me over.

"Now, Nicholas," he said, "I remember visiting John over in Princeton while he was in attendance there, yet I cannot determine for the life of me why and how we missed each other. You were friends then, I'm sure."

"Friends nearly from the first day," I said.

"Same club? Were you in Ivy?"

"No. I didn't join a club."

"Ah! Too bad," he replied with a turn of his head. He grew another six inches or so as I fell a notch in his estimation. Legacies were obviously important. "Nevertheless, the fates have finally brought us all together, and I assume it's for the betterment of us all. Time shall tell us, no?"

"I'm sure it will," I answered, trying to be polite. I didn't quite care for him, and I'm sure he felt the same of me.

We stood staring in stifled silence, his eyes never moving from mine, until Johnnie R. burst out with, "He was in the Foreign Service, Pop. London."

"So you said, John. And I hope, Nick ..... May I call you Nick?" he asked as he carefully picked a piece of lint off my dark, ill-fitting suit.

"Of course." I was fuming.

"Well, I hope, Nick, that I can hear about your adventures abroad," he said, taking my hand again and squeezing it hard. "But for now I'll leave you to continue your tour. Good luck."

And then he was gone, basso, blue eyes, frail frame and all. I could only ask myself, *Who was that masked man?* True, as he walked away he lost some of the luster of power, became a mere mortal, a slightly palsied older man, but he was a breed apart. Throughout my tenure at the bank his presence always delivered the same troubling impact. I was never able to accommodate the fact that this ballsy guy shared his unequivocal demeanor with such a worn body.

"He doesn't like me," I said to Johnnie R. as we continued the trek.

"He's just distant. It comes with the territory," he said, unconcerned. "Let's finish the orientation."

The bank itself was quite nice, really, and the facility was modern enough to be both comfortable and alienating. The desks were new and the carpet and walls, clean. Unfortunately, the many windows weren't made to open. Shut off from the world, the only connection with the balance of civilization was the dreaded telephone or the long walk down the quietly carpeted hall to the elevators and the world beyond. We walked in and out of every department. Face after face appeared before me; name after name rang in my ears (including the name Gretel which belonged to a starch, dark-featured Germanic woman of

61

fifty who was to be my secretary). We chatted throughout the morning with executives and clerks and tellers, and I was granted no reprieve over lunch when several of his cronies joined us in the Executive Dining Room where office gossip and talk of sex mixed with chatter concerning interest rates and treasury coupons and bond money. This was definitely MBA country.

"And now to work for a bit, Nick," Johnnie R. said to me by mid afternoon as he walked me back to my department where, above the door, were the words: Economic Analysis, Investments and Financial Markets.

"Do you think the title is long enough?" I chided him. "Maybe you can squeeze in *and other important stuff.* What do you say?"

"If you must know, smartass, its history is even more ludicrous," he offered with a smile. "Before the department was re-structured, the name by which it was known was Economic Analysis, Trusts, Markets and Estates."

"But of course in the age of sleekly packaged finance such a rambling and incoherent title wouldn't do," I suggested.

"Nick, buddy, you don't get it. The problem was less that of a nonsensical hodgepodge of unrelated areas of banking than it was the creation of an unfortunate acronym: *EAT ME.*"

"But good fun for disgruntled employees," I suggested.

"Well, when this rather delicate literary state of affairs came to the attention of the old man the acronym was banished with the creation of the new department name."

"And the moral?"

"There is none, Nick. Such is the story of normal corporate life."

In my office, the view from the single window, where not entirely blocked by adjacent buildings, was of the west. The cloud cover was thick, and in the distance a few birds flew near the roofs of the smaller buildings, disappearing eventually into the gray vapor as small lost specks of dust twirling about meaninglessly. Dead eye material floating in and out of direct vision. On the streets below, traffic began to congest in anticipation of the Friday afternoon rush hour. Back in the room, the walls had been furnished with vague watercolors depicting farm life, all of which would have to go. There was one small bookcase, nearly empty, against one wall. A credenza to match the desk was placed behind the desk chair and beneath the window. Two small chairs faced the desk.

"Sit and enjoy, Nick," Johnnie R. said before turning to leave. "And remember, buddy. T. S. Eliot worked as a banker during his early years. Wallace Stevens worked for an insurance company in Hartford, Connecticut all his life. Two of the greatest poets of the century. You're in good company, sport."

He'd certainly anticipated my mood with talk of Eliot and Stevens as he left me to hunker down with my new banker's life. I ventured that even Johnnie R., the consummate banker, might occasionally have felt some uneasiness born of the loss of the Word, the realm of poetry, where, incrementally, one might discover meaning on ever-wider inner scales. Hard to do, though, while developing financial forecasts and studying interest rates, inflation rates, unemployment figures and the GNP. Recession or growth. Higher inflation or stable prices. Increased housing starts or a glut. After all, economists weren't, as a general rule, interesting people. Keynes was the greatest exception, and that had more to do with his Bloomsbury connections and sexual preferences than with his well-known economic theories. So it was back to dishing up the same old grub. Move over Rilke! Make room for treasury bonds, junk bonds, blue chips, securities, certificates of deposit, commercial paper and financial instruments! Because, though not included between the glossy covers of the bank's annual mission statement, the unspoken corporate goal was simple: mold the individual into a pliable portion of the greater collective piece of anonymous human machinery. Bank motto: Insert a card, withdraw a soul. Once lost within the mechanical innards of the great machine, hidden deeply within, all meaning would become associated with the heartbeat of the newly created Being. It was a mirage, a gallant corporate feat. Amusingly, it seemed real, but it had no pulse, no brain waves. And even if you were lucky enough to survive, to make it through the maze of the digestive tract of the beast, finally excreted, retirement papers and pension in hand, filthy yet alive, with what compromised will would you meet your new world as you nursed your aching vitals and a tainted soul?

*   *   *

Johnnie R. retrieved me from my office in the late afternoon and pressed me to join him for a drink. We walked to a bar two blocks from the bank where the air was warm and the smoke was stiff. It contained the usual mix of Friday afternoon urbanites - businessmen, lawyers, bankers, a few women sprinkled among the men. A jukebox played for the festive crowd, the holiday season and the weekend reprieve helping them to dodge the corporate beast. We grabbed the last available table near a window and ordered drinks. Once delivered, Johnnie R. held his glass high. "Welcome to the bank," he shouted above the crowd. I toasted him in return, taking a sip of the vicious drink. Johnnie R. surveyed the bar and then turned to me to ask, "What are you thinking, Nick?"

"That I'm glad I'm here and not in London," I leaned close.

"So I gathered from your letters."

"There were genuinely good people in the service, but the dreary landscape and dead-end job were too much bear."

"And Londoners?"

"The British play well with what they have, but what they have seems to be dwindling by the day."

"So much for Her Majesty's Empire."

"You know, there's an odd similarity to the American South. A reserve, a class consciousness, something deeply ingrained, a gentility of sorts. In that sense, I wasn't nearly as far from home as you might think."

"And female friends, Nick-o?"

"What do you want me to say? That I sneaked off alone to St. Anne's Court in the wee hours of the morning for some good old fashioned British porn with the likes of Miss Fifi, Cathi Clit and Madame Sixty-nine?"

"At least you still remember their names."

"My point is that there were a few lusts, but no great love."

"Then tell me about the lusts!"

"Just reflect on those names and extrapolate." He laughed, cheering me again. Then I changed the topic. "There's a pub very similar to this one where I went to escape."

"Escape what?"

"The drudgery. The nine-to-five stuff."

"Drudgery," he offered impatiently, "is the sacrifice you make for money."

"You like it more than I do."

"You deny its ameliorating effects?"

"I don't deny that it feeds and clothes me, but I dislike its power. It speaks against me."

"You mean it's not poetic," he countered, shaking his head. "Nick, you haven't even begun!"

"Come on, you've never questioned where all of this is leading?"

"To the bank, of course!"

"I'm serious."

"I know you are. And so am I," he said, taking another sip. "Hell, Nick, I love the numbers' game. There's power in numbers, like there's power in money. I get all worked up over diverse portfolios, collateral security, treasury bills, promissory notes, Euro-dollars and Form 9's. Give me a financial statement. You can have *War and Peace*. Hell, while the rest of us are out creating the foundations for the twenty-first century, you're a hundred years behind, masturbating with words!" He checked me for a response, gulped his drink and added, "Nick, there's no longer power in poetry. Can't you see? We've got all the leverage. We've got 'em by the balls. They need us more than we need them. We're the money guys. We feed their dreams."

He meant every word of it. While others found themselves docked forever in their unchosen careers, he was quite happy with his own fate. He did love it, his bankers' world. And I frankly expected him to continue waxing philosophical about the great romance of power while providing me with an inspirational talk combining Vince Lombardi and Adam Smith. But at the moment there were more pressing concerns.

"Jesus, look over there!" he blurted out, grabbing my arm and pointing beyond the window. 'Do you see the guy on the corner, the guy without a coat?" I followed his pointing finger and spotted a man of medium height wearing an elegant but rumpled pinstripe suit. He appeared distracted, ill at ease, though I couldn't get a good reading on his features. We watched him fidget, glancing from side to side, and then the light changed and he walked beyond our view.

"So?" I asked. "A guy has no coat. There are lots of wacky people on the streets."

"This guy's no street bum, Nick. And it's worse than I thought."

"Do you mind starting over?"

"He's a big shot at the bank. On his way out," he frowned. "And you might say he's the reason we're having this drink."

"Christ, I hope the rest of top management's in better shape."

"No laughing matter, Nick."

"What does this have to do with me?"

"The guy's going off the deep end, and he'll have to be replaced."

"With whom?"

"Me, of course," he said. "And I'll need your help. We'll knock 'em dead together."

"What does he do?"

"Executive VP - Operations."

"Pretty big shoes to fill. I mean, at your age."

"You mean at *our* age, sport."

"Christ," I said, shaking my head in disbelief. I pressed him to elaborate.

"Not here, Nick," he said, scanning the crowd. "I can't talk over this noise. Let's go to a quieter place, have some supper."

He touched base with Charly and we grabbed our coats and stepped out into the cool air. We'd taken only a few steps in the direction of the bank when the man we'd been observing stepped in front of us to block our passage. Jolted, we both stopped. I glanced over at Johnnie R., searching his face for a clue. He gave me a quick nod, tapping me on the arm as he offered, in a casual whisper, "It's okay."

"John, a word with you," the man ordered, quickly placing a hand on Johnnie R.'s arm and pulling him to the side. I followed, noting the expression of growing alarm on Johnnie R.'s face.

"Mike, are you alright?" Johnnie R. quizzed, leaning forward as he removed the man's hand from his arm. The older man didn't immediately respond, his mental lag time out of kilter as he shook his head slightly, his bearings seemingly shot. While he gathered himself, I took him in from head to toe. For a banker, he was certainly in a wild state of disrepair. Hair askew, face a ruddy red from the cold, the navy pinstripe suit a bit rumpled, his tie buffeted about by the wind. Still, he was no bum. The threads were first rate. Perhaps in his early fifties, he sported silver hair and deepening lines around the lips and eyes, and on another day he would have appeared as not unlike Johnnie R.'s father in terms of elegance and sophistication. Yet, here he was, disheveled, a real mess.

"Are you alright?" Johnnie R. repeated.

"No, of course not, as you well know," he answered curtly, grabbing Johnnie R.'s arm a second time as they walked closer to the building. I remained to the side, a couple of steps away.

"Mike, meet Nick," Johnnie R. said calmly, hoping to defuse him. Mike glanced over but said nothing. I said hello and offered my hand, but he ignored it, continuing to stare in silence. I noted a pair of delicate brooding brown eyes with prominent crow's feet, bagged and bloodshot. His firm chin and strong square jaw couldn't quite counter the weakness of his eyes, and his sanguine face offered the impression of a drinker's complexion. Without acknowledging me he turned back to face Johnnie R., saying in a loud, quivering voice, "He's going to fire me!"

"Mike -"

"- And don't play coy, goddammit. You're in on it, you sly son-of-a-bitch!" Johnnie R., appalled, backed away. Mike's antics were attracting attention among the rush hour crowd. Some turned to watch while others stopped to listen. Mike looked down, shaking his head slowly, and when he looked up there were tears. He began to tremble. "Help me, John."

"It's out of my hands."

Again, Johnnie R. removed Mike's hand from his arm, and for a long moment Mike was silent, his head still shaking, his eyes a watery blur. He stared at Johnnie R. for a long stretch of time, their faces only inches apart. He then turned as if prepared to walk away and Johnnie R. glanced at me, rolling his eyes. But Mike wasn't finished. He turned quickly toward Johnnie R., his voice rising like acid in the throat. "I taught you everything you know, you punk. Everything. You owe me everything!"

He grabbed Johnnie R. by the lapels, but Johnnie R., far stronger, quickly pulled his hands away and shoved Mike back. "You're drunk," he said, brushing the wrinkles from his suit.

Mike, off balance, nearly tripped, so I reached to help him. Though he pushed me away, he faced me while bitterly baring his teeth, a cornered animal. Then he smiled, speaking in a soft voice. "You're Nick, aren't you?"

"Yes."

"I've heard so many things about you," he said, taking a step forward. "Ivy League. Princeton, of course. A long time friend looking to move up in the world."

"Knock it off, Mike," Johnnie R. intervened.

"Ah, yes. The well-educated Princeton man. Ready to take on the world. And what, might I ask, does John get in return?"

"I said knock it off, Mike," Johnnie R. warned, moving closer.

"A lover? Or just a fuck buddy?"

"Shut the fuck up!" Johnnie R. yelled, pushing Mike against the wall.

"Testy," Mike replied, laughing it off. "I see I hit a nerve."

"You're drunk and you need to go home," Johnnie R. said evenly, regaining composure.

"It won't work, John. Education has nothing to do with success at the bank. It takes savvy, something you don't possess."

"You've lost your mind. Just look at you."

"Quite the contrary, John. I'm as lucid as I've ever been. I see everything now. Everything," he said, loosening Johnnie R.'s grip and then straightening his collar. He brushed his hands over his suit as if to remove lent. He smiled. "Yes, John, I understand. You bring in your slick Ivy League buddy to hold your hand." He paused again and then looked at me, his smile widening as he shook his head ever so slightly. "But you two can't do it without me."

"Watch us."

"You're punks. You're not ready."

"You've lost it, Mike," said Johnnie R., shaking his head as he turned away.

"Fuck you, John," Mike yelled, stepping closer. The shout brought more attention our way. A few more people stopped to watch. "You knew nothing, John. You couldn't wipe your ass without my help."

"You didn't teach me everything," Johnnie R. said with a slight grin, turning.

"If you had balls you'd go to bat for me. You can do that. The old man listens to you now."

"The old man listens to no one," Johnnie R. whispered, his smile gone. "But it doesn't matter, Mike. I can't."

"You're right, John. I didn't teach you everything. You have no balls."

"Go home, Mike. Sleep."

"You're weaker than I am, John, because you fear him. You kiss that old man's ass out of fear. Can't you understand? That's why I lasted so long. I never kissed his ass."

"We're leaving, Nick," Johnnie R. said, turning again.

"You weak fuck!" Mike yelled again.

This was too much for Johnnie R. He took a quick step toward Mike and pushed him against the building facade. Firmly, he took his hand and placed it over Mike's mouth and said, inches from his ear, "It's over. It was over month's ago. Now show a little dignity and let's walk away quietly." When Johnnie R. released him, Mike was quiet, looking down. Johnnie R., in a softer voice, said, "Mike, let me take you home."

"Please. Go on. Please leave," Mike answered, his eyes still watery, his voice thin and weak. When Johnnie R. stepped toward him, the older man said, "Leave, John," before turning around and slowly walking away.

I glanced at Johnnie R. and then at the dispersing crowd and then back at Johnnie R. His expression registered panic and puzzlement both. "Let's go, Nick," he said, turning to walk in the direction of the bank.

"What in the hell was that all about?"

"It's bad," he answered, walking faster. "I'll tell you over supper."

*   *   *

"Look, I know that wasn't a pretty scene back there, but that's the last we'll see of him," Johnnie R.offered not long afterward as we ordered dinner and sipped another drink at his father's favorite club just off the Circle. "I'll need help when I take over. We'll be a team."

"This seems a bit more complicated than simply making plans to move into a larger office."

"Look, Nick, understand that Mike's is a story of an obsession. He came up the hard way, quietly worked his way up the ranks at the bank, and he's been second in command to my old man for over ten years. A dreamer who actually realized the American dream."

"A dream gone sour."

"Yes, a tiny problem of sorts in that ..."

"Yes?"

"He likes boys, preferably in their middle teens."

"Ouch."

"Yeah, he was able to remain low profile for years, but then he made the unfortunate mistake of choosing from the pool of available applicants a streetwise hustler known in the trade as the kid."

"As in Billy? Is this turning into a bad western?"

"Knock it off, Nick. It's serious," he answered, taking a sip of scotch. "Typical tale. Mike was in love with the kid, the kid was in love with money."

"And what about this kid?"

"A hick, for starters. An urban redneck," he said, shaking his head. "He's manipulative and selfish, a hustler and a thief. I think that adequately describes the major traits."

"Something's not right," I suggested. "The genteel banker and his honky-tonk kid?"

"Love is slippery, Nick. Human nature tends toward the inexplicable."

Dinner was brought, and as we ate in silence I entertained further questions. What was it that had consumed Mike, the kid or the kid's image? The mystery which is *beauty* or the beauty of the kid? Was it a question of youth only? I glanced at Johnnie R. as he ate his filet and wondered if Mike's fate was to be his own. In his prime then, how would Johnnie R. react to the changes of his body in a decade? Eventually, he would lose his hair or the gray would begin to show.

His stomach would paunch; the moles would grow. His body would lose its tone, the skin would forfeit its resilience, the shoulders would droop, the hips would grow wider. He would suddenly be unattractive, no longer one of the chosen. Beauty becomes a memory, something located beyond the elementary abyss of middle age. And at that point will he attempt to replace what he can never again possess with his own version of the kid? And once you find it, can you ever it let go?

"No one doubts youth is attractive, desirable," Johnnie R. said between bites. "But I agree, the question is *why* does he choose in this way?"

Ah! But why do any of us choose as we do? Why did Johnnie R. choose men and women both? Why had I, up to that very evening, chosen no one? Sometimes the difference in choices comes down to the simple turn of the lips with a smile. Sometimes we are caught and mesmerized by sweet and delicate eyes. Others are captured by the curve of a strong cheek bone, the smooth extenuation of the jaw, shades of auburn in the hair, the sleek thinness of the neck or the tight protrusion of the ass. When we'd finished eating, the waiter brought coffee. We sipped and I asked, "Does the kid have a real name?"

"Danny. An eighteen-year-old high school dropout from a deteriorating neighborhood, and for all practical purposes he's been a truant all of his life. Abundant streetwise skills, a child of the night."

"You'll next be saying he's from Transylvania, Johnnie R."

"Nick, he's a walking social aberration, king of the fucking hill. A punk, a hustler, a course lewd manipulative impertinent little shit."

"But he's just a kid, Johnnie R. Do you remember yourself at eighteen?"

"Look, Nick, you don't get it. The kid would've developed in the same manner if he'd spent his entire goddamned life sharing a room with Wally and the Beave." He sipped his coffee, straight-faced. "Wise up. There *is* evil in the world. Laugh if you will, but whenever near the kid I experience a nonbeliever's paradoxical recognition of *Old Testament* evil, undiluted wickedness."

I did laugh out loud, spilling my coffee.

"That's right, go ahead. I know I can't *rationally* explain it. You can speak in terms of sociological causes and psychoanalytic structures, but believe me, in the end our modern vocabulary falls short when attempting to describe him. His skills are of the street, of the don't-bullshit-a-bullshitter variety. And it helps that he's uncommonly good looking, understands the force of his sexual powers. A perfectly packaged commodity, an extravagant item in the marketplace of sexual desire. And Mike, for a time, was the highest bidder. But naturally a problem arose."

"Naturally."

"Mike was blind to the fact that he wasn't the only bidder in the sexual marketplace. Imperfect laws of supply and demand, mind you. Allows for erratic behavior. After all, the kid wasn't a box of detergent. Mike made his bid at the auction of flesh, and the rules of the game were up for grabs, changed as often as interest rates. And to keep the goods safely stashed away, out of the hands of the corporate raiders ... now that's the slippery trick. Mike couldn't contain the kid's sexual appetite, and the kid wouldn't keep his dick in his pants."

"Well, he's a hustler."

"Bingo. The facts are elementary. Hustling is his chosen occupation, a genuine career move, something in his blood. It's a banging good time! The kid isn't Mike's exclusive plaything. He belongs to the world. But the problems began in earnest when Mike tried to clean him up a bit, take the rough edges off. He bought the kid expensive clothes, wined and dined him out of the way in Chicago, tried to teach him not to scratch his balls with the dessert fork.

"But the kid isn't one to be educated in the ways of Mike's world. Far too pretty and clean. The kid's in chronic need of a quick fix, a doper's desire for elementary nastiness. Easy street sleaze. He demanded entertainment, but his conception of diversion precluded the stuff of Shakespeare and your mighty Rilke, Nick. I mean, to mold the mind into an appreciation of the arithmetic Bach is one thing, superlative as that may be, but to play the games of the city streets is quite another. Mike subscribed to the mistaken theory that the kid could be caught and kept with the lure of money only, but the kid couldn't be expected to sit at home eating Godiva bonbons while awaiting the older man's chivalrous return. There were greater enticements. Sex for money, sex for free. It all depended on his mood and his immediate emotional needs. So, Mike's status at being the highest bidder never meant the goods were solely his since he couldn't enforce the terms of the contract. He never absorbed the fact that the kid was of a separate world. Mike was unable to conceptualize a world without the scent of brandy and the pathos of Beethoven. The kid functioned in a nether world of sex-for-hire, street money, and *Mad Dog 20/20.*

"Mike was once suave and self-controlled, but by the time the kid began to play his game those attributes were no longer relevant. Eventually, they had ugly scenes, some of them played out in public, and they more than once became physically violent. Then the kid, once a part-time live-in, left. After all, he always had an ace in his pocket, or in his pants. Try to imagine it from his point of view. He'd hooked a big fish, and this one didn't want to get away. It just kept coming back for more! And if the line should break the kid knew there were other such fish in the swarming sexual sea." Johnnie R. paused and took a final gulp of coffee and then leaned forward, allowing a slight smile. "But the kid gambled, and here it gets a little silly, Nick."

"Imagine that."

"The kid being, after all, just a kid, he agreed to return, but there was a price."

"And what was the asking price?" I asked, finishing my coffee as well.

"Why, a car of course! What better steal for a teenager, even one as old as the kid? But Mike, his faculties still somewhat in tact, understood that new wheels would merely entice the kid to cover more sexual ground in less time. He could fuck at more than twice his former speed. Or hit the road, if he weren't first killed in a final sexy joyride. Mike lost either way, and now you've seen the results. He's way, way out. His lack of discretion came to the attention of my old man. And now he gets the boot."

Johnnie R. became quiet, slouching down in his chair. I reflected on his story, all of which was fine and good if you enjoyed a cheap night out, *Enquirer* style. It contained all the proper ingredients - homosexuality, sauciness, lurid obsessions, jilted lover, a bit of *good versus evil* for proper measure. But my instincts told me he was holding something back. So I pushed him. "And?"

"I'm associated with Mike, socially and professionally. It can affect my career as well."

"So when's he out?"

"Christ, I don't know. Soon," he answered, playing coy. "It's such a damned pity, Nick. He was a good man. So bright and charming and witty. He's helped hold the bank's operations together for years." Johnnie R. leaned forward again, stretching his neck from side to side. He popped his knuckles gingerly, and then looked at me squarely. "Plus, there's a problem."

We were close, almost there, I thought. He must've been tired, letting the goods loose so early. I waited for the clincher.

"Look, Nick. The kid's dangerous, no good. He gets under my skin."

"Yeah?"

"And I roughed him up pretty good a few months back."

Bingo! We were nearly there.

"Needless to say, the kid hasn't forgotten. He's a trouble maker, and I don't need trouble. As long as he's got Mike on the run, he's dangerous to me, and to the bank."

"Whoa! Back up," I said. "What do you mean you roughed him up?"

"It was at a party," he offered. "One of those *Big Deal* parties you have to attend every month or so to talk trash with clients of the bank. You know, you start with polite introductions, exchange views on the state of the economy, maybe get a bit technical with treasury bills and the prime rate, finally someone cracks a joke and the next thing you know the guy next to you is talking about a piece of pussy. No big deal, right?"

"So far."

"Problem is, the party was at Mike's, an annual event in the community. No one misses it. Everything was going well until about eleven, and then bang! The kid showed. Mike was nearly drunk. Hell, everybody was nearly drunk. I was too. But I had to act. I was able to get the kid aside, pushed him out the back door and beat the hell out of him. I mean I punched him pretty good, Nick. Broken nose, black eyes, a few stitches. I just went crazy. Simple as that."

"I've never seen you violent."

"Everything got out of hand, Nick. I was worried about the bank, Mike's reputation, my own, for that matter. I lost control."

"Yeah, Johnnie R. Everybody goes to a party to talk bank loans and takes time out to beat the shit out of a teenager."

"Nick, I'd had too much to drink. The kid was out of control. Mike was looped. I had to take over," he offered casually. "Besides, nobody saw it happen. None of the big wigs. Just Charly."

Double Bingo! Time to cash in. I'd hit the jackpot. "Charly?"

"It was a business party for spouses too. Social stuff."

"And how did she take this *Thrilla in Manila*?"

"Funny boy, Nick. You ever think of stand-up comedy?"

"If the kid hasn't forgotten it, she hasn't either," I suggested.

"It's not a topic we discuss."

"Something's missing," I said. "Like a motive."

"Dammit, Nick, I told you the kid is dangerous."

"He's a kid!"

"You still don't understand, do you? I mean it's useless to go on with it."

"Mike's an adult, Johnnie R."

"But he's not in control. He's lost it. I was angry about that, frightened of what the kid might do with his power over Mike. I got carried away. End of discussion," he finished, voice raised, face flushed.

*   *   *

Moments later we were northbound on Meridian with Johnnie R. riding in the passenger seat, slightly drunk. As we passed Tenth Street and the inner-urban neighborhood became darker, somewhat forbidding, the neighborhood transformed from earlier scenes of women in minks to leggy whores working their strolls. The street-toughened faces conveyed the message that you were in the wrong locale if sex wasn't on your menu. Plus, there was the foreboding signal in the slit of the eye warning of doom should you decide to trade in the underworld currency without the streetwise savvy to know from whom to buy, or when to quit.

As we passed Sixteenth Johnnie R. came to life. "How about another bar, one more drink before we call it a night?" The booze was still taking its toll, but he'd discarded his earlier agitation, ready to move on.

"What about Charly?"

"She said she wouldn't wait up if we weren't in before eleven."

"I'm tired Johnnie R."

"Come on. This is special. It'll knock you off your feet."
"I've already been knocked off my feet, thanks to Mike."
"It'll bring back some memories, let loose some irony."
"The memories I don't need right now," I said lamely.
"Then settle for the irony."
"You're relentless, Johnnie R."
"I take that as a yes."
"We can't stay long. I'll be worthless tomorrow."

"Good sport," he chirped, leaning back as we continued north on Meridian. He surprised me when he had me turn east onto Twenty-second street as we drove through a ghetto with a smattering of garish neon lights where hustlers and whores negotiated their fees. Johnnie R. was playing games. A drink, a simple nightcap with a buddy, was one thing, but slumming in that risky neighborhood for the sake of slumming was quite another. I glanced at him as I turned the corner and drove slowly along Twenty-second, Johnnie R. sporting one of his easy smiles made sinister by the flashing neon lights.

Once off Meridian, the streets were darker, but on the periphery I could still make out the ghetto houses, most of which lay empty in disrepair, secured by boarding. Many were quite large and obviously had been favored by the wealthier families many years back, but by that evening urban flight had left behind chipped paint, broken beams, collapsed roofs, termites. Occasionally, a faceless figure could be seen scampering up to the entrances and disappearing within.

We drove two blocks further east before I realized why we'd come. I didn't notice the street sign until later, because dominating the dark horizon was a large neon marquee above the entrance of a nondescript one-story building facing the street. The red neon and flashing multicolored bulbs announced, simply, Talbott Street. The building was in fair shape compared to the surrounding structures and the dirty street. Across the street from the bright marquee lay a small gravel parking lot. The neighborhood was a combat zone with torn shutters and broken street lamps, garbage and decay.

"The promised irony," Johnnie R. said with a smile.
"What is it?" I mused.
"Just a bar. Another simple bar," he answered. "You can't escape the past completely, Nick."
"How did you find it, this far off the beaten track?"
"That's another story you'll understand soon enough," he said. "But for the moment imagine my surprise when I received your first letter postmarked with the return address of 755 Talbott Street. I roared with laughter. I mean I really howled."
"Just a coincidental piece of trivia," I said. "So why the title, Talbott Street?"

"Look at the street sign."

I glanced over at the sign at the corner intersection and read the words, Talbott Avenue. I looked around the neighborhood again, taking note of the urban decay - shattered glass and ruptured houses. Someone behind me honked and Johnnie R. pointed me toward the parking lot across the street from the marquee. "Why the difference in avenue and street?" I asked.

"Who knows?" he answered without interest. "Let's go in?"

"This is it? We're going in here?"

"Yeah, unless a gay bar disturbs you." The smile left his face for only a moment, and as it returned he leaned toward me, patting me on the leg, and added, "Too scared."

"It's not the best neighborhood, Johnnie R. It doesn't look safe. Besides, what use have I for a gay bar?" I answered, meeting his drunken gaze. Was he merely registering my reaction to his alternative environment? Pushing me? Was I the buddy he was taking out for a drink and a laugh, or was I the convenient cover in his deception? After all, Charly was alone at home that we might travel to the bar.

"Come on, Nick. Lighten up. It could be any bar anywhere, gay or straight, in a ghetto or on the Circle, and with that goddamned name I'd have to take you in. It's just too good to pass up. You just spent a few years of your life on Talbott Street in London. Now compare."

Johnnie R. was a master at playing the disarming, well-meaning buddy, so good, in fact, that with all the booze we'd had I couldn't quite determine if he were being disingenuous. His smile never left his face, just as his voice never faltered. He was cunning and shrewd, that pal of mine, skillful and crafty in the human relations department. He had me if for no other reason than that he played the game so well.

"Admit it, you didn't bring me here for a drink?" I said, my anger fading. He caught the change in my tone and ran with it.

"Well, I didn't bring you here for a blowjob either, Nick. Come on, where's your sense of adventure?" he asked playfully. When I didn't respond he said, "Listen, while at Princeton you once asked me where I whored around. Do you remember? I nearly punched you for saying it that way. Remember?"

"Yeah."

"Well, this is it. This is the other side. A place of refuge. We'll go in and not talk of it again."

I finally agreed, opening the car door and glancing over at the bar entrance to see men enter beneath the marquee. As we walked toward the door I asked, "But why is the bar here?"

"Too risky to have a gay bar in the open, especially in the corn belt. The ghetto is perfect because it's off the beaten track, out of the public eye. In the slums, Nick, no one talks."

"It's still dangerous."

"People are willing to battle the possibility of petty, nonideological crime, even violence, because it's easier than battling the disapproval of public opinion."

When Johnnie R. opened the bar door, the disco bass hit us hard. Inside, the place was packed. We threaded our way beyond the foyer and into the smoky interior where the music was overwhelming, pounding away rapidly in battle with my heart. It was too loud to hold an intelligible conversation, so Johnnie R. simply signaled for me to follow. In the inner room, heavy with smoke, my eyes adjusted to the moving shadows circulating through the darkness. I followed Johnnie R. as he ambled toward the battleship of an oaken bar, a great mass of polished wood strategically centered and dominating the view from all directions. Drinks were being served from four sides, but there was little space between the counters and the dark walls on two sides. As a result the flow of traffic halted in places, creating uncomfortable bottlenecks.

There were no available spaces at the bar where we could stand and enjoy a drink, so we stepped into one of the makeshift lines where the crowd gathered seven and eight deep. As I stood behind Johnnie R., I took in the unfamiliar surroundings as we inched forward. The dance floor was in the front of the bar, though my view was blocked by the bar's thick beams and the countless bodies surrounding us. There was little ventilation, and cigarette smoke hung like a fog in the stale air. Johnnie R. and I were obstructing the passage of others trying to reach the tables and dance floor, and although most politely asked to get by, others simply elbowed their way between and around us.

And the crowd was fascinating to observe. I caught the eye of several who glanced at me searchingly as they tried to pass. Some passed by quickly; others lingered. A few allowed their casual glances to settle into long, inspecting gazes. Words weren't necessary. Expressions conveyed unambiguous messages, inviting a conversation or pursuing an acknowledgment of interest. Most moved on, but others were more daring, even brash, their determined eyes settling on mine; a proposition was occurring without so much as uttering a word. As we continued the slow shuffle to the bar, I was reminded of Johnnie R.'s powerful gaze from that Princeton evening of long ago when I'd lost my own virginity. The same expression of hunger. And more than one, as he slowly continued his sexual journey, allowed a roving hand to pat my ass while passing by. Johnnie R. simply snickered at my fate.

Eventually we made our way to the counter, and the bartenders themselves were an intriguing lot. There were three men and a woman behind the bar. Two of the men you'd expect to find serving drinks anywhere, dressed in jeans and t-shirts. On the other hand, the remaining two couldn't be easily duplicated. Though one was male and the other female, their apparent sexuality differed only in the smallest degree. She was masculine and stocky, dressed in blue jeans and a wild, multicolored top. Her hair was cropped, bleached blond. Deep, black lines marked her eyes and lips; her voice was husky and demanding. She wore an expression that dared you to fuck with her. But the fourth bartender was as nearly asexual as a man might be, if indeed he was a man. He matched her clothing as well as her hair. He also wore the make-up, but much more lightly and without exaggeration. And although his voice had the depth of a man's voice, he spoke very softly and sweetly, with a hush, as the words came in small wisps escaping painted lips.

With drink in hand I followed Johnnie R. as we maneuvered away from the bar. Just beyond it we found space near a banister separating the bar area from the tables below. Two steps down and past the banister lay several rows of small tables and booths, and beyond the last table was the large dance floor. At the front of the bar was a stage without curtains, and a large white projection screen was nearly hidden at the back of the stage. As we settled into the cramped space by the banister, sipping our drinks, I continued to inspect the bar as Johnnie R. coolly watched the men. Above us and to the side of the dance floor the DJ sat behind a plate of hazy glass dishing out synchronized disco tunes with heavy bass and rhythmic erotic lyrics. Above the dance floor hung a large display of various lights, including a glittering mirrored ball and a strobe. There were rows of other colored lights as well, and tucked in among these were red and blue patrol car lights twirling about and cutting the darkness around the stage. The dark walls were nearly blank but for a few mirrors and nondescript pictures. Above, the ceiling was painted black, the venting vanishing into the depthless heights of the bar. And to one side, close to the DJ's box, there was hung a large pink neon sign in delicate script spelling out the word *diva* which was further softened by the lingering layers of smoke threading around the neon tubes.

"So what do you think?" Johnnie R. shouted in my ear.

I shrugged and looked away since it was far too loud to talk. Still, I was conscious of Johnnie R. gauging my reaction to the bar, and I too was intrigued as he cruised the men, watching as he occasionally returned gaze for gaze. He would take a drink, chew on the ice and then turn subtly toward a passing body, cocky and aloof, before turning away and scanning the crowd. He still had it, the muscular build and refined good looks, the casual swagger and erotic stance which solicited without effort the second glance. In fact, he attracted the eye of nearly everyone who passed, his finely tailored suit made to seem less formal by his open collar and loosened tie.

I was intrigued by the bar's large, diversified crowd, its extraordinary mix of men. The ages ranged from below the legal age of twenty-one to post-retirement. Dress varied, as did occupation and wealth. There were businessmen and students, professionals and laborers. Some wore suits like Johnnie R. and myself while others wore jeans or leather or casual clothing. While scanning the crowd I managed to find a little bit of everything. Standing not far from us near the banister, a group of very young men who apparently had entered with the help of fraudulent IDs chatted above the bedlam about school, money and men. They were college kids dressed in tight faded jeans and bright Polo shirts, clean cut and washed with an excess of cologne. They'd arrived as a group, but I noted that each was in tune to the swelling crowd around him, open to the sexual signals from those who passed by. They laughed and shouted and drank their beer with an eye open to a new encounter. And near them were several businessmen still dressed in suits, quite interested, it appeared, in the small clique of college boys nearby. A couple of the luckier ones had made contact with a younger man, buying drinks and flashing money.

"Ah, but will the beverage-bribe pay off by evening's end?" Johnnie R. joked, leaning close.

There were several men dressed in black leather, a few of them in complete gear - hat, vest, chaps, collar and boots - and neither body type nor age seemed to matter as far as the leather was concerned. Or, as Johnnie R. observed for my benefit, "Leather never requires good taste." Each of these men seemed a bit more brash than the balance of the pack filling the bar, cruising aggressively, grabbing college boys by the ass as they passed by. A few carried tambourines which they tapped against their chaps at the thigh or against their free hand high in the air as they danced through the bar.

On the dance floor several of the men had discarded their shirts, wrapping them around their waists. As they passed us coming off the dance floor, smelling of smoke and musk, their sweating bodies dampened our jackets. Many approached the bar for a quick drink and then returned to the dance floor. Others, still shirtless after dancing, cruised the crowd in a fashion not unlike Johnnie R. And when I noticed that a few of the men occasionally sniffed from a small bottle, Johnnie R. enlightened me. "Amyl nitrites, Nick. Also known as *poppers* in modern parlance. They deliver, shall we say, a light-headed rush of temporary ecstasy. Good for dispelling inhibitions on the dance floor and delaying an orgasm in bed. A couple of deep sniffs and off they go."

I noticed that a certain type of man caught Johnnie R.'s attention. He allowed his eyes to follow the big-muscled men, those who apparently worked out regularly in a gym. These were for the most part the same men who sported tank top shirts tucked into their tight blue jeans. Their bodies were their major asset, and they were obviously proud of them. Most of them remained apart, rarely mixing with the more effeminate crowd. Still, the bar contained its fair share of what Johnnie R. referred to as *regular Joes*. "They comprise the silent, invisible majority, men you might meet in any bar at any other time. They come for drinks and conversation, for dancing, for the possibility of sex. Or to take a pee, Nick, which is what I need to do now."

"Don't be long?" I said, less than ecstatic about the idea since we appeared to be together and for that reason were not up for grabs.

"You're a big boy," he said, slapping me on the back.

When ten minutes had passed and Johnnie R. hadn't returned, I circled the bar in search of him, found some stairs and walked up to the small balcony located directly over the oak bar. At the top a young guy in jeans and tennis shoes nearly blocked the stairs, cocking his head as if to ask if I were interested. I moved past him and circled the balcony with its plastic palm trees, small counter bar and smattering of tables and chairs. I walked toward the banister at the edge of the balcony and looked out over the bar, and from there I spotted Johnnie R. standing near the dance floor, near the stage, with his sleeves rolled up and his suit coat over his shoulder.

I waved, but he didn't see me, and moments later I lost him in the crowd as the strobe lights slashed the darkness. When I turned to leave the balcony, a siren blared from the stage and red and blue patrol car lights began twirling about as smoke billowed from beneath the stage. It was all part of the evening's program controlled by the overwrought DJ. The smoke spewed, the music blared and the strobe lights sliced the thick air, reflecting from the frenzied bodies below. The stage screen filled with images barely visible through the murky distances, though eventually I made out the image of naked men. One after another filled the screen, and the crowd reacted with enthusiasm, cheers erupting from all corners.

There was still no sign of Johnnie R., but the young guy who'd earlier blocked the stairs walked up to the banister next to me. A good-looking kid of medium height with blond hair and blue eyes, I was struck at how young he was as he stared at me with lips parted, tongue slightly moving between them. He winked, a no-nonsense invitation to pleasure. I looked away, scanned the floor below for Johnnie R. and then maneuvered my way down the stairs and back to the spot where he'd left me. When he didn't show I settled in to one of the few empty spaces against a wall to the side of the bar, leaned back and scanned the crowd.

The evening was slowly turning into a prolonged Fellini moment. A woman approached the bar by an aisle leading from the dance floor. She was tall and large and broad-shouldered and wore heels which matched her dress of turquoise sequins, an extraordinarily garish getup which wrapped tightly around her narrow hips. Her make-up matched the color of the dress and shoes, and she wore innumerable rings and bracelets along with a large necklace dangling obtrusively from her thick neck. Still, her unimaginable *coup de grace* was a large silver tiara balanced precariously on her head. The crown of bogus sapphires sparkled as the lights from the dance floor reflected back. As if this weren't enough she also sported a huge black wig which hung in a long straggly sweep down her back and shoulders and curled back up in incomprehensible fashion into a bouffant of immense proportions. She was Elvira with yet less class.

As she approached I noted she was much taller than I'd at first thought, the bouffant fully visible after descending from the heights of the smokey bar, and it was as I heard her speak that I realized my grave error. She yelled to the bartender for the desired drink in a grand resonating basso. The poor tasteless girl was no girl at all. She was very much a he in drag. Yet, the husky deep voice notwithstanding, his manner of speech was quite effeminate. He yelled to a male friend, "Girlfriend, come here! Give this old girl a kiss!" This, my first experience with a drag queen, was most amusing, and as he passed to return to his throne below he paused long enough to blow me a wildly ostentatious kiss. My eyes followed him to a table of like-minded queens holding tea near the dance floor.

There was still no sign of Johnnie R. as anonymous faces continued to pass in the near-darkness, many slowing their pace and glancing over, hesitating and then moving on as tune after tune bellowed from the speakers. A rousing rendition of *Thank God It's Friday* brought shouts from all corners of the bar, and it was as *MacArthur Park* began to play that I heard a voice ask, "What do ya like?"

I turned to find the blond kid from the balcony now at my side. "What?" I asked.

"What's your game? What do ya like to do?" he repeated, leaning close.

"You've got the wrong person."

"No, I definitely got the right one, man. And you got a chance to have the right one too. So, what do ya like?"

"Nothing."

"Come on!" he shouted, leaning closer yet, sporting a broad smile. "Everybody likes somethin'. Fuck or suck or golden shower. There's always somethin'."

"I'm not gay."

"Then why the fuck are ya here?"

"I'm with a friend," I said sternly. "And I'm not interested."

"I heard that one before, buddy. A lot of guys think they ain't interested, but I always found they was willin' to pay for a good piece of ass. I say your interested or ya wouldn't be here."

"A hustler? You're hustling me?" He was too puzzling to ignore.

"No, I'm sellin' ice cream. What the fuck do ya think I'm sellin'?"

"Why?" I asked, incredulous. It was my first hustle. I was genuinely interested.

"Huh?"

"Why do you hustle?"

With an expression of pure disbelief on his face, he said, "Is this an interview or somethin'? Shit, man, I do it for money. Sometimes for kicks."

"And since I'm wearing a suit you figure I've got the money," I laughed. "God, it's not your night. Not only am I not gay, I'm broke. You'd better scoot on."

"Nope. I'll do this trick for kicks, man, just to prove my point."

I turned to look him fully in the face. He was serious, and I was both stunned and saddened. He was only a kid. That he was streetwise and confident there was little doubt, but the fact remained that he was very young. "Go try someone else," I said, turning away, and as I did so he grabbed my crotch. I pulled his hand away and shouted, "Knock it off!"

"I'll suck your cock."

I began to walk toward the banister where Johnnie R. had left me, and I hadn't taken two steps before the kid tugged at my arm. "Who're ya with," he pushed as I kept walking. I looked up to see Johnnie R. finally coming from the dance floor. With tie and coat over his shoulder he looked at me with a smile, drenched and drunk.

"I'm with him," I said, pointing to Johnnie R. "Now leave."

"Holy shit!" the kid shouted and turned.

Johnnie R. had been watching me while walking up the aisle, and when he spotted the punk following me he ran forward. The young guy in turn tried to run, but the crowd was too thick. Johnnie R. caught him by the shirt tail before he could wriggle away, pulling him over to a spot against the wall where I'd been standing moments before. The commotion caused a stir in the crowd, but in the corner against the black wall they were nearly invisible. No one intervened, and within moments the faces turned away from the corner where they'd vanished. As I approached them, barely visible, I saw the punk struggling. Johnnie R. held him securely by forcing one arm behind his back, and the little guy was hurting.

"What are you doing?" I couldn't believe my eyes. Johnnie R. was roughing him up a bit.

"Have you met?" Johnnie R. asked, ignoring my question.

"Let him go, Johnnie R., and let's get out of here. I want to get some sleep."

"He propositioned you, didn't he," he demanded, anger rising in his voice.

"He's a punk. He didn't cause any harm. Let him go."

"Not before I introduce you."

"Let go of my fuckin' arm, asshole."

"I'll break this fucking arm," Johnnie R. shouted. "You know I will. So shut up." Then he turned to me and said, "Nick, I'd like you to meet Danny. Alias, the kid. This is Mike's kid. Mike's beautiful worthless shit."

"Fuck you, John."

"I said shut up."

"Let him go, Johnnie R."

Ignoring me, he'd managed to lock the kid's hands between his body and the wall. With his free hand Johnnie R. held the kid's face, thumb pushing against one cheek, the forefinger against the other. He pulled the kid's face close to his own. "I should break your goddamned arms and that sweet little neck," he shouted over the music. "I thought I told you never to come back here. I told you not to bring your cheap little ass anywhere near where I might be. And that means here. If you fuck up again -"

"Look who's whoring around, man. Least I ain't married."

Johnnie R. tightened his grip and then slapped the kid hard.

"Shit! Let me go, man, or I'll scream bloody fuckin' murder!"

"Get out of here," Johnnie R. shoved him away. The kid walked a few paces backward until he was safely beyond Johnnie R.'s grasp, and as he rubbed his sore jaw he yelled back, "Fuck you, man! I've got your fuckin' number! You'll pay!"

I grabbed Johnnie R. before he could make a move toward the kid who quickly disappeared into the crowd. The strobe lights began their cyclical game, and I caught sight of the rage on Johnnie R.'s face in and out of the darkness. The music screeched as the DJ played an encore of *Last Dance*. All around us it was New Year's Eve. The dance floor lights zapped on for the finale, synchronized to the rhythm of the song, and for a second time smoke poured from beneath the stage like a mysterious winter fog. The dance floor overflowed; the aisles were full. Men who couldn't reach the dance floor began to dance in place as shouts went out from every corner of the bar. The tambourines beat out the rhythm of the tune, and above the dance floor the siren sounded. It was unbearably loud as I grabbed Johnnie R. by the arm and guided him toward the door. It took five minutes to thread our way through the crowd and finally out the door into the cold dry air.

"Sorry. I'm drunk," Johnnie R. slurred as we walked to the car. "I fucked up."

"Yeah. And thanks for leaving me alone."

"I only wanted you to know where I sometimes come. That's all."

"Christ. He's just a kid, Johnnie R. A punk," I said, still bewildered by his violence.

"He's a hustler, a worthless slick little shit."

"Let's go. I've had enough for one day," I said. We entered the car and sat as it warmed. Johnnie R. slouched back into the seat, shivering in the cold.

"Nick, I just wanted you to understand that there are two Talbott Streets."

"Come on, Johnnie R., don't give me any of your jazz. You wanted to shock me. You brought me here for kicks. The famous Johnnie R. jazz. This so called kid notwithstanding, you're still the slickest operator I know."

"Johnnie R.'s jazz," he whispered, smiling. "Hmmm, I think I like that."

"Self-delusion is the key, Johnnie R. One slip, one false move, one thought taken for granted, a hesitation in timing, and it all comes tumbling down."

"Leave Charly out of this."

"I'm not referring to Charly. I'm thinking of you," I said. He was silent, and a few moments later I glanced over and found him with his eyes closed. He was finished, nearly asleep.

I drove out of the parking lot and half a block from the bar I spotted the kid near an alley. He recognized Johnnie R.'s car and gave the finger as I passed. Still, I wasn't able to understand Johnnie R.'s anger. Sure the kid was a cocky street hustler on the make, maybe a bit of trouble, but he was a teenager loose on the ghetto streets. If anything, his circumstances were tragic.

I turned north on Meridian and drove out of the ghetto. The thriving evening commerce seemed to be gaining strength by the hour. It was a dusk to dawn economy, nighttime capitalism. Cars stopped to pick up whores or hustlers or drugs. Deals were openly made on street. The neon continued to flicker above the doors of the adult porno shops and third rate liquor joints, and a few who were taking a respite from the chores of the evening gathered themselves into the tiny twenty-four hour dives which sold coffee and stale donuts and warmth. As I drove beyond the margins of the inner city slum, I reflected on the two Talbott Streets and wondered what Johnnie R. had hoped I might find in the way of comparisons. And how can you compare a small flat on a dreary London street with its contradictory, a garish ghetto bar in Indianapolis?

I drove further north beyond the grasp of the ghetto's mirage, Meridian by then lined by the soft white street lights leading to Johnnie R.'s home, and it was then that I entertained a likeness. I remembered the bleak, gray tones of London's Talbott Street, and I instantly encountered the lonely insatiable eyes of the men cruising the bar. Downcast eyes meeting the unforgiving street. Unrelenting eyes chasing dreams never replete. They shared the habitual hunger, the persevering pain. Searching, always searching eyes. They were despondent eyes in the end, Mike's eyes following years of toil, and I couldn't quite shake them as I drove quietly north on Meridian with Johnnie R. asleep beside me. Nor could I ignore their constant and reinforcing image as I continued up Meridian Street. In the distance my eye caught a narrow depthless spot of darkness, a dark circular point on the linear axis, just a tiny simple apex, and this small round black point on the horizon, drawn and outlined by the rows of lighted street lamps which merged far ahead into a halo surrounding it, created an absorbing image during that late-night-hour drive, the unforgettable image of the simple and sacred abyss which is the center of the human eye.

7

Indianapolis, 1991

As I returned from the distant past and that night at Talbott Street of long ago, I again picked up Johnnie R.'s journal and thumbed through it while waiting for him to wake, and I was touched as I read from his most recent entry:

I live!

Oh, not for long, admittedly, but for this moment and for perhaps a series of longer moments - a few weeks, perhaps - and well, who can know? I only know this: I live now! And Nick lives, and so our memory shall live through him long after I'm gone, and with this I feel an immense satisfaction, a contentment not known to me since our days together at Princeton when I was dreamy-eyed about him and first learned to love him deeply. Mine was an irreversibly deep love, furrowed into depths untouchable, and it has stayed with me all these many years, following my marriage and my son's birth and my divorce and now this illness which shall kill me soon enough; I still love him beyond measure, just a sentimental pup, and probably will die with his smile as the final image flickering before the lights go out.

I like that.

But here's one thing love does to you that I'd not been prepared for. Not only does love contain the power to jettison all difficulties, both present and past, in favor of love's virtual reality, love also forces you to contemplate its cessation, and the only form of cessation to which a truly great love might surrender is death. Yep. Love requires a meditation on death. Swear to God. Love asks: Are you afraid of death? And from there you can form your own derivative of the question, such as: Are you only afraid of certain species of death? I rarely gave death a second thought until I got it. AIDS.

I've never been in the business of dwelling on my mortality, and as a banker, and a man with a banker's temperament (two separate considerations) you might imagine why. In a nutshell: Never dwell on the possibilities of a loan just closed; it's out of your control. You only muse and mull over the possibilities of a not-yet-closed loan - the long process stretching between application and closing - since that's the window period during which you continue to control the destiny of the question, Will it turn out well? But damn if the Great Banking House of Mortality hasn't come early to foreclose on me - ME - and now I'm forced to face nonexistence. Odd, the facing of death with not altogether well-honed skills following years of treating the Great Experience (that's from Henry James, I think) either as a remoteness bordering on the impossible or as a certainty as fixed and natural as the cycle of the seasons, something to ponder, fleetingly, and then to forget.   But now I am told I shall die soon enough, all these new medications notwithstanding, and so I've recently begun to dwell on it - the unspeakableness which is death - and have been known to howl wildly in protest during that isolated stretch of hours between midnight and dawn. But today's different.

Today Nick's coming to offer his farewell, and so all my thoughts are directed toward him. I can only think of Nick: Nick leaving, Nick coming back and Nick in the past. Ah, the past!   Now, there's a pretty picture. Seneca said death is either a transition or an end. But maybe death is merely an invitation to reflect, a metaphysical posturing forming a meditative mood. If that's so I do think of death, for all reflection has as its end (and all memory eventually finds safe harbor) in the present, and maybe death is that place where memory used up meets the here and now, and so life, like a spurned lover, seeks other worlds for the playing out of all that which was never properly lived Maybe that's death.

Jesus! I've got so much to think through, so much to get off my now-enfeebled chest, yet so little time to do it in. To make matters worse these meds make me soar a bit now and then. I'm a bit cagey at times. I mean, exploring death isn't easy work! But here's the trick: To write this journal as a forum for sorting out my thoughts but in a manner which recognizes that someone else might read them (someone like Nick) and so taking into account the fact that the reader has his own death to ponder - if not soon, then soon enough - and might be thinking: Shit, I'm not gonna do this twice, die with you and then die my own death! Fuck you! And that would be fair enough. So I try to imagine Nick reading what I have to say - a most liberating thought by one now totally liberated from self-consciousness, a gift offered in advance by ever-politic death - and this in turn mutes to a certain degree forms of self-pity. Not that I don't dwell on leaving this life in my prime - about that I remain pissed - but the overtures of death, like certain lovely mating calls, sometimes order the passions into forms of selflessness.

I'm a man who believes in ultimate forms of human redemption, and what's more: I've been redeemed. Or, that's the feel of it. I suppose this would strike many as just plain screwy, since more often than not we consider redemption, if we consider it at all, in terms of a spiritual change which manifests in all realms of life. Like Scrooge, everything changes - the approach, the voice, the desire, the mode. But that's not what I believe redemption to be. (Besides, we were never given a peek at Scrooge's goings-on during his first post-redemption Christmas. My guess is that he back-pedals a bit, maybe even slides all the way back into his former emotional isolation, and then finds a new plateau, say, three Christmases hence.) My point is this: I believe redemption refers to perceptual focus, a subtle broadening of conscious awareness which embraces a larger spiritual realm. But I can still lie here dying and think of doing the nasty, and there are moments, when my energy is up, in which I feel like a quick hop in the hospital sack might just do the trick. Even a finely minimalist hand job will do if I can wade through all these tubes and I'm not catheterized. This becomes less and less a biological exercise and more nearly a spiritual exercise as I slowly fade into oblivion. Because redemption is not a declension from, but rather an embrasure of, everything we are: bitterness and dark, sweetness and light.

I lay the journal down again. It was really just too much to bear, as were the questions which followed. When will this ghastly battle be over? How long will he live? How long will I need to stay? What will the end be like? And when I tried to escape such questions another entered. When will Charly arrive? By noon she was nowhere in sight, and I was famished. So I ditched the sanitary outfit, grabbed some lunch in the cafeteria and then took a walk.

Outside it was gray and getting colder as the flakes continued to fall, and I noticed that the naked trees with their spindly brown arms appeared as enormous upside down sweet gum pods sprinkled about the gray landscape. I found a lone bench where I sat as snowflakes dotted my forehead. With hands in my pockets I tried to concentrate on the small muffled sounds of traffic from the street, but it was no good. I couldn't quite get out my mind off Johnnie R.'s words, nor the image of his dying in that hospital bed.

And then there was Charly. I reflected on that odd image of an aperture found on Meridian street nine years earlier and noted a similar image as I watched a row of street lights flicker on in the distance, the penetrating light ripping through the afternoon darkness right to my feet. I fought the cold for a long while, but the wind picked up and the snow fell harder. Though it couldn't have been much after one, the sky seemed dusky, a gift from the shortest days of the year. I tried to outrun the mood as the snow fell harder still, muffling all sound.

Charly was sitting next to his bed when I entered the room, wrapped cellophane-clean in sanitary robe, cap, gloves and mask. I stood at the door, unnoticed, while watching as she leaned close to Johnnie R. trying hard to understand his slurred speech. When Johnnie R. heard the rustle of my clothing, he stopped talking. I walked close to the bed, opposite Charly, and following her eyes he slowly turned his head toward me. As I rested a leg against the side of the bed Johnnie R.'s eyes met mine with a squint. Tilting his head ever so slightly, oddly, he asked, in a thin raspy voice, "Is that you, Nick?"

"Yes," I said, nearly as weakly. There was an adrenalin rush when I realized he could barely see me. Only yesterday he'd said that his vision was impaired, but could blindness come so quickly? I leaned closer, looking into his eyes. He in turn looked at me as if I were a shadow. I glanced at Charly for help, but her gaze was focused on Johnnie R.

"I'm afraid I can't see too well this morning," he said softly. His voice was weak, hinted of terror.

"Take it easy."

"Where the hell have you been?" Unlike the day before he seemed to chew his words. He'd declined overnight.

"I was here early, just after eight, but you were asleep," I answered, touching his arm lightly. I wanted to hug him then and there, knowing he was losing ground quickly. He'd be gone much too soon. "I watched you snore for two hours. Same ole guy."

"And?"

"You were really sleeping soundly, so I grabbed a sandwich and went for a walk."

He lay his head down on the pillow and closed his eyes. His breathing was labored, irregular. Though talking was a chore, he spoke. "When I woke up I told Charly that I'd had this strange dream that you'd come to visit. After all those years. My best buddy. It was like old times. I cried like a kid," he said with a snicker, laughing it off. It hurt to hear him say it just that way, all dream and innocence, and I was moved to look away as I caught a peek of his watery eyes. Most of all it pained me to discover how quickly his mind was wasting away. The regression from only the day before was remarkable.

"I'm here!" I chirped, trying to be cheerful.

"Yeah, Charly reminded me that it was real. That I'd asked you. Then it came back. Fuck this is scary," he said, his voice shaky.

"Dreams are like that."

"Now life is like that," he replied in a tone reminding me that he wasn't to be patronized.

"Now John," Charly said, patting his arm while maintaining her focus on Johnnie R.'s scrawny face.

"Okay, okay," he shrugged her off, eyes still closed. Then, trying for good cheer himself, he said, "Hey, I can order supper for both of you. Right here in the room. They do that now. Did you know that? It's like a restaurant at the morgue. Don't chew too loud, you'll disturb the corpse!"

Charly smiled, like me, so that she wouldn't cry.

"So you'll have supper?" he asked.

"Of course," I said. Charly was silent.

"Good. Now say hi to Charly," he ordered.

I walked to her and awkwardly took her hand. I saw the old eyes, brown with golden specks. They seemed sadder, worn and weary. I noted very narrow lines at their corners, small wrinkles, nothing unpleasant, but they hadn't been there nine years earlier. Just another reminder of how much time separated us. We both smiled through the masks, but we had to work hard to perform it, something soft and shallow.

"I see you've discovered my journal?" Johnnie R. said, saving us from more discomfort. I turned to see him thumbing through it. "That you'd left it open was Charly's proof that you'd arrived."

"I should've asked first," I said.

"My way of dealing with this."

"I hope you don't mind my thumbing through it."

"Are you kidding? I mean, where will you take my little secrets? To Zelda?" We smiled. "That's why I left it out. Maybe you can give me some pointers on the poems."

"I'm anxious to read them."

"Better hurry, tough. I'll be gone in a month."

"Quit," I said, as Charly tapped his arm lightly.

"Funny. I can forget yesterday, but the memories of our time together stay with me."

With every opportunity he pushed us back, eight years, nine years, fifteen years. The great unadulterated past. It seemed to bolster the waning present with a sometimes lovely scent. Yet, if only he'd remember it fully, he'd eventually catch a whiff of the putrid scents as well. Ah, the imperfect little past. The scene of a thousand emotional crimes. The life that once was ours.

"More complications, Nick," he said.

"CMV or herpes has damaged his eyes," Charly quickly offered.

"What she's trying to say is that I'm going blind. I'm fucking going blind!"

The adrenalin, again. Harsher, more piercing. Little tears, ducts bleeding HIV, trickled down his hollowed cheeks. So it was true; he would go blind. "But just yesterday -"

"Nick, I live in a different category of time now. Don't you understand? The pace has doubled, tripled. I'm like a dog. Seven years for every one you live."

I glanced at Charly and this time she held my gaze. She was better prepared than I. She'd had months to absorb the reality of his illness, the changes in his mind and body, the slow death, the eventual emptiness. But there wasn't room for my pain as well. I was on my own. "They can give you medication," I said.

"It's stronger than I am now, with or without medication. It's what I feared most, and now it's too late." He paused to take some water and then added, "I knew it was happening. I knew it a month ago and tried to ignore it. But my eyes just got cloudier."

"We'll all fight this," I offered weakly.

"Remember when I told you I wanted to die before my sight went? I meant it, Nick. I can't stand the darkness. It's too much."

"We'll stay by you."

"Just be my eyes, huh?"

"Hey, you're never alone. We're always here."

"Good. Then be my lungs and my brain and my heart and my guts....."

He was too weak to cry, but Charly's eyes teared and my guts were on fire. It crushed me to hear his anger, the stand-in for fear. It dawned on me that from that point forward there would always be something. His illness was a brush fire out of control.

"Let's change the subject," Charly said softly, trying to take control.

"I brought the picture," I said to Johnnie R., taking her cue.

"What picture?"

"The photo with the two of us outside the Firestone library. Remember? You knew the date, exactly when it happened."

"Let me see it."

He took a long look at the picture, bringing it close to his face. Though the room was bright enough he could only make out a few muted colors. He put a finger on it, tracing a line down the border of the photo. "It was warm, unseasonably. I'd just finished a finance exam. Aced it. Forced you to give up on Rilke and go for a beer. We got shit-faced," he said with a little laugh, shaking his head on the pillow. "God, I wish I were back there. I wish we were there again, starting all over."

"Na, you called those the days of two dimensional existence. Remember? You lectured me for romanticizing them."

"But I was wrong, Nick. They're real. They're as real as anything I've known. They were the best days of my life."

He was quiet again, and I could see the tears at the corners of his eyes. The moment was getting away from us. Charly shifted in her seat; such talk made her uneasy. The college days weren't her days. She'd met him later, and to hear her former husband talk of such sweet memories had to hurt her. After all, she'd lived with him for a decade.

"What about your son? Show me a picture."

That brought him to life. I'd hit on the right connection, something they could both enjoy. Johnnie R. perked up and Charly pulled a picture from her purse. I looked at it under the light for a long while.

"My eyes and Charly's face, huh?" Johnnie R. said.

"He's a beautiful kid," I said. But Johnnie R. was wrong. His kid was Johnnie R. all over again. Eyes, brows, cheeks and chin. The hair. Even the spunky look of the eye gave him away.

Charly said, "He's in one of those awful stages."

"They call it the fearsome fours, right?" Johnnie R. said.

"He's difficult at times, but he's a good boy," Charly said. "John's a good father."

"For an absentee father I wasn't bad."

Before he could run with the thought I said, "Johnnie R.'s temperament, I suppose."

"Alas, yes," Charly chimed in.

"Then he'll be a great success," Johnnie R. played along.

"I can't wait to see him," I said.

"Yeah, Charly. Bring him here tomorrow, okay?"

Suddenly, the bottom fell out. She struggled for a minute, trying to find the right words. She nearly spoke, debated, was silent. Then she offered, very quietly, "He doesn't do well here, John. You remember the last visit. We agreed it was best."

"But you could bring him to the waiting room. Nick could see him there."

"We'll see."

"He did ask about me today, right?" he asked. Charly said that of course he had, and Johnnie R. took the photo from me and held it silently. We said nothing for a long moment as he traced a finger over the shadows on the photo. "My kid's afraid of me, Nick. My kid's afraid to see me. My father won't see me. My friends are no longer friends. Except for the two of you."

"Then the two of us it is," I said.

"You've no idea what loneliness is until you've been disowned by your family, ignored by friends," he continued. "They no longer see a human being, just a disease."

"Okay, that's enough," I said.

"It's like the movie *The Fly*. Did you see it? The guy transforms into an insect. That's me. One big Kaposi's. One large virus to go."

Fortunately, Zelda made an entry at that point. She was in a ball-busting mood, and Johnnie R. was forced into silence. She chatted about the weather while she checked his vitals, the IV, his bed pans. She did quick efficient work, straightening the sheets, checking his gown, wiping his face with a cool wash rag. Ignoring me, but kind to Charly, she informed us that Johnnie R. must rest, but when he said he didn't want to be alone she didn't attempt to resist. Instead, she walked out with a hint of an authoritarian smile, and Johnnie R. mimicked her as best he could. It was good to see the sudden change in mood. Temporarily, we put the difficult matters behind us, and the three of us spent the next couple of hours chatting lightly about absolutely nothing at all, avoiding the past. There was no talk of Princeton, the old honor of pals, the *good old days*. We swept the afternoon along with small talk and little jokes and pep talks and TV. And later, as the sky began to darken, Johnnie R. tired. We watched him sink into a stupor with the help of xanax as he was shipped him off to the land of sleep and temporary hope, the first stage on the journey to acceptance of inevitable death. Ten minutes later we were listening to his shallow, thin, raspy breaths. I counted each labored one, but when his breathing became more regular I looked at Charly with relief. She suggested that we grab a cup of coffee while he slept, and we left the room, two nicely wrapped mummies, and rustled down the hall where we heard an orderly say to a buddy, "Shit, man, that HIV, it's a bad motherfucker."

We de-robed in a changing area, two silent adults in adjacent cubicles listening to the swish and flutter of fabrics as we changed. How odd it was to share that intimate space without sharing so much as a word. So much to say and not a word. So I thought about her eyes and face. During the walk down from the room, masks off beneath the bright fluorescent lights, I for the first time in eight years caught a good glimpse of it. The soft blush, the smooth complexion. But those eyes held a great deal of pain, a great deal of suffering. In the changing area I remembered when I'd first seen them with just that depth and expression. It was on a Saturday, a week following my initiation to Talbott Street, the winter weather playfully toying with Indianapolis. It had been a day not unlike that snowy afternoon, and the weather and Charly's eyes carried me back as I took yet another reading from the past.

8

Indianapolis, 1982

During that first week of my stay back in December of nineteen eighty-two I'd quickly come to appreciate Charly. I enjoyed her intelligence, the dry wit, her soft charm. I was enamored of her simple beauty. Friendships, of course, grow in many ways, and ours blossomed over the span of one memorable Saturday which began when she knocked softly on my bedroom door, paused to hear me wake and then cunningly bribed me. "I have a proposition, Nick. I'll make the world's best brunch if you'll join me for a day of shopping."

Johnnie R. was still sleeping, recovering from yet another hangover. During the previous evening the three of us had gone out for dinner, caught a movie and grabbed drinks afterward. The night had ended with me lugging Johnnie R. into the house and up to bed. He'd sleep for hours, leaving me to fend for myself. That's when Charly extended the invitation.

"I made him swear that he'd Christmas shop before the day's out," she confided over breakfast.

"Ah, you worked him over."

"No, it was the work of guilt. I told him to do it for his dad. And if he happens to pick up my present too, well....." she smiled as she took a sip of coffee. "We'll keep each other company, and then there's the bonus of having you carry his present to the car. I'm buying him golf clubs."

"Surely he doesn't golf!"

"He told me that being a golfer fits the banker's image. He's going to learn. Always the opportunist!"

It was a peaceful December day. Several inches of new snow lay on the ground, and not even the slightest current of air was perceptible. The snow had settled delicately upon the hidden surfaces as if placed by hand, flake over fragile flake. Snow cushioned the car tires, muffling all sound from Meridian Street. There were no birds, no children, no barking dogs. Just soft silence and a splash of white. And Charly was irrepressible as she maneuvered the car across the stark white landscape. Once we'd left the car she insisted that we take a winter walk around the Circle and parts of Downtown before hitting the stores. Arm in arm we tip-toed around the icy patches and mounds of snow until we reached University Park and its diagonal walks, imitation turn-of-the-century gas lamps and a fountain of frozen nymphs. "In the spring John and I occasionally meet here during the week for a picnic lunch. I'll prepare a basket, and we'll spread a blanket so that he can lay on the ground in his suit. It's wonderful, though I think its more beautiful with the snow," she said as we circled the fountain.

We made our way back to the Circle where young carolers whooped it up as we bought hot chocolate and a pastry from an old vendor with a makeshift cart. Then it was on to the stores where I discovered that Charly was a shopper's shopper, sporting a list both categorized and alphabetized. She used it as her bush guide and treasure map as we traveled up and down escalators and in and out of department stores. We stalked the shopper-infested aisles as if on safari, Charly playing the indefatigable huntress shadowing and tracking and circling until the clerks relented and the presents were wrapped snugly in their holiday bags. She continued in hot pursuit, checking off the captured quarry one by one from her exquisite hand-written lists, and it wasn't until she'd bagged the *Big One* that she called it quits. With a sparkle in her lovely eyes she seized those exemplary tusks, Johnnie R.'s golf clubs, and ordered the sales clerk to toss them over my shoulder. With the magnificent beast in hand she led me out of the vast, synthetic hinterland of the American department store. `

"That's it, Nick. Another year of shopping completed," she announced triumphantly. "Safari's over!"

We waddled back to the car like a pair of penguins with the Christmas bounty, and moments later she whooshed us off to dinner on the outskirts of the city where there was only the snowfall and the icy road and the car skating over the wide-open flat spaces of the midwestern prairie. Yes, and pink-faced Charly.

The German restaurant where we ate was a Bavarian affair of dark brown rafters, old brick walls and bookcases housing antique steins and knickknacks from the Rhine. The tables were old and worn; chairs didn't match. But each was covered with a white linen cloth and topped with a candle. There was German classical music, an open kitchen and a glass-enclosed case of pastries which we eyed throughout the meal. We ordered the works - roast pork, potato pancakes, red cabbage, rye bread and beer. Afterward, there was coffee and conversation.

"What do you think of Indy thus far, Nick?"

"It'll make a nice home. I like the prairie. Farms, lots of snow and Frank Lloyd Wright!" She smiled, raising her brows. "But I don't want to interfere. Johnnie R.'s taken me out nearly every night. You two should just go on with your lives. I'll be fine."

"It's not a burden for either of us," she insisted. "But tell me, what late-night sights have you visited with John?"

With her eyes on me, cheeks still rosy with the warmth of the food and coffee, I was evasive. "He's taken me to a couple of bars. We've grabbed a couple of meals out. But I'm getting too old for boozing in the middle of the week."

"Talbott Street?" she asked casually, surprising me with the sudden, nonchalant reference to the bar. I was silent as I drank the coffee and looked out the window, feeling the awful pull of mixed alliances. Their troubles were none of my affair, though I'd already begun to sympathize with Charly's position. "I'm making you uncomfortable. I'm sorry," she said, taking a sip. "Frankly, it usually takes a couple of drinks to get me started. We need not discuss it."

I smiled, and she ended it there, though we were quiet for some time as we ordered more coffee and listened to Beethoven. My eyes wandered to Charly's and then scanned the restaurant, the dark wood and rough brick walls adding a sturdy dimension to the contrasting softness of the lace curtains and Charly's face. "I haven't felt this good in years," I broke the silence.

"Wonderful! You're at home. I had a hunch, remember?"

"I'm at a disadvantage when you invoke your ethereal sources."

"Well, as I said, it all comes back to the eyes."

"There you go again!" I laughed.

"I'm not relying entirely on intuition. John did share your past with me," she said. "Let's see, how did he describe you? Oh yes. An exile from the South hooked on Rilke. A numbers man who loves his poetry more," she offered.

I leaned back and looked up at the rafters. "Last week he was more succinct. Over drinks he simply told me to get over it." She laughed with me, and then I asked, "What else did he say?"

"I can't remember," she confessed, shaking her head. Against the backdrop of the lace curtains and snow she was stunning. She took another sip of coffee and then, with a wide smile, said, "No, I do. I do remember more. He said, Mobile was that hellhole on the Gulf."

"Ah, yes, but he was wrong about that. Mobile is beautiful, genuinely beautiful."

"I'm sure it is, Nick."

"I probably did say something like that years ago, though. That's all so distant now. Damn, we were both so cavalier at Princeton, playing with words - time, identity, nexus, purpose. Initial urges. Silly little elemental causes. It sounds so generational, so baby-boomish," I said, still smiling. "But you know, Charly, we were very attached then. A fragile covenant binding us together."

"Which is why he asked you to come."

During a lull we ordered apple cake with more coffee as German waltzes replaced Beethoven. When we'd finished I said, "Now tell me how you met Johnnie R."

"You won't believe it," she laughed.

"Try me. I know all of his tricks. The original smooth operator."

Charly described their romance between sips of coffee. At times smiling widely, occasionally quite serious, often wearing a simple and puzzled expression, she began with the day they met in the lobby of the bank four years earlier. "Nick, it all happened so quickly, with fireworks and lots of anger. I entered the bank in a rage over an incorrect bank statement, the fifth computer error in as many months, and John, all polish and pizazz, happened to be in the vicinity. Of course, I insisted on talking with the manager, and instead I was received by the bank president's son!" she laughed. "Thus hath fate intervened."

I enjoyed the details, including Johnnie R.'s disposition as he attempted to console the woman he would marry. Johnnie R., casual and confident - and sporting his sexy smile and sensual charm - was poised as ever. "I'd call it a swagger," she said. "And he didn't allow himself to become angry when, after he introduced himself as the owner's son, I said, 'For that I forgive you.' He took it as a challenge, both professionally and romantically.

"I became angrier and decided to close my account, demanding a cashier's check then and there, and in the end he acquiesced. And the angrier I became the cooler he appeared, which made me all the angrier!" Johnnie R. was a master of that ploy. He liked such contests when the heat and passion of argument developed into a mental, or sexual, tug-of-war. "My small account didn't amount to peanuts." True. The banker in Johnnie R. knew the loss was meaningless, hilariously forgettable in the world of high finance, and yet it was his duty to attempt to keep the account. Business school capitalism versus banker's etiquette. But there was much more to it than that. "He liked my spunk." And of course, it didn't hurt that he found her very attractive.

"He stood in line with me while I waited for the next available teller, attempting to hold a conversation, and when he reached for my bank statement I shouted, 'Don't touch it!' When he apologized for the bank, I said it was too late. When he offered me a cash benefit for my troubles, I said I didn't want it. When he suggested that he would ask his father to send a letter of apology, I asked, 'Do they give you small jobs like this throughout the day to keep you busy?' And Nick, he only laughed. I'd never been angrier."

When she finished with the teller, cashier's check in hand, she walked hastily to the door. Johnnie R. charged ahead of her and held it open. She froze, refused to walk through. Realizing he wasn't going to back off, she said, "I'm not moving until you close the door. And then I want you to leave me alone."

"Come on. Be nice. Let me make it up to you. I'm not a bad guy. Let me take you to lunch."

"Forget it. Rich kid innocence doesn't work with me."

Charly looked at me with a wide smile, leaning on the table with her elbows, chin in hands. She tilted her head slightly, saying, "You know, Nick, I hadn't expected him to battle in just that way, all politeness and poise. And when I made that last comment he looked at me almost wickedly, still smiling, and his smile said everything. It was an expression that suggested 'Then why not a rich kid romp in the sack.' That's when I left. John, ever the chivalrous gentleman, was still holding the door and waving when I looked back."

I laughed. It was vintage Johnnie R. Charly said that she was convinced that he'd begun plotting his next move immediately. He apparently obtained her address and phone number from the account information stored on the very computer which had abused her. From there it was easy. Johnnie R., never previously the romantic, sent her a dozen roses every day for a week. The card he attached to the flowers contained the same word every day: "Lunch?"

"My God, he must have been watching re-runs from the Forties! I've seen it done a dozen times, but always in the movies!" she said, chin still in hands. "Still, in the end, I called him. Can you believe it, Nick?"

I shrugged.

"Admittedly, I found him good-looking and sexy. My motives weren't beyond reproach. Although I'm not one who naturally falls for the poised, arrogant type, his wit compensated for the fault. As I thought about the incident during the following days I realized he was only trying to help. After all, he only became smug and patronizing after I'd become difficult. He'd taken my barbs generously, and I'd been difficult. So after the seventh day I began to feel badly, and I gave him a call.

"You called him out of pity?"

"And I wanted to see him," she admitted. "I can still hear him snickering as I said, without introduction, 'I hate roses.' "

"I thought you would," he'd answered.

"And to force you to stop we must have lunch together?" Charly had asked.

"Today."

"And it's that easy? I begin to picture the women you entertain."

"Will you?"

"Of course not."

"What?"

"I can't. I'm booked for lunch today, but I wouldn't anyway. That would be too easy."

"Tomorrow?"

"Maybe."

"Shapiro's. Twelve-thirty," Johnnie R. had announced, naming his favorite delicatessen.

"Make it the King Cole. You're a banker. You can afford it."

I picture Johnnie R. somewhat in shock as her voice came over the line without the anger and sarcasm of their previous encounter. "The King Cole it is," he had agreed. "But why so easy?"

"I'm nearly broke."

"I don't believe it. I saw the money you withdrew last week. You didn't blow the entire wad!"

"But would you believe one of your competitors will not allow me to withdraw money from my brand new account?"

They laughed together for the first time and later had a smashing first date. They continued to see each other daily, and within six months they were engaged to be married. Charly led me to believe that those were the happiest six months of her life. Yet, Johnnie R.'s undisclosed bisexuality lay ahead. Although Charly didn't then divulge to me when she'd discovered his secret, and once discovered, when he'd begun to revert to his old habits of trading men and his woman interchangeably, the unspoken was noticeably present. The facts lay just beneath the romantic surface. Her expression gave it away.

"It was a wonderful beginning," she said at last, forcing her words, her smile slowly fading. I said nothing and she was quiet. I watched her for a long moment, took note of her expression, her lovely eyes, and as her smile passed, the strain was palpable. I knew she had no desire to continue with the conversation, though I'd been informed that the wedding early the following spring had been a real beauty - "A lavish, gala affair sponsored by my father," Johnnie R. had written to me in one of his infrequent letters. And somewhere between that letter and my move to Indianapolis their marriage had collapsed, only later to be partially mended - a delicate web of tenuous threads holding the shattered pieces loosely together. Charly's expression conveyed fatigue, an example of the price she'd paid for the compromise and the energy expended in its name.

"My God!" she said as the waltzes gave way to folk music. "We've been here for nearly three hours. We need to get back."

And so we left. When we slid away from the icy streets near the restaurant the snow picked up again, and as the headlights sliced through the empty prairie on the way back to the city I seemed to catch a glimpse of her eyes in the snow shadows cast by the lights of the car.

9

Indianapolis, 1991

Johnnie R..'s Journal

from Love Fever

and see the arc of ages
and see the arc of aids
and see the arc of love
squeezing within an elliptical frame
the orbits of desire

*   *   *

Yes, that was the first time I detected sadness in her eyes and sensed the grief which informed the depth of her expression. I again caught a quick glimpse of her eyes as we walked from the AIDS unit dressing area and toward the elevators. How odd that the memory of that vivid expression returned so easily, and how curious that she should wear it again, as one would an old worn hat, nine years later as her ex-husband lay dying of AIDS. Johnnie R. might have been losing his mental functioning to dementia, but he was still sharp enough to know that she was still haunted by her love for him.

On the elevator I examined her closely. She was still slender, a tall, small-breasted, subtle beauty. Her small, thin nose made her cheeks appear sharper, better defined. As always, I enjoyed seeing how the fine line of her dark brows accented her eyes. It wasn't until we reached the cafeteria minutes later and grabbed a small table where we drank our coffee that I noticed for the first time how long she wore her hair. It seemed darker as a woman's hair can sometimes become darker after having given birth. The harsh lights of the bright cafeteria were less forgiving than the lights in Johnnie R.'s room, and the small wrinkles just surfacing around her eyes seemed a bit more prominent. But they were the baby wrinkles of a woman in her mid thirties. At the table she was quieter than usual, concerned, distant. She maintained her composure, but in garnering the energy to do so she appeared starch and businesslike, removed and serious. She broke the silence.

"You've lifted his spirits, Nick. He's happy you're here."

"I still love him like a brother. I couldn't have stayed away."

"Still," she said. "This must be difficult. You have a job, other obligations. He could live on in this state for some time."

Her words were offered with genuine concern, but her stiffness made them seem harsh, uncaring, even crass. "It doesn't matter," I said. "I've made arrangements with the university."

"You're teaching?"

"Yes, and someone has taken my classes. It wasn't difficult getting away."

"Don't get me wrong," she said, perhaps aware that her tone and manner weren't quite right. "It's good that you've come."

"Believe me, I had no choice in the matter. Love for an old friend. Guilt from the past."

She looked at me oddly, nearly frightened, and I immediately understood her reaction. Implicitly, we'd agreed to carry over into that conversation the earlier rules of the game as applied in Johnnie R.'s room. We'd silently agreed to ignore the past. She'd been especially adept at keeping all of us focused on the present where she was most comfortable. But never the past, though we all knew it was lying in wait just around the corner, silently stalking its prey. To touch the issue even slightly would be too much for her. She might touch on *IT*.

"What about his prognosis," I moved on. This placed her back in her element. The business mask was secure. She was all no-nonsense reserve as she spoke.

"You obviously understand that he doesn't have long to live. Two days ago the infectious disease specialist said it could be a matter of days. It's the pneumonia. Most people don't survive the third episode. This is his fourth."

"Christ!" I said. There it was again, right before me. His death. The cold facts.

"But Nick, if it's not the PCP it will be something else, possibly something worse. He's been infected with a particularly virulent strain of HIV. It's very aggressive. He has meningitis, perhaps toxoplasmosis. His sight's already going. And his mind."

"You're saying get it over with," I suggested, angry at the situation, though it sounded harshly critical of her.

"I'm saying he will die soon," she answered. "I've watched him for eighteen months, and in that eighteen months I've seen several people die of AIDS. It's never pretty, and it's never quite the same. I've seen all of its phases. The malignancies. The infections. From ARC to AIDS. From swollen lymph nodes and night sweats to death by suffocation."

"I'm sorry."

"I know," she said, her natural warmth showing through.

"Then I'm glad I came when I did."

"I am too, Nick. He's losing ground quickly. This last week has been very bad. He's not the same man. To make matters worse, he's so isolated. His friends have vanished. His father has disowned him. You hear stories of such things and never imagine it could happen here, to him."

"What about the old man?"

"He's taken the moral high road, and self-righteousness is easier when it's also convenient. He loved John, deeply, and I'm sure he feels betrayed. After all he's from the old school, unthinking though that may be. He's far too bright to believe the Far Right's theory of God's vengeance, but he's always expressed a somewhat patrician attitude about what a real man should be and stand for. Being gay isn't one of the items on the list, and John's dying of what he calls a gay disease doesn't help. So he disowns his son and at the same time attempts to save the bank's image. In the end, and this should come as no surprise, he loved the bank more than he loved his son."

"Have they spoken?"

"Not in six months. They had words after John's diagnosis. He actually tried to fire John at the time. His own son. Can you believe it?"

"Yes."

"Then he attempted to disinherit him, as if that mattered when it became obvious that the father would outlive the son."

"And?"

"And I intervened," she said, still smooth and controlled.

"The old man can be a real terror. I remember all too well," I said.

"It was quite easy. I threatened never to allow him to see his grandson. He adores Ian."

"The new heir-apparent," I offered.

"Yes. At four years of age. Good God, Nick, it's all so ludicrous. John had to remain with the bank. He'd never find insurance to cover his treatment. The divorce was costly for him. His funds were running low. I've helped, but he needed his father's help."

"And the compromise?"

"John remained on the payroll but was forced to stay away from the bank. For most people that would be a dream come true. No work and all the money. But it nearly killed him. He loved his work at the bank. He was very good at what he did. Anyway, his father's also picking up the costs beyond what the insurance is paying. Experimental drugs. Black market drugs. A new protocol every few weeks. So, he pays, but he won't see John. It's a stand off."

"And we all wait for him to die," I said, pissed. "There's nothing that can be done?"

"Nick, you really don't understand the disease yet, do you? It's not a matter of fighting off a bug, washing the system clean. His immune system has collapsed. He has no defense against even the most harmless infection. He's been dying since the day he was infected."

I shook my head and looked away. I watched the orderlies come and go, nurses take a break, doctors grab a quick sandwich before the next surgery or round. When I looked back at Charly she was still stiff, but in control. Her defenses were way, way up. There had been a time when Charly would've broken down and cried at that point. I'd seen it before. But she was stronger by then. She'd been through a lifetime of sorrow at the age of thirty-four. The dream had been shattered more than ten years earlier. She simply built a fortress out of the emotional ruins. That's all she had.

"When it's over I don't want John's father to see Ian," she said suddenly, full of anger. The reserve was temporarily gone. I looked at her closely but said nothing. I understood.

She said, "He created John, you know. And I'm not talking about the biological stamp. Nick, I loved John very much, you know that, but there was a monster in there. You know? I'm not referring to his sexuality or orientation. I mean his temperament, his drive. A lust for power. The life of making money. I've seen it in both of those men, and I've benefitted from it financially. But I want no part of it any longer. My son won't be exposed to it."

"And the deal with the old man?"

"The deal can be broken, Nick. I did what was right for John. I'd do it again. It's like, what do the lawyers call it, a life estate? It's good for as long as John's alive. That's how I see it."

"You're fighting a tough old man."

"Yes, and I'm surprised he didn't have me sign something that he could take into court, though I don't suppose it would hold up there, do you?"

I shrugged, uncertain.

"Anyway, I can fight too. I finally learned to do that. It's not unethical. What his father did was unethical, even evil. So I did what I had to do, for John and Ian both. It was a pact among family members, and as far as I'm concerned once John dies the family is gone."

"What will you do afterward?"

"I'm not sure. I may move. Fortunately, it's not a question of financial security."

We sat in silence for quite a bit longer, listening as the intercom paged physicians, watching the medical crowd come and go, seeing family members of the ill whisper and cry and console. Everyone was waiting, just as we were waiting.

"Thanks again for coming, Nick," Charly eventually said as she scooted her cup to the side and stood. Her voice was warm, thoughtful. But she just as quickly replaced that warmth with the old mask as she added, "We'd better get back. John's probably awake."

Back in the room Johnnie R. was awake, and pissed. He thought we'd left him for the evening, and he was difficult for nearly half an hour. It wasn't until supper was brought for the three of us that he settled down. We ate in silence while watching the evening news, Charly and I stationed across the room since our masks were off. Afterward, masks back on and chairs pulled close to his bed, we chatted for a bit until Johnnie R. tired. A new nurse entered and gave him his medicines, checked his vitals, did the nasty duty with the catheter and bed pans. Later, Johnnie R. had me turn the television selector to *Nick at Nite* so that he could watch the fluff which was his daily menu: *Get Smart, Green Acres, Andy Griffith, Patty Duke, Dobie Gillis, Mr. Ed, The Beverly Hillbillies, The Addams Family.* He wanted something unthinking, not of this world. He needed this tube pudding, a generation removed from where we sat, which was the stuff that baby-boomers grew up on. So the three of us trudged through episodes of *Bewitched* and *Gilligan's Island* before Johnnie R. fell asleep. He missed Maxwell Smart talking into his shoe, just as he missed Charly crying not long after.

When I looked over, only her wet eyes were showing above the mask and beneath the large cotton cap, and her head was shaking as she doubled over in her chair. I stood and walked to her, but as I touched her shoulder she pushed my hand away. She waved me off, and after I withdrew she stood and walked out the door. I followed her into the hall where she mumbled through the mask that she'd return tomorrow. When I tried to console her again she again pushed me away. Bewildered, I stood in the hall and watched her disappear into the dressing area. I didn't move until I saw her come out of the area and walk to the elevators. Only when she disappeared behind them did I walk back into the room.

Johnnie R. was awake when I reentered. He had the look of the eyes of a wild animal, frightened, confused. He hadn't found his bearings yet. He was somewhere between childhood and his death bed, and he couldn't find his way home. "I thought I heard somebody crying. It's not my boy, is it?" he asked, looking at me but only seeing shadows.

"Just a dream, Johnnie R.," I lied.

"Nick, is that you?"

"Yes. I told you I'd be here."

Hurriedly, I pulled the chair up next to the bed and took his hand. He held it tightly.

"Thank you," he said softly, closing his eyes again.

He didn't say another word, but he wouldn't let me withdraw my hand. I held it firmly and leaned against the bed and waited for him to sleep as Max Smart bungled his way to victory in the background. Yes, I sat there with Johnnie R.'s hand in mine and thought of his death, reflected on the sinister manner in which the virus kills. I thought of Charly and her tears, compassion and the fragile human heart. I thought of how strong she'd been, yet how weak we all could become in the face of this ghastly syndrome. And those tears? They weren't new. She'd cried in my presence more than once, the first time being on that unusual evening nine years earlier after we'd returned from the German restaurant. Yes, with Johnnie R.'s hand in mine I reminisced again. He breathed those shallow little breaths as the oxygen forced its way into the receding air sacs, and I remembered.

10

Indianapolis, 1982

And what I remembered was that Johnnie R. didn't return until very late that evening. When Charly and I reached their empty house after dark we sat and talked over a bottle of wine. I still retain the image of her flushed face, her alcohol-bright features presenting a sharp contrast to her dark eyes. The den light chiseled out the shallow hollows of her cheeks, and everything seemed perfect, her thick dark hair, the small nose, her coloring.

After finishing the bottle we brought in the gifts from the car, and I hauled the golf clubs up to her drawing room where Johnnie R. wouldn't find them. She directed me to a closet full of art supplies and some of her paintings, and when I leaned in to put the clubs away a large canvas fell out onto the floor. Putting the golf clubs aside, I reached to pick up the canvas but drew back quickly. Charly stepped to my side, staring along with me as I deciphered its simple message. It was an oil painting of the buildings surrounding Talbott Street and of the bar's facade. Amazed and distressed both, like a child who peeks into the forbidden drawer as the scornful parent draws silently near, I felt guilty and embarrassed. Many thoughts raced through my mind at that moment but none more moving than those accompanying the image of Charly as she stood alone in the gravel parking lot across from Talbott Street while painting the canvas. A mission of expiation? I tried to imagine her sentiments as she'd stood before the plain building with the gaudy marquee mixing the colors on her rainbow palette.

When she knelt to pick up the painting moments later, rather than put it away she carefully placed it against a chair in the open room, playing with it as she sought just the right light. With her back to me she stepped away from the canvas for a better angle. "You can put the clubs away, Nick," she said without turning her head, her tone unchanged from our earlier conversation. When I returned to her side she looked up and said, "Surprised?"

"Yes," I mustered.

"You needn't worry about having found it, though I suppose it calls for an explanation."

"It's not necessary."

"No. I think I'd like to," she insisted. "I told you earlier I needed a couple of drinks before I could talk about it. The wine will do." When I said nothing she added, "Perhaps it will prove interesting to you."

I shrugged my shoulders noncommittally, looking at the canvas closely as the light picked up what previously were only shadows. Every detail seemed excruciatingly studied, just as every color seemed appropriately applied. The

103

marquee of the bar held center stage with its bright lights and red neon which announced *Talbott Street*.   She painted the plain facade in drab colors.   She illustrated the poverty of the ghetto with severity, all filth and dilapidation along declining Talbott Avenue.   Broken windows, torn shutters, hanging gutters, shingleless roofs.   Trash and other debris lay strewn along the curbs, and she'd carefully painted in the chipped and broken walks beyond.   It was a study in browns and grays with the lone exception of the garish marquee which was free-floating above the decay and putrefaction beneath.   Looking closely I noticed that she'd painted the door beneath the marquee slightly ajar with an anonymous hand clutching it.

She placed the painting back in the closet, and when we'd made it back to the den, sipping more wine, she offered, "Obviously, the painting came afterward. After I discovered everything."

I was silent, stunned that I was being drawn into the mire.

"You might say that early on John was eager to make his mark on the world with his wife by his side and his personal fortune in his pocket, but it eventually became clear that he wanted both worlds, the world of marriage and the world of Talbott Street."

How easy it was for me to entertain the image of Johnnie R., ever confident and poised, even brash, as he attempted to balance the two worlds, juggling his love for Charly with his desire for men.   After all, I'd seen him in action at Princeton.   And if anybody could pull it off, it was Johnnie R.

"Early on, during our engagement, there had been a lost weekend here, an unexplained series of absences there.   There were ugly scenes.   The wedding was once called off.   But of course we made up, though I remained unaware of John's bisexuality.   It turns out that I believed I could change a man I didn't really know, and for a long while I believed he'd had one last fling with some unknown woman.   It pleased me to believe.   I desperately wanted to believe."   She hesitated a moment to sip her wine as she ran a hand through her hair.   A slight smile came over her face.   "We were a good match, it seemed.   We were able to accommodate our careers, tastes and hobbies.   We enjoyed mutual friends, and our home life was unruffled by outside concerns."   And then her smile slowly vanished.   "But within a year, the tension began to build.   His unexplained absences increased, and although I didn't immediately confront him, I began to draw distance between us.   And then his conspicuous absences made a scene unavoidable, and I had no choice but to confront him."

As Charly held the glass of wine she described the confrontation as she waited up for him one week night after he'd failed to return home early, and as he entered the house, two a.m., she stood before him with tears in her eyes.   "What should I say?" he asked.

"You bastard," she yelled.   "I believed you had given it up, John.   I believed, foolishly, that your final goddamned triumph as a bachelor had ended.   I was willing to go along with it. The lenient modern times. One for old time's sake, you know? But you've been screwing around with other women from the beginning, haven't you?"

"No," he answered.

"You don't have to lie now, dammit. I know! Lies no longer serve their purpose." When he didn't defend himself she said, "Wasn't I quite enough for you? If together we weren't sexually compatible, couldn't we have discussed it? Wasn't there a possibility that we could work out a solution?"

"It's not what you think," he said.

"You son-of-a-bitch!" she yelled. "Damn you! You're going to tell me, John."

"There are no other women," he said, raising his voice to meet hers. When she said nothing, simply standing there with her head down, crying, he finished it off. "Men, Charly. The infidelity is with men."

And as quickly as he said it she charged him, straight-arming him full in his chest, knocking the breath from him. He bent over, and she slapped his face and then his back with her open hands. When he raised himself, she used her fists to pummel his stomach and arms. "This isn't a joke, you bastard! How dare you make light of this."

Johnnie R. grabbed her arms, surrounded her with his own. He turned so that her back rested firmly against his chest, her arms pressed to her sides. She struggled for a moment and then became limp as if it no longer mattered that she should escape him. And as they stood together in that fashion she cried, and then he too began to cry, squeezing her tightly, rocking with her. He leaned forward to kiss the back of her head and then whispered her name. And then she loosened his grip and walked to the bedroom, leaving Johnnie R. behind in the den.

"The days following were silent ones," Charly continued, putting her wine glass down and leaning forward in her chair, head back as she looked up at the ceiling, stretching. Then she looked at me squarely, without a hint of emotion. "He took a guest bedroom, and we avoided each other. We ate separately, and in the evenings I stayed in my drawing room while he remained in the den. It was like sharing the house with a shadow, a ghost. Those days now draw a blank, a horrible vacuum without voices or time. Night after night after night it was the same."

It was the same, that is, until one evening during the following week when Johnnie R. left the house around ten. Charly followed. Johnnie R. drove to Talbott Street and didn't notice Charly pulling up behind his car as he entered the bar. She turned off the car and waited, though she didn't have to wait long. Perhaps he'd left the house simply to escape the silence, to get away from those ghosts, but he stayed only long enough for a drink and then left. When he crossed the street he saw Charly.

"He pulled me from the car," she said, still leaning forward in the chair. "He shouted at me, shaking me very hard. When I wouldn't respond he walked to his car and left. I just stood in the street, leaning against my car for a long while. Later I climbed into the car and locked the doors, and for hours I watched men walk in and out of the bar, remaining there until the bar closed. I wasn't frightened or upset. It's as if I had to memorize that small space, permanently commit to memory the picture of what was there. That's when I realized the truth. And you know, Nick, I wasn't even angry. I was beyond that. I just watched the marquee flash and the crowd go in and out until three a.m."

She drove around for an hour, parked at University Park, sat on a bench until dawn and then drove home. When she reached the house she found Johnnie R. on the floor in the den, passed out with an empty bottle of *Lepanto* nearby. "I just stood there watching him breathe for a long while, but the night began to catch up with me and I felt very weak," Charly offered. "I felt so lonely and I needed to touch him. So I walked over and knelt and touched his shoulder, and then his face and neck. I began to cry and when he woke he cried too. And then I laid down beside him. However hopeless the situation might have been I felt the need to hold him, and so I did."

Johnnie R. didn't go into the office that day. At noon they woke, and they began to talk. Charly, surprising even herself, wanted to know everything, the smallest of details, and as the day wore on Johnnie R. offered it all, freely, as if the burden could be removed only with the honesty which he'd never been able to give. He recounted his first homosexual experiences in high school and ended only when he reached the previous evening's flight to Talbott Street.

"Nick, I remember that day with a great deal of clarity, the mood and his words and the surroundings," Charly said, leaning back in her chair. They groped through the many emotional changes, not unlike, she said, the ever-changing patterns viewed through the den's large windows as the sun passed from east to west in its slow descent to dusk, and in doing so passed the imperceptible point just beyond innocence where there is no emotional space allowed for remorse. Their lives had changed in an afternoon.

"But I didn't leave him," Charly said, without emotion, while rubbing her neck as she slouched in the chair. No, she didn't leave Johnnie R., and the smooth passage of a few weeks beyond that evening made it quite clear what Charly's choice would be. She remained silent in her workroom where she labored among her art, and within a week she began therapy. She wanted to save the marriage.

During those first few weeks following their confrontation Johnnie R. stayed in with Charly during the evenings, usually away from her, but only a room away, a floor away. He returned from the bank each evening and ate supper with her, only to part soon thereafter as she closed herself behind the doors of her drawing room and he walked to the den to watch the tube. She believed him when he said he wanted to save the marriage, and they slowly began to take up their earlier lives, attending parties, dining out, catching a film, having friends over. A month later they again slept together.

"We returned one evening from a party, somewhat overdone by the booze, and we suddenly found ourselves embracing," Charly said with a coy smile. She didn't, of course, elaborate, but I found myself trying to imagine that evening. Was it an embrace of pure lust? Did she resist? Did they slowly walk arm in arm to the bedroom, or were they suddenly too taken with the idea to do anything other than grab wildly at their clothing and fuck savagely on the floor?

Charly continued with her therapy sessions twice a week. She made no demands, no requirements, and Johnnie R. offered no commitments. Though never telling him directly, by her actions, and through his silence, impliedly she'd agreed to share him with those anonymous men. For weeks at a time they found themselves comfortably together, at ease, deeply in love by any standard, and then it would happen. He'd leave for an errand and usually return early enough not to appear to be late. But of course, she knew, and she said nothing as the circle took another inevitable loop.

"On occasion, if John were out later than usual, I'd stay up with the lights out in the den, waiting but not waiting. I sometimes cried, but I cried in parody as if what had been lost actually had been forgotten, somehow, somewhere, leaving behind only a vague outline of some former beauty with which I might trace my thoughts."

She was silent for a moment, and as I glanced at her I couldn't help but believe that she was reflecting on the growing distances accumulating between them. I thought about their watered-down marriage contract, marked at the appropriate blanks by human need. By that evening, only the skeletal outlines of the marriage remained as they lodged in their little prison with its unending cycle of tattered hopes and dying dreams. When did they first begin to detest that part of their love which had hardened with it? I of course would never know, any more than I would ever know how Johnnie R. could compromise the marriage, or how Charly might silently agree to its terrifying terms.

Charly stood and walked to the kitchen. When she returned she handed me a soda and sat again, smiling. She'd exhibited amazing control as she'd told of the unfolding of their marriage, her voice never faltering, but the conversation had taken its toll. She was tough, but she wasn't invulnerable. "I'm sorry. Where was I?" she asked.

"I suppose you've finished with all but the painting."

"Of course, the painting," she said casually, leaning back in her chair. "The beginning and the end. For a long moment she was silent as she gathered her thoughts, and then she crossed her legs as she leaned forward a bit in the chair. "Talbott Street became an obsession for me, a symbol for the breakdown in our marriage. And you know, Nick, the problem wasn't simply that I found his bisexuality appalling, because my views toward his orientation transformed over time, but the fact remains that John had lied. For a year afterward I was skeptical about every word he uttered. True, I continued to love him, but the lack of trust made that love brittle. As I began to sort out my thoughts and to live with the fact that our marriage never would be the same, I found Talbott Street at the center of my thoughts.

"One afternoon following a particularly bad morning alone in the house I felt the need to escape. I drove down Meridian simply to get away, and I ended up at Talbott Street. I parked in the lot across the street from the bar, and you know during the afternoon there's not a soul visible there. The place was frighteningly empty, and during the day the building is quite plain, ugly in fact, and there's absolutely nothing about the scenery that I find appealing. It's in the middle of the ghetto, and I was taking a chance with my life sitting there alone in the car. But I was attracted to it, compelled to return to it time and again. Eventually, I drove there daily.

"My therapist began to worry about my frame of mind, and eventually she suggested that I do a painting of the bar. So I did. For a month I drew sketches in the parking lot. Occasionally I returned in the evenings when I could get away and knew that John wouldn't be there. I was able to get a better feel for it during the evenings, because the atmosphere after dark is dramatically different from what I encountered during the day. In fact, it's of the night, the bar and neighborhood both. Surely you sensed that when you were there," she said, intensely holding my gaze.

"Yes, I understand what you mean."

"The people come for their pleasure. The marquee brightens the ugly surroundings. There's a heightened sense and fear of crime, and I became as obsessed with catching the mood as I did with sketching and painting the building itself. Later, I set up my easel in the parking lot during the afternoons and began to paint it based on the daylight facade before me and the memories and sketches of the night. A month passed by before I completed it," she said, looking down and away from me. "And now you've seen it."

She was quiet, and during that silence her face flushed, her eyes darkened, her lips moved slightly though she said nothing. Moments later, with her head down, she began to cry softly on the edge of her chair, cupping her hands over her face. I didn't move to her right away, playing instead with an image of Charly in the dusty seclusion of the ghetto, encamped in the hollow spaces of the gravel lot near Talbott Street, palette in hand, as she gazed at the building through the slicing glare of the mid-afternoon sun. With the wide open sky above and the dusty breezes below, I too sensed the invisible spaces suddenly separating her from her husband, wordless spaces filling slowly with the slow recognition which precedes the awful grasp of horror.

As she wept louder, her hands wet with tears, I walked to her and knelt beside her and touched her shoulder. "It's okay, Charly," I whispered as I leaned closely and lay her forehead against my chest and held her.

"It was my choice," she strained as she wept. "It was my choice to stay."

"Yes," I whispered, holding her long after she'd dried her tears, the room an empty hush save for the intermittent drone of cars on Meridian Street. It was troubling to find myself suddenly involved in the darker side of their marriage. For over a week Charly had extended the hand of friendship, warm and generous. Openly, she'd suggested we shared a great deal in common, soul mates as it were, and had insinuated that a bond held us together. With Johnnie R. on one side and Charly on the other, my best friend and his lovely wife, I felt the guilt of dual allegiances, and the thought frightened me. Perhaps that's why she slowly pulled herself away from me, wordlessly, and then turned away and walked to her room.

11

Indianapolis, 1991

Johnnie R.'s Journal

*from **the nap***

in a sleep without dream
in a life without sum
in a room without time
in a world without hope

i'm sheathed in shrouds
of plastic tubing
swaddled in clothes
of altered meaning
of what it is to be human

or rather
what it was
to have once been
human, though dying
inhumanely, like the winding
down of a century's metabolic clock ...

*　*　*

I tried to forget Charly's tears as I glanced at Johnnie R., his hand still in mine. He was sleeping, feverish again, his breathing very shallow, and perhaps that's why I began to panic. Remembering his near-blindness and Charly's warnings, every waking moment now seemed infinitely precious. I wanted to hear his voice, needed to talk with him about our years apart, the past, our years together. I needed to discuss forgiveness. But he was out and I could only think of Charly crying and imagine a world without Johnnie R. as I left the hospital for the evening.

But on the following day I arrived at the hospital early, hoping to squeeze consciousness from every living moment Johnnie R. had left with me, and when I entered his hospital room I was in luck. It remains as one of the great mysteries of AIDS that a dying man may temporarily cast away the fast-forming death mask long enough to reach curious levels of lucidity. Temporarily, the effects of the illness somewhat recede; momentarily, the mind and body find short but significant reprieves. Such was a time for Johnnie R. on that hopeful morning as he gained a transient upper hand on the pneumonia. He was in a wonderful mood, having slept well the evening before. He breathed easier, the pain was less pronounced, his mind was clear. When I entered there was an old *Father Knows Best* rerun playing on the television. Tubes still sprouted from his body, and the monitors still buzzed and percolated, but he was propped up high in the bed with a big smile on his face. His eyes had recaptured some of the lost luster, though his vision was nearly lost.

"Breakfast?" he asked gingerly, his voice still weak but containing an enthusiasm I hadn't heard since my return.

"I grabbed fast food on the way over."

"C'mon, have some oatmeal. I ordered special."

I relented, and we laughed through the end of the tube pudding as I ate. Johnnie R., though he couldn't see me well, listened to my every move and kept tabs on me with his peripheral vision, a curious and mischievous expression on his face. He was up to something, and once I'd finished and the nurse had taken away the tray he was all official business. "You still love her don't you?" he asked out of the blue. His tone wasn't in the least accusatory, contained no jealousy.

"What?" was all I could muster.

"You still love Charly," he said quite calmly.

"Not now, Johnnie R. We can't go through all that. It's been eight years now. Let it lie," I said very softly, almost in a whisper.

"Don't get me wrong, Nick. I'm not angry. Hell, I dropped the anger before you left town. You know that."

"Don't do this."

"But you do," he pursued.

"I'm here for you. You know that."

"Still, you do."

"If you weren't this sick I wouldn't be here. It's as simple as that," I said, standing. "I have no other reason for being here."

"Sure, I understand. If I had the mumps you'd still be in Princeton, right? But I'm dying so you came. And you came due to guilt."

"That's not true."

"But you don't need to feel guilty anymore because I'm not angry."

"Goddammit, quit it!"

"And because you've responded like this it means you still love her."

"What do you want, Johnnie R.?"

"The future."

111

"What are you saying?"

"You and Charly," he said.

"What?"

"I want you two to get together when this is over."

"For Chrissake, Johnnie R.!"

"Why not?" he asked. "It's perfect, makes complete sense. Maybe you've got no choice."

"First of all you're making assumptions you have no business making. Like who I love and don't love."

"But you love me. I'm your best pal. Even when you hate me you love me. Right?"

"Secondly," I ignored him, "she's not yours to give away."

"Ah, but she is, Nick. She still loves me," he said, the smile fading. He was all seriousness. "I don't mean she loves this dying shell. It's the memory. She still loves me through the memory. If I consent she'll let herself love again."

I said nothing, looking away.

"That she still loves me surprises you, doesn't it?"

"No, not at all," I said. I nearly left it there, but cruelly added, "She always loved you more than you loved her."

"Bingo!" he laughed, immune to my anger. "That proves it. You never get mean unless you're hurt. And you don't get hurt unless love's involved."

"Leave it."

"Okay, for now," he answered, letting it drop with a smile. "But I mean it."

He'd gotten to me, and I left the room under the pretense of using the toilet. Walking the halls instead, I became angry with myself since there was precious little time for disagreement. Still, I wondered why he'd wanted to push it. I was there, after all, to erase our differences, to resolve tensions stemming from the past. We'd forgiven each other; the anger had vanished. My being there was proof of my love and friendship. Was his peculiar offer proof of his?

When I returned, he'd changed masks again, ready for more fun as he turned his attention to lighter fare. He shared some dialogue form an earlier *Three Stooges* episode, hammed it up, carried on with the nursing staff. The word quickly spread that Johnnie R. was having an uncommonly good day, and the real fun began after we'd settled down for more tube pudding. We heard a rustle at the door and looked up to find floating into the room three gaunt but spry-in-the-eye fellows, two dressed in thick terry cloth robes and the third in a pink chiffon gown with faux fur at the wrists and collar. Each was thin and sallow, apparently battling his own version of the illness, though none was as wasted as Johnnie R. Sporting grand smiles as they spied Johnnie R. propped up in bed, the man in pink in particular seemed in a mischievous mood, his thin-lipped camp smile giving ample warning of the unpredictable as he shuffled to the bed with the others in tow.

"Girl, get up! We're going to dance!" he effervesced, clapping his hands for emphasis.

"I'd love to accommodate you," Johnnie R. mustered the energy, "but, as you see, my plaid pajamas clash with your gown."

"Then take them off, silly!" the fellow in pink retorted.

"Oh, just let me help, sweetie," said another.

"No, it takes at least two," said the third.

The man in pink moved yet closer to the bed with a pronounced swish made all the more remarkable in that he was also lame. Turning to face me, and touching me lightly on the shoulder, he said, "Ooooh, you're new aren't you?"

"Nick," I answered, standing to offer my hand. He took it gingerly, held it but for a moment and then twirled around in a whoosh of chiffon, the bad leg notwithstanding. "And we're the Three Queens. Upper case. Or, if you prefer, red robe, green robe and pink gown!" He then circled me, lame foot dragging a bit, and tapped me gingerly on the ass as he purred, "Forgive me, dear, but I must be tactless and ask you something."

"By all means," I played along.

"I *mean* I have little time for anything but a simple and direct question. I *mean* time is of the essence. I *mean*, after all we're all just *dying*!" he said with a wave of his arms, feigning a swoon. "So do tell. Straight or gay?"

"Straight," Johnnie R. chimed in.

"Dear, let him speak for himself," the pink gown camped it up, hands on hips.

"He doesn't play your game," Johnnie R. insisted, still smiling.

"You're loss, sweetie," the pink gown tapped me again on the ass before turning to Johnnie R. "And that answers my second question which was, "You're new boyfriend?"

"No," Johnnie R. said, playing it to the hilt. "But I get first debs if he changes his mind."

"Tut, tut! Methinks you've had first debs once too often."

"Vicious queen," Johnnie R. laughed as the others moaned.

"My point was simply that safe sex is important. You don't want to *kill* the little sweetie."

"Tact, girl. Tact," the green robe chimed in, winking at me.

The pink gown said, "I told you we have little time for such formalities. In our state, it's a waste of precious moments."

"Where did you get the threads?" Johnnie R. pushed on.

"It's for the cotillion, dear" said the pink gown. They all snickered.

"I couldn't possibly," Johnnie R. continued the game. "The catheter."

"You just let little ole me undo it," the pink gown said, lifting the sheets. He glanced down, held his nose, turned his head and raised his brows. "On second thought." He then turned and walked to me in a pink flourish, sitting on my lap. "Such a big strong man," he said, tilting his head all the way back.

"Be easy on him," Johnnie R. warned.

"Shush!" said the pink gown, standing and walking back to the bed. He tilted his head, all seriousness, and then smiled widely. "I've an idea! Since none of us save for *moi* can put her hands on a proper cotillion gown we'll have a night club act instead." There were cheers all around. "We can all dress as our favorite drag queen, except for Nick, of course, who might agree to perform as emcee."

"I'd be honored."

"Lovely," he chirped, hands high in the air. "It will bring back my nightclub days at Talbott Street when I was queen of the runway on Thursday evenings."

"She was a drag queen once upon a time," Johnnie R. informed me with a wink.

"Once a drag queen, always a drag queen!" the pink gown replied. And then, as if on cue, the red and the green terry cloth robes joined him, standing side by side, and began to belt out a rousing version of *Tomorrow* from *Annie*. They bellowed out every word of the song, and afterward Johnnie R. and I clapped as they gestured their thank yous with a bouquet of kisses.

"Nick," Johnnie R. hammed, "whatever you do, don't yell 'Encore'!"

"Bitch!" the pink gown retorted. "Men used to pay top dollar to hear me sing."

"And bottom dollar too!"

"Ah, those were the days," the pink gown mused. "Even the surreal-gaudy bars in Cincy were fun to play. A decorator's nightmare, to be sure, from the shiny cheap beads a la *Casablanca* to the ever-farting vinyl seats, but by God, those were the days. I can still see those lavender palaces and their shiny half-moon naugahyde booths with specks of lime green to match the shag carpets. Ah, to be a lounge lizard again!"

"Once a lounge lizard, always a lounge lizard!" Johnnie R. cackled.

"Now you're catching on, sweetums," the pink robe continued. "They were all so lovely, the way their heaters in the winter were turned up full blast so that the heat and smoke would make you puke. Bar bulimia, I used to call it. And no one hangs multicolored tinsel anymore! What's become of us?"

"A whole lot less than before," said the green robe.

"But no harm came to us then, as opposed to gay baiting now, because no one dared enter those clubs of long ago for fear of doing battle with the vast synthetic lavender and lime surfaces." He feigned deep reflection and then added. "And I have only one more thing to say on the topic. God bless naugahyde!"

"Hear, hear!"

"But where were we?" the pink gown mused. "Oh yes, nightclubs acts." He clapped his hands. "And if we're to have a nightclub act we must have stage names. So pick your favorite stage names, girls."

"Leona Sofa," said the green robe. "Or perhaps, Rhoda Botashore."

"You've plagiarized, dear."

"Then Heidi Hoe," the green robe suggested.

"And I'll be her sister, Ida Hoe," said the red robe.

The pink gown glanced at Johnnie R. and said, "How about you? Perhaps Leda Horstawater? Or Eda Brownic? Phyllis Up?"

"Speaking of plagiarizing," Johnnie R. said, rolling his eyes. "No, as a salute to these wonderful robes I think I'll be Terri Cloth."

"Good! Good!" said the pink gown. He then pointed to me and added, "And Nickie-poo. You'll be none other than the emcee - Mike Hunt!"

This game continued until a staff person entered to take Johnnie R.'s supper request. He was a very shy young man, quite intimidated by the trio of queens, and before he was able to get to Johnnie R.'s food form, the pink gown grabbed it, pretended to take out a pad and pen and then, in preparation for taking the order, asked, in his best Paul Lynde impersonation, sibilating, "So, then, gents, what'll you have to eat, hmmmm? Or dare I ask?"

"Must I order from the menu?" Johnnie R. asked.

"Honey, it's obvious you've ordered off the menu once too often!"

"Turkey and dressing then."

"Oh my mercy!" he screeched, flitting his wrists, arching his brows, the whole nine yards. "So unimaginative. Girl, you've simply got to get with the program, and take it from a sister who knows. That will bloat you."

"Of course, I'd rather have five *White Castle* burgers."

"Well, if you're going for bloat, you might had as well go all the way," he said. "Anything else?"

"What are you offering?" Johnnie R. asked, arching his brows.

"Oh, you terrible tease!"

"A special request?" Johnnie R. ventured.

"For you, anything, love," the pink gown said, feigning light-headedness as he brought his hand to his forehead, feigning a swoon. But as he leaned back, balance unstable, his bad leg gave way and folded beneath him like a little broken pretzel. He screamed shrilly as he began to topple over, none too gracefully, and his arms wriggled about above his head as his good leg cast about the slick floor for support until all balance was lost and he crashed down onto the vinyl scrub land below. In unison, as if the chorus had been preplanned, red robe and green robe joined in with their own high-pitched screams, hands on their cheeks, mortified. He wallowed about, squirming like a wounded little bird, until I stood and pulled him up. "Oh, heavens! Thank you, Nickie-poo," he said, patting me again on the butt as he attempted to regain composure. He gestured to the others, hands still on cheeks, indicating that he wasn't hurt, and then calmly brushed the gown as he added, "I haven't fallen like that since I tried to breakdance!"

"Are you okay?" I asked.

"Yes, you little angel," he cooed, returning to form. He pinched me on the cheek and then added, "Now, where was I?"

"Taking my order, unless you can provide us with another trick," Johnnie R. laughed.

"Oh, you little cunt!"

"You said for me *anything*," Johnnie R. said with a hint of seduction.

"You naughty boy. I'm twice your age."

"Three times my age!"

"Little bitch!" the pink gown screamed as he flounced and scuttled and swayed, nearly losing his balance again, his lame leg slightly lingering like the dragging blanket of a small child. He seemed as fragile as a tiny china doll. And then, finding his bearings again, he mused, "Did I ever tell you the story of my girlfriend, I mean a real girl, a rather robust one, hefty as a heifer, who was taking orders for fast-food carry-out from about ten of us? The order came to fifty-two burgers and at the last moment someone also ordered a chocolate malt, and she said, 'If you think I'm going into *Dairy Queen* and ordering fifty-two burgers and *one* chocolate malt -"

"What's going on in here?" Zelda interrupted, appeared at the door as a large sinister presence wrapped in white and fear, the great damper amid all the good cheer.

"Ah, oh! It's the gestapo!" the pink gown shrieked. "Hurry girls, against the wall."

"Rules!" Zelda bellowed, shaking her head. Deep down she'd rather not be the heavy, I thought. Still, she didn't crack a smile.

"Please. Please don't beat us," the pink gown camped yet more.

"Two visitors to a room. No exceptions," Zelda the Impregnable ordered. She placed her hands on her large, battleship hips for emphasis. She was all human glare, mortal terror.

"But Zelda, dear, we're planning a party."

"Not here," she said, placing a firm yet kindly hand on the pink gown and then gently scooting him toward the door.

"A cotillion, perhaps. Or night club act," he explained as he neared the door. And Zelda, you can be security!"

They left the room in a roar, giggling all the way down the hall, and Johnnie R. was still snickering when Zelda peeked into the room. "Mr. Thayer, don't you need your rest?"

"Nope. I need to talk with Nick."

"Anymore outbursts and Nick leaves. Understood?"

"Heil, Hitler!" Johnnie R. yelped, and she turned around quickly and left.

*   *   *

Johnnie R. was still smiling when we later set up the backgammon board on the edge of the bed. I made room among the wires and tubes, and we played and joked as I told him the value of his rolls and moved the backgammon pieces the allotted number of spaces. It was like old times, the smoothest afternoon of that long month of dying. But later, after we'd eaten and he had tired, his eyelids drooping, I shifted in my chair and he jolted awake, looking my way with wild animal eyes, full of terror.

"Don't leave me, Nick," he said, reaching for my arm.

"I'm staying right here."

"And you'll be here for supper too, right?"

"Yes," I said, and he stretched so that he could touch my shoulder with his hand. Minutes later he was sleeping soundly. With the television blaring away - he insisted on background noise - I picked up his journal again and read fragments from a poem entitled, ***Elegy for Charly****:*

> *And yes, dear, it does hurt*
> *to know that you continue,*
> *against all odds, to love me.*
> *I'd prefer that you remarry.*
>
> *Yes, guilt is the culprit here.*
> *That you might find love again*
> *releases the fetters of guilt, helps*
> *me to prepare for the long sleep.*
>
> *But I'd not exchange any of it,*
> *not even the bad moments*
> *following your discovery*
> *of my once-tightly-held secret.*
>
> *Because love is unworded mystery*
> *and fate is the word now lost to us,*
> *we must embrace what is given*
> *rather than pine for what is not.*

Those words hit me hard as I put the journal away, bringing back with clarity our earlier conversation regarding Charly. The ever-encroaching past was on the move again. He'd taken me there, and as he slept longer I surrendered to its pull.

117

12

Indianapolis, 1982-83

Those early weeks in Indianapolis were very good ones. Johnnie R. and Charly insisted that I put off seeking an apartment until after Christmas, so I remained in their home beyond the New Year. For nearly a month Johnnie R. and I drove to the office together each day, met for lunch and usually stayed in with Charly during the evenings. Occasionally Charly cooked a meal; often we dined out. Christmas albums, hot chocolate, pastries, a warm fire. It was the finest holiday season in memory.

On Christmas eve I attended the family dinner at the home of Johnnie R.'s father, becoming further convinced that the old man had it in for me. True enough, before dinner Johnnie R.'s father was generous to a fault, exuding irresistible charm as he poured drinks. "Drink up, young man, drink up!" he ordered happily. "And, again, welcome to Indianapolis!"

We all had several. Even the rather staid old man appeared a bit tipsy as we ate our dinner among much laughter and good cheer, and the dinner was a magnificent feast, the old man's goodwill continuing. But later that evening a bit of the mean streak surfaced as we sat near a roaring fire sipping his expensive brandy, though things began innocently enough. The Christmas carols played in the background and the fire popped and sparked while we chatted away. The old man took up his perch on his aged Chesterfield throne and held court, all eyes focused on him. He led the conversation, changed topics, prodded agreement, pontificated. I watched as he elegantly swished his brandy in the snifter and puffed on his rare and regal cigar. While others talked he pondered their words, blowing large and perfect rings of smoke across the room where I sat wheezing. Yes, he was enjoying himself, an adoring sister to one side, a passive brother-in-law to the other, his only son imparting signs of fealty, his daughter-in-law revealing her lovely charm, nameless others looking on and me sneezing away as he continued to blow the smoke my way. It was obvious at that point that he was going to have fun with me.

"Now, Nick, correct me if I'm wrong, but is it not true that you were unable to attend John and Charlene's wedding?"

"I'm afraid so, Mr. Thayer," I answered through the smoke, leery. "I was ill."

"Ill?"

"Yes, at the last minute I had to cancel," I said. He knew damned well why I hadn't been able to attend. He was playing games.

"You were to be the best man, correct?"

"Of course he was Dad. You remember. We had to scramble at the last minute," Johnnie R. tried to save me. The old man waved him off with his huge cigar.

"Of course," the old man agreed, his eyes full of mischief. He wasn't done.

"I was so angry at the time," Johnnie R. continued. "Do you remember, Nick?"

"How could I forget. I badly wanted to be there." It was true. The wedding was to provide my first return trip to the States since leaving for London. I called Johnnie R. upon receiving the telegram announcing his wedding, and I agreed then to be his best man. I made all the plans. Tickets were purchased. The itinerary was set. And then less than a week before I was to leave I came down with, of all things, epididymitis. One of my testicles ridiculously swelled to tangerine size, and now that I was captive to this fruit out of season my doctor ordered me to bed with medication and an ice pack. The painful swelling continued, and I finally had to call off the trip. When Johnnie R. heard that I wasn't coming he exploded.

"What do you mean you can't come. You've got to come."

"Johnnie R., I can hardly walk I'm in such pain. I'm stooped over like an old man. My ball's the size of an orange."

"Take some aspirin and get on the plane, Nick. Come on. This isn't cancer. Order a fucking scotch on the rocks and let the stewardess put the ice on your nuts. Just come, goddammit!"

"I'm on medication. The ice pack is as big as a brief case. I'm not supposed to walk."

"Fuck, Nick, we'll have the ice pack sewn into your underwear. Just come!"

"I'm in pain, Johnnie R. I'm bedridden. I can't."

"Some best friend. Some fucking best man!"

He hung up at that point, only to call back later in the day to apologize. So my trip was canceled and I missed the wedding. I was in bed for over a week with frozen balls and dusty books. All this Johnnie R. knew. I was certain that Charly had been told. The old man remembered as well.

"What was the illness. It slips my mind," he said with feigned sincerity, puffing away. His blue eyes were wide and daring. He was having a blast.

Johnnie R., the proud inheritor of his father's power games, played along at that point, saying, "A pulled muscle, wasn't it. Stomach muscle. Lower stomach muscle. I mean *really* lower stomach muscle."

I glared at him and turned to see the old man smiling widely, puffing away, awaiting the kill. I glanced at Charly who turned away, pretending not to be embarrassed.

"Hmmmmm. I just do not seem to remember it being a pulled muscle," the old man said, shaking his head. "I thought you had caught something."

"It wasn't a pulled muscle," I finally said. "It was epididymitis."

"My god, son, it sounds like death itself. What is it?"

The old fart knew exactly what it was, and at that point the women excused themselves, taking dirty dishes with them into the kitchen. When they left I said, "It's a swelling of the testicle."

"Oh my," the old codger said, wincing. "Quite painful I suppose. So painful that you missed your best friend's wedding."

"I was on ice packs," I said, my voice rising.

"How does one get it?"

"It's bacterial, I believe," I said, running out of patience.

"Sexually transmitted, eh?" the old fellow said, cocking his head, showing a wry smile.

I rolled my eyes and slouched back in the chair. Johnnie R. could hardly contain his laughter. I said, "It can be. Not always."

"Oh well," he finished, pausing to blow a final series of perfect circular rings my way. "I hope the swelling didn't go all the way down, young man. What we need at the bank is more men with big balls!"

That was Johnnie R.'s father. Old time *machismo*. The wealthy's version of good ole boy humor spiced with a typical power play. Yet, his humoring me aside, I was still convinced the old guy had it in for me. I hadn't been hired on merit, and I'd failed the cronyism test by missing his son's wedding. I was outcast, in limbo. A week later my suspicions were verified.

The old man had demanded that Johnnie R. and I join him for dinner at his favorite club. "A gentleman's club, very exclusive," Johnnie R. had informed me. "And Nick, it's not exactly an invitation. The old man never invites, he demands. Your presence is required. No backing out."

I took this not-very-well-veiled reference to the missed wedding in stride, saying, "What is this, an initiation?"

"No hazing, I promise."

"He hazed me at our first meeting, and on Christmas eve, if you'll remember. He obviously doesn't like me. You remember our first encounter. Christ, he picked lint off my suit. Face it, the old man wants to work me over."

"You're too sensitive, Nick. He just wants to get to know you, get a feel for your talents."

"He already knows my talents don't include de-linting my suits or attending his son's wedding."

"Anyway, the place is a Republican bastion. Very conservative. Elitist."

"Is Charly joining us?" I asked. "Or are women not allowed?"

"Of course, they're allowed. But this is to be a working supper. Man to man stuff. He's very big on that kind of thing."

So we met the old man in the foyer of his club, its inner sanctum an enormous smear of polished oak and shiny brass, and no room was more richly polished than the darkly masculine Harrison Room, the club's main restaurant.

"Named for the second most easily forgotten of American presidents, Benjamin Harrison," Johnnie R. allowed as we entered. "Millard Fillmore shall always bring up the presidential rear."

On the way to our table (reserved, as usual, for Mr. Thayer) I felt as if we were in a reception line since the old man shook hands with nearly everyone in the room. Apparently, there wasn't a face in the place he didn't know. And once we'd settled in, the casual aura of a long buried era began to stifle me. It was as if we'd stepped back into the Gilded Age. I could nearly hear Mark Twain spoofing its Victorian pretensions; this was definitely robber baron country. Lots of deep pockets. Cigars, scotch, pinstripe suits and Adam Smith's invisible hand. Still, it was an admittedly grand room. The restaurant boasted rich textures in its fine woods, carved stone, thick draperies. A definite aristocratic bearing came with the preferential atmosphere provided by the impeccable service. And it was hard to resist admiring the notable mahogany paneling, not to mention an added tincture of decadence: medium-blue tucked leather tacked into the wood. Well-crafted furniture, muted recessed lighting, a grand piano, brightly illuminated coffee service, chandeliers, unobtrusive sconces. It all added up to English clubbishness, Republican style.

When we were seated, the waiter, an efficient and warm young man, quite effeminate, brought our drinks and took our dinner orders. Not long afterward, the old man set the tone for the evening. He asked for the manager, something I assumed he did on a regular basis, and the overly anxious fellow nearly ran to the table moments later. "Raul," he said, when the manager arrived. "A piece of advice."

"Of course, sir."

"Mind you, personally I have no problem with our waiter, and homosexuals are found in the food service profession as often as not ... they must after all work somewhere ... but I hardly think it's the image the club hopes to convey to the public. Manly virtues, understand."

Oddly, though I had no evidence of it and assumed the old man knew nothing of Johnnie R.'s sexual ways, I took this as a jab at him nonetheless. Johnnie R. glanced at me, anger flaring for a moment, as the manager asked, "Has he done something wrong, Mr. Thayer?"

Ignoring the question the old man said, "I'm no longer on the board, far too busy, but I must say this young fellow seems a bit too effeminate for the club. They really ought to take better care. When I was on the board there were certain, shall we say, unwritten rules. Let the Democrats hire him down at their club. Do you understand?"

"Would you like another waiter, sir?"

"Just pass it on," he said, and without skipping a beat, abruptly turning away from the embarrassed manager, he turned to me and said, "Distasteful business, but these things need to be said."

"He hasn't done anything wrong, Pop."

"You miss the point, John. Perceptions are important. As with manners, there are forms to be followed." Having dismissed his son, he looked at me and said, "Now, Nick, please refresh my memory. You were, or were not, in Ivy with John."

A reference to the family legacy in one of the elite Princeton clubs. He knew full well I wasn't in a club, and so I braced myself for the game he was about to play. "I was not."

"Which club, then? Cap and Gown? I understand you were quite an academic."

"I wasn't in a club."

"Oh! No legacy from your father."

"Pop, you know Nick's story."

"Oh, how forgetful. My apologies, Nick. You were orphaned."

"Yes, a character out of Dickens," I jabbed, releasing steam. Johnnie R. kicked me under the table.

"Then why Princeton, if I might ask? I find that most southerners desire to remain in the South."

"I read a lot of Fitzgerald as a kid and fell in love with Princeton through books. And I had no family, my mother having died in childbirth. I wanted to escape, an eighteen-year-old seeking adventure. Plus, I had scholarship money. It all came together."

"And your father?"

"Pop," Johnnie R. said, glancing at me. He knew the story.

Why did he dislike me so? What was his game? Flustered, my anger growing, I said, "I don't know who my father was." And then, unable to resist, added, "Though perhaps he was a prominent midwestern banker slumming in the South over the holidays."

"Unlikely," the old man mused, unfazed. "How terribly tragic, though. No relatives on either side." He paused to wave to a club member before adding, "And the scholarship. Was it awarded by the state? A program for the orphaned?"

Fortunately, the mayor stopped by our table on his way out and chatted up the old man long enough for our dinners to be served, and I'm not sure which was the hotter - the old man's steaming French onion soup, or me. I tried to take my mind off his jabs with a glance around the room, but it quickly took on the old man's aura: stolid parochialism, aristocratic impulse, autocratic bearing, lack of compassion, Republican fervor. When coffee and cognac were served he continued with his game. "Nick, you say Fitzgerald helped to form your Ivy League aspirations?"

"You might say that, yes."

"A real Horatio Alger," he mused. "I must say that I do enjoy a story involving a fellow who is able to climb -"

"Beyond his social station," I offered.

"What he means, Nick - "

"Hush, John. He knows very well what I mean," the old man said, sipping cognac.

"I worked very hard," I said.

"I'm sure you did, Nick. In the cafeteria, John tells me. I think it's wonderful that Princeton has opened the doors to the economically disadvantaged."

"Hard work is the gist of the Horatio Alger stories."

"Although some interpret them as a common passion play concerning the role of luck in human affairs," he smiled, knowing he'd gotten to me.

"When you're not born with a silver spoon, Mr. Thayer, you'll take anything. Even luck," I finally said, my anger too great. Still, the old man refused to be insulted.

"That's why I mentioned my surprise at Princeton. Very blue blood. Most who have no legacy don't succeed. It could have been so helpful to you after graduation. You perhaps could have landed a job in the private sector rather than struggle in public service."

"I had offers in the private sector," I said. "I chose public service."

"Ah, so Kennedyesque."

"No, the Kennedys had money," I said, thankful that dessert was served. And during the silence that followed, I glanced at the room again. The old man was right about one thing. Few were immune to the enticements of money's underlying representations of power. Perhaps that's why I noted the strong libidinal impulses, a puissance which seemed so easily sublimated within the fine grains of the room's wood and carpets. Here, High Art was defined in terms of power, a distillation of esthetic feeling into the hard currency of the old man's world, an oligarchic realm as privately guarded as the Fed chief's office. And negotiable instruments? Well, poetry wasn't one of them. That I knew. No, here they ruled and ate and drank and gossiped and planned their extravagant infidelities under the influence of the smoky glow imbuing the magnificent room. And as soon as the old man finished his last bite of souffle he said, "But as I was saying, Nick, public service does not always offer security, and never financial reward."

"I was seeking something other than financial reward."

"Yes, all fine and good, but my experience with public employees has been nearly universally negative. And I trust you won't take this personally, but didn't you find your fellow employees -"

"Slothful?" I ventured with a smile. "Yeah, they were the dregs." Poor Johnnie R. simply shook his head.

123

"My point, young man, is that in the public sector there is very little incentive for excellence."

"You believe that monetary incentives are necessary for people to enjoy their chosen professions?"

"No, they are necessary to force one to perform at the optimum level. And of course one cannot be content without wealth."

"I was quite happy in the service."

"Which is why you left and came to my bank?"

"Please, Pop," Johnnie R. said. "Can we discuss something else."

"I was ready for a change," I said.

"Another trait of the public employee is lack of loyalty, not to mention impertinence."

"Pop, quit. Every man has the right to choose."

"Why do you dislike me, Mr. Thayer?" I finally said, figuring that it was best to openly discuss it. The most he could do was fire me. "Do you feel I haven't earned my place at the bank?"

"Nonsense. You're being overly sensitive, young man. I'm simply exploring and ask that you help me," he said, taking a drink. "Your major was not in business, correct?"

"English and history."

"He loves Rilke," Johnnie R. piped in. "A German poet."

"I prefer American poets. Sandburg, for instance. The prairie poets. A bit of Frost. No mumbo jumbo."

"You really ought to try him," I said. "I could translate him from the German if you'd like."

Johnnie R. kicked me under the table again as the old man responded. "Poets, Nick, you'll be sad to know, don't make the world go round. Remember, Plato banned them as a danger to a civil society."

I didn't respond; it was useless. So we finished our coffee in silence and left the restaurant. But in the foyer the old man finished. "Nick, the bank isn't likely to provide as romantic a venture as the Foreign Service, the monetary rewards notwithstanding. I hope you're able to find comfort in that."

"I was an economic officer. Not much romance there."

"Surely you were you involved in free trade negotiations, economic security arrangements, trade agreements?"

"Not at my junior level."

"Political intrigue, then. I understand Foreign Service officers are often simply CIA in thinly veiled disguise."

"My name is Bond. James Bond," I cracked as Johnnie R. winced.

"I take that as a no," the old man said as we stepped outside. "How unfortunate. I was hoping I could tell the board at the next meeting that I've hired someone who helped to overthrow communism." He offered his hand and as I took it he asked, "But tell me, what is it you seek, Nick?"

"A meaningful career. A life companion," I said, unable to retrieve my hand.

"Companion?"

"Pop, Nick still believes in Rilke's *others*. The perfect companion."

"Pardon me, but is that not a euphemism for ... how shall I say it .... homosexual pairings?"

Ah, another dig, and now I was certain he was on to something.

"Pop," Johnnie R. complained.

"If you are asking if I am gay, I am not."

"Why no woman?"

"That's what I'm seeking."

"May you then find her, Nick," he said with a smile, releasing my hand. And as he walked off he added, "Though not on bank time, of course."

*   *   *

On Christmas evening Johnnie R., Charly and I celebrated in the den of their home with drinks, hot chocolate and a roaring fire while Johnnie R. practiced putting golf balls over the soft carpet, the first test of the new putter Charly had bought him. I was genuinely touched by their big-hearted gestures, their familiar hospitality. In particular, I was moved by the gift which they'd given me. It was Charly's gesture, actually. She'd painted two watercolors for my office.

"John told me your walls were empty. Perhaps these will help," she offered with a smile. They were beautiful abstract pastels. I was stunned that she'd taken the time and effort to paint them.

"Look at him, Charly!" Johnnie R. shouted as I examined the gifts. "Like a kid playing with toys!"

When I glanced at Charly, I caught something vaguely expressive in her face. Certainly, she'd cemented our newfound friendship with her kind gesture, yet I was conscious of more. Her expression conveyed the idea that we had, after all, shared a secret, unknown even to her husband. Oddly, the watercolors created a bond between us, a wordless vow, as I remembered the hard, literal portrait of Talbott Street and its great contrast with the soft delicate abstract pastels. The watercolors carried no grief, none of the emotional baggage associated with the portrait of the ghetto bar, and it was difficult to reconcile the bright warm splotches of pastel color with the biting neon images from the garish marquee. The portrait of the bar demanded attention, rubbed your nose in its nastiness, dared you to taste of its underworld flavor. The little pastel puffs merely floated off, somewhat whimsically beyond the barriers of the paper itself. She studied me, and I felt at once that she understood my thoughts.

125

And her influence over me increased with time. Two weeks into the new year it was Charly who found my rental. I'd begun house hunting the week before, the three of us having spent several days going through the ads and walking through houses. I'd hit on nothing, and then came that surprise call at the bank. Charly told me she'd found the perfect place for me, something affordable on my banker's salary.

"It's within walking distance from our house, and I took the liberty to walk through it myself this afternoon," she offered.

"As long as it's not a brownstone," I said. "Too dreary, like London."

"Stucco," she announced. "A small bungalow painted beige. It's in good condition and sits on a hill. The view from most angles is very good. It's affordable."

And the proximity is right, I thought. I wrote down the address and left the office early to meet Charly there, and she was right. I liked it the moment I stepped out of the car and walked up the drive. It was small, but the two bedrooms were all I needed.

"I want it," I told Charly as we walked through.

"I thought you might," she said, parting the drapes of the front windows.

I shielded my eyes from the western sun and saw the light catch the tall steeple from a church on Meridian. Our line of sight was even with chimneys and treetops surrounding the house, and the steeple's perfect proportion underscored the fuzzy, rambling lines of the drab grays and browns and greens of the distant roofs and trees. There was a great sense of depth and space and light. It was an immense change from the claustrophobic flat on Talbott Street.

"It's a marvelous view. You can see my church from here," she said.

"So, you're a church girl?"

"Yes. John hasn't totally debauched me," she answered, realizing immediately that her response was clumsy. She didn't smile.

"On Sunday mornings I promise to look out the windows at precisely eleven as a courtesy to those who still believe," I offered, changing the subject.

"If you're up at eleven, perhaps," she answered quickly, reminding me of my habit of sleeping in on Sundays.

She and Johnnie R. helped me move into the bungalow on the following Saturday, and on Sunday, usually ever-blue Sunday, I had little time to ponder the intrusive silence of my new home because they showed up just after noon with carry-out Chinese food and beer. They remained the entire day and helped me unpack and organize and make a home. Afterward, we went out for dinner and a drink, a typical practice during the months to come. I saw Johnnie R. daily, and Charly nearly so. My friendship with Johnnie R. resumed effortlessly, and we talked easily and freely, occasionally had drinks, attended a few ball games together.

Yes, early on we got on marvelously. He was in my office - or I in his - each workday, and we usually lunched together. As he prepared to take over Mike's functions as Executive V.P. I worked closely with him, and we maneuvered our way through the maze of corporate operations, often working late into the evenings. He seemed to find a reason to drop by my house on the way home from the bank two or three times a week, staying for a couple of hours to chat or to watch a game on the tube. It wasn't uncommon for him to call Charly and have her meet us at a Broad Ripple restaurant, or in the alternative, Charly would call and ask me to join them for dinner. The weekends offered more of the same. Often we followed the meal with a movie. Occasionally we opted for coffee or drinks. And I was as content as I'd ever been.

*   *   *

Danny, alias the kid, popped up again only a week after I'd moved into my place. Ah, the kid! The little ripple in the unassuming pond spreading the pulse which met us. To be sure, he was a mere man-child in years, but shrewd, quite sly, with an insidious streak for trouble. And I unwittingly served as audience for the kid and his antics when he surfaced one cool afternoon at the public library. On the only Sunday in January which I spent alone, I combed the stacks for over an hour and walked out lugging several books under both arms. As I began to descend the steps I was stunned to hear my name called out.

"Hey, man! Hey, over here," a not-quite-recognizable voice echoed over the traffic below. I awkwardly turned and spotted the kid strutting just a few feet away on the limestone stairs. He swaggered over to me while I tried my best to prevent the entire load of books from falling.

"Hey, man. I know ya!" he shouted, coming close. "You're the dude with John."

I took a good look at him for the first time in daylight. He couldn't have been over eighteen, good looking and with a nice build. He wore tight faded jeans and a bomber jacket. Though there was still a bit of snow on the ground, he was wearing tennis shoes. His light blue eyes were all confidence and pizazz, sporting an odd tic of the lids which opened widely, as if surprised, and then narrowed before returning to normal. I couldn't help but invoke a bit of Freud to explain it, a sign from the libido's dark side, a hint of the power of the irrational.

"Yes. And I remember you," I said. "Danny, right? Alias the kid."

"I'm not just a kid. Maybe you'd like to try me out for size just to see," he answered quickly, slightly smiling, quite serious. His eyes widening and then closing. The library steps were congested, and the kid's voice carried. Several people who were walking close cast a quick glance toward us.

"Keep it down, okay?" I said as we continued down the steps.

"So, it bothers ya to talk about it, huh?"

127

"You don't remember me very well, do you?" I said, stopping briefly to find a better grip on the books. "If you'll think back, I told you I wasn't gay."

"So what are you doin' here?" he asked, undaunted. I started down the steps again, the kid in tow.

"Obviously, I'm getting books to read. The better question is, 'Why are you here?' You don't appear to be the literary type."

"Ya think I'm stupid, don't ya?" he demanded, the tic working overtime. The smile was gone from his face, but his eyes were wide as moons.

"No. I don't think you're stupid," I answered, stopping to lay some of the books down on the steps. I was nearly losing them.

"Another fuckin' banker, right?" he said more than asked.

"Listen, I'm afraid its a bad time to socialize, kid. I've got my arms full," I said impatiently, trying to pick the books up again.

"Then give me some to carry," he ordered with a smile, changing tactics altogether. Before I could protest he picked up a few books and began walking toward my car. I caught up with him at the bottom of the steps.

"Why do I keep runnin' into ya at the homo spots? Sure looks curious to me," he said as we reached the car.

"This is a library," I said, putting a few books down on the hood of the car while fumbling in my pockets for the key.

"And a cruisin' spot."

I turned around to glance back at the library steps while I continued to fumble for the keys, and as I did so I remembered Johnnie R.'s reference to the library as a notorious stomping ground for hustlers. The front sidewalk and the library steps were spotted here and there with perhaps ten young men milling about, most dressed as the kid was dressed in tight jeans and slight jackets. One of them winked at me when I glanced over. Another whistled. The kid just laughed. I turned away and studied the passing traffic, primarily solitary older men scanning the library steps as their cars crept by. "I begin to see what you mean," I said, finally finding my key. "Thanks for carrying the books for me, Danny."

"What's the hurry?"

"I've got to go."

"Always on the run, huh? I suppose I'll be seein' ya at Holliday Park next."

"What's that?"

"The biggest cruisin' place in town. I ain't got a car to get there, though. That's why I'm here."

"You better get off the streets, kid," I said, putting the key in the lock.

"Nowhere to go, man."

"That's right. You no longer live with Mike."

"So, ya know all about it, huh? John told ya. You're a banker for sure."

I opened the car door, leaned in and placed the books in the seat. The kid shuffled around to the other side of the car. When I stood up again I could only see his head above the roof of the car.

"He thought he owned me, if it's any of your business," he said, giving me one of his none-of-your-fucking-business looks. "But nobody owns me. Nobody."

"That somehow doesn't surprise me."

"Well, when ya see him you can tell him he fucked up, man. He fucked up big time. He fuckin' shit in his roost. You tell him that."

"I don't even know the man. I only know *of* him. I'm sure you'll tell him yourself," I said, leaning against the roof of the car.

"Shit, you'd think he'd know how the game's played, man. Nobody keeps me wrapped up alone in a house. I gotta get out and see the action. He's fuckin' it all up."

"How?" I knew better than to get into it, but he intrigued me.

"All I wanted was a car, man. Especially one of them sport's cars, like maybe a corvette I seen at the dealers, but I'd a settled on a Camaro. And now he fucked it up."

"How?"

"He said no car. He wanted me to stay at the house, off the streets." He paused for a moment and then said, "Well, fuck him!"

"A car is a pretty expensive toy."

"That's right, and there's other ways of gettin' a car."

"Undoubtedly, you'll find them."

"Don't be a prick, man," he warned. His eyes narrowed for emphasis and then his lids opened widely, his Freud-tic an aperture seeking a panoramic view. I was about to get into the car and he added, "I earned it fair and square. It was the logical next step."

"A car for a hustle?" I asked.

"Hey, I paid my fuckin' dues. I deserve it. I paid with my ass."

"No need to give me the details."

"Listen, man, ya don't understand. It goes back before I even met the fucker," he said loudly, anger rising in his voice. He began to attract attention again. I looked up and toward the steps. Disapproving glances turned our way. In order to avoid a scene I quickly said goodbye and jumped into the car. When I turned the ignition the kid leaned down and knocked against the window. He was smiling broadly as he pointed to the books in his hands. In the commotion I'd forgotten them. "Ya forgot I don't read!" he yelled through the window, shaking his head. I unlocked the door and told him to place the books on the seat, but after he opened the door he jumped into the car and closed it.

"Don't mind if I do, man. Thanks," he said casually, placing the books on his lap as he looked over at me.

129

"Get out of the car," I demanded, my patience running low. I grabbed the books from him and threw them in the back seat. He didn't budge as he played the game, enjoying himself immensely.

"I said out!"

He leaned his head back and laughed loudly.

"Ya look scared," he said.

"Pissed. Get out or I'll put you out."

The kid continued laughing, his eyes widening with each new breath. I sat for a few moments longer trying to decide the best tactic to take; that he continued laughing made the decision much easier. I was too angry to consider a softer approach. I grabbed him by his arm and squeezed hard. With my free hand I grabbed for the door handle. I'd nearly reached it when he yelled.

"I'll yell fuckin' rape, man. I'll yell to the top of my goddamned lungs and then give em your fuckin' name. Ya dig?"

"Christ!" I let go of his arm and leaned back in my seat. "What do you want?"

"It's cold, man. I just wanna sit for a minute. That's all," he said, his voice smooth as silk.

"For a minute," I agreed, outraged.

"I mean, until the car warms up. Don't ya have a heater in this old thing?"

"The engine needs to warm first."

"Good. Then we can just sit and talk."

"About what?"

"Don't ya wanna know why John hates me?"

"I think I know why?"

"No ya don't."

"Tell me and get out."

With a whimsical expression on his face he said, "Hey, man, look at those dudes over there. They're damned sure jealous I got me a trick on a cold day."

"You don't have a trick," I said flatly.

"Yeah, yeah. But they don't know that."

"You're running out of time. You better talk fast."

"Well, like I said, all I wanted was a car -"

"We've already been over that. Talk about John and get out."

"I gotta work my way there, man."

"Quickly."

He turned in the seat and faced me, relaxed and poised. "Okay, it started out as a joke, way back before Mike, that car idea, but I'd a taken it in a second if it'd been offered. I wasn't too proud for gifts like my old man was. So what the fuck if it was free? " He looked at me closely, hoping for a response. His antennae was positioned for signals, but I said nothing. "Hey, I'm not talkin' about today.

It wouldn't be free today. I worked for it with Mike. But back then, when I first got the idea, before I was hustlin' full-time, you might say it was for free."

He continued gazing at me, trying to find in my face some form of recognition, of understanding. I merely looked beyond the windshield, hoping he would quickly finish. "Okay, so it was a joke at first, but it got real serious after awhile, and soon enough I really wanted that damn car real bad. If ya had a car, a good car, no offense," he paused, looking around at the interior of mine, frowning, "if ya had a good car it was a sure sign that you'd made it. I could always find a place to eat and sleep. I was willin' to do odd things to get it, but what does it matter if ya can have what you want? Especially a sports car. So, fuck em if they can't take a joke. Goddamn, I just wanted a car.

"My old man couldn't afford one and when I started hollerin' for it he gave me three bags of shit about how ungrateful I was and how unfortunate it was how I liked cars instead of books or some kind of intellectual shit. He called me a no good brat and when I'd go on about it he'd yell so loud that he'd get all red and sweaty and once he hit me real good in the face and it took away the trade for a week. Shit, nothing for a week. I was pissed."

"Yes, I know that feeling."

"So, I got real quiet about the car idea, and soon enough I worked up in my mind this idea about how I'd get that car just like those rich prick kids in Carmel get em from their swanky and filthy loaded pig parents. I'd show em, and I nearly did. I bet I still got a chance, but not as good as before since Mike started gettin' crazy and fuckin' everything up. That old fart deserves a bad end. He was a fuckin' liar and cheat. I was just a hair from a car, and his rich ass goes and screws it up. Fuck 'em. Besides, he got what he wanted from me. A deal's a deal. He wanted a hot body and he got it. Plenty of it. He wanted a nice sweet ass and I let him have it. Man, he's the one who screwed it up. If I had that fuckin' car I'd a stayed and he wouldn't be goin' off the deep end. Why should I feel sorry for that jippin' Jew bastard who never wanted for a dime. He was filthy rich and all the time talkin' about good blood and good education and lots and lots of sophistication. The goddamned *S* word. I hated it. Everything had to be the best, but ya see he decided what was the best. The best wine. The best meat. The best bread. The best clothes. And especially the cars. And he was too stingy to give me a car. Fucker!"

"So?" I prodded him, looking at my watch.

"So, the chance finally comes along and the shit fucks it all up over a piece of ass he don't wanna share. And I'm out of a car. It was like it was all a waste. All those years of dishin' it out. All the clap and the piss in the face and the smelly pricks and the rest -"

"Please," I said, shaking my head.

"Well, it was like it was all wasted and a joke. I remember it from the beginnin', plannin' it out, plannin' it real good. And then Mike comes along and the plan goes along smooth-like and then he cracks up. Listen, I wasn't stupid like most of 'em. I ain't educated, but I know how to do things. I know how to carry out the plan. Hey, I ain't a real queer, man. Ya see there's faggots and there's queens and there's hustlers. A faggot is a goddamned nelly thing who likes bein' a sweet little girl and to be treated like a lady. A queer is a regular guy except he can't suck enough cock to please 'em. A hustler just fuckin' gives for the dough and sometimes he likes it fine and sometimes he don't. I liked it some and hated it some. But I ain't stupid. I had it all planned out and then Mike started makin' trouble and it all went to hell. It ain't my fault."

"And that's why Johnnie R. dislikes you?"

"Johnnie what?"

"John."

"That's just the latest reason. He blames me for lots of stuff. Fuck him."

I was silent, hoping he was done. When I said nothing he asked, "Do you wanna hear more? There's more. It's pretty juicy."

"No, I've got to run."

"Your loss, man," he said, stretching. I caught his eyes doing that little thing they do, opening and closing and taking the world in, and he rubbed his thighs and then added, "Anyway, thanks for the warm car."

He finally opened the door and stood. Before closing it he leaned over and looked in, saying, "Hey, ya can tell that prick John to kiss my shinin' ass. Ya hear. Tell him to just kiss my sweet ass!"

"Close the door," I said.

"And ya better not keep hangin' out here, man. The cops are liable to pick ya up for solicitin'!" he yelled, slamming the door with a bang. I heard him laughing loudly as he walked off toward the library steps.

When at lunch with Johnnie R. on the following day, I mentioned that I'd run into the kid at the library. He sipped his tea, put down the glass and shook his head, a touch of anger rising in his voice. "Stay away from him, Nick. He's trouble."

"I wasn't exactly seeking him out, Johnnie R. "He saw me as I was leaving the library."

"I told you it's a cruising ground. Avoid him."

"I'm not going to stay away from the library simply because this punk hangs out there."

"Just don't talk to him again, Nick. I mean it."

"Okay, okay."

"And don't mention him to Charly."

*   *   *

I had little time to ponder the kid's shenanigans, nor the fact that he seemed to carry around with him a steamer trunk's worth of bad luck, inviting premonitions, because things were heating up at the bank. Mike was canned at the end of January, and on the day he was terminated, Johnnie R. walked into my office to share the news. "It's finally done," he said, his expression a composite of relief and sadness both. "It hurt Pop to have to do it. His right-hand man for so many years."

"I'm only surprised the old man didn't move earlier, Johnnie R. Christ, I've never seen Mike at the bank. He's been on leave since the day he made the scene outside that bar."

"The unofficial story was that Pop was giving him another chance to dry out. In reality, Pop was biding time, hoping Mike would land another job. After all, he'd been forewarned."

"It's still puzzling. I mean, your father doesn't exactly have a soft spot for homosexuals."

"I don't think the old man was aware that Mike was gay until near the end."

"Oh, come on, Johnnie R.! He insinuated that I was gay since I'm not married. Remember the dinner at his club? When you spoke of Rilke's companions he thought you were referring to -"

"Homosexual pairings, he called it," Johnnie R. agreed, shaking his head. "Look, Nick, the old man hired a private detective three months ago to keep an eye on Mike. The guy was to report anything unusual, and of course there was plenty to report back. At that point he felt he had no choice other than to fire Mike." I didn't respond, shrugging. "My point is, the old man didn't *want* to believe. It was Mike's behavior at the bank, his lack of polish, his frequent bouts of drunkenness, that first Pop's eye. Dad didn't want to fire him before Christmas, for obvious reasons, and he twice postponed dumping him this month before finally handing down the verdict."

"So the old ball buster has a soft spot after all."

"A small one, Nick. Very small."

"So I've noticed."

"It had to be done, Nick."

"You seem to be trying to convince yourself."

"What a waste. Mike was there from the beginning," Johnnie R. said, standing and walking to the window behind my desk. "Remember when Mike said he'd taught me all I know? It's nearly true. He did."

"So now he goes under and you feel like shit."

"He was part of the master plan," he replied, returning to his chair. "A mental configuration conjured up by the old war horse himself, something never put into writing."

"And what were the terms of this verbal high-finance agreement?"

"A transition plan with a twist," he answered. "Fearing that he might kick off before his young capitalist pup was prepared to take the wheel, Pop entrusted Mike with the transition."

"Ah, the future regent who warms the throne until the babe comes of age."

"Nick, his many demons aside, Mike performed admirably, always the dutiful servant. His gifts were highly valued by Pop, and he willingly roamed within the wide circumference of the old man's shadow. After all, he enjoyed the boss's confidence, and he was well compensated for his efforts. He wielded enough real power to find the arrangement satisfactory."

"He was a tutor. You were being groomed."

"For years, the hallmark of Mike's personal ethics had been self-discipline, total discretion. He'd quietly gone about his personal business well out of the public eye."

"But he was still ... well, how would your old man describe it, a confirmed bachelor?"

"And Pop turned his head, ignoring the rumors. That is, until the kid made it impossible to do so. Mike cracked, and when he failed to pick up the pieces of his life, Pop's finely chiseled corporate facade began to crack as well. When his piece of art was in danger of being called a corporate fake, the old man took action."

"You don't need to tell me. He's a seasoned player from the big league, tough as nails."

"Nick, the day of the scene with Mike was the day Dad told him he was on the way out. There had been a private conference; I wasn't involved," he said, standing to pace. "But I know he was told to look for other employment. And remember, this wasn't the first time the issue was discussed. Dad sent Mike to dry out on two separate occasions to one of those plush BIG IMPORTANT FUCKING PEOPLE alcohol abuse clinics. The required stay each time was two months. He had his chances."

"Why didn't he demote Mike? Put him over in residential loans?"

"Wouldn't work, Nick. Mike was too big for that. Pop had to get rid of him altogether."

"So Mike was banished from the money kingdom, and now you're on the hot seat."

"We're on the hot seat. You and me, pal," he said with a smile. I only shook my head. "And when Pop called me to his office to tell me Mike was canned, he said, 'These difficult situations must be handled quickly and efficiently. As of this moment your title is Executive Vice President - Operations. It's a big man's job, goddammit, but I expect my son to meet the challenge. And, by the way, would you like a cigar?' Swear to God."

"Gosh, do you think anyone will be shocked, Johnnie R.," I deadpanned.

"There I was, Nick, sitting on this mammoth Chesterfield leather sofa with my father next to me, and suddenly I felt as if I were sixteen years old and asking permission to drive the car. There he was, perfectly dressed, manicured and combed and perfumed, a man of real power, a grave expression on his face, and he put his hand on my shoulder and told me he was about to put the bank in my lap. Christ, I almost shit my pants!"

"C'mon, you've known for months.!"

"Nick, I've always planned to take over the bank. I've never wanted to do anything else. It's been in the plans from the day I was born. He wants it; I want it. But I know I'm not ready. Eventually, yes. I've got what it takes, the brains, the balls, the bullshit. But I expected to be preparing to take over at forty, not at twenty-eight. What was worse, he knew it! The entire goddamned house of cards could come tumbling down, perhaps it was probable, and yet he held me tightly by the shoulder and said to me very forcefully, 'You won't fail.' I've never felt so inadequate in all my life."

As I sat there watching Johnnie R. confessing his feelings of inadequacy, I thought, You'd never know it from your daily performance. His mask of bravado was totally convincing. On any given day he could've persuaded you that he might easily manage the country. Vintage Johnnie R. - brains, yes; charisma, without doubt; but barges and barges of bullshit. If all else failed he would bluster his way through.

"So what now?" I asked.

"*We* take over!" he said, a smile finally surfacing. About this he was quite serious. He opened the door, winked, gave me two thumbs up and then turned and walked away as he whistled down the hall.

13

Indianapolis, 1991

I bolted out of this revery when Johnnie R. woke with a scream. A nightmare. A nurse rushed in, and I leaned over his bed, holding him by the shoulders, as the nurse combed a hand through his hair. I then took one of his hands as she played with the sheets and then gave him water. He said that he could just make out our silhouettes, find the shadows which were our faces, but it was enough to help clear the gray haze of the dream. How quickly his earlier energy had vanished, and yet, when Charly appeared in the door with their son moments later, Johnnie R. once more gathered his energy as he put on his father's mask. Time to be brave.

Yet, the boy was terrified, frightened by the strange illness of his father, the vague shadows of death which a child intuits better than he understands. Charly was nearly as distraught as the child, caught between Johnnie R.'s desire to be with his son and her kid's fear. Johnnie R. excitedly called for his boy to come to him, but the child remained glued to Charly. She held him for the first ten minutes, and when she put him down he stood next to her with both arms wrapped tightly around a leg. He never took his eyes from Johnnie R., staring as only a child can gape with that blend of fascination, curiosity and horror.

The kid was his dad, blue eyes and all. His nose and chin and dark hair completed the picture of a mini-Johnnie R. The fine pencil line of his brows, however, was from Charly. He was a good looking kid, though at that the moment his expression only gave notice of terror. Johnnie R. called to him again, and this time the kid hid behind Charly, staying there.

"Won't you come and say hi to daddy, Ian?"

"No."

"Then just come close and sit in the chair and talk to daddy."

"I don't want to."

"Don't be scared. Daddy's just sick. Remember when Ian was sick with measles?" he coaxed the kid. When the child didn't answer he tried again. "Come on, buddy boy. Daddy just wants to say hi."

As this continued I watched with interest as Johnnie R. played the pop. It was an intriguing sight, his display of paternal instincts. His smile, even though obstructed by his gauntness and the Kaposi's, was convincing. His voice, soft and comforting. But since Johnnie R. could only see shadows, he was forced to face the kid in an angular fashion as he tried to focus with peripheral vision, playing with the light. This odd angle spoke of his vulnerability and the kid understood that something was askew. Still the ever-patient papa, Johnnie R. maintained his smile and composure throughout. He badly wanted to carry it off.

"Let's sit in the chair next to the bed, Ian," Charly said, taking his hand.

The kid instantly let out a big yelp, his wide eyes filling with terror, and then he began to cry. Charly picked him up and rocked him a bit, drying his eyes. He stopped crying moments later and then turned to watch Johnnie R. once again. He wanted no part of his dad, fearful of the changes he saw, and yet he seemed captivated by the transformed man, the vaguely familiar scent of death. He wanted to watch from a distance, though not touch.

"It just won't work, John," Charly said, shaking her head as she wiped the kid's nose. I gave him pep talks all day. I've been trying to do this since nine this morning."

"Want to see the Christmas lights, Ian?" Johnnie R. asked, still trying to salvage the visit. The kid said nothing, hiding his face in Charly's hair.

"Come on. We can all go down to the lounge and see the Christmas lights on the Circle. Okay?"

"No."

"Hey, listen to this," Johnnie R. pursued. Even as he was dying he was relentless. "Nick will push you in a wheelchair like we used to do. Remember that? Mommy will push daddy's chair and Nick will push Ian's!"

The kid looked over at me for the first time, squinting his eyes to see me better. He cocked his head, sizing me up. Apparently, he was on better ground with me. He was the type of kid who wasn't shy around new acquaintances. He looked me over hard and long, his radar out for signs of trouble. I smiled and then he smiled.

"I'll get a wheelchair, Ian. Okay?" I said.

He said nothing, but the smile was his approval. We called the nurse and told her of our plans. There was a long, drawn scene during which Charly finally had to leave the room with the kid as Johnnie R. debated with the staff. Arguing that this was perhaps his final opportunity to see his son, the final familial stand, they relented. After all, it had been a good day and he wanted to make the attempt. So they wrapped him up in blankets and a mask, unfastened tubes and monitors and catheters, and then stood by as an orderly carefully picked him up and placed him in the wheelchair. Two mobile IV stands were brought in. Then they hooked him back up to some of the gadgets, and after twenty minutes of this we were ready to travel the short distance down the hall to view the Circle Christmas lights from the lounge window.

The orderly pushed the wheelchair out into the hall, and a parade of nurses followed with the IV stands and monitors. Charly plopped the boy down into a second wheelchair. He giggled as I pushed his wheelchair ahead of Johnnie R.'s and down the hall, off like a rocket. Charly stayed behind with Johnnie R. as his chair was slowly maneuvered down the hall. I reached the lounge, doubled back to catch up with Johnnie R. and then swept by him again as we raced down the hall. The staff was aghast, but Ian loved it, temporarily tossing off his fear. When we reached the lounge again, the boy jumped from the wheelchair and pushed his nose against the cold window. In the distance were the Christmas lights from the monument.

"There!" he pointed to the lights cutting through the darkness. "Over there!"

I knelt down and put my face up to the window too, watching his excitement grow as he pointed to the lights. Still snot-nosed from his earlier cry, he plastered mucous on the glass as he placed his face fully against it. Then he played the kids' game of fogging up the glass and drawing with his fingers until the fog evaporated. He repeated this several times, and then he placed a hand on my shoulder and said, "There's daddy's bank and grandpa's bank too."

"Yes, and Nick worked there too once. Right Nick?" Johnnie R. chimed in behind us. They'd finally made it.

"That's right," I played along, looking up at Charly as she watched her kid. "I worked there once too. One day you might work there."

"I want grandpa's office," he said.

"I'm sure that can be arranged," Johnnie R. said, smiling.

The foot of Johnnie R.'s wheelchair was just inches behind the kid, and when the boy turned to see Johnnie R. in mask and blankets and tubes and wires, a modern concoction which was half beast, half machine, he became frightened again. With Johnnie R. to one side and I to the other, the window now behind him, he had nowhere to go. He just looked in fear and uncertainty at Johnnie R.

"Describe the Christmas lights for daddy," Johnnie R. said, trying to ease his son's fears. The kid, without taking his eyes from Johnnie R., pointed toward the glass. Snot still ran from his nose. He looked closely at Johnnie R. eyes, noted the odd angle of his father's head as he spoke and finally seemed to recognize that Johnnie R. couldn't see. He put a finger to his mouth and kept the other hand on the window as he continued watching his dad's face.

"That's right, Ian," Johnnie R. said. "And what color's do you see."

"Red."

"What else? What other colors?"

"Why is your head funny?" the boy asked out of the blue, tilting his head to meet the angle of his father.

"I'm just a little sick, Ian. Like the measles."

The kid wouldn't turn his back to Johnnie R. He just watched him closely, hawked him, tried to understand, saying, "Your eyes is funny."

"I can't see too good," Johnnie R. said, reaching for the boy.

Ian watched Johnnie R.'s hand approach and backed against the glass. He peered over to find Charly. He was getting his bearings, testing his environment. Johnnie R. brought his hand back to his lap and prodded the kid to interact. But the boy was elsewhere just then, attempting to absorb the strained knowledge of physical infirmity. He had no words for what he saw in the shell which was his father, but his expression indicated that he was connecting, instinctively, with death. That's when he began to whimper again. He backed against the window - hands in the air as if surrendering - while his face reddened with terror.

Johnnie R. reached out to console him, but the boy screamed when his father's hand touched his arm. Then Charly picked him up, rocking him in her arms, and when he continued crying she walked out of the lounge with him. Johnnie R. was quiet in his defeat, blindly glancing down at his lap. I said nothing and the staff stood in silence. We watched as he looked out of the window toward the lights that he couldn't see, by far the most difficult moment I'd yet shared with him. I couldn't find words strong enough to allay the disappointment, only watch helplessly as he wept and his mask became damp with the tears.

"Take me back to the room," he said quietly.

The orderly turned the wheelchair away from he window, and the entourage marched out into and up the hall as if the burial already had occurred. Charly said goodnight from the room, telling us that she'd be back the following day, and I watched as the kid looked over her shoulder, wiping his eyes, as his dad was rolled out of sight. At the elevator Charly waved and the kid stared. Back in Johnnie R.'s room the orderly and nurses went through the procedures again, this time in reverse, as they prepared to put him back into the bed. Once there and hooked up to the contraptions, he was quiet.

Demoralized, his energy sapped, he wouldn't respond when I tried some small talk, and an hour later he fell to sleep, though not before whispering, "It's over." The failure to bond a final time with his son had broken his spirit. I suppose that was the moment he surrendered. Before I left the hospital I thumbed through his journal again, pausing to read fragments from a poem entitled, ***Ode to my Son***:

> *They don't make it anymore, or if they do I've not seen it in years,*
> *but as a kid of five or six, or six or seven, it was my favorite toy -*
> *beanie cap they called it, from a cartoon dubbed Beanie and Cecil,*
> *a much-watched show by kids my age when your age I once was.*
>
> *Two buddies, these. Cecil was a sea serpent and Beanie ...*
> *well, son, Beanie was just a boy who wore a funny cap,*
> *a beanie with magical powers and small propellers off the top*
> *and an invitation to fly. Ah, son, to fly! Like Icarus and Daedalus.*
>
> *True, an unhappy myth, as some myths are, now best left alone,*
> *but nonetheless I desired to fly with propeller atop my beanie head;*
> *yet in the end I made due with more nearly mortal forms of pleasure,*

like polished tokens of muted love and little ditties from the heart.

But listen: beanie caps were made of plastic - a tiny red cap,
a yellow chin strap and a propeller like sprouting goldenrod!
And at the center a tiny compartment, a storehouse for secrets
and childlike wares, bugs and paper and wishes and prayers.

And later, distraught that his father had never been able to utter to the boy who was Johnnie R. the simple words, *I love you*, he feels the need to share with his son something the boy can remember him by:

.... And that's when I remembered the beanie cap again
and understood that I could send along to you secrets of the muted heart,
secrets nourished for a lifetime, hidden from everyone until now,
everyone, that is, save for my beanie-induced imaginary friends.

By the way, they all suddenly disappeared as I entered kindergarten,
and I often wonder whatever happened to them. There were three in all,
nameless to me now. Did they become bankers too, or perhaps poets?
Do they still tread somewhere in an internal circuit, an imaginary path
within?

Or have they been released for others to use, boys just like you, son?
Who can say what becomes of imaginary worlds once we've let them go?
But as I was saying, for years I sent messages to imaginary friends, and
then they joined me in sending messages to anyone else who might listen,
find my message, respond in kind with one of his own.

And now I've found him, following all these many years of silence. Yes,
now I know I was waiting for you, just beyond the generational fence, a
lifetime between us, and a good thing I've kept the secret message stowed
away and polished and shorn of all unnecessary words.

In this way you might pick up the beanie propeller that is this poem
flying over you now, like a miracle, and open it, like the secret
compartment, and find in it a short message scratched in six-year old
script, a message I've held for a lifetime. It's very simple and reads: I
love you.

14

Indianapolis, 1983

As the January cold gave way to the February snows, Johnnie R. and I continued our long hours at the bank, and our threesome continued meeting regularly. Occasionally, I'd bring along a date, but already time spent as one of a foursome was never as enjoyable for me as time spent with the two of them or, more nearly correct, time spent with Charly. Yes, as the weeks flew by I began to connect with a solid point of reference for my previously directionless emotions, and the allusion was to Charly. She was just around the corner and a few blocks away. I'd come to Indianapolis to work closely with my old pal from Princeton, and what I'd found as my stay in Indy continued was the constant nagging desire to be with his wife. Certainly, I had no passion for adultery. I'd never been a party to it. But there it was, the desire for Charly. I of course found her physically attractive, wanted her sexually. I certainly wasn't immune to her understated beauty, but she moved me primarily in other ways as one is moved by the affinity of kindred spirits. I fancied that I'd found a Rilkean *companion* after all, one who shares the spirit, sustains the view from the identical angle, but it was enough for me at that moment to consider my affection in terms of her quiet talent, calm wit and lucid intelligence. When I'd held her for those many moments at Christmas I'd been unable to allay the need to find such closeness once again. I wanted nothing more than to be alone with her on a long drawn Sunday - listening to her voice, following her lovely movements, detecting the strength of her intelligence, making love. So as winter passed in my small house I began to fight the realization that I was so easily falling in love. True, it was a chimerical love, Keats's nonconsummative variety, but it was love nonetheless. The fact is it that existed, and I expended a great deal of energy sparring with it.

As a result guilt began to play a direct and abiding role in my friendship with Johnnie R., and I attempted to combat these dual feelings for Johnnie R. and Charly by plowing into my work at the bank. Also, I tried to counter my growing attachment to Charly by going out alone or double-dating, and one memorable attempt succinctly sums up my efforts. In February I made my first trek alone to an Indy bar. My libido had raised its cunning little head and was looking for the appropriate release. So it was off to a pick-up bar to find a kind voice and a warm body. For an hour I threaded my way in and out of the Friday night meat market crowd, fighting through the warm masses of bodies and the thick layers of cigarette smoke, but as the evening wore on I began to lose interest. It all seemed such a waste, and within an hour I decided to call it quits.

"Going home alone?" a silky, sexy voice caught my attention as I put my hand on the door to leave. I turned to find behind me a woman in her late twenties sporting a pair of inviting hips and large breasts. She winked as I caught her eyes, and as she smiled two sensual dimples appeared at the corners of her mouth. She was expensively dressed and apparently drunk.

"I'm calling it a night," I answered as I pushed the door open.

"But it's so early and you look so lonely," she countered, walking closer to me. When she reached me she took a finger and drew a circle around each eye. "And these eyes are so downcast. I think you need company. Wouldn't you like Marlene's company?"

I looked at her disbelievingly and then nearly laughed. Instead, a voice from within began to ask the silent question over and over: "What are you waiting for, idiot?" Well, I knew the answer to that one. In my own distorted and twisted fashion I was waiting for Charly. I knew as much as Marlene stepped closer yet until her breasts touched my chest. She kissed me fully on the lips, wet and hungry, and as she did so I gladly tossed off my thoughts of Charly by embracing her just as hungrily. Angry and flustered with the play of my emotions I merely murmured beneath my breath, "Fuck it", and we left together.

At three in the morning I lay awake as this wild banshee with whom I shared my bed slept soundly. For hours we had not so much made love as simply fucked, one of those incredibly long salty wet animal affairs. Still, this gifted and acrobatic woman, even as she spent me, couldn't quite release Charly from my mind's hold. How odd, lying there, the heavy, humid scent of sex in the air, and thinking not of another round with Marlene but of Charly's face and voice. That's when a sickening sense of depravity quickly rose within, guilt associated with my having coveted my best friend's wife. I wrestled with the thought and the banshee until dawn.

On the following weekend Johnnie R. and I agreed to a double-date, and I was to bring along Marlene. It was a fiasco. I was to pick her up at six and we were to have drinks at Johnnie R.'s until seven. Dinner was to follow. When I knocked on her door, however, I found her quite drunk. But drunk with a flare. She met me at the door naked but for a gaudy, gold tiara perched atop her tangled hair. She somehow managed to drag me through the door and over to the couch where she pulled me atop and yelled into my ear, tears in her eyes, "Fuck me now! Fuck me hard and now!"

Though not prone to intercourse on demand I was still less immune to the sweet enticements of mysterious Marlene. While plowing toward orgasm she took to quoting lines from an old Katherine Hepburn movie, the gold tiara still somehow, miraculously, balanced atop her wildly moving head. We eventually managed to finish, and then I learned the reason for the tiara, sex and tears. A failed actress, Marlene was wallowing in self-pity after losing a role for which she had auditioned. Her specialty - southern belles and English queens, of the royal variety.

So on that peculiar evening she had a penchant for Katherine Hepburn, for she remained nude on the sofa for some time mumbling scenes from *The Lion in Winter*. She seemed to be stuck in the scene where Katherine as Catherine tells Peter O'Toole as Henry that she has made love to his father. She played it for all it was worth, down to that favorite of lines, after Henry leaves, "Every family has its ups and downs." Ditto, every double-date. After having coupled like rabbits I tried to sober her up, an exercise that ate up the better part of two hours. When we reached Johnnie R.'s two hours late, both he and Charly were in foul moods.

"Where the hell have you been?" he whispered to me as Marlene stumbled into the house.

"It's a long story," I said, shaking my head. I did the introductions, and then Johnnie R. and I went to mix drinks.

"What's that smell?" he prodded, sniffing about me.

"What?"

"It smells like.....sex!"

"Let's just get this over with. It's a nightmare, really," I said.

"And what's wrong with your hair?" he asked, touching the top of my head. I walked to a mirror to comb my hair, and noticed with partial horror that somewhere between entering and leaving Marlene's house she had managed to mousse it. Johnnie R. suddenly appeared by my side as I combed.

"You're supposed to fuck *after* dinner!"

"Thanks, I'll remember that the next time she plops on the couch and orders me to fuck her."

"Liar!" he laughed.

When we returned with drinks Charly was sitting on the sofa with Marlene, attempting without much success a coherent conversation. Charly politely asked questions. Marlene answered them all with a line from a movie. The theme seemed to be Irene Dunne since I recognized a line out of *The Awful Truth*. This continued for some time, Charly and Johnnie R. eventually looking at me for a sign. I could only shrug.

"I think perhaps it would be better to eat in," Charly finally announced.

We did. Charly and Johnnie R. and I all helped in the kitchen as Marlene shouted more lines from the sofa. We ate, Marlene eventually passed out and I sat in embarrassed humiliation before them both as we later watched a movie. When we left, Johnnie R. helped me with Marlene, and I heard him chuckle when Charly said from the door, "Nick, ask her to change movie themes next time. Perhaps *film noire*."

I took Marlene to my house where she immediately resuscitated. And although she was prepared for yet another evening of the old rough-and-tumble I couldn't perform. The evening was not so much a total disaster as it was, perhaps, a non sequitur. The problem I encountered, both physically and emotionally, is best summed up as an elemental proposition of logic. Simply, the conclusion, the sexual inference, didn't follow from the given premises. I was to have sex yet again with an attractive woman I didn't much like, and instead I was thinking of Charly. With such thoughts came again the guilt, the baseness, and the unconscionable thought transformed the desire to perform into something less substantial than an erection. I was left limp and angry in the face of my powerful confusion, and eventually I was left alone as well, for soon after Marlene parted for more tropical climes in the mighty sexual jungle.

Such was my state of mind by late February. My single attempt at romance had failed miserably, and the single emotional attachment I desired to nurture was with the one woman I most surely couldn't have. Guilt, ambivalence, love. I gave up on the singles bars after the initial fiasco and spent a great deal of time with Johnnie R. and Charly, though of course we did things apart. Occasionally I went for drinks with the guys at the office. I played cards, attended a few ball games. For the most part, though, we remained a threesome, though even this became difficult after a time as the discomfort arising from the impossible situation destroyed the prospect of an enjoyable evening with them. The crushing guilt which pressed down on me as I looked into Johnnie R.'s smiling eyes made matters worse. When I returned home I entertained the guilt and obsessed over Charly, and it was as the envy and anger grew that hostility toward my buddy began to grow as well.

If it's true, as Congreve has suggested, that *Heav'n has no Rage like Love to hatred turn'd*, it's doubly appropriate to mention in my case the point made by Tacitus that it's human nature to hate the man whom you've injured. Until you've both intensely loved and despised the same person it's difficult to understand this. Sure, I'd come to Indy without any real innocence, well aware of the sometimes slick games played by my old buddy from Princeton, but on one crucial point I plead innocence: I never expected to find Charly. I never believed Johnnie R. and I could love the same woman. Then the question arose: how could I disdain my dearest friend? My love grew, the question came, my anger flared and the guilt became all the more pronounced. And it didn't help that in mid-March Charly wanted to paint the landscape spreading between my house and the church steeple on Meridian.

"Do you mind?" she asked over the phone one Saturday morning.

"No, of course not," I said, ecstatic. Often during those early months I'd found myself at the living room windows parting the drapes and taking in the view, particularly on Sunday mornings when, at the promised hour, I'd cast a glance toward Charly's church and its white steeple peeking out from the rooftops. I'd keep the drapes open for the remainder of the day, and near dusk I'd watch the horizon change colors from bright orange to subtle violet as winter shadows played against the windows and arthritic tree branches threaded through the dusky pigments. Later, the steeple lights were turned on, and the steeple appeared as a thin silver needle among the crooked thorns lingering above the rooftops, a small sliver of light. I always thought of Charly when it peeked through the darkness.

So I was more than happy to have her over on three successive weekends to paint that landscape. Johnnie R. was usually in tow, and he helped lug her easel, canvas, brushes and paint supplies into the house. The two of us usually talked or watched ball games while Charly sketched and then painted the landscape. We'd take a coffee break and then go for supper to finish the day. On the few days when Charly came alone I pretended to read as she painted. As she positioned the palette in one hand and applied oils to the canvas with the other, I sat in silent amusement, following her frenetic movements. Sitting behind her and to one side I was able to take in both views, the skyscape and her interpretation of it. Occasionally she would simply stand near the window, silent, brush and palette remaining in hand, as she contemplated the details of the larger picture, and her lovely silhouette before the window destroyed what little concentration I had. When she pushed her hair back and down on her shoulders, I simply gave up, absorbing the contours of her elegant body in her snug-fitting jeans. Trouble was, she knew I was watching her, so when she turned and smiled, only to return to her work, I took the cue and left the room, usually ending up at the kitchen table with my book open and unread. I was sinking fast, my distraction nearly complete, so it was a blessing when she asked to finish the painting one weekday afternoon while I was at the bank. When I returned home, she'd finished, but I could smell the light fragrance of her perfume lingering in the air. I wanted her badly.

Then spring plopped down on the prairie, and I managed to take a deep breath, recapturing the frame of mind of my first weeks in town. Life at the office continued to be hectic as Johnnie R. and I walked the new corporate turf. Our lunches continued, as did our evening talks. With the warmer weather in April and May the three of us took long walks in the evenings or grabbed a coffee. Weekend films, short trips through the countryside, antique hunting, romps through used book stores.

We took in Chicago over Memorial Day weekend, driving over the drab, flat farmland of the vast empty prairie in order to escape the minor insanities of the *Indianapolis 500*. Silos, cattle and corn gave way to Gary's steel mills where rust-colored smoke spewed into the air like a rusty Wyoming geyser, a caustic, eye-watering, soul-disturbing odor lingering all the way into Chicago. The city of Sandburg and Daley and Bellow offered three hectic days of fun and an abundance of time with Charly. We spent an afternoon at the Art Institute, toured the Frank Lloyd Wright home, shopped at Water Tower Place, attended a Cubs game. We walked and drove the vast cityscape from the haughty Magnificent Mile to Old Town. We ate at *Berghoff's* and danced into the early

145

morning on Rush Street. There were late breakfasts at the Hilton, jaunts along the Gold Coast at three a.m. and shopping in between.

Back in Indy, a beautiful spring transformed into an even lovelier summer. June took hold, and life carried on in the fashion of the previous few months as the summer danced away. Picnics, concerts in the park, swimming, the sun. But in late July, with the heat and humidity intensifying, there was a great transition. The weather began to mimic the heavy Gulf summer days of my youth, the long, hot days exhausting us all, and the kid surfaced again as Mike went under.

15

Indianapolis, 1991

Johnnie R.'s Journal

from Ode to Three Queens

So camp it up,
if you must,
triumvirate sojourners
on life's royal path,
sometimes kings,
sometimes queens,
and don't be afraid to say,
like Norma,
'I'm ready for my closeup, Mr. DeMille!'
Just don't shoot
the lovely young man
who can never quite understand
your ambiguous needs,
and raise your chin,
if you must,
and click your heels
like Dorothy in Oz,
and force the world
to follow you back to Kansas.
That's where the real work must yet be done.

* * *

Although Johnnie R.'s condition deteriorated during the following days, there were a few good moments, such as the impromptu party thrown by the three men in robes. Since their first outrageous visit of some days back had done him good, they'd made a practice of stopping by once a day to check on Johnnie R. Now that the word was out that he was fast losing ground to pneumonia, not to mention his near-blindness, they decided to perk him up.

"Girls, sit up straight!" they ordered, erupting into the room like a volcanic explosion as I sat chatting with Johnnie R. This time all three wore terry cloth robes, the pink gown now festooned in white, and they entered in conga-line fashion, swaying back and forth, their white, red, and green robes complete with matching fluffy slippers. They carried with them balloons, horns, hats and a variety of party favors.

"What's this?" Johnnie R. yelped, attempting a smile. "I can hardly see you."

"We're billowing in the wind," said the red robe. "Can't you guess what we are."

"Nick will have to be my eyes," he said. "What do you see, Nick. Besides three queens."

"Three men in terry cloth robes swaying as if performing an exotic Polynesian dance."

"But what are we, collectively?" said the green robe.

"A gaggle of queens," Johnnie R. played along.

"No no no. Now concentrate," said the white robe. "We've dropped the idea of cotillions and night club acts for more intellectual fun. This is our new collective costume. We're to be thought of as a single entity. Red, white and green. Get it?

"No," we said in unison.

"Well, call us three queens if you wish, but we prefer to be called, collectively, Italy. Get it? Red, white and green!"

"Oh, the Italian flag," I said.

"Are you sure you two attended Princeton? You're both awfully slow!"

Johnnie R. shrugged with an attempted smile, saying, "Well, if you can't have Greece ..."

"Honey, you've eaten Greek once too often," the white robe said. "But we have little time to argue. Ratchet's around the corner, rounding up the usual suspects."

"What this time?" I asked.

"An unnamed source - and I absolutely refuse to divulge the name, torture me or not -"

"Oh, to be manhandled right this moment -"

"Shush, silly queen!" the white robe ordered. "I was saying that a reliable source tells me that a certain half-demented queen set off the smoke detector in the public lavatory as cover for party noise rumored to be coming from this room, poopsie."

"Party?" Johnnie R. tried to sit up.

"Surprise party for the birthday boy!"

"It's not my birthday."

"Details, details. Now, sit up." As the last one in shut the door, the three began a feeble, whispered rendition of Happy Birthday. Then the white robe brought forward a platter of scones, one of which had been speared with an enormous, high-flamed candle the size of a sparkler.

"Now blow it out!" they shouted, moving the platter close to Johnnie R.

"And don't pretend that you're not a world-class blower."

"I can barely breathe!" Johnnie R. wheezed. "Are you trying to kill me!"

"Oh, honey, it's too late for that!"

"Nick will blow for me."

"Oh, if only it were true!"

"Yes, blow for us, Nicky-poo. Pucker up and blow!"

I stood and tried to blow out the candle, one of those eternal-flame gag gifts a hurricane couldn't put out.

"Two Ivy leaguers, and neither one can figure out how to blow out a simple candle," the white robe said, pinching the wick.

"We didn't take that course," Johnnie R. said.

"Nor the safe-sex course, methinks."

"Low blow!"

"All good blows are, silly!"

"And now it's time for gifts," the white robe said, reaching into a small sack. "Let's see, here's the penis enlarger. Oops, hear tell from the really cute orderly that you won't be needing that. But here's some hot lube, just in case. And a fashion magazine of prom dresses for those special occasions."

Johnnie R. chuckled as the green robe said, "I remember my first prom as if it were yesterday."

"Me too," said the red robe. "I always stayed home so that I could dress up in my bedroom. I went for the Liza-Minnelli-in-*Cabaret* look. Quite striking. So svelte in those dark stockings."

"It was Marilyn Monroe for me," said the white robe.

"With those legs!"

"Hush! I too was rather svelte and happened by chance to find at Goodwill a near replica of that tight little number Marilyn wore in *The Seven Year Itch.* You know, the one she wears while swooning at the piano with what's-his-name."

"Tom Ewell playing Rachmaninov's Piano Concerto Number Three, I believe," I said.

"Just like a straight boy to concentrate on the tune rather than the dress."

"But you as Marilyn Monroe?" the red robe pursued.

"Far more believable than you as Betty Grable. Remember, someone mistook you for Edith Bunker."

"But the judges threw you out of the Halloween contest that year due to the Ugly Factor. Pimples, remember?"

"I had developed a horrid rash, a reaction to some tainted mascara."

"Pimple? You had a boil the size of an apricot."

"A mere flesh wound, as the saying goes," the white robe defended himself. "Besides, I was still able to get laid that night. Over a keg of beer, no less."

"Which reminds me of the night I lost my virginity," said the green robe.

"Ten, were you?"

"I was in a fraternity -"

"Sorority, dear," the white robe said. "Fraternities are for men."

"But that was back when I *was* a man."

"Sweetie, describe it as *male*. *Man* is a stretch."

"Anyway, a frat brother I'd had my eye on for two years followed me down to the basement, drunk, in an attempt to fetch yet another keg for the party upstairs. Damn, one thing led to another, and eventually I went down on him."

"So, he'd obviously passed out."

"Oh my, no. Quite willing, and eventually he took me from behind, straddling me and a barrel of *Bud*."

"Good heavens."

"It's true. He insisted I repeat over and over again, *This butt's for you.*"

Johnnie R. joined in the laughter, wheezing as he laughed, waving them off. It was hard to keep up with them.

"The poor boy needs his rest," the green robe said. "We can't stay much longer."

"That's right. We have things to do," said the white robe. "Let's see, we must dress our Kaposi's at ten, inhale pentamidine at eleven, juggle our protocol at noon and pray to our silent god before napping."

"And then there's the afternoon talk shows. Can't miss 'em, hon. Today's guests are fringe groups from Montana. And Oprah has a trio of Southern Baptist ministers with shiny, slicked-back hair and voices smooth as silk. Delicious."

"Which one is having those two not-well-dressed individuals from the religious sect, the one's that are going to prove that HIV is programmed with a moral code?"

"That would be Jerry Springer."

"Oh dear, yes. Remember the one last week? Those good ole boys from out west somewhere. A dude ranch I believe -"

"Oh swoon!"

"Save it, deary. They were flannel-shirted, card-carrying NRA members. Remember the one who said AIDS is God's punishment of lefties? Especially the Greenpeace Commie types, most of whom are queer anyway?"

"And then there was the show entitled *Gibbon's Rome Redux*. We've badly declined and all of that."

"Or is that *reclined*?"

"Once too often, I'd venture, sweetie."

"And there's always Bill Buckley's tattoos!"

"Well, call me Hester Prynne!" said the white robe.

"A scarlet letter to go with my robe!"

"Girls, you're forgetting the best of the week! Remember the sweet little lady from down in Mississippi who suggested in a sweet Christian voice, "If someone likes to taste fecal matter - and I understand that all homosexuals do - or receive oral pleasure from the genitals, well, oh my stars! They should be left alone to die. It's God's way."

"Tongues on fire, honey, or perhaps speaking in tongues, because I can't understand a word they say."

This went on and on until Ratchet walked in, and even Johnnie R. had tears in his eyes when they lined up against the wall as the white robe pleaded, "Please be kind to us! We're Italy! Can't you see? We once were fascist too! Have mercy!"

* * *

After they'd left, though, there was no laughter. The infectious disease specialists marched in and out of the room. There was talk of a new protocol, a different regimen of drugs. The nurses further medicated him as his fever rose, but he couldn't sleep. The oxygen whooshed and the monitors clicked and the IVs dripped, and after I helped him drink water and then sat on the edge of the bed as he held my hand, he spoke in a very light voice.

"Do you think AIDS is a form of punishment?" he asked, gripping my hand harder. "As the queens were saying earlier?"

"We've been over this, Johnnie R., remember? It's a disease, that's all."

"What was it I once read? Nature compensates for population gluts by unleashing new diseases. When disparate populations come into contact new diseases flourish. Nature tries to keep tabs on raw numbers in some inexplicable way."

"Perhaps."

"But maybe Nature also practices a form of, I don't know ... call it moral equilibrium. Nature kills and makes a moral choice. Maybe I'm paying for the past."

"Then we all do because we all die, Johnnie R. The kind of death we die doesn't relate to the quality of the life lived. The world's not made that way. If you feel guilt it's because you're not giving yourself a break."

"What about the kid?"

"Your boy? Ian?"

"No. Danny. *The* kid," he whispered. "What I did was wrong."

"But that's done now. There's no one sitting in judgment waiting to call your name. We're not that important."

"Like I said before, that's more frightening than the idea of sin. I'd rather have something, even if negative, than nothing at all." He paused, and when I said nothing he added, "I wonder how it will all turn out. I mean the cure."

151

"It will happen."

"And I won't know. Just like I won't watch my boy grow. It'll be too late. You know, someone will become infected with HIV in twenty years and it will be curable. Future generations will know it like we know the clap now. It will be embarrassing, that's all."

I had no answer for that. I just sat back and held his hand, helping him to more water, trying to console. After he'd fallen to sleep I scooted to my chair and sat by the bed reading fragments from his journal such as this one from Swift's *Thoughts of Various Subjects:* "We have just enough Religion to make us hate, but not enough to make us love one another." Then I put the journal away and thought about his reference to the kid. The past, again. I remembered why Johnnie R. was plagued with guilt as he lay dying.

16

Indianapolis, 1983

On a Saturday in late July, a real scorcher, the heat was so intense that Johnnie R., Charly and I decided to forego a day at their pool, and I remained in my bungalow, stirring about, until I heard a knock on the door around noon. It was the kid, dressed in cutoffs and tank top. Barefoot. "Long time, no see," he said with a smile, his eye-widening ticklish tic as prominent as the sweltering heat pushing through the screen door.

"How did you find my house?"

"I got my sources," he answered, hands on hips.

"I bet," I said, closing the door a bit to keep the cooler air in and the kid out. "What do you want?"

"Oh, nothin' in particular. Just to chat," he answered, placing his hand on the screen door handle as he studied me, his eyes doing that little two-step ditty. I reached over and held the handle firmly. "About what?"

"Stuff," he said, backing off and ambling about the porch. "Somethin' smells mighty good."

"I'm leaving."

"I'd love a soda. Damn hot."

"I'm not inviting you in."

"It's about Charly's brother. I've got some shit you wanna know," he said, placing his hand on the door handle again.

"Tell me from there."

"Too fuckin' hot out here. I don't think good when it's hot."

I pondered his motive, even thought that he might be casing the house. Still, I was curious, and against my better judgment I let him in. "Ten minutes. Tops," I said, swinging the door open. He sauntered into the living room, looked around, inhaled deeply. He caught the scent of the coffee and followed it. Before I could stop him he had scampered into the kitchen.

"Don't mind if I do," he said, picking up a sweet roll on the table.

"That was my last one," I complained, picking up the wrapper and throwing it away. He leaned against the counter, eating the roll.

"Hell, you're a rich banker. You can afford it. I'm just a hustler."

"And hustling doesn't pay like it used to," I said, finishing my own coffee.

"Man, you're almost as much a smartass as ole John. Must be the line of work."

"So tell me about Charly's brother."

"How 'bout a soda?" he asked, turning to rummage through the cupboards.

"One soda. That's it," I said, grabbing one from the frig. He licked his fingers after he'd wolfed down the roll in two large bites. He grabbed the soda and chugged the entire bottle.

"Thanks, man," he said, glancing around the kitchen, his eye tic doing double time as he scavenged for food. When he sensed my patience was growing thin he added, "Like I said, man, I know somethin' about Charly's brother." He paused and then scampered out of the kitchen and back into the living room, standing before a bookcase as he fingered through a book. "Lit-a-chur."

"Some of it, yes."

"Just like Mike. That's all I ever heard from him. Cul-chur. Mo-zzzzzart. Lit-a-chur. All that bullshit. Like it was going to make me a better person."

"It might."

"Yeah, just like Mike, right? Look where it got him? Lost his job. Drinkin'. Whorin' around. He's gone all crazy. Lot of fuckin' good it did him."

"What about Charly's brother?"

"It'll cost ya."

Bingo. The money hustle was on, not that I thought he'd come to discuss Mozart. "It's time for you to leave," I said.

He ignored me, pulling a volume of Rilke's *Elegies* from the bookcase. He glanced at the cover, turned a few pages. "Who's this faggot?"

"A poet."

"With a queer name."

"Out, kid. I'm tired of being hustled." I took the book from him and led him by the arm back to the door. When I opened it he said, "I'll give ya part of it free. Part ya gotta pay for."

"Tell me the free part."

"Let go of my arm first."

I did, making certain he remained between me and the door. He smiled one of his leering, mischievous smiles, rubbing his hands together. His tic was in overdrive with all the excitement, or perhaps the sugar he'd consumed.

"Charly's brother. Randy. Ya know about him?"

"He's dead."

"Yeah. And he was a friend of mine. We even had a thing for awhile. Rich kid and poor kid. Did ya know he was gay?"

"No, but thanks for telling me," I said, scooting him out the door.

"I was there the night he was killed. I saw it all."

I stopped pushing him, and he knew he had me as he casually leaned against the door frame, stretching, taking his time as the hot air poured in. He was all smiles and nervous tic.

"That's what I tried to tell ya back in your car. Remember, at the library?"

"Get on with it."

"It's simple. John hates my guts 'cause he thinks it's my fault Randy's dead. Just like he blames me for Mike goin' off the deep end. That's what I'm gettin' at."

"And?"

"It ain't fair. I didn't do nothin'. I was just there. And John's tryin' to fuck me over for it. It wasn't my fault."

"So tell me about the death."

"Happened last summer, man," he said, cocking his head. "I thought ya was John's best friend. Ya sure don't know much for a best friend, do ya?"

"How did he die?"

"He was stabbed. Right in the fuckin' back. I seen it happen in an alley behind Talbott Street. Three guys robbed him and he fought and they stabbed him right in the fuckin' back," he said, voice rising. As his eyes widened I thought they might swallow me whole. He paused a moment, looking out at the street. "Damn filthy niggers."

"And why do they blame you?"

"Because they don't fuckin' like me. At first they said I done it, but ya can look at the police report. I got all cleared from it. They got the guys that done it. It was a robbery, that's all. It coulda happened to anyone. Anyways, they caught two of those niggers and they confessed about the robbery part and said the third nigger done the killin'."

"So you two were tight."

"Yeah, he was my friend," he said, looking away. "And they blame me for it. They said I was bad company to keep. Well, fuck 'em. They don't know how tough it is. They're too fuckin' rich to know how tough it is." When I remained silent he asked, "Ya want some juicier scoop? It'll cost ya fifty bucks."

"Goodbye, Danny," I said, leaning toward the door and opening it.

"It's hot stuff."

"No thanks."

"Twenty."

"Get out."

"Last chance," he said, walking onto the porch. He turned and grabbed his crotch, his eyes clicking out a wild Morse code. "I'll throw this in for the twenty."

I closed the screen door and locked it. He walked down to the sidewalk and then turned and faced me. Smiling, he put his hands to his mouth and yelled, "Thanks, Nick. It was great. Maybe next time I can be the bottom!" And off he went, barefoot, laughing, clapping his hands. That was the kid. King of the hill, still hooting it up. Everything he touched seemed to go bad, and his latest information was troubling. Had Charly's brother really fallen under the kid's spell? Did they meet at Talbott Street? And what about this friendship? A street-smart hustler and a north side rich boy. Was it simply a case, as Johnnie R.

155

had implied, of a rich kid slumming? One thing was certain. The kid offered a life of intrigue, the endless possibilities of the night. Perhaps that's what so angered Johnnie R.

*   *   *

Less than a week later Johnnie R. stormed into my office, winded and worn. He closed the door hard, walked to my desk and threw a bundle of papers on my desk. Then he leaned forward, his face only inches from mine. His warm sour breath struck me in sharp little bursts. "Mike was picked up yesterday for soliciting a minor at a place called Holliday Park," he said. "Christ, Nick, the guy's life the past few months reads like a cheap detective novel."

"So you've been keeping tabs on him?"

"I've got a contact on the police force who has it all documented. Unsavory public scenes with the kid, drunkenness, occasional violence. After the kid split there were drinking binges, porno shops, bath houses. He cruised for male hustlers where the undercover cops were known to work. They were on to him. He was throwing wads of dough for a young piece of ass. And to make matters worse, Nick, vice has been seen speaking with the kid who, it seems, hasn't quite escaped the law himself. He was recently hauled in for solicitation."

"Ah, that explains his visit," I said. "He somehow found out where I live and came by offering information in return for money."

"Like what?" Johnnie R. asked, leaning yet closer, his eyes little slits of anger.

"He told me he was friends with Randy and that Randy was gay?"

"That little motherfucker!" He banged my desk top with his fist, stood and banged it again. I'd never seen him so angry. "I told you not to talk with the little shit!"

"Why didn't you tell me?"

"Nick, it wasn't necessary. Randy was gay. Hell, ten percent of the population is gay. So what?"

"It just seems odd that you didn't mention it. He died near Talbott Street. You took me to the bar. Damned coincidental."

"It's in the ghetto, for Christ's sake, Nick. Crime is rampant in the ghetto. The real issue is the kid. He's trouble, a detestable little shit. He was there when Randy died."

"That's what he said."

"And what else did he say, Nick?"

"Nothing. I kicked him out."

Johnnie R. grew suddenly subdued, distant. When he spoke again he was calmer, smiling. "Well, I'll deal with him soon enough."

"What do you mean?"

"Nothing, nothing," he said, evasively. "Look, the important thing is that this guy on the force thinks the kid's made a deal. He helps catch Mike and he goes free."

"What do you mean, he helps catch Mike?"

"Guess who Mike tried to pick up? The kid, of course, but the kid on the make. The plain clothes guys from vice used him as bait. It was simple entrapment. Read it. It's all there," he said, pointing to the police report on my desk.

"Take it easy, Johnnie R. At least Mike's no longer associated with the bank," I said, reaching for the report.

"Look, Nick, the kid's dangerous. They paid him money. The department keeps dough stashed away for these occasions. What else did he offer?"

"What do you care? What are you hiding?"

"He can lie, Nick. That's as bad as being guilty. It could kill my career."

"Why did the kid do it?"

"Wise up, Nick. He did it for the money, for revenge, for kicks. It was a banging good time. The kid and the law fighting on the same team. A real gasser, huh?"

"How did you get this report so fast?" I asked, still thumbing through it.

"People will do anything, at any pace, for money, Nick," he said, shrugging his shoulders. "Just read it."

I did. Although the papers would never publish his name, it was true that the kid played a starring role. Of course there was no mention of money, but it smelled of payola. Two cops staked out the park, hiding beyond the wood line. The kid remained visible at the edge of the woods, near the pavement. Mike spotted the kid and followed him into the woods. He fell to his knees, attempted to fondle the kid and asked to perform fellatio. Then he was arrested.

"And now Mike, the big fish, ends his career by dashing to the surface to perform the consummate super splash in the big sexy pond," Johnnie R. allowed as he left.

* * *

This day was taking on a Fellini feel, and it became all the more pronounced when, within an hour, we were both summoned to his father's office. When I entered I noted Johnnie R.'s expression at once. Caught off guard, he was fast losing composure. And for good reason. The circumstances surrounding Mike's arrest were worse than we'd been led to believe. Not only had the old man been independently informed of the essential facts, he'd been given much more. I understood at once from the tenor of his voice that he was angry with us.

The old guy was dapper in his finely tailored pinstripe suit. His thick white hair shined brightly under the dome of lights in his office. His face may have been wrinkled and somewhat pale, but it still carried strength in the powerful square jaw and high proud forehead. From behind his formidable desk he dominated the room with his genteel features and still-strong voice. I immediately realized the extent of the trouble by the manner in which he addressed me. "Sit down near John, Nick," he ordered without a smile. I sat and glanced at Johnnie R. who in turn simply raised his brows as the old man continued. "I wanted you present also, Nick, for the simple reason that your name seems to be involved as well in this abominable and garish affair. That makes the count three when you include Mike and John. We must talk."

The old man remained behind the battleship of a cherry wood desk, standing for emphasis. His slight carriage loomed large in those environs. He was no longer playfully pulling wings off flies as he'd done during my previous encounters. No, he was clicking along on an altogether different level that morning, totally within his element as he cleared his mind of all but the essentials of the scandal which loomed before us, a tight-fisted capitalist maneuvering within his autocratic realm. I'd never felt more the transient guest than at that moment. And as he paused I happened to remember the conversation described by Johnnie R. concerning his imminent promotion, and I too began to experience the same taut weakness, the inadequacy.

"Men, as you know we are faced with a highly serious problem. You both are aware that Mike has been arrested for accosting a minor, a male, for sexual purposes. I need say no more than that. The topic is totally anathema to me. It should be to both of you. That we shall discuss in due course." He paused and turned to his sprawling credenza and opened a drawer, pulling from it a delicate wooden cigar box, quite old, and laying it on his desk. He took from it one cigar, slowly cut it in preparation for a smoke and then lit it. He took several puffs, held the cigar before him as if he were inspecting a garment for flaws and then inhaled again. Always the mannerist, a man of blue-blood forms, he scooted the box across the vast tarmac of his rich desk as an offering. Neither of us desired one, nor were we expected to take one. He then picked up the fragile box and returned it to the credenza, continuing to puff on the cigar as the room filled with smoke.

"Fortunately, Mike was terminated some months ago, but a great deal of harm may already have been done. I expect no further words with the man, nor do I expect either of you to make contact. This practical directive is both a management decision and the professional advice of counsel. Do you both understand me?"

We both said that we did. He paused a second time and walked to one of the large windows of his office which overlooked the city, puffing away. I was amazed that at that distance, and far from his desk, he appeared much less formidable, in fact, quite ordinary and unassuming with his old man's slight stoop. Undoubtedly, he realized this as well, having refined the art of social intercourse to his advantage over years of such experiences. After all, I'd experienced first hand his talent for psychological nuance. De-linting me, retaining my hand as he spoke, jabbing me at Christmas, slicing me up at his club. The power of his position afforded him a species of dominance which somehow shadowed his physical ailments, his aging frame. I was certain that's why he didn't resume the conversation until he'd returned to his looming desk. Still standing, while behind the desk he seemed once again quite imposing.

"There are two remaining problems, and they are somewhat interconnected. First, the bank shall reap some bad press over this episode; of this there can be no doubt. Mike was very good at what he did. He developed a great rapport with many powerful men in this city over the years. He is widely known, and until now, respected. His fall from grace, for it is surely that, will send shock waves throughout the business and banking communities. We must be prepared to mitigate the damages. We shall weather the storm; of this I entertain no doubts. I depend on each of you to assure our success." He paused and puffed and then added, "Secondly, you both, to a degree, have been implicated in this charade."

"What?" Johnnie R. blurted out, standing with arms in the air.

"Sit, John. And don't speak until I've asked you to do so," the old man roared. I was amazed at the power of his voice, the energy informing his anger. That mean streak again. Diminutive but ferocious. Slowly, though, his frown transformed into an ironic, subtle smile, a twinge of wickedness apparent at the upturned corners of his mouth. Johnnie R. was silent and sat down.

"It seems the boy, the minor involved in this liaison, has stated to the authorities that both of you also have shared in these, shall we say, unwholesome desires. Of course, I need not remind you that Mike has been destroyed. This is not to say that either of you could be prosecuted. Obviously not. No one intends to do so. I've taken care of that possibility and it has successfully been put to rest. The mayor and prosecutor need to continue receiving my political contributions and financial pull, you see. Still, such talk is damaging to the bank, and we cannot allow it to continue. You are both put on notice that I will not allow such activity to occur."

Johnnie R. shifted forward to the edge of the sofa. He nearly spoke, but the old man held up a defying finger as he shook his head, those old blue eyes twitching. Johnnie R. said nothing, looking down at the carpet. I, for my part, was aghast.

"Now, boys do lie. That is a fact of life. This particular boy is a male hustler as I understand it. I assume he is lying. It would be the natural thing for him to do. I, of course, do not believe a word he has uttered about my own son and his Princeton colleague. I have no knowledge previous to this information to make me believe otherwise. However, listen closely," he warned, his eyes narrowing to little cat slits, "listen very, very closely, both of you, to what I am about to say.

I do not know if this information is true. I do not want to know. But I do know this. It absolutely shall not be true tomorrow. Do I make myself understood?"

His frame shook as he bellowed, the bass nearly too deep and strong to have come from his small frail body. He was all anger and fire, leaning over the desk as best he could, cigar in one hand as he pounded the desk with the other. Angry and dumbfounded both, we agreed that we understood. As he leaned over the desk, the smoldering cigar still balanced in one hand, ashes precariously balanced on the tip of his cigar, I caught the glint of blue in his strong icy eyes. Those were Johnnie R.'s eyes. Within that old, failing frame was the young man who was Johnnie R., all spunk and daring and bullshit and confidence, and not even the wrinkles could hide the vestiges of the charismatic young man from whom Johnnie R. had inherited. The fiery demeanor was frightening, and the contrast between the image of the young man behind those eyes and the now-frail fellow before us allowed a glimpse of history in the making.

"Men, just to be certain that I am properly making my point with you, let me add this detail. Pansy boys, as I shall call them, or homosexuals, if you prefer, have been with us for centuries. They always shall be with us. There is no changing history, nor, I think, human nature. Some of these individuals have become contributing, worthwhile members of society. Many are quite famous. But, you see, none of them are Indianapolis bankers. Understand, please, that pansy boys may be hairdressers and artists, waiters and poets, but they most emphatically cannot be bankers. It is not in their constitution. I hope this is clear."

The point he was attempting was quite clear, of course, and I wasn't the one being undone by the old man's words. Johnnie R. held his father's gaze for a very long time, icy blue eyes meeting icy blue eyes a generation removed, nearly half a century of experience and wisdom separating them, and it was Johnnie R. who first looked away. There was nothing more to be said; no threats needed to be made. The rule contained the implicit punishments. "I believe we understand each other," he said casually. "And now, men, we must be tough as nails. Let us return to our work. There is much to be done."

We left the office without a handshake, and Johnnie R. followed me to my office where, embarrassed, hurt and angry, he began to plot again. "Now you know why I was worried about the little shit! You see what he's done? He's even implicated you, Nick."

"He lied, Johnnie R. Your old man said he took care of everything. Forget it."

"He must be put away. It should be fairly easy," he said, pacing as he sorted his thoughts.

"Put away?"

"Jail. Or reform school. Whatever it is that keeps adolescent criminals. He's obviously not yet eighteen. He's a hustler with a record. He's a born thief as well. That's how I'll get him," Johnnie R. said. He rapped his knuckles on my desk for emphasis and then turned and walked to the door, but before leaving he added, "I'll call you before I leave so that we can meet for a drink."

And this long Fellini moment continued gaining surreal strength when Johnnie R. later buzzed my office with news of Mike's suicide. It was all far too macabre - the need, the vengeance, the suicide, the waste. The meaninglessness of an obsession, the lustful haunting of the heart. I pitied him, a man I never really knew but whose choices touched my life, a man lost both to the world and to himself. Johnnie R. said, "He was found in his garage with the car running. The mailman smelled fumes and called the cops. Christ, he was still dressed in the suit and tie he'd worn to the park. His slacks still had mud on the knees."

We left the bank moments later to get drinks, and I spent the evening cooling him off, calming him down, talking it out. And I hadn't looked so forward to a drink in years. Life in Indy had become so very complex - Mike's death, the mystery surrounding Charly's brother, the kid's pranks, Johnnie R.'s mysterious secrets, my desire for Charly. It was a world out of control. And among the torn napkins, empty beer bottles, peanut husks and half-full plates the night passed slowly; we both drank too much. The more Johnnie R. drank the angrier he became and the angrier he became the more he seemed to be plotting. Around midnight I began to experience one of those ghastly, dizzy, topsy-turvy drunks, the likes of which I hadn't known since my college days. I was a mess, and Johnnie R. wasn't much better. And the only item of our hours-long, rambling discussion which I clearly remember is the comment Johnnie R.'s father made once he'd learned of Mike's suicide: "It was quite the honorable and right thing to do. No question."

* * *

I was in a ghastly, hungover state when Johnnie R. knocked at my door at ten the following morning, walking to the door dressed in the clothes I'd worn the previous day. Johnnie R., however, was all fire and energy. "I need you to come with me," he said with a booming voice. My head throbbed with each word he spoke.

"I'm sick. You'll have to go without me."

"We've got some business to do, Nick."

"I need coffee and aspirin and sleep. Come back later," I said, walking toward the bedroom.

"Make it coffee and aspirin, Nick. You can sleep this afternoon. You promised." Apparently I'd agreed to accompany him to Mike's house for some unspecified reason, another one of his madcap schemes to even the score with the kid. The relentless one, he prodded for half an hour, and following two cups of coffee I finally agreed to tag along. "No need to change. I'll bring you right back," he said.

During the drive to Mike's house he elaborated. "I'm the executor of his will, Nick. Can you believe he never thought to have it changed? I can get into the house under that pretext," he chirped. He was running off the nervous energy from the day before. That and his desire to destroy the kid.

"And what, precisely, are we going to do there?" I asked, gingerly leaning my aching head back and closing my eyes.

"I need to check on a few things."

"And you have a key?" I asked. My head ached and Johnnie R. managed to find every bump in the road.

"No, but I know where he hid his extra keys."

Of course he did. We arrived, he parked the car and then found the keys. He was in the house before I could close my car door, and when I entered, the stench sent me reeling. Exhaust fumes lingered in the air and in the carpet and the fabric of the furniture. "Goddamn!" I shouted, holding my nose. "I can't take this."

From somewhere in the house he shouted back for me to be patient. I left the door open and then opened a window and pulled up a chair. With my stomach already teetering on the fragile balance, the acrid odor sent me over, and moments later I charged to a bathroom and knelt at the toilet. As I wretched, the bathroom walls spun around in a solemn salute to my old college days. Remaining near the basin, I could hear Johnnie R. exploring the house as he opened and closed doors. I listened as he walked from the silent carpet onto the hard wood floors and back onto the thick rugs. From deep in the house I heard his rummaging through drawers and cabinets and the clink of metal on metal and glass on glass.

Back in the kitchen, I breathed the fresh air from the open window and thought of Mike's death as shadows fell on the lawn. Such a reservoir of nothingness, not to mention that long moment of impatience as he waited to die. And the old man again: "It was the honorable thing to do. No question about it." It was all so troubling, the thought of a man swallowed by the darkness. "Come on, Nick," Johnnie R. interrupted my thoughts as he entered the kitchen, hands full. He wore gloves, and he carried various valuables - rings, a thick gold chain, a silver medallion, gold jewelry, some small pieces of art, a money clip, cash and credit cards.

"What in the hell are you doing?" I asked, moving away from the window.

"Getting rid of the kid. Come on and open the door to the garage for me," he answered calmly. There was a tone of simple sweet victory in his voice. He knew exactly what he was doing.

"What do you mean?"

"Just open the door, Nick."

162

"This whole thing is so goddamned tragic."

"I'd rather not talk about it. It merely makes be angrier," he said as he walked past me and to the door leading to the garage, leaning against it as he waited for me to open it. I remained near the window, shaking my head. Anger was his emotive response rather than remorse. He was more interested in his little scheme than Mike's death. "Come on, Nick," he ordered.

I walked to the door and opened it as Johnnie R. breezed past me and into the garage where I followed. The carbon monoxide fumes lingered, biting and harsh. I closed the door and watched him maneuver among three cars. He walked past a Cadillac, Mike's killer and temporary tomb, and brushed against a Jaguar sports coupe before coming to a stop beside a third car covered by a protective canvas. He placed the goods on the cement floor and then wrestled the canvas from the car.

"What in the hell are you doing?" I walked closer.

"Just help me, Nick. We don't have time for questions," he ordered. I grabbed a corner of the canvas, and we pulled it from the car. It was a real beauty, a refurbished candy apple red Stingray.

"Nice, huh?" Johnnie R. said, stepping back. "New wheels, new engine, new paint job. He spent a lot of money on this baby, and to think he originally bought it for the kid." I only shook my head. "I talked him out of it, of course," he said, self-satisfied. "The kid would've been dead within a week. That, or he would've skipped town."

He opened the car door sat in the driver's seat. I leaned against a wall for a long while, looking at the car and watching Johnnie R. fumble around with several sets of keys before finding the right set. "The car the kid never got," I said, breaking the silence. I wondered if the kid knew he'd been that close to victory.

"Maybe not. He might have it yet," Johnnie R said with a slight smile.

"I don't get it," I said. Before he could answer, Johnnie R. slid the keys into the ignition. The car started right up; the engine roared; the fumes came pouring from the exhaust. "Goddammit, Johnnie R., turn it off!"

"Can't. Have to make sure its running smoothly," he yelled over the rumble.

"I'm going to be sick," I said, running back into the house. I slammed the door and ran to the bathroom where I heaved into the toilet. Minutes later, while still on my knees, I heard the car engine sputter and then stop. I moved back to the open kitchen window and sat with my chin on the sill. Johnnie R. stirred in the garage, but the engine was off for good. I heard the clink of metal and then car doors open and close. Next I heard the sound of fabric being rubbed over a hard surface and realized he was returning the canvas to the Stingray. Moments later, he walked to the door, opened it and entered the kitchen.

"That's it. We're set," he said, satisfied.

"Set for what?"

"The kid. He'll come for the car. I'm sure of it." He walked to the refrigerator and grabbed a soda.

"Then hide the keys."

"Jesus, Nick, you're slow. His taking the car is just the point," he said as he pulled the top off the can and took a drink. "Sure. I hid the keys to the larger cars. He'll never find those. But I left the keys in the Stingray. All he has to do is remove the canvas."

"You're setting him up!" I yelled. "Don't do this, Johnnie R."

"It's not a setup, Nick. He'll come for the car. I know he will. I simply want to make sure he takes it."

"And then you'll call the cops," I finished his thought. "It stinks Johnnie R. I want no part of it. I want to leave now."

"We're done. No problem."

"And the goods you took to the garage?"

"I've hidden them where he won't find them, of course."

As we rode in silence back to my house, I wondered just how long he'd stewed over the possibilities before this particular idea had come to him. He had me along, I finally realized, as an alibi. Of course he didn't need one. He was the executor of Mike's estate; he'd been a friend. To the cops, and over the kid's objections, he wouldn't need to explain. It was the word of a prominent banker over the slick words of a street hustler. Still, ever-cautious Johnnie R., like his father, was taking every precaution. And now the kid would pay.

* * *

Johnnie R. called late on Sunday afternoon, energy personified. "Nick, he took the car," he said excitedly. "I'm going to report it missing."

"Why are you doing this?"

"He's stolen the car, Nick. The kid deserves this. First I find him. Then I call the cops. It's as simple as that."

"Just report the car missing and stay away from the kid."

"Come on, be a sport. I've got a little thing to settle. It's almost over."

"Then pick me up and take me with you," I said. "I don't want you alone with him."

He picked me up and we drove to University Park. When there was no sign of the kid, we slowly circled the mall. Still no sign of the red sports car. We parked at the library for a few moments, but he didn't show. Near six we left for Holliday Park. "He must be there," Johnnie R. said, speeding up Meridian and entering the park just before dusk. He slowly drove around a horseshoe-shaped road as we looked for the kid. There was little traffic in the park by that hour, though a few stragglers remained. As we reached the top of the horseshoe we spotted the empty Stingray on one of the loops off the top of the bend. Johnnie

R. drove to the nearby pay phone and placed a quick call to the police to report the car stolen and then drove to a parking lot not far from the Stingray.

"Let's find him," he said, quickly opening the door.

"Wait for the police."

"Stay if you like. I'm going to find him."

Fearing what he might do with the kid when he found him, I jumped out and caught up with Johnnie R., now walking in the general direction of the Stingray as he eyed the wood line for signs of the kid. In the distance were a couple of men loitering near the woods, both of whom scampered away as we approached, and moments later, perhaps twenty yards from the car, Johnnie R. spotted the kid walking off a path and onto the road. He didn't immediately see us as he strolled along the edge of the asphalt, and Johnnie R. picked up his pace as the kid neared the car, breaking into a full run as the kid reached for his keys. The kid heard footsteps as Johnnie R. closed in, and as he tried to open the car door Johnnie R. slammed it closed with his foot.

"Not so fast, you little fuck," Johnnie R. shouted. The kid tried to run, but Johnnie R. caught him by an arm and threw him back against the car.

"Leave me alone, John. I'll fuckin' yell rape," the kid raged as he tried to shake off Johnnie R.

"And I'll yell thief. Got it?" Johnnie R. was enjoying himself as he pinned the kid against the car, their faces only inches apart. "And this time you're in over your head," he said, tightening his grip. He laughed loudly, his voice echoing through the park.

"You're hurtin' me, man. Let go."

"The pain's just beginning, kid. Wait until you reach the reformatory. Do you know what they'll do to that sweet young ass of yours? You'll think it was reamed by a jackhammer before they're done with you. They'll fuck you every day, every night."

"Hey, I didn't steal nothin', John. I was takin' it back. I was takin' it back tonight. I was goin' right now," he said, resting against the car rather than continuing to fight.

"Sure, Danny boy. And maybe you're finally telling the truth. But the cops won't believe it. You're going to pay now, and not just for the car, really, but for the lives you've ruined." He hesitated a second and looked at me with a puzzling expression, slightly shrugging his shoulders as if to apologize. Then he turned and slapped the kid hard on the face.

"Goddammit!" the kid yelled, trying to protect his face with his free hand. Johnnie R. released the kid's arm.

"Go ahead and run," Johnnie R. said. "Let's have some fun."

The kid looked at me disbelievingly and then at Johnnie R. suspiciously. He took a few hesitant steps backward, away from Johnnie R., and then turned quickly to run. Johnnie R., much too quick for him, grabbed him again before he'd taken ten steps, bringing him close to his body. "Now you know the feeling of being trapped, don't you? You know that awful pressure of being holed in with nowhere to go. You know how Mike felt now." Johnnie R. then reached back and slapped the kid hard a second time.

"Quit, man. Goddamn."

"Johnnie R., cut it out," I yelled, walking closer. He maintained his grip on the kid's arm and turned toward me. I'd never seen such wrath.

"Stay out of it, Nick. This belongs to me and the dead."

"Come on, Johnnie R.," I said softly, touching his shoulder lightly. He shrugged it off, turning back toward the kid.

"I said stay out, dammit."

"Pull him off, Nick. Come on, man," the kid begged, all false innocence. I stood and watched, saying nothing. Johnnie R. pulled the kid in front of him, a hand on each of the kid's arms, as he spoke again.

"It doesn't matter whether Nick or anyone else pulls me off. It's over. The cops are on their way," Johnnie R. said. He slapped him a third time.

"Goddammit!" the kid shouted. Johnnie R. turned his head toward me and laughed again, and the kid, thinking quickly, brought a knee up to Johnnie R.'s groin, hitting him hard in the balls.

"Shit!" he yelled, losing his grip. He doubled over and nearly fell to the asphalt. Freed, the kid started to run.

"Dammit! Get him, Nick!"

I grabbed the kid as he tried to pass. He fought me with wild punches and a few kicks, though I managed to bring both of his arms down, pinning them to the side of his body with his back against my chest. Cursing and screaming for help, he kicked my shins, forcing me to release him, but Johnnie R. was there to nab him. As the kid swung around he caught my eye. "I knew ya was a faggot, man," he yelled. "I bet you like it up the ass nice and sweet like John here."

"You shouldn't have said that," Johnnie R. said softly, almost delicately. He pushed the kid down, and when the kid scrambled from the ground Johnnie R. grabbed him and slapped him hard on the face once again.

"That's for Nick," Johnnie R. said. The kid stumbled but continued standing. He yelled out again, and then Johnnie R. hit him harder.

"That's for Mike."

The kid fell back and nearly down, but Johnnie R. held him up tight. The kid stumbled about, and as he regained his balance, ever so tenuous a balance, Johnnie R. slapped him on the face yet again. The kid screamed for Johnnie R. to stop as he fell to his knees and held his face. Johnnie R. pulled the kid up from the ground, brought his face close to his own and before he could speak the kid spit on him. Johnnie R., undaunted, smiled as he wiped it from his face.

"This is for me," he said. Again he slapped him. The kid fell down, his nose bleeding. He was cursing wildly, his arms flailing the empty air, hoping for a shot at Johnnie R. Before he realized what was occurring Johnnie R. pulled him off the ground a final time. Again, he brought the kid's face close to his.

"And this, you little fuck, is for Randy," Johnnie R. shouted, out of control. He slugged the kid full-fisted in the face. The kid dropped to the ground immediately, and when he turned toward us I saw blood flowing from both his mouth and nose. That's when I walked forward to stand just behind Johnnie R.

"That's enough. You'll be thrown in jail too."

"I said stay out of it goddammit."

I inched closer and he reached to push me away. "I'm warning you, Nick."

I didn't move as he pulled the kid from the ground and dragged him to the car. The kid was still cursing Johnnie R. When they reached the car Johnnie R. pushed the kid's face against the hood. "Kiss it," he demanded. "It's the pretty little car you always wanted. Now kiss it!"

The kid resisted, cursing between the heaves.

"It cost a life, you little fuck. Now, kiss it!" he shouted, slamming the kid's face hard against the hood. I heard a sickening pop and then the kid screamed, a terrifying, echoing shriek. I ran to the car and put my arms around Johnnie R., pulling him away from the kid. He fought free and pushed me away, hard. I pushed him back, and then he swung lightly toward my face but missed.

"Don't do this, Johnnie R."

"Don't push me," he shouted, taking a step toward me.

"The cops will be here in a minute. Let them take care of him."

Before he could answer the kid managed to stand straight up and turn to face us, leaning against the car. Johnnie R. continued looking at me with his back to the kid, but I watched the kid over his shoulder as the blood oozed from his mouth and nose onto his clothes and the car. A thick dark red stream slowly descended the perfect curve of the candy apple hood. His face was a mess, bloody and bruised. The blood had smeared into his hair and over his face, dripping from his chin. I noticed as he looked up that he was no longer crying. In fact, as I focused on his expression I managed to catch his attempt at a smile, a slightly malicious turn of the lips. His watery eyes twitched with his tic, and then widened before a squint formed litttle slits. With the blood and matted hair against his face his smile was ghastly, a gruesome mask.

"Hey, Nick," he shouted. Johnnie R. didn't move; I stood absolutely still. "Hey Nick, ask John about his secret lover. Come on, ask him," he yelled, trying to laugh, though coughing up blood instead.

"Shut the fuck up," Johnnie R. shouted back over his shoulder, still looking at me.

"Come on, Nick, ask him. Ask him why he *really* hates me. Ask him why he hit me so hard for Randy," the kid said, playing his last trump card.

"I said shut up you little shit," Johnnie R. shouted, turning toward the kid. In the background I could hear sirens, perhaps a mile away but closing in fast.

"Okay, then. I'll tell ya," he said. "Want me to tell 'em about Randy, Johnnie boy?" He tried to stand without leaning against the car, but he stumbled and fell back against it, slipping slowly to the ground. With a great deal of effort he stood again, this time remaining against the car. Even with the looming shadows of dusk beginning to cover his face I could clearly see the freakish tic and macabre smile. The blood had begun to crust in large splotches near the corners of his mouth, making his appearance all the more hideous. Eventually he pointed a shaking finger our way as he tilted his head from side to side, a mad puppet.

"You little fuck, I'll crush you!" Johnnie R. shouted. Before he could step forward I grabbed him from behind and held as tightly as I could, but he was bigger than me, bulkier, and he wrestled free with an elbow to the ribs. When I bent over he stepped toward the kid who'd maneuvered to the far side of the car.

"Hey, Nick, they was fuck buddies! They was fuck buddies! That's why he hit me so hard. That's why he don't want me around. 'Cause I know too much," he said, trying to keep the car between himself and Johnnie R. Johnnie R. lurched forward to grab him but missed, and then he chased him around the car.

"They was lovers, Nick," the kid yelled, laughing. "Randy and John was fag lovers."

"I'll destroy you!" Johnnie R. yelled as he neared the kid.

"It makes ya sick, don't it. And I know. That's why he hates me. They was lovers!"

The kid barely uttered the last words before Johnnie R. caught him from behind. He pulled the kid to the middle of the small paved street, turned him so that the kid faced him and slugged him hard with his fist a second time, catching the kid's jaw. I heard it break, and the kid screamed as it shattered. He fell hard to the pavement, on his knees, the blood dripping to the asphalt. He sprayed blood with each word he tried but failed to utter. Johnnie R. walked to him, leaned over to pick him up again and then thought better of it. Instead, he kicked him in the side, and the kid fell on his stomach, moaning. Johnnie R. then leaned over and turned the kid onto his back, straddling him as I ran forward. I saw him pull a knife from his pocket, and simultaneously I could see the lights from the squad cars as they entered the park.

"No!" I yelled, trying to pull him off the kid a second time.

"I'm not going to use it on him, dammit," he shouted as I pulled him away. "I've got to cover myself."

He pushed me back, and I watched as he placed the knife in the kid's hand, tightened the kid's grip and then jiggled it loose. The knife landed a couple of feet from where the kid lay on the ground. Then, before standing, Johnnie R. punched the kid in the gut, and he erupted with a long guttural yelp and vomited.

When the police didn't immediately see us, Johnnie R. whistled and waved to attract their attention. With lights on and sirens blaring, they rushed forward, and as they neared I heard the kid mumble very softly, nearly incoherently, "They was lovers, I swear it."

"Goddamned! What happened here," one the cops demanded of Johnnie R. as they approached.

"I called in the stolen car," Johnnie R. said coolly. He introduced himself as they neared, holding out his identification. "When I approached and tried to stop him, he pulled a knife. There it is," he pointed to a spot near the kid. The cop leaned over to inspect the knife.

"And who are you, buddy?" one of the officers asked.

"I'm with him," I answered, pointing to Johnnie R.

"Tell me what happened," he said to Johnnie R.

Johnnie R. gave them a spiced-up recap, painting a picture of grand theft and falsifying the knife attack.

"You shouldn't have roughed him up."

"It was self-defense," Johnnie R. countered, giving his best shot as the innocent underdog.

"His face looks like hamburger. It doesn't look like a simple case of self-defense," the officer said, belching.

"I have a witness," Johnnie R. said, looking at me.

"You'll probably need one, son."

"Tell him," Johnnie R. ordered, looking at me squarely. I held his glance for only seconds, long enough to assure him of my anger. I hesitated as I tried to find the right words.

"It's true, officer. The kid stole the car," I said simply.

"I was goin' to take it back," the kid mumbled, barely intelligible.

"Whose car?" the cop asked, ignoring him.

"A dead man's," Johnnie R. began. "The guy who owned it died Friday. I'm the executor of his estate, and when I went by to check on the house I noticed the car was missing."

"You know this kid?"

"I understand that he's a hustler and a thief," Johnnie R. said. "He has a record."

"You're going to have to answer some questions," the officer said.

"As I said it was self-defense. Check the knife for prints. The kid's nearly mad, a common criminal," Johnnie R. elaborated, all polish and poise. "But I'll of course be happy to answer any questions you might have."

The kid rolled over as one of the officers knelt to check him. The bleeding had slowed, but the dried and crusted masses near his mouth were larger. The kid mumbled a few unintelligible words which the cops couldn't understand, but I knew he was repeating the last sentence again: "They was lovers."

"He took more than just the car," Johnnie R. continued. "While at the house I noticed some of the owner's valuables were missing. Jewelry, some art work, money and such."

One of the officers walked to the car and began to rummage through it while a second one opened the small trunk. I began to feel sick as I watched him pull several items from within, all of which I recognized. They were the goods which Johnnie R. had taken into the garage the day before. He'd put them there after I'd left the garage. The setup was complete.

"Is this the contraband?" the cop asked.

Johnnie R. walked over to the car, feigning innocence, and after inspecting the goods, confirmed that they'd belonged to Mike. Afterward the cops read the kid his rights. The kid mumbled throughout the entire affair, realizing what was occurring but helpless to stop it. One of the officers called for an ambulance, and we stood for ten minutes awaiting its arrival. As the cops huddled Johnnie R. came close to me and spoke softly.

"You don't believe any of that shit," he said, looking at me helplessly.

The kid was a liar, I knew, but Johnnie R. had cried wolf once too often, and on that evening I knew he was lying. The charge that he'd been involved, sexually, with Charly's brother pushed me beyond belief, yet I knew it was true. It explained everything. As I looked at him squarely, my eyes not leaving his, he knew I believed it. "You set him up, Johnnie R."

"Don't be so goddamned naive, Nick. What I did was necessary," he whispered in anger. "He had it coming, Nick. You know its true."

"It's wrong."

He took a step closer, his expression one of anger blended with supplication. "Perhaps, but it's done. If you speak up I go to jail. Choose between me and the kid." I just shook my head. "You don't believe any of that shit from the kid," he said softly, his voice uneasy. I held his gaze, saying nothing. "He's a liar!"

"I think I do believe him. It all fits now."

Johnnie R. was speechless as he held my gaze, though he visibly made the effort to pull his considerable forces together, and in that short span of time he seemed to be making one last glorious attempt to save the patterns of a fading world and the many dreams informing it. Already, we were bidding farewell to our friendship, though he didn't forfeit the past without a fight. He seemed to be taking my measure, hoping to find that singular weak spot which he might manipulate to his advantage. If only I wouldn't completely believe. If only I would partially doubt. Yes, if only I would agree to keep my mind free of judgment he could save it yet. But I'd heard the kid's words clearly, and as we stood in the dusk light I thought them to be true. He'd been sexually involved with Charly's brother. It was one thing to be a libertine, but it was quite another thing to become involved sexually with the brother of your wife. If that fact alone weren't enough to persuade me there was my love for Charly to carry me well beyond the brink. Moments later, understanding that I was lost to him, he very slowly backed away, closing his eyes as he shook his head from side to side. And I too was speechless, numb with the knowledge that he who I'd loved as a brother was lost to me as an irreducible distance shimmied between us.

When the ambulance arrived we stood in silence as they hustled the kid onto a stretcher. Johnnie R. and I were requested to drive down to the police station for statements, and we remained there for two hours as we each described the evening's events. I corroborated Johnnie R.'s story. Then they let us go, but with the suggestion that we might be called for testimony at a later trial. There was also the unspoken but lingering possibility that Johnnie R. might be prosecuted for assaulting the kid. Then he drove me home, the silence along the way a short bitter accent on the undoing of our friendship as I contemplated the malicious streak from a malevolent man I'd never known. He suddenly seemed foreign and unfamiliar, an echoing memory from another time.

When he dropped me off at my house he turned off the car engine, though he continued looking straight ahead. I remained seated, very anxious, saying nothing. Perhaps thirty seconds passed before he said, "Don't judge me."

"I've said nothing."

"You judge me by your silence."

"There's nothing to say."

"I'll no longer deny the truth to you, Nick. But you can't judge me. You can't understand what I've done unless you've been where I've been."

"And Charly. What about her, Johnnie R.?"

"I can't go into that, Nick. Just don't judge me now. Please. You couldn't possibly understand," he said. He was quiet for the moment, but when I reached for the door handle he said, "In the span of less than a year I've lost two of the closest people in my life. Tonight, you choose to be the third, and now that you elect to end this friendship I have only Charly. I won't lose her, Nick. I promise you that. I'll do anything to keep her. Anything." He very coolly turned to face me, his anger having faded, and I observed the terror of a man backed against a wall. He spoke as if he had nothing to lose, and he was as serious as I'd ever known him to be. "She's not to hear what you've heard tonight."

After I'd left the car and began walking to the porch he opened his car door and stood. "Nick, goddammit, did you hear me?"

"Yes," I said, turning to face him.

He leaned against the top of the car and looked up. "It's forever changed, Nick."

"Yes, I think it is."

"I'm aware that I fucked it up. I'm not so crass to believe otherwise, no matter what you think of this. You've got to believe that."

Words wouldn't come to me.

"It's too bad, too. It could've been good, you and me. We had the world before us. It had slipped right into our hands, and yet we won't share it. I'm sorry for that."

"I'm sorry too, Johnnie R."

"I find that hard to believe, Nick. The tone's all wrong. You know, it's not like you to be so heartless. Your compassion was your greatest virtue," he said very softly.

"And you see where that's gotten me," I replied. "Caught up in this fucked up scheme because I trusted you. You've lied to me from the beginning about nearly everything - your marriage, the reason you brought me here, Mike's problems and now this. You don't need compassion, Johnnie R. You need help. Therapy. A total character overhaul."

"Nick!" he said, his voice cracking. He leaned slightly against the car door and when he didn't speak I took a step toward him.

"Why did you bring me here, Johnnie R.?"

"Because I'm so fucking lonely, Nick," he said, his voice choking.

"We all are, Johnnie R.," I offered weakly.

"I love you, buddy," he said softly and then slipped into the car and drove away.

In the dark I looked up at the stars as he'd done moments before and thought of Johnnie R.'s words, his loneliness. And then I remembered Rilke again. The *First Elegy*. Below the great dark expanse of the night sky, dotted infinitely with the twinkling specks of stars which marked out the inhuman spaces beyond our world, I thought of Rilke's question. So bold. Striking so very hard at the core. *And if I cried, who'd listen to me in those angelic orders?* Indeed, who would do so? Johnnie R.'s loneliness was the monumental Nothing. The consuming night sky wouldn't answer. It would give nothing save for the fear of infinite space. I suddenly felt very weak and small, incredibly lonely myself, as I entered the house.

17

Indianapolis, 1991

Hours had passed in silence as I remembered the kid and thought of Johnnie R.'s earlier question concerning AIDS and guilt and punishment. Difficult emotional work, this - bringing the past to the surface as I watched Johnnie R. slowly die. He was sicker, and getting sicker by the hour. He couldn't eat, and the single attempt to do so ended in a ghastly spectacle of vomiting. Charly stopped by for a short time and left early, but I remained until nine. He came to as I prepared to leave, making me promise to return early the next morning, and as I stepped outside his room I turned when I heard him maneuver in bed. In silence, I watched him attempt to sit up as he looked in my direction with a curious expression, frightened and nearly blind, and then he lay his head on the pillow as I heard him ask in a soft weak voice, "Where did it come from?" Later that evening, while alone in Johnnie R.'s apartment, I read two entries from his journal that gave a partial answer.

* * *

Johnnie R.'s Journal

Entry, July 1991

From where did it come? It is the question a man may ask when he wishes to know the origin of that which shall kill him. They call it the cradle of civilization. The great African continent. From the Valley of the River Omo, those vast ancestral jungles, our evolutionary links clang and clamor toward a beginning. This is the fertile ground of our human, and pre-human, ancestry. It all began here. Somewhere within those bogs and swamps and thick forest shields there were parallel beginnings for other life forms, some complimentary to the human race, others parasitic, still others diametrically opposed to us. Some hypothesize that HIV sprang from here and rippled outwardly. Perhaps, perhaps not. Only Nature's private history book provides the answer. However, we know that HIV has been in Africa for a very long time: Decades? Centuries? Isolated and endemic, it slumbered, lying in wait, patiently stalking time and humanity while awaiting the kill.

And how did it spread? Strictly modern conditions paved the way: changes in lifestyle, social disruptions, modern technology and modern medicine, alterations of the natural environment, modifications in sexual habits. So HIV escaped its original niche, found a medium conducive to transmission and then exponentially reproduced. Was it born of simple mutation? A degenerative evolutionary processes? And I ask by what quirky turn of fate did the awful beast awaken to find its way to my door? By what method has it reached Me? The medium was sex, but what was its raison d'etre? And if perchance it does have an African origin, how might it have escaped the region of, say, Lake Victoria? How did it move through the continent, and then from continent to continent (by plane or boat?) finally reaching the U.S.? How did it reach Indy? Through how many unknowing, vulnerable veins did it course? How many hosts did it utilize in order that it might one day deliver its uniquely lurid form of death to me. How many viral scripts had to be written and rewritten before it had transformed from endemic jungle habitat to urban killer in Indy? It is the great why behind the eternal frightful echoing which is the awakening of the awful beast.

*   *   *

Entry, September 1991

*from **moments***

and I say this
when the rhyme's
done with
so am I
lack of meter
lack of rhyme
are enjambments
of the soul

as frightful
as an intersection
in Mexico
near where
once, years ago,
I laid with a man
who killed me

pushing his dagger in
sweetly at first
then harder
but with a sweet word

then not so sweet at all
just lunging forward
like a poet seeking
the word he cannot find

forward
into me
taking from me
as he gave me death
the memory of
what God used to be
before even that
disappeared
in the bleak light
of a midnight cigarette

18

Indianapolis, 1983

How odd were the newly-defined emotional distances separating Johnnie R. from me after our friendship had come to a crushing halt on that peculiar Sunday evening. We were coldly businesslike at the bank, avoiding each other when possible. He didn't call or drop by my office, nor did he stop by my house. Our lunches ended, as did our week night suppers and weekend romps. The friendship simply evaporated, an old image fading away, all silence and emotional debris, as he transformed from best friend to the husband of the woman I loved, and in return for this modulation, I hoped to take from him his wife.

For months I'd successfully fought my nagging desire for Charly, but as Johnnie R. fell away the single most potent weapon in my battle against my love had been lost, though initially this desire was thwarted for reasons altogether clear. The quixotic remoteness of those August days following my break with Johnnie R. resulted in greater distances from Charly as well. When Johnnie R. vanished, the trio vanished; when the trio vanished so did Charly. True, she occasionally called, but she didn't talk much, particularly if she were calling for Johnnie R. only to find he wasn't there. I volunteered no explanation, and we'd chat for a moment and then she'd say goodnight and another day would pass without seeing her. After a few weeks of such calls coupled with my conspicuous absence from their home, she understood there had been a rift, but there was more in that he was conspicuously absent from his home as well. Week night absences, weekend jaunts. He'd started running around again.

And then one evening Charly called, found Johnnie R. absent and suggested we meet for supper nonetheless. Eventually, there were movies, walks to Broad Ripple, coffee breaks, shopping. We'd meet, eat, see a film and drive home separately, and we didn't discuss Johnnie R. But the threesome didn't crumble for good until a warm evening in early September when I heard a knock at my door and found Charly waiting to be let in. Nearly as surprising as finding her alone on my doorstep was the staggering manner in which she was dressed. She was lovely in her long sleek red dress which hugged her hips and breasts and tiny waist. She wore black heels, gold jewelry and subtle hints of makeup which lightened her eyes and carved out deeper hollows in her cheeks. I stood gawking before she finally asked, tilting her head, "May I come in, Nick?"

"Of course. You surprised me," I managed.

"I'm not interrupting anything?" she asked as she peered in before walking into the room.

"Not at all," I said, still not quite in my element.

"Good. Then I'll make myself at home!"

She'd been drinking. I could smell the faint hint of scotch on her breath when she passed into the living room where I cold better observe the delicious patterns of her body in full light. And then, bingo, a couple of steps behind her came the faint scent of gnawing guilt. My former best friend's ravishing wife had just walked alone into my empty house, and I wanted her badly.

"A drink?"

"I've already had one," she said, stretching with arms above her head. She hesitated a moment and then changed her mind. "Perhaps I'll sip a second small scotch and water. But only if you'll join me."

In the kitchen I was in a daze as I sought the bottle of scotch and tumblers. I wanted Charly to be there, had dared to hope that she might visit without Johnnie R., and at the same time was well aware of the impossibilities as I searched for something to serve with the drinks. There were only crackers and some cheddar cheese, not quite the gourmet touch, but I put both on a hideous looking holiday platter which was the only available dish. When I returned to the living room with the goods, still awkward, I handed her a drink and placed the platter before her.

"Dear God, it's a turkey platter, Nick!"

"It was this or paper plates."

"Do you think you're overcrowding the crackers?" she poked fun. I looked down to find the food nearly lost within the platter's gaudy design as Charly took long sexy strides to the sofa and sat. I joined her and placed the enormous platter on the center cushion between us, my heart pounding as if I were plodding through my first date.

"You're all dressed up. Beautiful!" I cheered her, gulping the drink.

"I rarely do it."

"What's the occasion?" I asked. "Beautiful women haven't exactly been walking in and out of my house on a regular basis."

"Filling up your slow moments with books, it's no wonder," she quipped. "Anyway, I attended one of those awful women's civic group get-togethers. Frankly, I went out of boredom. But my God, I'd forgotten just how dull they can be."

"Well, you're lovely."

"It wasn't much of an effort," she said self-consciously. "I was tired of the monotony in my drawing room. Sometimes you simply have to escape. I mean, one can abide only so much silence." Such was her first public offering that all was not well. Not since the late-night Christmas conversation had she mentioned such loneliness. "Has John been by?" she asked in a nonchalant fashion.

"No, Charly. There's been a rift. We even avoid each other at the bank if we can."

177

"I thought so. He has said nothing, but its obvious there was a break," she offered. "But it's such a pity, Nick. You two are so close. You shouldn't allow what I assume to be professional differences to come between you. Maybe you'd like to discuss it."

"I'd prefer not to, Charly." Of course I couldn't. And professional differences? If she only knew.

She drank from the tumbler and then caught my glance with a sharp eye. "I'm afraid I haven't seen much of my long lost husband this past month either."

I caught the hardened tone at once. "Perhaps the bank," I offered weakly. We both knew it wasn't true.

"That's what he says." Her voice was icy as she slowly let the words fall, a form of subtle lashing out at Johnnie R. Even during the December conversation she hadn't abused him as she offered the cold hard facts without so much as a judgmental remark. Certainly, in the end she'd cried, but they were tears of release rather than tears of anger. But now the tone had changed and she'd been transformed. With those four small words I knew it, and I was both stunned and relieved to hear her utter them. "And there's no need to defend him, Nick. It no longer matters."

"I'm sorry."

"No need to be," she answered, amused, raising her brows for emphasis. For Johnnie R., just then, there was a problem, a very elementary and practical problem. For Charly it no longer mattered whether or not Johnnie R. was at the bank innocently working away or attending a business function or climbing the rungs of the corporate ladder, and it didn't matter because the truth was now a foreign object, unrecognizable after years of abuse. "Another drink?" she asked, handing me the glass.

"Are you hungry?"

"Famished!"

"All I have is pizza. Lot's of pizza."

"Then pizza it is!" she said as she returned my smile.

In the kitchen I placed the pizza in the oven, poured more drinks and played with my guilt. I'd managed to keep it at bay while next to Charly, but while away from her it attacked. It was one thing to silently desire Johnnie R.'s wife; it was another thing altogether to physically prod an infidelity along the way. After the pizza had cooked I hurried back into the living room like a five year old escaping the claws of a monster.

Charly, although a veteran of more than two drinks, still appeared in full control, poised and elegant. I placed the large platter of pizza between us, made a toast and then we chatted between bites of what the box had referred to as a *fresh-frozen treat.* Suddenly all smiles and laughter, carrying on like old friends, I nearly choked when she cavalierly tossed off her heels. And so went my wildly galloping heart. She was captivating with that intangible feminine allure, finessing me at every turn with her fluid movements, her slender body, the fine lines of her delicate neck, those dark intelligent eyes. And beyond the pull of erotic enticement I entertained the idea that we were, perhaps, kindred spirits. Rilke's *companions* again.

The hours passed swiftly, desultory conversation and all, as we were prodded on by the scotch and the mystery of our being together without Johnnie R. The measure of our repose was the ability to banter on about small meaningless things without touching upon the darker feelings concerning him. We talked and laughed past midnight, but then had one drink too many. Charly began to tire, her eyelids drooping as she became quieter. Then she leaned her head back on the sofa to rest.

"I'm done for, Nick. Too late, too old and too much liquor," she said, smiling with her eyes closed. "I'll have to call it a day." She leaned up and sat on the edge of the sofa with her face in her hands and said, "But I'm afraid I'm in no condition to drive."

"I'll take you home," I said.

"No," she said, hesitating a moment, hands on her temples, "No, I don't think so."

I was silent, my heart pounding so goddamned fast that I was shaking. Worse yet, my bowel suddenly announcing total surrender, and I very nearly shit my pants. Every muscle seemed to give way save for my sprinting heart.

"If you don't mind I'd like to sleep on the couch. If it's not a problem."

Those words were too much. My sphincter barely holding tight, a weakened corky projectile atop a warm bottle of champagne, I ran to the can, shouting over my shoulder, "Of course you can!" Ah, the frantic all-too-human biological functions. On the pot, though, as my mind returned to normal in the short span of finishing my frantic, mundane business, I began to play back the love and passion and mystery of the greatest friendship of my life - my life with Johnnie R. and the meaning of a vibrant world only a short memory away - and I debated the confusing issue which was swimming within my mostly-intoxicated head. As a result when I returned to the living room I asked casually, "Will Johnnie R. worry?"

"I don't know. Perhaps."

"Shall I call him?"

"He never called me. In four years he never called me to say where he was or who he was with, Nick," she said. She sat straight up and turned toward me as she added, shrugging, "So I think I'll continue the pattern."

I said nothing more as I searched for sheets and blankets and pillows. In fact, I was thinking only of her, of sharing the small house alone with her for a single night. With the goods in my arms I walked back to the living room to find her lying on her side, legs curled up, resting in the womb position. "Here's a pillow," I offered as I neared the sofa. She didn't answer, and as I stepped closer I saw that she was sleeping. I set the pillow on the floor near the sofa in the event she later awakened, and as I unfolded the blanket I studied her. She'd placed one arm beneath her head for support, and her face seemed to hold a slight smile. Her legs were covered to the knee by her dress, and she'd loosened her belt around her waist. Her black heels remained where they'd landed after she'd kicked them off hours ago. I covered her with two blankets, and she slightly shifted but didn't wake. I stood over her for a long moment while enjoying the uncommon features of her face - the high cheekbones, the slender nose, those lightly accenting brows. Only when she shifted again did I walk to my bedroom where I turned off the light and undressed in the dark, feeling odd as I stripped while Charly slept soundly so few feet away. The same method of undressing, the same habits night after night for nearly thirty years, and with Charly nearby I couldn't help but smile at my uneasiness.

Of course I didn't sleep right away. The tormenting guilt had disappeared somewhere during the course of the evening, but as I lay there, knowing Charly was soundly sleeping, it returned. I thought of Johnnic R. then and wondered if he were up pacing the floors. What was he thinking? How would he react if he knew she were sleeping on the sofa? How angry would he be if he knew I'd not called? These thoughts merged with the late-night noises of the house, the creaks and pops and other settling sounds of an old midwestern bungalow. Somehow, indescribably, the noises seemed different, the old house nearly alive, its innards organic. As the furnace fan turned on I was certain it sounded louder than usual. The refrigerator motor echoed a vibration which seemed more pronounced. The house was animated, yet nothing had changed save for Charly on the sofa. Thoughts of Johnnie R. eventually were lost among the mysteries of that Platonic slumber party, and later, as the furnace droned away and the refrigerator motor quieted, I listened for sounds from the living room. Perhaps she would shift slightly on the sofa, or turn from side to side, maybe sit up. I was all ears in the dark as I remembered that the last time I'd entertained such feelings was as a senior in high school. I remembered a warm spring evening in Mobile when I'd watched the stars from my bedroom windows, total darkness but for the quixotic specks of illusory light, and fantasized the soon-to-be-realized romance of Princeton - and the companion to that romance, an inarticulate anticipation of something wild, inconceivably extraordinary, totally absorbing of mind and body both. Yes, I thought of that evening long ago, smiled to myself in the dark and listened while the formerly lively house noises dissipated into the early hours of the morning as I fell to sleep.

When I woke at seven Charly was gone. I quickly put on my robe and tiptoed into the living room, and when I saw the empty sofa I peered out the window and saw that her car was gone. I sat on the sofa and picked up the pillow which she'd placed on top of the neatly folded blankets and brought it to may face and inhaled, but it offered no scent. As I lay it down I noticed something had fallen from it and onto the floor and found a bookmark nearly hidden beneath the sofa. I picked it up and noted her handwriting on one side: *Thanks for the blanket, the sofa, your friendship. No more melancholia, Nick! - Charly.*

I laughed, and the emptiness disappeared as her voice played in my mind while she uttered the words from the note. I lay down on the couch with my head on the blanket, daydreaming like a kid, and suddenly smelled her fragrance as the aroma which had kept me company most of the evening returned. I reached back and pulled the blanket from under my head and brought it near my face. I inhaled and caught the scent again. Near the frayed edges of the old cotton blanket, where Charly had pulled it close to her neck, the fibers had caught a soft bouquet. I looked at it closely and noticed traces of her makeup along the edges. I touched the smudges with a finger - rouge, lipstick, eye shadow. I inhaled again and then laid the blanket back beneath my head.

I lay there for some moments wondering when she'd left the house. Had she left not long after I'd fallen to sleep, fearing reprisals from Johnnie R.? Did she begin to feel guilty? Did she leave between a catnap and dawn? Perhaps, I thought, she'd written the note and then had scampered away as the first rays of light shot down the hall from the windows in the back of the house. And melancholia? What once had been imagined as a beast's large and fearful imprint, clawed and deeply depressed in the soft brown earth, I suddenly conceived to be much smaller, lighter, subtle and easy, as if a wild bear's heavy unforgiving footprint had been replaced by the soft and small imprint of a tiny bird's finessing foot. A few light indentations popping up here and there and then gone. Melancholia had discarded the muscular and vicious armor of anguish and despair for the light and deceptively harmless simple suit of love. It had temporarily, cunningly, exchanged sentiments. On that peculiar September morning, following many years of noncommittal responses, I'd simply and unequivocally fallen in love.

19

Indianapolis, 1991

Johnnie R.'s Journal

from **hiv**

hiv, can't you see,
it means all the world to me
enter here, oh my dear,
do you think they'll say I'm queer
viral flux, clogging ducts
caused by one too many fucks
biding time, such a crime
then to kill me in my prime
got no drug, for this bug
don'tcha hate a viral thug
retro-high, say goodbye
viral load so high I cry
T-cell rape, foot to nape
slimming down at quite a rate
soar throat here, large node there
what's that in my underwear
first I sneeze, then I wheeze
now I suffer Kaposi's
swollen leg, spit up egg
simple symptoms of the plague
rash on rump, stomach pump
still I had a solid dump
up so late, balding pate
T-cells down to thirty-eight
I won't lie, wanna die
tried and tried but couldn't cry
still it's time, such a crime
bought a casket, so sublime
by and by, soon I'll die
it's okay now, don'tcha cry
'til you know, what I know
ain't no god beyond this show

in which case, stone and lace
quite a thing, the human race

*　*　*

The work of the virus was nearly complete by the end of the following week. It was time for the vigil as Charly and I took turns bedside calling for medication and soothing Johnnie R. He was now blind, and although the pneumonia would kill him - his immune system by then long gone - it wouldn't do so before he began to manifest signs of AIDS dementia. He was often confused, spoke incoherently. He forgot words and occasionally forgot us as his always-sharp mind turned to jelly.

It was during this period, the last week of Johnnie R.'s life, that his father surfaced. Though I hadn't yet seen him during my return to Indy, I'd felt his presence at every turn. He lurked in the background like a stalking virus, ever-present, awaiting the kill. He was, after all, the legal guardian since Johnnie R. and Charly no longer were married. And of course the old man carried a lot of weight with the hospital administration, his bank endowment having funded a hospital wing as evidenced by his name on a large bronze plaque near the entrance. He'd known I was in town from the beginning, and his single visit to the hospital since my arrival had been timed to avoid me. He remained in constant contact with the doctors and staff, however, and it was all very hush hush. To the outside world the *official* story was imminent-death-by-cancer. This was true, of course, in a very limited sense, Kaposi's being one of the laundry list complications Johnnie R. suffered, but the old man wanted the AIDS diagnosis kept quiet. He knew the status of his son's health as well as Charly and I, yet he'd only once peeked in to see the sleeping Johnnie R. as he lay dying.

On a particularly bad afternoon as the wind blistered the city, Charly stopped by the hospital with their son in tow after Johnnie R. had taken a turn for the worse, and since she couldn't bring Ian into Johnnie R.'s room I agreed to watch him in the lounge as she visited. On that afternoon the boy showed absolutely no fear. When I entered the lounge, he didn't think twice about Charly slipping out and down the hall. He was spunky, gutsy, a real terror, and I had trouble focusing his attention. He ransacked the lounge, ran into the hall, shouted at will. My paternal instincts which in the past had occasionally surfaced were of the standard sentimental variety, part of the romantic machinery of a baby boomer somehow severed from the *real world* of fatherhood. I'd had no practice. Did I have within me the proper temperament of the modern parent? Patience, nurturing love, childlike imagination, an appropriate attitude toward punishment? Frankly, I think not, since those instincts, when they did infrequently arise, lingered only momentarily before fading altogether. So as I played baby sitter, those instincts having scurried far away, I was at a loss. As he shouted, a mischievous expression on his face, I realized he was testing me, pushing us both to the edge of boundaries separating his world from mine. Though spanking his little ass did briefly come to mind, I sought alternatives.

I waited for the proper moment, and when he made yet another of his daring passes I quickly grabbed him and lassoed him in. He yelped like a pup as he leered at me, but before he could pout I placed him a vacant wheelchair and swirled him in wide circles around the room. He loved it. He laughed and screamed, grinning broadly, and when I stopped to rest he begged for more. I talked him into a soda, but when we returned to the lounge he urged me to play the game again. I placed him in the chair, and this time I took him down the hall, past the elevators and then back to the lounge. Finally, tired and bored, I stopped and sat in a chair with the kid facing me. As I watched him plead for more, tapping my leg for emphasis, I looked at him squarely. Ah, the intensity of those beautiful blue eyes, his thin brows, the fine delicate line of his nose, that small sensual mouth. It was really too much to bear, observing that younger version of Johnnie R.

"Push me!" he demanded.

"No. You push me!"

"Okay," he said, sliding out of the chair and then tugging my arm to take his place. The kid, like his father, was relentless. To keep him quiet I stood, walked to the wheelchair and then sat with a thud. He tried his luck at pushing me, grunting and groaning, and finally I helped by moving the wheels with my hands. He was nearly hysterical, all playfulness and laughter, as we circled the room. We circled until he was dizzy, and after a rest we circled again. We were both red in the face and breathless when we came to a screeching halt at the feet of Johnnie R.'s old man. He'd obviously received a call as well.

"Grandpa! Grandpa!" the kid yelled as I looked up at the old guy. Ian ran to his grandfather, and I took in the old man. He seemed not to have changed in eight years. He was old then and he was old now, an aging lion sporting the same stoop, the same pinstripe suit, those Thayer blue eyes and the identical white mane of hair. His voice was stronger than ever.

"You're still alive I see," he thundered. He didn't smile, nor offer his hand. One hand remained behind his back as the other rested atop the kid's head.

"You were hoping otherwise?"

"I had thought it possible that the disease of my son might have killed you as well."

He'd worn his ball-buster mask that day, or perhaps, by then, it was a permanent fixture. I said, "Why so?"

"You both were implicated by a young hustler long ago, if you'll remember. The boy who was given jail time following a plea bargain as you and John remained untouched. Surely you remember?"

"He lied."

"Yes, at the time I thought so, and yet he was not lying about John, now was he? So I must assume that he was not lying about you."

"I'm sorry to break the news, Mr. Thayer, but I'm not gay."

"Oh, I fully realize you are enamored of women, Nick. Of *certain* women," he replied. A reference to Charly, no doubt. "But John was enamored of women as well. Bisexuality, they call it."

"What's that word, Grandpa?"

"Nothing important, Ian," he said, patting the boy on the head.

"It doesn't apply to me," I said. "I simply represent the past gone awry, though you disliked me long before my break with your son. I was never your type, your stock, your breed." He glared at me silently. Such depths of malevolence those eyes held. Perhaps that's why I added, "But in the end it's irrelevant that your son is gay."

"Quite relevant!" he retorted, raising his brows. "That's the entire point."

"Then the point's lost to me."

"Undoubtedly," he said, shaking his head. "But let me coax you toward some form of understanding. John has breached the code."

"Fuck."

"What's fuck Grandpa?"

"I demand that you watch your language in the presence of my grandson," he barked. I looked down at Ian. He'd caught the tone of the conversation, and circled his grandfather as we spoke.

"Which code is it, that of banker or that of gentleman?"

"They are one."

Of course he needn't have said more. I knew the score. He came at the issue not from the moral high road, but from a different angle altogether. He made his point clearly. "You don't understand," he said. "I'm far from a religious zealot. The so-called holy rollers are, of course, imbeciles. They lack imagination, education, culture, stock. Still, and this is important, they reach the correct result. I don't invoke their book, nor their creed. Inversion is no more a sin than banking. It is, rather, a breach of the gentleman's code."

"I don't believe this."

"Young man, I'm merely saying that we are not dealing with good or evil here. Instead, you must approach it in terms of nature's way. It is a question of the survival of the fittest. The laws of equilibrium in nature. Homosexuality is a weak link in nature. As a result my son will die."

"You're a very sick man, Mr. Thayer."

"It is a matter of simple indulgence. Gentlemen never indulge. Sexually or otherwise. Socratically speaking, of course. Love of the mean."

"And banking isn't a form of indulgence?" I asked. He obviously disliked that his authority was being questioned. It wasn't something which often occurred. His face reddened a bit, but he wasn't indignant.

"All aspects of my life are performed in moderation, including making money."

"And we certainly know you don't indulge your son."

His face was bright red, and I think I've never seen such hatred as he showed me then. "But I do have my grandson," he said emphatically, adding an artificial smile. He pulled the kid close to him, patting him firmly on the head again. A grab for history. He beseeched the laws of primogeniture. He implored all that the common law had to offer in the way of property rights and familial affections. You understand, the king was on soft ground, and he was angry for it. Eight years earlier the Regent-in-Waiting had been scandalized and then had died. The king's heir, the son, had fallen. The son's son, by virtue of those same invisible laws, was the heir apparent. Hopefully, the boy some day would take the throne. No, what the old man exhibited wasn't love at all. It was simple recognition of History's ineluctable power.

"The heir apparent," I said, glancing at Ian.

"And he shall not be despoiled by the likes of you."

"The times are leaving you behind, Mr. Thayer. In a world rampant with corporate raiders and takeover artists you don't have a chance. You're big, but you're not that big. The boy won't reach sixteen before you're either dead or the bank has been sold. It's nearly the Twenty-first century."

"You're shrewd, but unlearned. Power is something you know nothing about. I'll survive. The bank shall survive. The boy shall survive."

"But perhaps he shall decide to be a dancer, a poet, a waiter."

"He smiled, slits for eyes, and said, "The boy shall be what I want him to be."

"Only if he's within your grasp. There may be other plans."

"You're a fool. Out of your league."

"What do you want?"

"I want you to leave. I never want to see your face again. I never want you to make contact with this family again."

"I'm afraid that's not your call."

"I could easily make it my call," he said casually. "You've no idea, young man."

"No you couldn't, Dad."

We looked over at the door as Charly walked in. Speaking of cold masks. The kid ran to her and she picked him up.

"Please stay out of this, Charlene," the old man said in a softer voice.

"No, you stay out," she said. "You've no right to speak to him that way. He's John's closest friend."

"I have the legal right as his father."

"You have no son, dammit!" The old man jumped as high as I did. The kid whimpered, a nurse ran in and the old man burned in a silent red rage. Charly was all bright red terror. How potent and primeval her power just then. How odd that only moments before the old man had invoked powers much stronger than me, and yet Charly then petitioned a power greater than any of us. She called forth something raw, earthy, vibrant, ancient - the simple power of a mother's love. The force and dominion of the maternal bond, I reflected just then, is perhaps as strong as the unifying force the physicists are still seeking. I watched her carefully, her expression daring the old man to fuck with her. She was a lioness protecting her cub. She'd rip his heart out if she had to.

"Very well," he said, understanding his dilemma at once. "John has stabilized, so I will be leaving." He walked to the door, turned, winked at Ian, and added, "We'll continue this at another time."

He waved and then disappeared altogether, and the three of us stood in silence for a long moment, the kid staring at me and then at Charly and then back at me. Charly rocked the boy casually, and that ancient power of the womb, greater power than history, remained in her voice, only somewhat subdued, as she said, "I'm sorry."

"I'm sorry too. It's none of my affair."

"Yes, it is, Nick. It is, because you came. Because you love him too." I said nothing, my emotions running high. "We're all irritable and tired, Nick, and I need to take Ian home. His father is right, John seems to have stabilized. I think he'll be fine for now."

"I'll call you if there's a problem," I said. She smiled, walked to the door with the boy and then turned and said, "Thank you, Nick." In the hall, the kid kept his eyes on me during the walk back to the elevator. He apparently hadn't decided if I were a good guy or a bad guy, and his face was all mental calculation as it disappeared behind the elevator door.

* * *

But the old man wasn't yet done with me. At Charly's prodding, I slept in the next morning following a late night at Johnnie R.'s side, and I decided to clear my head with a quick run before returning to the hospital. It was nice to run again in Indy, even as the wind whipped up and small crystals of slush crashed against my face, creating little rivulets soon enough absorbed into my turtle neck. Yes, the pounding heart and expanding lungs released the death-vigil tension like the long-delayed unfettering of a long-stifled soul. Something within me seemed to unfurl as the widening breeze pushed me along the gray boulevard of the sleepy city. Such a physical rush to mirror the emotional surge which was the companion to those many memories of eight years past. Back then, before our break, Johnnie R. had run with me a handful of times, and though he wasn't a glider like me but a solid man of some muscular bulk, he kept up as we circled the north side, ending typically with a coffee and juice at an espresso bar near Broadripple. Ah, lovely times. And just as I thought I might just sprout a pair of

187

Daedalus wings and fly away into the gray dimensionless December air, I glanced back to find the source of a low hum nearing me, a stretch limo keeping pace a few feet behind. The mystery occupant, and his desire, didn't remain a mystery for long as the driver pulled up beside me, keeping pace, and a window rolled down to reveal the face of Johnnie R.'s father - a wizened face with a pinkish hue, a salmon-colored flesh born of a close shave and a spattering of cologne. He even went so far as to allow a cordial smile when he said, "Good morning, Nick,"

"Good morning," I answered, picking up speed as if to illustrate the intensity of my purpose. So he's going for a softer approach today, I thought.

"Unforgivingly cold for a run, young man, wouldn't you agree?" he asked, his face only a few feet away as the driver expertly kept pace.

"Refreshing."

"Won't you agree to enter the car for a rest?" he asked, his voice still pleasant enough.

"I'm quite comfortable, thank you. It's the rest that I'm avoiding."

"But I would very much like to speak with you," he pursued, a cold crack in his voice hinting at anger.

Looking over without slowing down, I said, "What is this? Something out of one of Coppola's *Godfather* movies?"

"A formula of gangster films, Nick. This is the real thing. The way I live."

"So I don't need to be concerned that you might have someone rough me up a bit?" I allowed with a smile.

He let loose a deep, gravelly chuckle, clapping his hands with relish as he replied. "Oh, young man, you really don't understand me, do you?"

"Oh, I think I do."

"That's not my style. I haven't in me to do *physical* harm."

"But you can do harm. We both understand that," I replied. I could swear the driver was inching ever closer, a smallish power play on behalf of his boss.

"Let's say I specialize in harms reminiscent of more ethereal qualities. Word of mouth qualities. Career-ending powers. But harm you physically?" he asked, a glint of white visible between his barely-parted lips. "Don't be ridiculous."

I stopped cold, forcing the driver to break. It was amusing watching the old guy's head wobble forward as he attempted to maintain a proper sense of balance, not to mention decorum. The street was empty as I walked forward to stand near the window. "Ah! You'd prefer to watch me squirm metaphysically, then. Perhaps watch my soul wither away."

"I am not a man who embraces metaphysics, Nick. Nor do I believe in the soul."

"But you do believe in evil."

"Why do you suggest that?"

"Johnnie R. once told me that he believed in old-fashioned biblical evil."

"Evil is a relative term describing those unknown factors not within our power to fight."

"As I said."

"Personal attacks never solve underlying points of contention, Nick."

"Yes, but why did you attack me only yesterday at the hospital?"

"A moment of weakness. Please get in."

"I'm sweating. Very wet."

"Really, Nick. A little bit of sweat is harmless. Why, I have gone to the sauna three times a week for thirty years now to sweat with other men. It is healthy. A form of male bonding they call it now in those ridiculous books so entitled. I was doing that before Robert Bly knew how to write mediocre poetry."

"Might tarnish those immaculate seats."

"You have no idea what these seats have seen, or what I have seen in them. Why, in this very limo I sat near John as we rushed him to the hospitable months ago now. He fouled his pants and then vomited blood on me. And then he cried himself wet thereafter. A bit of sweat seems quite harmless in comparison. So please," he said with a softer voice, "Please give me five minutes." I hesitated, still shaking my head in disbelief at his description of Johnnie R, and then I opened the door and climbed in, taking a seat opposite the old man, my back to the driver. How surreal the moment as Bach warmly played in the background to mirror the cozy, computer-controlled seventy-two degrees within. There was tea service set up nearby with a continental breakfast on display. Never, I thought, has so much leather been used for such an odd display of wealth. "What may I serve you?"

I thought, Serve me? Me? He poured two cups of tea and offered one to me. "No thank you."

"Suit yourself," he said, taking a sip. He placed the tea cup on the service tray and then pulled from his suit coat pocket a piece of paper. "I want you to have this."

I accepted it, inspecting it closely. It was a check written on his personal account. Written out to me. One hundred thousand dollars. "What is this?" I asked, leaning forward to give it back.

He waved me off with a grimace as if I were attempting to infect him with something quite disgusting. "If it is not enough I can increase it. Within reason, of course."

"What is this?"

"The money I assume you will be asking for soon enough."

"For what?"

"Why must you force me to say it? Hush money, of course."

"Christ. You're not evil. You're sick," I said, laying it on his lap.

He picked it up and observed it closely, saying, "I had hoped to be able to prove your own homosexuality, in which case I could have forced your exit more efficiently. That is, without the need for this dreadful encounter."

"No, you're evil and sick."

"So crass, wouldn't you agree, for two Princeton men to stoop so low as to play such games as these. But necessary," he said as I reached for the door handle. Not quickly enough, though. The old man locked it just in time. "Yes," he continued, "I could have simply proven your inversion. I believe that is the politically proper term for it."

"Though not gay, Mr. Thayer, right now I wish I were. I wish I were your son's lover, not simply his friend. I'd hold him and kiss him, perhaps make love to him one last time. Then you'd perhaps come to understand the nature of love."

"As I was saying," he continued, seemingly oblivious to my words, "I could have more easily forced your hand. If you had not cooperated I would have had your job at Princeton.

"Fire me?" I laughed.

"Nick, really! Your naivete surprises me. And I prefer the term *mutual departure.*"

"And how might you have achieved this?"

"I have given that university millions since I left. I have the current president's ear. I golf regularly with board members. I would have you out the door by the end of the day."

"And since I'm not tenured," I mused, shaking my head.

"Oh heavens, tenure would not have stopped me. Tenure presumes moral rectitude. I would have come up with an angle."

"Your son is my dearest friend, Mr. Thayer. I love him as a brother, the brother I never had. What is it that so very much disturbs you about this friendship?"

"Sometimes sibling rivalry creates the nastiest of stirs."

"You're deeply troubled by the fact your son is gay. I suggest therapy."

"Bisexual is the correct word."

"I'd like to leave now. Please unlock the door."

"Since I could not prove that you are homosexual, I was forced to dig deeper for something perhaps equally revealing of moral turpitude."

"I've not robbed a bank recently. Certainly not yours."

"Adultery." Ah, there it was at last. The old man was quite resourceful. The consummate poker player. I simply remained silent, waiting for more. "To be more precise, adultery with the wife of my son, your best friend, the brother you never had."

As I sat their in silence, my mind drifting back to those tragic days with Johnnie R. and Charly, I had to give the old man his due. He performed his victory speech without a hint of pride, his voice remaining steady, absolutely no gloating. That was the key to his many years of success: never allow pride to upstage cold reason. Treat it as a business proposition. Play your hand and rake in your winnings without a hint of a smile.

"You're stunned, Nick," he said, reaching for his tea and taking a long, slow slip. "Before terminating Mike I hired a detective for purposes of surveillance. The detective performed admirably, providing me with much more information that I cared to see, frankly. After Mike's death I learned, by way of the surveillance work, that my son might also be gay. I had him watched for months, and sweet Charlene by default. And then you entered the picture. And speaking of pictures, I do have photos. Oh, nothing lascivious. Just a kiss. I received the other lurid details by word of mouth only. Your affair - I believe that is what they still call it - lasted only a few days. I didn't want the details. And it's no longer appropriate to include John, though if he weren't sick I'd do so. He should know the nature of his best friend's interest in the family."

"He does know." The old man didn't exactly shake all over, but I'd caught him unaware. This time he was speechless as he placed the tea cup on the tray. I said, "Apparently your man was sleeping on the job. Have you no idea why I was hospitalized? Johnnie R. discovered my love of Charly. We fought. He won. I lost. I left."

"Then why did you return."

"He called me, asked me to return to help him die. He was lonely. I wanted to come say goodbye, make amends."

"To ask for forgiveness for taking advantage of his wife?"

"No, he forgave me years ago. I came back so that I might remember what it is to love someone intensely."

"So you admit that you love her."

"I was referring to your son."

"Men don't love each other, Nick. They simply abide each the company of the other."

"I'm sure you believe that, but you're badly mistaken, Mr. Thayer. Men who fear love can love no one, man or woman. But that's beside the point. I returned to see off the best friend of my life, and I'll not leave until he dies. I'm not here for Charly."

I reached for the door again."

"Perhaps you have other designs," he said. "For instance, her money."

"I'm not here for money either, though I'm beginning to understand the dynamics here. Freudian projection. Since money is the single commodity you do understand and desire, you assume my desire equals yours. But it doesn't, and I don't want it."

"Ridiculous ," he said, anger rising in his voice. "Money does matter, and you are not wealthy. You're worth very little. I know these things."

"Why do I frighten you?"

191

"Young man I do not frighten."

"Ah, yes, heart of stone."

"I want you away from her."

"I told you that I'm not here for her. I'm here to mourn the loss of her husband."

"Allow me to be more precise. I would consider it a crime if you were to attempt to remain here to marry Charlene following the death of my son."

"Charly is a friend, nothing more."

"And I want it to stay that way," he said. "But let us get to the point. I do not want my grandson sullied by you."

"Ah, back to the heir again and the laws of primogeniture."

"Precisely. I want you away from my heir, my bank, my city, my life."

"Keep your money and let me out."

"Leave now, Nick. With the money. Be gone. It is best."

With this the old man unlocked the door. I reached forward to open it, and as I did so he grabbed my arm and offered the check to me once again, silently. I shook my head in amusement, not, as it turns out, due to his persistence but rather due to the fact that they had returned me to Johnnie R.'s apartment. He was efficient if nothing else. "In the movies," I said as I opened the door, "when they do this they always return you to the spot where they picked you up. That is, if they don't kill you."

"In this manner you might pack your bags all the more quickly."

"I won't be leaving, Mr. Thayer. I'll be at the hospital. And I'll be with him when he dies. If I'm not mistaken, Charly will see to that." And she did.

*   *   *

Johnnie R.'s Journal

from **Elegy for Charly**

As to the other thing, the thing with Nick,
you were merely human, lovably so,
and who could have known his visit
to us would have created such unusual
energies, such force fields of desire,
leading inevitably to that tragic end?
I couldn't have foreseen it, and I'm
the one who invited him after all.
No regrets, here, Charly. None.
There is nothing to forgive, for there
is no judgment to enforce, only a recognition

of our humanity. Love is forgiveness.

* * *

I returned to Johnnie R.'s room later that day and found him awake. He appeared to be just hanging on. His blindness had left him depressed and frightened, and he didn't even turn his head to follow my footsteps as I walked to his bed. He breathed in shallow little spurts. His chest moved imperceptibly. He'd been crying.

"What can I get for you?"

"New blood?" he tried to humor me.

"The tube?"

"No. I've got a better idea," he said. He spoke so softly I had to lean close to hear him. "Promise me."

"What?"

"That you forgive me."

"There's nothing to forgive."

"I forgive you," he said. "Say it."

"I forgive you."

"I love you," he said.

"And I love you, Johnnie R."

"Thank you, Nick," he said in a broken voice. "And, Nick. Get together with Charly."

"Johnnie R., this isn't the Home Shopping Club."

"No, it's your best friend talking. Just think about it."

Then the light went out again. Here one moment, gone the next. Once again he'd come to, revealing a heightened sense of awareness only to quickly fade. That's how his days were structured now. There were moments of lucidity regarding the past, his present dilemma, his hope for the future. It was good to see the light shine through, but it was awful to watch it fade into the dullness of dementia. Moments later, he escaped me once again, and I turned on the tube. The nurses entered and left, Johnnie R. dozed and I kept vigil near his bed. And as evening came, the memories scurried back yet again. As the oxygen hissed in the background and Johnnie R. turned restlessly in the bed, I thought of why he'd made his peculiar request. And so returned the early autumn of nineteen eighty-three.

20

Indianapolis, 1983

On the morning of Charly's departure from my living room sofa, her freshly written note hidden away, I sauntered through my department in such exuberant fashion that even Gretel, the stoic secretary, noticed the change as I walked by her desk. Whistling and grinning, I threw her a wink. She glanced back, astonished. But I couldn't contain myself while evading the most obvious questions and pressing problems: What indeed had occurred between Charly and me the evening before? How could I presume that she might feel the same way? How dare I interpret the loneliness of my best friend's wife as a protestation of love, or lust! Instead, I dove into my job with abandon. I hadn't known such energy since my days at Princeton, nor such eagerness since that starlit southern kid of long ago awaited the incomprehensible romance of pure possibility as he prepared to leave Mobile.

This mood began to fray and frazzle as the morning wore on, however, and when the lunch hour neared I found myself squirming in my chair. By the end of lunch, thinking of her no longer seemed enough. I needed her voice. I returned to my office sooner than usual intent upon calling her, but for a second time I delayed and then hung up. I hesitated off and on throughout the afternoon as I drew the courage to call and then lost it. By three in the afternoon, having done nothing but stew over her, I was a wreck. I couldn't see her; I couldn't call her; I couldn't concentrate.

That evening I pulled a chair up to the living room windows and tried to read, all the while listening for signs of Charly. I held out hope that she might return, though she never came. And of course I couldn't sleep. For hours I lay awake, and my mind wouldn't release the impressions from the evening before - the red dress, her soft face, the tiny fine hair on the back of her neck. I scrolled up and down her body as I revisited her calm eyes, the thin nose, those sensual lips. I rekindled the sexual fire as I visualized her firm breasts, the small waist wrapped by the black belt, her inviting hips. I followed the shape of her legs at the calf and the slow slender curve from knee to ankle, remembering how she heaved her heels across the room with a burst of laughter and a sip of her drink. Yes, it was all there, the gorgeous body, the magnificent face, the elegant feminine features. Her laughter, her voice. For the remainder of the week that unnerving pattern continued. I awoke thinking of Charly. I remained distracted while at the office. I drove slowly by her house after leaving the bank. I waited for her to return as I ate before the front windows. I slept fitfully.

Funny, when I awoke on Saturday this emotional battle seemed to have ended. I drove through the city while running my usual weekend errands, buying groceries, running to the hardware store, picking up dry cleaning, driving through the car wash. I visited an auto store, the mall, even a flea market. And by evening, following an entire day wasted within the mire of the widening consumers' trenches, I found that my desire for Charly was no longer finessed by the trawling guilt associated with Johnnie R. With Johnnie R. already lost to me, what more did I have to lose? The possibility that she might react with horror when she found that her husband's best friend was in love with her seemed better than the alternative: doing nothing while lying in wait for that which would never come. Realizing that Charly wasn't going to return unless I forced the issue, and perhaps not then, I decided to act; as I slid between the cold sheets that night I knew my duty, and for the first time in days I slept peacefully with the thought that I would see her the following day.

On Sunday, I showered, dressed, ate breakfast and skimmed through the paper, eventually sitting and watching the sunlight play with the steeple in the distance. I'd seek her out there. By eleven-thirty I could wait no longer and left the house and drove the few blocks to her church. I turned into one of the parking lots, and on the horseshoe drive bordering Meridian I spotted her car and parked nearby. "Johnnie R. be damned!" I yelled as I waited for the service to end, and end it soon did as the congregation emerged and Charly came walking toward the car. Initially she didn't notice me, but as she gained on the car with her fine long feminine strides she looked up from the walk and spotted me. I waved to her. Startled, she stopped in mid-stride.

"Shocked?" I asked. "Is it the sermon or me?"

"Nick! What a surprise," she said, forcing a smile.

"I'm not often seen in these environs."

"We've had greater surprises, believe me," she said. Gaining her composure, she walked around her car and to my open window.

"What brings you here?" she asked, back to normal.

"You," I said candidly, deciding not to play games. She looked down and away. "I didn't hear you leave the house a few days back. I wanted to make sure you were okay."

"Thanks. I'm fine," she said without emotion. She nervously scraped one heel against the asphalt as she crossed her arms.

"Since I'm out why don't we grab a bite to eat," I suggested.

"I should be getting home."

"Or we could just talk," I said quickly.

She glanced at her watch but wouldn't look me straight in the face. She placed her heels together but kept her arms crossed. She looked up, taking in the rays, and then glanced up Meridian. She waved to friends in the distance, hugged herself tightly as if she were cold. Finally, she caught my eye and smiled. "Okay. For a short while."

"How about University Park?"

"That's fine. I'll follow," she answered, glancing again at her watch.

What was she thinking as she followed me south on Meridian? What were her feelings toward me? Did she perceive my attraction for what it was, or did she feel I was just another lonely guy out for a hustle? And her husband's best friend, for Christ's sake! These questions continued until we parked and I jumped from my car and walked to hers. I opened her door and laughed, saying, "One of us is inappropriately dressed."

"I wish I were the one wearing the jeans right now," she said as we walked toward a bench near the fountain. .

"Would you rather sit in the car?"

"The bench is fine."

We were alone in the little park as the fountain spewed and the water nymphs danced around the basin. The sun was soothing, but the breeze from the north was cool. "I was worried about you," I said after we'd sat. She shifted slightly but didn't move away. "You were so quiet that I didn't hear you leave."

"I didn't want to wake you," she said, hesitant. She looked away and then back at me. "Did you find my note?"

"Yes. I got a kick out of it."

"Thanks for taking me in. Obviously, I wasn't in the best of shape," she said, slightly smiling. She was distant, a far cry from the woman of verve and grit who'd slept on my sofa. She was uneasy and anxious, her speech still forced.

"I wish you'd called," I blurted out.

She hesitated before answering, her smile disappearing altogether. "I didn't think it was appropriate."

"Was there trouble with Johnnie R.?"

"A bit, yes. But he seems to be over it now," she answered. "He's very distant lately. He probably hasn't given the incident a second thought."

"Did you tell him you slept on the sofa?"

"I told him I stayed with a girlfriend. Whether he believes me or not I can't say. We didn't discuss it."

"Beautiful day. A hint of autumn," I suggested, trying to relax her.

"I love the park," she said, leaning back on the bench. She smiled when she added, "Did I tell you about the picnics we had here?"

"Yes you did," I said. I hesitated a moment and then decided to go for it. "I thought you might come back, Charly."

"I've been busy."

"I enjoyed our evening together."

"I was lonely. I shouldn't have come. I'm sorry," she said, leaning forward to sit on the edge of the bench. She placed her fingers on her temples and rubbed gently.

"No. I'm glad you did. You saw that I was lonely too."

"It's not good, Nick," she said softly, taking her hands away from her face. She looked at me squarely, holding my gaze.

"Do you love him?" I asked. She shifted on the bench and then looked out into the open spaces of the mall to the north where we could see the bright outlines of the war memorial and the obelisk and the library further beyond The church crowd traffic was picking up on Meridian. Still, we were alone in the park, and it was due to that isolation that I was able to say what I'd wanted to express for months. It no longer seemed difficult, nor wrong. "I love you."

"No, please," she said, quickly standing. Her arms were wrapped tightly about her, and she tilted her head back, eyes closed. I stood too, though I didn't walk to her.

"You've known for some time, Charly. I love you."

"Nick, it's impossible," she said in a soft voice, taking a few steps toward the fountain before stopping, her back to me. I watched her from behind for some moments as she regained her composure. Yes, it was impossible, but I couldn't let go. I stepped forward and touched her arm lightly from behind.

"I'm sorry, Charly." She didn't move. I took her other arm as well. "But I love you."

She shook herself free, and without uttering a word she began to walk quickly toward her car. I didn't move immediately, but as she picked up the pace I ran after her. "Don't follow me, Nick. Please!" she shouted when she reached her car. I stopped and watched her fumble with her keys, drop them and then attempt to unlock the car again.

"Dammit, do you love him?" I shouted as she opened the car door. She closed the door quickly and started the engine, though she didn't drive away immediately. She was crying. I began to walk toward her car, but as I neared she looked up, shook her head and drove off. I stood there for a long time watching her car disappear into the traffic and then walked for an hour along the mall. I had no desire to return home, dreading the silence I'd find there. No, I preferred congested Meridian and its street noise just then. I needed the cold brisk air, the noises of the city, the bright warm sun. And later, when I did return to my car, I drove for most of the afternoon, returning home after dusk. There, I sat in the chair near the western windows and thought of how I'd bungled my stay in Indy beyond repair.

The following week I made a few phone calls back East to check on job opportunities. Chaos was everywhere; I had to get out. I couldn't remain at the bank with Johnnie R. Charly was lost to me. Staying was futile. So I waited for word about job prospects as the week drifted on, a vacancy surrounding me as deeply disturbing as the fine gray void of an overcast prairie afternoon, depthless clouds and all.

On Sunday, the drapes remained closed; I wanted not so much as a glimpse of the damnable steeple. But the claustrophobia returned (would Burton have described this as *Solitude-Melancholy*?) and I decided to spend another day in the car, perhaps drive old country roads as I took soundings of the rustic prairie spirit, losing myself to the isolated embrace of provincial midwestern life. Solitude, upper case Nature, Rousseau's challenge. I poured coffee into a thermos and grabbed a stash of cookies, and with my jacket on and my hands full, not three feet from door, I heard a knock. There was a deep wrenching in my gut as I walked to the door after the second knock, set down the thermos and bag and then opened it to find Charly standing alone on the porch. She'd come directly from the church, flawlessly dressed. I studied her eyes, the flush of her cheeks, the trembling of her hands. And in the breeze pushing through the door I heard a fragile little ditty scored by the chords of loneliness. She'd made the decision to come, and with that resolution she'd left behind the battered innocence which hadn't entirely escaped her throughout the years of marital turmoil with Johnnie R. I opened the screen door to let her in.

"I'm sorry," I managed to say before Charly walked close and put a finger to my lips. Only for a moment did she keep it there, long enough to create the hush she desired. I held her gaze as she quieted me. She said nothing. She placed her arms lightly around my waist, her head resting on my shoulder, and I could feel her tremble. I wrapped my arms around her tightly. Neither of us spoke. I simply listened to her soft breathing, felt her chest expand and contract, smelled the scent of her perfume, saw the deep autumn sheen of her thick clean hair. All the while there was that silky breeze playing its tune and the shadows cast from the leafless trees. Nature, I thought, would have to console Herself.

She loosened my hold and walked me to the bedroom where we remained until after dusk, and in that short span of time the wacky world had changed again. First with her strong gaze on the porch, then with the slight finger to my lips and finally with her warm slender body next to mine. As she undressed in the bedroom, I softly touched her soft perfumed skin, a moist sheath of hope, and when she in turn pushed her hands along the lines of my body she sent me off. She lay naked on the bed wrapped loosely in the sheets as I finished undressing, and when I pulled back the linens to find her flushed and ready she lead me by the hand and wrapped me in with her. I held her for a long while, stealing kisses, daring to touch, slowly moving along the fine afternoon silhouette of her body as my lips scampered along the sweet hollows and the moist earthiness there. With her fine deep feminine odor filling the air, she pulled me atop and kissed me hungrily. Then I dove into her, hard and clean and full, and we fucked wildly and temperately in turn.

Later, resting, I tried to speak, but each time I did so she placed a forbidding finger upon my lips. And each time I obeyed, implicitly agreeing that all I might desire to communicate could be delivered with a kiss, a hug, the soft easy stroke down the length of her back or the easy rhythm of my cock within her. And we were content in our silence as I played with her delicate neck and the fine softness of her hair. She rested on my arm as we watched the afternoon shadows slowly pass from wall to wall, moving solemnly across the cold hard wood floor. The shadows slowly finessed the lingering patches of light on the walls, melding into the larger cape of darkness, the twilight. But this nearly funereal passage was lightened when from beneath the comforter I touched her softly, cuddling and gathering her warmth into mine. We dozed off more than once, our damp bodies together, and how beautiful it was to find the surprise of Charly in my arms as the dreams slid away. Twice more I brought her wildly awake, entering her with a frenzy, and in the cool casual darkness of dusk we dozed a final time as she rested her head on my chest.

After dusk I crept out of bed long enough to retrieve the thermos full of hot coffee, and we ate the cookies and drank coffee from the single cup which was the thermos lid. As the crumbs escaped and fell onto my chest Charly vacuumed them with her teasing lips, and I in turn explored her breasts to see what droppings I might find. Afterward, I pulled her close, the cookies and coffee long gone, and we made love a final time, shuddering deliciously, and Charly hugged me tightly and rose from the bed as the street light cast its eery glow, creating new shadows out of the darkness.

She stood near me as she dressed, close enough to touch, and I watched as she slipped into the lovely clothes she'd worn to church. I wondered then what thoughts she might have entertained that morning as she'd sat on the uncushioned pew? What emotions had splayed her distracted mind with the passage of that awful hour? Did she ponder the possibility of driving to my house and lying in my bed? Did she know as she awoke that she would make love to me? Had she grappled with such thoughts all week? These were my unspoken questions as she placed each delicate item of clothing on the wonderful silhouette which moved through the darkness of the room.

Watching her prepare to leave I asked no questions; I knew she would return. I put on my robe and walked her to the door where we embraced a final time. As she opened the door I nearly broke the silence, but before I could utter the words she reached up again and placed a finger on my lips. I took her hand and kissed it, whispering, "Thank you," and when the door closed I returned to the bedroom and slept until morning.

On Monday afternoon I rushed home from the office hoping to find Charly at my front door. All day long I'd imagined finding her in the drive and taking her to me, walking hand in hand into the house and lying on the sofa without saying a word. I dreamt of going to bed with her again and crawling from bed wild and wet and worn as we shared a long hot shower and then cooked dinner together. I wanted to sit and talk, listen to music, chatter on about absolutely nothing at all. Instead, I ate supper alone, and waited. I sat on the porch while looking at the moon, but by ten I realized she wasn't going to show. Moments later I entered the house, turned off the lights and sat in the dark. I peered back out at the moon from my chair, and then found the steeple in the distance as I vacillated between anger and remorse. But there was no more guilt; my need was greater than my guilt, well beyond the threshold of regret.

Much later, as I lay in bed beyond midnight, a more immediately absorbing emotion surfaced as my thoughts took an obsessive turn. The raw nerve of irreversible jealousy had been pinched as I grappled with the fact that Charly was not my own. Yes, I burned with a raging jealousy, the product of the twisted midnight meanderings of an uneasy mind. Eaten by hostility, a blazing fury, I became bitter at the thought of nothing more than the possibility that Johnnie R. might be playing the role of husband to his exquisite wife. Yes, a simple question and its addendum arose. Was Charly sleeping alone, and if not, was Johnnie R. touching her?

This frame of mind was cast aside on the following evening when Charly returned. At dusk she pulled into my drive and knocked at my door, wearing faded jeans and a light jacket. She held me tightly when I closed the door, and unlike the encounter two evenings earlier we sat on the sofa and talked openly without trouble or fear. We went out for a quick dinner, and when we returned we drank wine and lay on the sofa. Later yet, I led her once again to my bedroom where we placed the wine glasses on the bed stands and then made love. Though I was hungry for her, we went at it slowly as I explored her body, all freshness and symmetry. Call it Pythagorean love-making. I touched her carefully, almost cautiously, a woman of such internal delicacy, and even the ravenous chaos of orgasm brought nothing but a strangely protective thrust, a cautious sexual reply, the easy and tender rhythm of love. We lay quiet in the bed for another hour, talking little, sipping the wine, and the silence was good, as was the somber flavor of the soft, mellow cadence of our love. She nourished me, completely, and as she came, finding her orgasm with a sing-song voice, a wonderful playful whimper, I said goodbye to the dissolving image of a kid lost within the humid confines of the flatlands near Mobile. Only somewhat drained by the play of our sexual appetites, we rose at midnight and she left me with silence and a kiss.

I spent the following evening alone once again, and as I'd done two evenings earlier, I entered the house and prepared my supper in a blind fury and then sat in the living room darkness steeped in a blustery rage. As my jealousy gained strength I obsessed over the possibility of Johnnie R.'s touching Charly sexually, exerting his marital rights, picking up where I'd left off. And later, in bed, I became stormier as pondered whether she were happily relenting to his desire. I cast about in bed, stewing over the imagined possibility that she was making love to both of us, a woman of great appetites, insatiable desires. I boiled and fumed, several times leaving the bed and walking the post-midnight floors. I cursed the fates and their ambiguous gifts - the two closest friends of my life - and it was at dawn that I stormed out of bed and made the decision to confront her when she returned. I'd force her to make a decision. I badly wanted her for my own.

*   *   *

What is it in a man which tempts him to take more than he may have? What exceptional power requires him to possess another human being only for himself? Which of those uncommon, hidden, exacting emotions demands total control? And once the desire to do so, to control the loved one, has been made manifest, what blinding influence intervenes which prohibits him from discerning the truth and recognizing its imminent shattering results? I asked these questions of myself only much later, long after I'd left Indianapolis, but I've occasionally reflected back on how my stay in Indy might have differed had I asked them during that unusual autumn as the cool air swept over the prairie.

Looking back, I wasn't totally blind to the lessons in human behavior then being taught, but nor was I able to discern the finer elements of Descartes message when he said:

> *Jealousy is a species of fear which is related to the desire we have to preserve to ourselves the possession of some thing; and it does not so much proceed from the strength of the reasons that suggest the possibility of our losing that good, as from the high estimation in which we hold it ...*

I didn't attempt to analyze the covetousness that pulled me through those last days in Indy, but oh how easily I remember the fears I entertained at the time. A quote from Ovid came to me even then, a bit of classical literature recalled from my Princeton days:

> *No pleasure is unalloyed: Some trouble*
> *ever intrudes upon our happiness.*

I wouldn't say I entertained a perpetual state of paranoia during those few days in Indianapolis with Charly as my lover, but I greatly feared losing her once she'd shared my bed. Every moment she spent away from me allowed her to change her mind and return to Johnnie R. So although I perceived the impossibility of continuing the relationship, the tragedy for me was the fact that I unwittingly pushed her away, an enigma in the mystery of love.

At the time I conveniently pointed to Talbott Street as the direct reason for the failure, as if an inanimate ghetto bar could control a decision or mold a fate. The rationale was this. Had Talbott Street not existed there wouldn't have been a final scene played out there, and all would have been well. This false association contained the virtue of easy redress and worked quite well for a time, but it prevented me from seeking the answers from within and avoided the final truth that Talbott Streets do exist, shall always exist, though under ever-changing guises, and that in the final analysis it isn't the scene where the action is played out but the frame of mind brought to bear which seals our fates.

Certainly, I knew the score. I hadn't fallen into a trap not of my understanding; the facts were out on the table. I knew the history of those unstable alliances creating the infamous triangle, and I couldn't beg to plead innocence. I'd freely made a choice, and Charly herself had walked through my hopeful door quite freely. She'd never once implied, much less promised, that she would leave Johnnie R., but I easily convinced myself that justice was on my side. After all, Johnnie R. had whored around for years, and he'd topped it off, so to speak, by making it with Charly's younger brother. With this secret I lay claim to fairness and truth and equity in love. Oh how naive and self-righteous I was while so very deeply in love. Oh how much I needed to deceive myself in order that I might deceive Johnnie R.

It wasn't enough to look deeply into Charly's lovely eyes and recognize her affection for me. Once she'd climbed into my waiting bed I couldn't afford to be gallant in love. Those lovely moments spent with her in my bed spoiled me like an only child. Her divided allegiance tore at me. That's why I became demanding of her time, uncaring of her delicate position, selfish in my concern for my own feelings. That's when I allowed that gnawing jealousy and parasitical anger to envelop me. Blinded, I was confident that she'd choose me over Johnnie R. She was in love with me, I told myself. She'd knocked on my door. She'd entered of her own will. She'd stayed. So when she returned on Friday evening my mind was made up. Again, she came to my door without warning just after dusk. I took her to me. We sat and talked, drank wine, made love, left for dinner. Back at the house we undressed hurriedly and fucked intensely like young desperate hungry teenagers. We rested and glowed, chatting easily arm in arm, and around eleven, as she made the motions of leaving, I confronted her.

"Dammit, why must you leave?" I asked, standing naked before her as she gathered her things.

"Nick?" she said softly, trying to ease me with a smile. She walked to me quickly and planted a quick kiss on my cheek, and just as quickly she casually turned away to see if she'd forgotten anything in her preparations to leave. At the time this seemed an uncaring gesture, quite cavalier, and it made me all the angrier.

"Are you sleeping with him?"

"Nick, don't do this," she pleaded, holding my gaze for a moment and then looking away.

"Are you?" I persisted, taking a step back and putting on my robe.

"I'm leaving," she said.

She walked briskly by me and to the door, but my ire was up and I refused to back down. I beat her to the door and stood against it. "Are you going to leave him?"

"Nick?" she said my name again with a question, softly.

"Are you going to leave him?"

She said nothing, turning to stand with her back to me. I could see her trembling. She was crying. I felt for her then, badly, and yet, for the moment, just a moment, a little sliver of time, my anger was stronger than my pity. I needed to know. "You're really unable to make a decision, aren't you?"

"Why must you do this?" she answered, turning and taking a step back.

"Because I love you, dammit!"

"It's much more involved than that, Nick. It's much more confusing. Please give me time to think," she said, her eyes on the door, hopeful that I'd move.

"You're afraid to leave the security arrangement he offers," I announced matter-of-factly.

"Don't be a bastard, Nick."

"Who's the bastard, Charly?" I slammed the wall with an open hand. "Johnnie R.'s the one who's pimped you over all these years. I ask you, who's the bastard?"

"You've no right. That's for me to decide, not you!" she said, tears welling in her eyes again.

"I have a right because I'm your lover, Charly. Because I love you," I answered softly, trying to diffuse my own anger.

"Then you'll step aside and let me by," she replied, tears on her cheeks.

"I love you."

"Please!" she nearly shouted, turning her back to me once again. Her voice broke, and it was of the tenor of regret. Several minutes passed with the silence broken occasionally by the whimpers she tried to suppress. Moments later I walked to her and lay my hands on her shoulders. She was warm, her body still shaking. Guiltily, I hugged her, kissed her head, buried my face in her hair, but she seemed distant from me just then, wrapped in thoughts which spoke of change and regret as she remained with her back to me.

"I love you, Charly. I've never loved like this. I need you," I said, hugging her from behind. I regretted making a scene.

"Nick, don't do this, please."

From behind I kissed her on the cheek. She turned and held my gaze for a moment, wiping her eyes. She took a step forward, hesitated, and then opened the door and walked out. When she didn't look back as she reached the car, in a hushed voice, I said, "Please come back tomorrow."

And she did return on Saturday, but she returned changed. Oh, certainly not greatly changed. It was a change of nuances, a transformation of subtle degrees, small deviations, intricate variations on a theme. Modifications in a relationship sometimes occur in the form of small acts and deeds, the vagueness of languishing love. They come, for example, in the form of a kiss which lasts not quite as long as the one before, an uncertain hesitancy suddenly present which was never previously noticed. It is as if a small vacant space, a nothingness, separates the before and after, and you're helpless to transform it or turn it away. These changes also manifest themselves in the short strange lulls in conversation which never presented in earlier times. You both sit in silence, and quickly an unusual awkwardness jumps out before you, cavorts before your eyes, a mad puppet dance upon the stage of love. The resulting mood contains a mixture of embarrassment and sadness, for life is changing, as is your love. These small changes cunningly feed upon the energy of intimacy, and once that fuel has burned away all that remains are the cool, newfound spaces between you and your lover. Also, they play with your mind, these little goblins of lost love, by convincing you that the carnal act of sexual intercourse has begun to take on the heavy mask of pure lust, only somewhat present in the beginning, yet perceptibly so, and the lust inhibits the softer side of love-making as that emotion begins to dominate the earlier aspects of love: hope, charity, pity, concern, sacrifice. The kisses during the act are hungrier, yet they are also less caring. The orgasm, once a tool of both the body and the spirit, begins to spit out both suppressed anger and powerful, ambiguous cross desires. The after-glow is not as mutually satisfactory as it once was, briefer, less giving of the energies which make the love stronger. Yes, the spaces crop up and widen like a late-night yawn, and in the little things you perceive a change. That is what I found when Charly returned the following afternoon. I feared the resulting void which I knew awaited me on the other side, immeasurable distances erupting where there was none.

I still remember that as I arose on Saturday the textures within the house seemed thinner and cooler, taking from autumn the drier, crisper air. Maybe it was only the placement of the morning shadows upon the walls and floor or the refracted glare in the seasonal slant of the sun in the southern sky. Perhaps it was only the melancholy hints of shorter cooler days or the first scents of autumn or the echoing sounds within the mild breeze. But it was there and it was palpable as I dressed and walked to the living room where I opened the drapes and gazed at the clean lines of the steeple in the vague distance.

Charly arrived in the late afternoon, Johnnie R. apparently out of town while cavorting in the great capitalist jungle. She was lovely, quite made up and expensively dressed, touched here and there with gold and diamonds. I held her for a long while and then apologized for the scene of the day before. She kissed me lightly on the cheek, but her eyes didn't rest long on mine. The casual glance lacked warmth and intimacy. It was a defensive glance, thin and isolated. Yes, I saw a change, a slight and subtle difference, and as she sat on the sofa sipping wine she seemed a bit removed. She was loving, but as she touched me she seemed more reserved in her affection. She was caring, yet less responsive. When we later made love she participated as if she were doing so due to habit rather than desire, and such were the after-shocks from the tremors of the evening before. These were the original spaces of exaggerated distance which grew between us, and as I walked from the bed to the kitchen for more wine an internal alarm sounded as I imagined the cocoon of immeasurable space growing more prominent and boldly defined.

Later, we rose from the bed and sat on the porch where she was very quiet and the sunset seemed to parody the growing space between us. As the sun fell beneath the tree line, a violet glow beyond the tree tops, I coaxed Charly to join me in a short walk, but I couldn't bring her to talk. When we returned to the house she seemed irritable, her moodiness surprising me as she snapped, "Not again, Nick," when I suggested a restaurant for dinner. I sat for another half-hour mulling over the strange flavor of the day - vacancy, apprehension, isolation, discomfort - and when Charly finally made a dinner suggestion I immediately agreed, hoping for a reprieve from her capricious mood. We ate late, ordering a bottle of wine before the meal, and Charly drank it rapidly, suggesting that we order a second bottle not long into the meal.

"Charly, we've had enough."

"I'm a big girl, Nick, and I'd like another bottle," she replied, scanning the room for the waiter.

"But I don't, and you can't drink it alone."

"Then I'll have another glass," she said curtly, raising her hand for the waiter. She ordered the wine, and within twenty minutes, our meal complete, she ordered yet another glass. I simply drank coffee as I uncomfortably watched her slowly get drunk. She was somewhere beyond me by then, and I couldn't quite bridge the distance between us. But near eleven, as we prepared to leave the restaurant, she perked up, and outside, as we reached the car, she said, "Let's dance!"

"What?" I asked, unprepared for both her sudden uneasy smile and her unusual change in mood.

"Come on, Nick. Let's dance."

"I'm not up to it."

"Don't poop out on me," she said, rolling down her window and looking out.

Though I was growing angry, it was useless to barb with her. After the wine she'd consumed it would have been a losing battle, so I relented. We drove north on Meridian Street from the downtown restaurant, and as we neared Twenty-second Street she said, "Turn here, Nick."

"You're not serious," I answered, slowing down. I hadn't turned off Twenty-second since Johnnie R. and I had visited Talbott Street nearly a year ago.

"Yes. I'm quite serious."

"Why?"

"I've always wanted to go in," she said casually. "I've obsessed over it for years, Nick. I've stared for hours at its garish marquee, and now I'd like to see the interior."

Why was it that I then thought, She'll be gone tomorrow? And the farewell song? Funny that it should all come down to where it had nearly begun, to where so much had occurred before I'd arrived in their city. The old ghetto bar, that uneasy melange of mystery and discontent. The great exeunt. It already had served such a wide variety of purposes: a place to come to for Johnnie R.; the kid's playground; Charly's obsession; the deathbed of her brother. Ah, Talbott Street. How fitting that she would want to enter there so that she might help to prepare an ironic and fitting end to my stay.

I knew at once that she'd planned the excursion from the beginning, the booze only one of the many energies needed to push us there. So I turned onto Twenty-second and drove past Pennsylvania, stopping at the corner of Talbott Avenue where the marquee at Talbott Street lit the sidewalks with its gaudy, bright colors while announcing in bold, flashing neon the ubiquitous schedule of events. The surroundings were as dark and dirty and foreboding as I'd remembered them. The avenue seemed not to have changed in the least since my December visit as the breeze swept debris about the street and walks. Yes, the ghetto still served up an abundance of broken promises, and at the edge of the cool evening there was a gnawing fear of crime hovering about us. Still, I turned onto Talbott Avenue and searched for side-street parking, the spaces along the street were nearly invisible since most of the street light had been shattered by vandals. Only the moon afforded a bit of dim light as Charly grabbed my arm and we walked in silence through the shadows toward the bar. At the entrance there was the deep vibration of the bass and the frenetic rhythm of the music, and as I reached for the handle of the door I paused and asked, "Are you sure you want to do this?"

"Yes."

I opened the door and followed her in where the bass and the smoke gave us a quick blast. The bar was full, it being Saturday night, with bodies crammed close from wall to wall. The thick smoke choked us as I paid the cover charge and we walked beyond the foyer. The large oaken bar was peopled four and five deep on all sides, so we decided to forego a drink. Charly held close to me, but the bar was far too crowded for us to walk side by side. Instead, she held my hand and followed as I threaded a path beyond the entrance and toward the dance floor, and the deeper we entered the louder the music became and the harsher the bass pounded. Smoke hovered at eye level, distorting our sense of depth, and there were high-pitched screams in the form of disco lyrics from the large black speakers near the front of the bar. Masculine and effeminate, young and old, boisterous and quiet, alone and in groups, the men slithered through the dense crowd seeking conversation, companionship, an available body. We passed a group of leather-clad men inhaling poppers and beating out tunes on tambourines against the black coverings on their thighs. Others stripped themselves of their shirts and passed through the bar bare chested, seeking some action in the daring slit of an eye. The mood of the bar was frenzied, nearly too loud to bear, as we passed beyond the sitting area and moved closer yet to the dance floor where faces disappeared into the smokey darkness.

I occasionally looked back at Charly who seemed not to have prepared herself very well. Surprised and curious, I noted in the slight creases at her eyes that she was afraid, and yet she'd had to know. Quite removed from her by then, I wasn't really part of the picture at all, and as we pushed on I wondered whether it was as she'd imagined it to be. When she'd painted the bar's exterior had she guessed that this might be what she'd find within? I guessed that she cavorted with a long lost image of Johnnie R., far far away, sampling the many mysteries of his once-hidden world.

We forged further ahead as she held my hand tightly, squeezing it when she found herself boxed in by the larger men who occasionally pushed between us. Each time we were separated I stopped to find her hand, and then we continued our trek through the bar. Ahead of us lay the stage, and upon the screen to the back of the stage were the same naked models. This didn't shock her, though she seemed particularly embarrassed as we passed two men who were embracing, kissing long and full on the lips. We circled the bar once as the strobe lights and smoke and men on the stage creating a curious montage. Near the bar we tried to maneuver in position for a drink, but it was impossible. She tapped me on the shoulder to suggest that we not bother, and I then followed her away from the bar and back toward the dance floor.

The bass, again, and the layers of smoke billowing from beneath the stage and the wild throng on the dance floor as we reached it. Strobe lights, synchronized to the beat of the music, began to flash as the lights above the dance floor flickered frenetically, and in this syncopated fashion, the men surrounding us clapping away with hands above their heads, Charly and I danced - or, rather, we shuffled our feet since the floor was far too crowded to allow for much movement. We both occasionally glanced at the screen of naked men and then turned to scan the crowd; the smoke continued pouring from beneath the stage as the strobe lights danced about. The balance of the stage and dance floor lights began to flicker, joined by the sound of a siren and whistles and tambourines. Organized chaos. Song after song continued, Charly still a bit tipsy from the wine, but as the heat rose and the smoke pushed between us she slowly loosened up with the music. She danced more freely, less self-consciously, as the tunes roared from the speakers. The crowd on the floor increased as the more popular tunes played, and we stayed there dancing for nearly half an hour while watching the men beside us inhale their poppers, chant with the music and become lost in their own wild gyrations. The music, the shouting, the poppers, the smoke, the lights and the unusual release of emotions all created a surreal ambience, an otherworldly milieu.

I asked myself why she'd wanted to come on that particular evening? Idle curiosity? Genuine concern? Out of an obsessive sense of history, a narrative which had consumed both a brother and a husband? Years had passed since she'd discovered Johnnie R.'s bisexuality, so why finally visit the bar on that peculiar evening? What did she hope to find within? The meaning of her brother's death, her husband's infidelity? Perhaps, I thought as the speakers continued their torturous vibrations, perhaps she'd wanted to enter it for the very reason that she'd painted its exterior - she was merely trying to disarm the beastly image which the bar had invoked. Familiarity weakens the mythical foe. Knowledge tames the monster. Perhaps she hoped for a reprieve. And as I played with these thoughts I glanced just off the dance floor, at the very edge near the bannister separating the tables from the floor, and there I spotted Johnnie R. Seeing him there, unexpectedly, sent me reeling; a deep sinking feeling splaying my gut. He wasn't due back in town until the following day, but good ole Johnnie R. had found a way to surprise even himself.

He'd seen me first. When I glanced in his direction I found his disbelieving expression awaiting me, and from that distance, even with the dark shadows and smoke separating us, I could make out the hard outlines of pain. And the pain, as I held his gaze, slowly transformed to anger, an anger most memorable in that it resembled exactly a particular expression from another incident in our recent past. His cold blue eyes were the eyes of his father. They were the eyes of a calculating man trained never to lose, suggesting qualities associated with an intention to win at all costs, capitalist eyes which knew the score and the prevailing winds on both the economic front and within the market of human concerns.

Charly didn't see him immediately. She noticed that I'd stopped dancing, staring in Johnnie R.'s direction, and when she followed my eyes and found Johnnie R. only a few feet away she stopped dancing as well, standing completely still. For a long time I didn't hear the music nor voices nor tambourines. I didn't smell the poppers, see the men dance about me, notice the smoke hovering near my face. I only saw Johnnie R.'s eyes, and I watched as his expression conveyed a variety of emotions, anger always intermixed with the others, which like a kaleidoscope constantly seemed to change. It was finished. Everything was finished. I took Charly's arm and led her off the dance floor. So she'd finally seen the bar. She'd wanted to see the beast face to face, but had it lived up to its billing? Her face was blank as I turned to glance at her. I tugged at her arm and led her very slowly toward the door. We'd exited the dance floor on the opposite side from where Johnnie R. had stood. He couldn't reach us from there. He wouldn't be able to catch us before the door. I looked back through the crowd to see if I might follow his movements, but I lost him among the people and shadows and smoke. Minutes later we managed to reach the door, and when I looked back I found Johnnie R. only a few steps behind. I opened the door and allowed Charly through and then followed. We stood just outside the door, and within seconds Johnnie R. rushed out.

"What the hell's going on here?" he demanded, still dressed in suit and tie. He stepped close to me, his eyes wide with anger.

"We might ask the same of you," I said.

"Fuck you, Nick."

"We were out for a little fun," I said casually, holding his accusing gaze.

"Like hell!" he shouted, red-faced.

"Please, John," Charly said, shaking her head, but he wasn't to be soothed.

"I'm taking you home, dammit. That's a stupid stunt you pulled, both of you, going in there," he said, looking at Charly and then back at me. I realized immediately that he hadn't grasped the details. He hadn't yet put all of the facts together. He preferred to think of our being together in his old haunt as a matter of bad taste only.

"Johnnie R. -"

"Some fucking friend, Nick," he interrupted me, spitting out the words. He took Charly by the arm and turned to walk away.

"Charly!"

"Never mind, Nick. Please!" she shouted back, turning to look at me. Which was stranger, the distance in her echoing voice or the blend of pain and remorse in her soft face? Her eyes were frightening, so full of emptiness, so lacking promise.

I stood still as they walked off and watched Charly wrestle her arm loose from Johnnie R.'s grasp, though she chose to continue to walk by his side. I heard him swear, but she didn't respond. He looked back once to find me standing alone where they'd left me, then he quickly turned his head and continued on. Seconds later they disappeared around the corner of Twenty-second and Talbott. I maintained my gaze on the empty space where they'd been just a moment before, and it was only then that I realized the door to the bar had continued to open and close during our heated scene. Several men roamed in and out of the bar, the music hitting me with a blast each time the door released. A few who had heard our discussion stood by and gawked curiously, though I didn't move from beneath the marquee until I saw Johnnie R.'s car driving past Talbott and back toward Meridian. Suddenly, a strong conviction entered where there had been only weakness moments before. I knew it no longer mattered whether I hid my love or not. Johnnie R. was no fool; he'd soon guess the score. And as for Charly, it was now or never - Johnnie R.'s presence at Talbott Street had changed everything, and I would force her to choose.

I ran back to my car, and seconds later I was racing up Meridian, passing out of the ghetto and toward the ritzy neighborhoods lying north of Thirty-eighth. I stomped the accelerator to the floor, hoping to catch them before they entered the house. I hoped to have it out on the wide open spaces of their vast lawn, and my wish was granted. When I turned up their drive they were just climbing from the car. "What in the hell are you doing here?" Johnnie R. yelled, slamming his door.

"I came for Charly," I said as I took a few steps forward.

"What in the hell do you mean you came for Charly?" he asked, taking a step toward me.

"Nick, please don't," Charly said.

"I came to make her choose, Johnnie R. She must choose between remaining here with you or coming with me," I said, looking at Charly rather than at him.

"What are you saying?" He badly wanted to deny that it could be true. Though he took another step toward me, he was still some ten feet away.

"I love her, Johnnie R. I'm in love with her," I said calmly, my eyes still on Charly.

"You fuck!" Johnnie R. screamed, slowly walking toward me. I knew he would fight me as he came to understand the total terrifying picture. He'd allow himself the liberty of another rage. Like an animal he knew only violence then, the essential inarticulate nature of pain, its practical uses, its easy recourse. His eyes said as much. It wasn't enough to reason it away; only the urge to hurt could satisfy his own languishing pain. Soon it would be done.

"Tell him, Charly. Tell him we're lovers. Tell him, dammit!" I said, holding her gaze. She was mortified, speechless.

"I'll break your fucking neck, you bastard!" Johnnie R. yelled, nearly upon me. Like a charging bull, head lowered and his strong shoulders set, he was ready for the kill.

"I love you, Charly," I said, slightly smiling, and the words were barely out of my mouth before Johnnie R. hit me. Charly screamed as Johnnie R. slammed into me full in the chest. He yelled as he hit me, wildly cursing. We both fell to the ground, he on top of me, and he hit me hard in the stomach and ribs, his face a distorted image of mild madness. I fought back with punches of my own, connecting at his face and neck, but he was bulkier than me, stronger. His appetite for violence was much greater than mine, his need to injure, purer. I remembered then his large appetite for vengeance at Holliday Park as he'd beaten the kid. I could fight better than the kid, but I couldn't beat Johnnie R. He continued pounding me, cursing loudly, and in the background I could hear

Charly screaming for him to stop. Eventually, I saw her soft outline just behind Johnnie R., and as she cried I watched her pulling at his shoulders, trying to take him off me. He pushed her away, and as he did so I hit him hard in the jaw.

"Bastard!" he yelled loudly, swiftly giving me two great jolts to the ribs. With the second swing I heard bones break and yelled with the pain, a searing breath-taking pain. Never had I experienced such pain as this. Yet, what I see now when thinking back isn't Johnnie R. climbing from me, knowing he'd accomplished what he'd hoped to. No, I see Charly's eyes, still crying, as she pushed Johnnie R. further away from me. He took a few steps back, remaining silent, but already he was remorseful as he placed his face in his hands. Charly's eyes came into focus again as she knelt beside me, and there was in them only distance, total vacancy. What I saw was great pity and remorse, but no love. They were not the eyes of love. Those ever-growing spaces between us had widened beyond measure, and at the opposite end of that vast space I saw her beautiful eyes blink away her love with sadness and regret. It was a great sadness, the sadness of goodbye. Her tears fell onto my face, rolled down my cheeks. That was all she could give then. That and her few broken words.

"I'm so sorry, Nick. I'm so sorry," she said between sobs.

"I love you," I replied softly, barely able to let the words escape. As I said them she shook her head and cried louder, and I understood then that she was gone.

I turned my head as she rose. The pain in my chest began to spread, a raking scratching unbearable shooting pain in my upper chest. I knew he'd broken some ribs, and since I was finding it difficult to breathe I supposed I'd ruptured a lung. As it collapsed and the tissues within began to rub, the air escaping into my chest cavity, the pain became greater, unbearable. "I need a doctor," I uttered the raspy words very slowly, as I rolled on the ground.

"John, call an ambulance, now!" Charly ordered, turning to him.

Johnnie R. allowed his hands to fall from his face, and after pausing for a moment, a slight hesitation as he tried to find words to say, he ran toward the house to make the call. Charly eventually returned to kneel at my side where I lay cuddled, trying to manage the pain. But I refused to look into her eyes, wanting no part of her loveless pity, her infinite regrets. She tried to comfort me with soothing words, and at one point she ran a hand through my hair.

"Please, don't," I whispered. "Not if you don't love me."

She took her hand from my hair, but she continued kneeling. Within five minutes I could hear the siren in the distance as it traveled down Meridian Street. Closer and closer it came, its echo growing louder and louder as it cut through the late-night autumn air. All the while Charly continued kneeling beside me, hoping to console but unable to do so. I was more accepting of Johnnie R.'s soft, broken apologies in the background. I could hear his quivering voice, both angry and bereaved, as he stood somewhere behind Charly. Over and over he apologized. How strange, I thought. How strange that he should be apologizing to me after I'd taken his wife. How amusing that we all three were crying by then. We all three had loved, but we'd loved the wrong people. We were all lost, incredibly lost in our newly strange world, and our chorus of cries and tears was a group farewell to all that we'd shared together, our little cosmos rapidly disintegrating, tumbling, tumbling, tumbling away.

The ambulance entered the drive moments later, and the attendants slowly maneuvered me onto a stretcher as I heard Johnnie R. describe most persuasively a fictional accident. It was a late-night game of touch football, you see. Lots of shadows, a hole, a stumble, a break. Charly followed the stretcher to the back of the ambulance where they slipped me in. I caught her eyes one last time before the doors were closed, and still they were filled with pity and regret. The attendants secured me, and I tried again to find more in her gaze than pity, yet nothing more surfaced. Then the doors to the ambulance closed, the siren howled and the ambulance hurried me toward a hospital south on Meridian Street.

21

Indianapolis, 1991

Johnnie R.'s Journal

from **Elegy for Nick**

*Such a lovely man, unduplicable, to use a favorite word, so very graceful in
your ethereal way, a rarity of some dimension in this era of gracelessness, of
inhumanity, of the grossest form of snow-pallored heartlessness.*

*Ah, Nick. What if the book could be rewritten? Would you rewrite it with
me? Would you help me to red-line it, chapter by chapter, and then begin
again? Agree to edit this life as the consummation of your philosophical
endeavors?*

*That's a tough one, I know; all questions in the shadow of death are tough.
Believe you me, death's preparatory procedures require tenacity of soul,
fierceness of resolve in the face of fear dressed by the simple emollient of
love.*

*Speaking of love, I must tell you again, and then be done with it - I love you.
There, now the rest shall be easier, no more heart-fluttering moments
between words, no more emotional enjambments or forced rhythms in lieu of
simple rhyme.*

*   *   *

I read those fragments of a poem from Johnnie R.'s journal as I continued my
bedside vigil during those dreadful last days as he barely hung on. Most of that
time his mind drifted far away, consciousness trapped in the deep, demented
furrows of his diseased brain. When he did come around he was usually
disoriented, often confusing me with Charly, his dad, his son, an old lover.
Sometimes he was in the hospital dying, other times he was at the bank, shopping
at the mall, attending classes in Princeton, playing with his boy. Charly and I
were able to provide little solace, just as the doctors were unable to provide a
cure. Our only resources were a warm hand on his hand and a voice for his
blindness. We simply waited for his death and hoped it would come soon.

I continued arriving in the early mornings, and Charly usually arrived around
noon. She and I ate lunch together, and afterward Charly stayed with him while I

took a walk around the medical center. She usually left by six, and I stayed until ten or eleven, each day's itinerary mirroring that of the day before. I sat close to him while I read his journal or watched the tube and listened to his shallow breathing and waited.

The infectious disease specialists continued to parade in and out of the hospital room wearing the stern expressions of the medicinal shield. Even stern Zelda mellowed as Johnnie R. slowly died, the room occasionally filling beyond the limit of two as the three robed queens paid their visits. Zelda would bring me a coke, pat me on the shoulder, share in the glint of the eye a medical professional's oft-buried sorrow. I watched as she and others checked his vital signs, and I wondered in my silence at the edge of the room what it was that informed their need to minister to those who, like Johnnie R., they couldn't heal. Obviously, it wasn't for money, and there's no pleasure in watching the dying die. Since the disease is incurable, did they attempt to comfort him in the name of the Hippocratic oath and nothing more? Or did they, perhaps, practice their craft in the name of larger causes and more ethereal powers, the alleged beyond, those forces of the ever-present, mysterious soul which danced at the edge of Johnnie R.'s physical pain? Charly continually reminded me that these questions were irrelevant, suggesting more than once that it was enough that Johnnie R. wasn't dying in a loveless world.

Just a few days before his death, he reminded me, unwittingly, that we'd swapped positions in the hospital. Eight years earlier, following the fight on his lawn, I'd been convalescing in an Indianapolis hospital bed while he'd sat by my side. He apparently heard the rustle of my gown and grunted something from out of a dream before turning his head my way, listening to find me through the web of blindness. I leaned over and touched his arm as his words came in little spurts.

"You okay, Nick? Is your side okay now?" he asked, slurring the words in a voice so weak that I wasn't sure I'd heard him correctly, mentally stumbling before I caught the reference.

"Yeah, I'm all better," I answered, taking his hand. He wasn't quite with me. By a viral turn of the mind he'd awakened in nineteen eighty-three instead of nineteen ninety-one. He summoned from the past my stay in the hospital, recalled my pain, remembered his own anguish.

"I meant what I said. I meant it. Okay?"

"Okay, Johnnie R.," I answered. That's all he needed for the moment, assurances. I watched him turn in the bed and slowly fall back to sleep. I held his arm, leaning forward with my head on the edge of the bed, and I'm not sure which was the more difficult - watching his mind dissolve or remembering the disintegration of eighty-three. For a long while I tried to forget, but in this - Memory's month - there is no forgetting. So I leaned back in the chair, still waiting for Charly to show, and I recalled that hospital stay and those final days spent in Indianapolis so many years ago now.

22

Indianapolis, 1983

After surgery, with my lung repaired and my ribs wrapped, I was placed for a short time in intensive care with oxygen, morphine and constant care. I can vaguely remember hearing Charly's voice as I lay nearly hidden among the monitors, just as I remember the somber tones of the doctor at the door to my room. Other times, while in my hospital bed, clean among the bleached sheets and sterile scents, the morphine would take me beyond the room, and I would escape the conversations near my door and float past the unusual fragrances, the palpable consistencies of air and matter, of noise and light and heat. My thoughts were directed inwardly to the calling voice which spoke unfathomable notes, and there I would remain for timeless stretches, uncountable moments, only to return to the present as Charly spoke to the nurses concerning my condition. The injuries were relatively minor, three broken ribs and a collapsed lung. There were no complications following surgery, so recovery would be full and fairly quick. I would be in the hospital for a week.

Charly wandered into my room ten minutes at a time while I remained in intensive care, and once I was moved to a private room she waited bedside for longer stretches. I lay for the most part in complete silence, my mind lingering at the edge of medicated consciousness. Sleeping intermittently, I continued to buzz in and out of awareness during the first three days, and whenever I came to from my drug-induced naps, the morphine having lifted me beyond the painful truth of the immediate past, I spoke little. The few times that I did gaze into her eyes through the cloud of medication, however, I noted the earlier distance and the emptiness of remorse. And while on the verge of consciousness, knocking at the door to daylight ,just before the threshold of reason, I thought long and hard about those pitying, loveless eyes of Charly.

At times I awakened as the nurses grappled with my oxygen or bandages or the pump feeding my weak lung with needed air. I can remember the small things as I lingered in the hospital: the discomfort and embarrassment of the catheter, the monotonous grinding of the oxygen pump, the constant whoosh of oxygen into my nostrils, the cool air about the room, the expression of Charly as she watched me move in the bed in response to the pain. All of these things come to mind. Twice I awakened and grabbed her hand, and each time I released it as I translated the message of her ambiguous eyes. She felt obligated to see me through my pain, the harshness of the physical injury, but she was there, again, due to pity rather than due to love.

There was always the gray silence to abide during that pathetic run of recuperating time. I played games with myself just as the morphine played with me, and I tried to rally with the simple power of hope (hope to a man on the verge of chaos being greater than the power of history). I even remembered Dr. Johnson then: *It is necessary to hope, though hope always be deluded; for hope itself is happiness, and its frustrations, however frequent, are yet less dreadful than its extinction.* However, this hope, this desire to dig myself out from beneath my despair, occasionally was gagged and bound in favor of the obsessive games presented by the darker side. I would think of Charly, remember that she was gone and face the thought that there was nothing left for me in Indy. It was over, and all that remained was a crying memory performing a little two-step ditty with the torn metaphorical heart. And the music? A soft echoing lament fed by the tendrils of morphine time.

"Why do you return if you don't love me?" I asked her on the fourth day as she sat in the chair beside my bed, smiling. Up to that point I'd been too groggy for conversation and Charly had said very little, had offered even less. But the morphine was long gone by then, and I no longer cared to avoid the emotional discomfort of our break. Bewildered, words wouldn't come to her. "Is it pity only?" I prodded, leaning up on my elbows.

"Nick, let's discuss this later," she said pleasantly.

"No. I want to know now," I replied, trying to sit up.

"Don't do this to yourself."

"You mean don't do this to *you*, of course." I finally sat up and then reached for her, saying, "I still love you."

"Nick." She pulled away.

"Did you ever love me? Or did you fall in and out of love?" I pursued. She said nothing, hiding her eyes. "Was it more convenient to make yourself not love? Was it more convenient to remain with Johnnie R., though you've lost your love for him as well?"

"Don't do this, dammit!"

"Why should I make it easy on you, Charly. Surely you've thought of these things. I have a right to know. We've spent months together. You spent nearly a week in my bed. I'm in love with you."

"You don't have a right to be cruel," she muttered the words softly, fighting tears.

"Ah, cruelty! A fact of love. I'm an expert at that now."

"If you've loved me you won't do this."

"And if you had any courage at all you'd leave him. You've compromised yourself, your integrity, by not taking the chance."

"You assume too much, Nick."

"What I assume is this, Charly," I replied, prepared for the wicked turn. Though I loved her I wanted to plunge the dagger in deeply. "If you'd come with me you'd embrace something authentic rather than the drivel of a fairy tale of easiness and sloth on mighty Meridian Street!"

Weeping, she turned and walked from the room, and for an hour my anger lingered as I lay in bed steeped in rage. She didn't even have the guts to end it, I thought. But later, as my anger fell away, the nurse fetched my omnipotent ally, that stalwart medicinal crusader, the ever-powerful morphine, and together we conquered the despair. The grogginess returned, and I willingly complied, preferring to stay under the ambivalent tutelage of darkness rather than remain awake to ponder my loss. There, I experienced little pain and fewer worries, just silence and darkness.

Still later that afternoon, slowly casting off *morphine-time*, I stirred with the sensation of having my hand strongly gripped, and I awakened to find this time not Charly but Johnnie R. sitting beside me. As I turned to glance at the chair nearest the bed he released my hand and turned his head away. I focused quickly enough to see tears. What I'd missed had been no small cry for Johnnie R.; he obviously had been at it for some time. Again, I entertained that happy mental state brought on by *morphine-amnesia*, forgetting entirely the confrontation of days before, and I initially saw not the husband to my lover but the closest pal I'd ever had. It was good ole Johnnie R., my buddy from Princeton.

"What's wrong buddy? Tell ole Nick what's wrong," I said as I raised my head, slurring my words, not quite with him.

"Just rest," he answered, wiping his tears.

I lay my head back down on the pillow, looking up at the ceiling in silence, confused. Then slowly I remembered everything, each aching detail, and the echoing vacancy returned. I said nothing, shaking my head on the pillow, eyes closed.

"I've been here from the beginning," he offered weakly.

"To make sure your old buddy pulls through," I whispered sarcastically.

"Yes. As a matter of fact, yes."

"Leave."

"No, you're going to listen. It's the last time, but you're going to listen," he said matter-of-factly. His voice was calm for the moment, no anger, no emotion.

"Then I'll have the nurses throw you out!" I reached for the buzzer to the nurses' station. When I couldn't find it I glanced over and saw it in Johnnie R.'s hands. I lay back down and closed my eyes.

"Not yet, Nick. You don't want to hear it, but you're the captive now," he said. He meant business. He cupped the buzzer in his hands as if it were a tiny bird or some small defenseless thing. It was useless to argue. "I've been here from the beginning," he repeated, no sign of the old enthusiasm, voice still tinny. He was as worn and weary as I, a different man. "We've both been here, sometimes together, sometimes apart."

"Ah, such a sweet married couple," I offered bitterly.

"I accept your anger."

"How noble."

"Sometimes I bring my work to the hospital, pour over the papers and make my calls in the hall. I can't concentrate at the bank. It's useless," he said. With my eyes still closed, I sensed him leaning toward me.

"I'm sure you won't be fired," I replied.

"They usually let me in a couple of times a day. I always come in when you're asleep."

"That's convenient."

"One of us is always here in the morning," he added, a slight quiver to his voice. "So you haven't been alone, Nick. From the moment the ambulance arrived we've been here."

"You're wrong, Johnnie R. I *feel* alone. I want to *be* alone again."

"I'm sorry, Nick," he offered, weakly.

"Get to the point, and then get out," I raised my voice. The simple strain of talking was nearly unbearable.

"I never wanted to hurt you. I'm so damned sorry I did this, Nick."

"It's a little late for that, Johnnie R."

"Please, Nick. Please listen." He tried to continue and then his voice cracked. I remained silent, my eyes by then open and staring at the ceiling. At another moment, another time, observing him in that state would've torn at me. And even then, deeply, somewhere very deeply, I was genuinely moved by his remorse, but for the moment I had to be unforgiving. It was easier to be angry than to allow myself to go under with him. Besides, at that point magnanimity wasn't at the top of my list. So I said nothing, and a long interval passed in silence. I knew he was far from finished, merely gathering steam. It was to be his last hurrah with his buddy. He wanted to make it good, and I was merciless in my silence. "It's all ended so damned differently than I'd planned. I had such high hopes."

"Such consuming needs."

"Yes, that's true. We all did. You know that better than any of us." This last comment wasn't offered cruelly. It was a statement of fact, a salute to history. A summary of my own feeble temperament. He felt my pain and compared it with his own. "And that's the point, Nick. This consuming need was shared among us. I thought we'd be good for each other. Fill in the emotional gaps. We all three were unhappy, so needy. I had to believe it would work."

"How, Johnnie R.?"

He didn't miss a beat, didn't even appear to hear me. He was far ahead of me. "I shouldn't be surprised that it all happened so quickly. You were ripe for it. Charly was ripe for it. I was busy trying to salvage my career. The kid came and went. I got lost in the job -"

"You whored around."

"True. And I wasn't a good husband with my late hours, the many trips." Pausing, he leaned his head back against the chair and looked up at the ceiling. Then he turned toward me, and with a much steadier voice added, "I wasn't a good friend to you, allowing too many opportunities for trouble. For that I'm sorry."

How could he be so damned magnanimous, so eagerly big-hearted, so fucking apologetic? Mr. Benevolence to the man who had made love to his wife? Oddly, the pain inflicted by his wife's adultery no longer seemed to burden him. For half a week he'd been given time to sort his thoughts, to place the blame. His gesture, just then, was too grand to bear. I would rather have faced him with his wild-eyed anger. Without it I was at a disadvantage. I couldn't win.

"I didn't anticipate that you'd fall for Charly."

"Please, Johnnie R."

He glanced at me and turned away. Again, he was ahead of me. Sitting on the edge of the chair he was now distant, his eyes scanning beyond the window near my bed. His expression changed to puzzlement. He was on to something. "Wait," he said in a near whisper, voice registering surprise. He tilted his head slightly. "Or did I?"

He stood and then lay the buzzer down on the chair, well out of my reach. He walked around the bed to the window. He leaned against the sill, and I turned my head on the pillow to watch his silhouette framed by the glare. I was silenced by his tone. Suddenly, the old rhythm of his voice returned. So much for his much-practiced speech, his little liturgy in memory of our friendship. Spontaneity always worked best for him, a free-fall of words. And now they'd come. "No," he said softly, his forehead against the window. He uttered that one word with such emotion that I lifted my head from the pillow. "I see now. I understand how appropriate it was. It's not unusual at all, Nick."

He continued looking out the window, and I knew I'd let him go on. The curiosity and the pain both crowded my anger, and I simply lay there listening while he added, voice rising, "It's almost as if I'd planned it. Oh, sure, the original plan differed, but now I detect the undercurrent that moved it along." He turned and leaned against the window, facing me. I looked away immediately, staring at the ceiling. Then, in an emotional torrent the words came. No reservation, no remorse. "Of course you'd fall for her, Nick. The right temperament. The right intellect. The perfect beauty. The talent. That damned poet Rilke's perfect companion? It was inevitable.

"I thought I was bringing you back for me. I needed you then, so damned badly." He slammed his fist hard into his palm. "My world was falling apart, Nick. He had died. He had died and then you were gone. Because he was you, you know. He even looked like you. Dark and tall. Just a kid, but he had these quiet features, emotionally I mean, and they reminded me of you. So I wasn't merely going after a kid. Not really. I was going after you, Nick. I needed you, and after I met her brother I found you again. Then he died and you were gone."

Strangely, though it hurt, though it was all so very bizarre, I wanted to hear him out. But as if to show I hadn't entirely surrendered I simply shook my head back and forth on the pillow as he continued. "It was simple absolution. Secular amnesty. Fuck, I understand it now." He was gaining energy as he vigorously pulled away from the window and began to pace the room just before my bed. "I see now. I wanted to make a go at it with you one more time. But ironically I wanted you back for Charly as well. I had to have known you'd love her. Jesus Christ, Nick. Can't you see it? It's right in front of us. I absolve myself by letting you fuck my wife."

"Christ, please, Johnnie R.," I tried to shout, but it was only a whisper. The morphine had worn off. The nurses were nowhere in sight. My mind was suddenly clear, but dizzyingly so. I felt all the more deeply the physical pain and the pain delivered by his words.

"I did this for the two people I loved most, the woman whose life I'd ruined, the man who couldn't love me. I bring back to her the one thing I can love more than myself. This lost soul, this dreamer kicked out of the goddamned South. My best friend. And I give her this gift. And I give him her. And they are both eager for it. They take it, hungrily. And I'm absolved."

"Please," I said softly, crying by then. It was too much. The loss of Charly. The physical pain. The anguish of my dearest friend. The lies. Emotional deceits.

"Christ, of course! I understand it now," he said, arms in the air. He began to cry too. Ah, how it hurt to cry. The silent sobs, the little heaves of my chest, worked against the torn tissues of the lung. My chest burned with the tearing pain. It was hard to breathe, harder yet to hold in the swell of emotions. "And yet it still hurts so damned badly." I could just make out the motion of his hand wiping tears away, yet he had to go on with it. He was driven. "It's not the infidelity that hurts, Nick. Christ, of all things that's the least important right now. It's you, Nick. You're gone forever, aren't you? How silly to have thought otherwise."

He stopped pacing at the foot of the bed and turned toward me. I caught his eye and saw the pain, wet and red and wild. Then he leaned over just enough for emphasis, just enough to catch my full attention, and while looking straight at me, hands on the bed rail, he added, "Just as you'll never have Charly."

"Fuck you!"

"Nick. It's a fact. None of us can have what he wants," his voice was very soft, nearly inaudible. "I love you. You love Charly. And Charly .... well .... Nick, Charly can't love at all, really. Not now. She used it all up on a dream. She loved a dream of love on Meridian Street, and now the dream's vanished. It's all over. She took a lover in lieu of a dream, but there's no more love to give."

"No!"

"It's true, Nick. She's told me as much."

"I said no!"

"It's not her fault, Nick. She simply used it all up. Couldn't you see? It couldn't last."

"No, dammit!" I shouted again. "I love her. Damn you, she'll love me!"

"She can't, Nick. I'm sorry ....," his voice cracked again. "I know how you feel. I swear it. I know the loneliness. The emptiness. How it is a person can drown in sorrow, really fucking choke on it," he offered in a near whisper. I remember that I lost the outlines of his face in my own tears. I cried a little whimpering echoing moan as my lungs burned. I wanted badly to resist him, deny what I knew already to be true. But all that would come was a weak compromise, a desperate yelp of four little words.

"I'm so fucking lonely," I said, shaking my head on the pillow. The room a blur. The sounds askew. Meaning nowhere, really, at all.

Johnnie R. walked to the side of the bed, pulled the chair close and sat. He took my hand carefully, easily, in his own. When he saw that I wouldn't resist he leaned toward me and rested his head on the edge of the bed and cried into the sheets. He tried to console me between his own heaves.

"It's alright, Nick. I know what you feel. We're all alone. That's how it is now."

For perhaps fifteen minutes he remained there, my hand in his, his head on the bed. We were a world apart, and yet really not distant at all. We each sobbed over our losses, our aching communal needs, and we both realized the meaning of that short sobbing dark duet. It signaled the end of an era, an era that had begun at the age of eighteen in a dormitory dining room at Princeton and which had ended only that afternoon, some ten years later, as we bellowed in that unforgiving hospital room over the knowledge of our companion losses. In the tension of a moment's harsh rendering we'd been thrown out into the wild retreat of a transforming world. Haunting, ambiguous, consuming. Yes, this duo of tardy emotional bloomers was finally delivered to the doorstep of that unbending master, age. We'd just grown up, having performed one last adolescent stunt before calling it quits. Emotional wrecks, we were simple flotsam on the human sea. That's why I allowed Johnnie R. to hold my hand tightly. The loneliness felt better with a human touch.

For a long stretch of time there was silence. I turned to face the window and saw the dusk light filter in. Pink and orange light, delicate airy pastels. It created an unusual glow, much less difficult to bear than the recent grays. It was fitting that the light should change at that point, with the day wearing down. It was appropriate because the light's transition matched Johnnie R.'s own. He released my hand and leaned back heavily in his chair, cleared his throat and pursued his desultory monologue.

"My greatest weakness wasn't that I cared so deeply about you but that I continued to love the faded Princeton image long after you'd gone," he offered, his voice light and wispy, an airy buoyancy in and out of my ears. "Crazy, huh? I mean you'd think that I'd be the first to know that I needed to cut my losses early. Ivy League training, you know. If you've made a bad loan take it to committee, access it and write the fucker off. Well maybe so, but I also learned that business school blabber doesn't coincide with simple emotional physics. So I failed the course."

How puzzling, this beginning. Yet how could anything take me by surprise following the events of the last few months? Mike's death, the kid's comeuppance, my love for Charly, my hatred and love for Johnnie R.? My world had unloosened and was spiraling out of orbit, so I couldn't be surprised by this. That's why I let him go on, waiting for each word as I looked up and away.

"And that, Nick, you'll never understand. Oh sure, you've had a loss, but until you've loved in a fashion which the majority calls *deviant*, loved a man who could never love you in return simply because you were also a man, ached with that double injustice, the lack of love *and* the intolerance, well, until then you'll never know or understand how I feel."

I hadn't thought of his torment in just those terms, but the ethereal tone of his voice and the cautious choice of his words convinced me immediately that he was genuinely suffering. He had put his bag of tricks away. That's why he could speak so readily, so easily, of what had haunted him for so long.

"You'll never know what it's like to be a scapegoat, banished to the kingdom of outcasts, in this monstrously bigoted world," he lashed out, voice rising. I braced myself for more fury, but this new-found anger fell away as quickly as it had risen. He was silent for a long stretch of time, and the room was so very quiet. And then came a calmer voice. "No. I won't do this. I won't allow anger to ruin the last moments I have with you."

He stood and walked this time not to the window but to the wall opposite the foot of the bed. He leaned against it casually. I looked up at the ceiling, but I sensed him watching me. His rambling monologue took yet another turn. "Do you remember the beginning?" he snickered. I could make out a small wry smile on his face. He was all memory and reflection by then, somewhere well beyond those hospital walls which echoed his voice back to me. Yes, he was somewhere between Nassau Hall and Indianapolis, somewhere within the webs of vanishing time attempting to recapture the improbable transience of a lost decade. "Ah, the beginning! The dining room. Ten years ago. I took a seat near the serving line and watched you dish up food for all the rich boys. You never once smiled, your expression one of unaffected scorn. Or resentment. Ole stone face. That's why you were so hard on me that first trip through the line. Ah, the easy life! Money. Expensive car. Instant career. Wonderful inheritance. But no free rides for you, Nick. You resented me for that difference. And ironically it was your distance that I took as a challenge. That's what hooked me. That and those big green droopy lazy eyes.

"Okay, I admit that in the beginning the attraction was primarily physical. I liked your type. Though I thought you were straight I spotted a deep-seated need for human warmth. You visibly ached for affection. That's what allowed me to make the move."

"I was drunk," I managed to interrupt. "There's no need to go back over it."

"No. It's important, Nick. This entire fiasco goes back to that night, explains why we're here today." He only wanted a final opportunity to vent, and in my pain and anguish I granted it. "Okay, so you were drunk and lonely. We were young and horny. But that's not the issue here, Nick. The issue has everything to do with what occurred after you passed out. Now I admit that in the beginning, of the many different thoughts going through my head, the most important had to do with how I was going to manage to fuck you -"

"Christ, Johnnie R.! Must you do this?"

"Take it easy, Nick. Nothing happened," he said quickly. "And that's the point I'm trying to make. You passed out. Sure, I could have fucked you good and hard then and there, maybe branded you as my own in exchange for my earlier comeuppance, but there was something else sneaking in too. Something that pushed me beyond the need for another casual sexual victory. That need to have and to hurt you was replaced by an odd tenderness. In me, of all people! I'd never encountered that sentiment, sexually, until then.

"So, Nick, worry not. Nothing happened. Although, quite frankly, there was enough Vaseline on my cock to lube a Buick. But all I did was get off on a casual exotic freshman frottage as you snored away. And after I'd cleaned up I did something I'd never done. I climbed back in bed next to you and cried these drunken little tears because I knew in the morning I'd be out of your sexual picture. But lying beside you at that moment was without doubt the most sensually pleasing encounter I've ever experienced. Can you imagine that? Ten years and an uncountable number of fucks later and I still believe that."

As Johnnie R. bitterly spit out those last words he walked to the window where the dusk light was waning. The room was much darker but the lights remained off. I could just make out the silhouette of his strong body in the weak light. He leaned against the sill again, this time looking straight at me. I could just make out the outlines of his face. The light was closer to gray and purple by then, true thick dusk light.

"Hell, you needed me as much as I needed you. *The Great American Alter Ego.* You liked my style; I liked your temperament. Whenever you'd start those ethereal time-chariot flights toward the *upper cosmic plains* in search of the perfect companion I'd pull you back to earth. Whenever you'd ask *The Great Fucking Question* I was there to answer, **'IT JUST FUCKING IS!'** But you weren't wrong to take it all so seriously. It all mattered, everything mattered," he said quietly, nearly a whisper. "And after a time I realized that when I was with you I mattered too. That's what I miss."

Those last words trailed off down the hospital corridor, got lost in the sounds of elevators, telephones, patients hacking up blood, crying away dreams. I tried to follow the sound of the words so that I wouldn't be forced to envision the loss that he'd described.

"We were a great team. Weren't we Nick?"

"Yes," I whispered. I thought hard about what he was saying, and I was touched by it. Though still angry, I loved him deeply, as a brother. And I knew the Princeton to which he referred. It is a fact that we had cemented the early fragile pieces of friendship into a very powerful bond. And the bond had kept pace with the galloping years.

"You know, after I came back to Indy -"

"No more, Johnnie R.," I whispered. "Please."

"Well, I could never quite get over the hump," he persisted, ignoring me. "Oh sure, I loved the work at the bank. Strategic plans, P & L's, net-to-gross, Form 9's. But I couldn't escape you. Even when I read your letters I was far less interested in watching you gallop away into *no man's land* with your beloved Rilke than in trying to imagine your hand guiding the pen over the page. And wouldn't you know it, when I finally started over and got lost in the job, dated some women, tricked with men and later got lost in Charly - suddenly I found her brother. That's when you came back, Nick. Loud and clear...."

He said those last three words very softly, almost inaudibly. He was silent for a moment, and I turned my head on the pillow to better hear him, perhaps to see his silhouette in the dark. He said, "Then he died, and later I called you. All those years trying to escape you and I called you back." His voice cracked. He hesitated. I heard a long sigh. And then, his voice still fragile, there was anger again. "Loneliness? Yeah, Nick, I know a little bit about that too. I've practiced it for years, buddy, but I didn't wear it on my sleeve like you did. I indulged you all those years and allowed you to share it, your petty sullen grief, your losses, but your old pal Johnnie R. never could let on to you because he'd made the irrevocable mistake of loving the best friend he'd ever had."

He paused and when he didn't immediately continue I looked up from my pillow and in his direction. I could see nothing, though he was near the window. I listened for any sound, and initially I only heard the shuffling of his feet on the tile, his quick short breaths and the far off noises of the nurses' station. But soon another sound entered in, made music with all the rest, a tragic little harmony, and Johnnie R. began to weep again, slightly, softly, choking back the tears. I could say nothing in my weak state, but I continued looking in the direction of the window as he spoke.

"So you see, Nick, when I was hitting you it wasn't for taking my wife. Not at all. It was for deciding to take her in my stead. I wasn't even angry with Charly. I broke your ribs for not loving me. And that's all."

Johnnie R. broke down completely, weeping loudly somewhere near the window. He balled like a kid. As I lay in stunned silence I thought about our tangled tiny universe and how monstrously out of whack it had become. Soft spots. Weak points. Blindness. How hopeful we'd all been when I'd arrived. How alone we now all were. Helplessly, I could do nothing but lean forward and look out into the darkness as I listened to him cry. Later, there was a long stifling silence. And later still there was his muffled voice piercing through the post-dusk haze.

"Goodbye, buddy," he said softly as he left the room. Strangely, the morphine and I raised a hand in silent farewell long after he'd gone.

23

Indianapolis, 1991

Johnnie R.'s Journal

from **Elegy for Nick**

I don't know, Nick. The smallest of things, the greatest of things - such considerations are now beyond me, dependent on a linear mind still seeking the future. I'm still stuck on the past, buddy. My mind's a maven of remorse. I'm still seeking simple redemption.

That's why I seek memory, our finest metaphor for redemption - a slow dredging of the lake beds of the past, the muck and slime of millennia, for the treasure-trove of immortality.

And the only image I have is the image of your eyes on the first night I met you, that first drunken night when I learned to love, and how it is you loved me back with the sharing of your secrets and the telling of your lies, and how in bedding you, once only, slender-bodied sweet-smelling Nick, murmuring so needily as I took you into me, you shared for a moment a gift of love, remembered always as a centrifugal pressure thrusting me out of the world of childhood, casting me deep-spaceward like a quanta of lonely light, pushing through the darkest ether before crashing through an aperture of utter brilliance, where, looking back, I see your eyes blinking in utter astonishment. Perhaps that's redemption.

*   *   *

Charly still hadn't shown as I shook myself out of the past and Johnnie R. shifted in his bed. He'd been sleeping during the entire stretch of my reminiscence, occasionally stirring. I slouched in the chair, drained from those weeks of remembering our shared past, and glanced at Johnnie R. He'd slightly lifted his head from the pillow, cocking his head to better hear, and when I leaned up and touched his arm, calling out his name, he spoke with a smile.
"Nick?"
"Yeah, it's me, buddy."
"You wanna meet for a drink after studying at the Firestone?"

He'd caught me by surprise, his disorientation so damnably difficult to absorb. It hurt to watch and hear him, wasted, his mind nearly gone, yet it seemed the better tactic to leave him where he was - Princeton, nineteen seventy-seven. Why disrupt his fantasy? So I played along, comforting him with his delusion. To love by playing the lie.

"Yeah," I said. "Let's meet after supper."

"Hey, my treat, okay?"

"Okay."

"Good," he said. He lay his head down on the pillow and was quiet for a moment before raising his head again, and this time I couldn't be sure if he were back in Princeton or there with me as we spanned that dreadful moment in time. He turned his head my way again. "Do me a last favor?" he asked.

"Of course. Anything."

"Hold me?" Those words airily escaped his lips, floating off lightly down the hall. His expression was half-smile, half-embarrassment. I said nothing immediately, still uncertain. I leaned forward and grabbed his hand and squeezed. He seemed to smile a bit. "No, I mean hold me. Please?"

I was shaking as I stood, uncertain what to do. I first leaned forward and tried to take him by the shoulders while standing, but it was no good. Tubes and wires were everywhere with little space within which to maneuver, and as I surveyed the situation he tilted his head and spoke. "I always wanted to ask. Is it okay? Just hold me and then we'll go to the game."

He was here and there and everywhere, and he wasn't going to relent. So I walked to the opposite side of the bed where there was more space, and I played with the wires and tubes and IVs, adjusted the blankets and pillows, moved a cabinet, scooted a monitor, fought for position. I sat on the edge of the bed and then lifted him easily, carefully pushing him toward the edge of the bed to make room for myself. He was so light and delicate and fragile, weighing less than a hundred pounds. Just a skeleton with some purple-dotted skin. For five minutes I maneuvered among the tangible barriers and the intangible emotions until I finally lay on the bed and held him against me.

He scooted around carefully and placed his head on my chest while he put a hand in mine. I lay there for a long time as he said thank you over and over, and I hugged him easily each time he said it. He dozed off and on, and it suddenly seemed good that he was in Princeton, swimming back to those happiest years of his life where time stopped for awhile. Yes, I obliged my old buddy from Princeton, and even the nurses who walked in, and later Charly, didn't dare to interrupt us. When I glanced down I saw that he was smiling and rocked him carefully, like one might rock a small child, and wondered what he might be thinking. Where was he just then? How was life where he was? Was there some form of meaning conferred in the land that he visited? I very much wanted to know these things as I listened to sounds outside the room, and slowly I too escaped the present. In my mind I saw the gutsy punk who I'd met nearly twenty years earlier in the dormitory dining room demanding his food. I gazed into those wise, bull-shitting eyes, the eyes of an eighteen year old, hopeful, spunky kid. My buddy. The best friend I'll ever had. I found myself holding the kid who had played with my own virginity, my old pal, my study buddy, the friend who had asked me to Indy. I held the man I'd fought, the friend I'd left, the companion that soon would die. Johnnie R.

It was an emotional moment, and I tried to cope by placing my mind elsewhere. This too was difficult, and as the moments passed I soon found myself returning to those last few days in the city back in nineteen eighty-three. It was time to finish it off, that long-winded revery three weeks in the making. So as I rocked Johnnie R. I returned to the day that I was released from the hospital. I was nearly there; Indy was nearly over. So I rocked and remembered.

24

Indianapolis, 1983

On the seventh day I was released. My lung was healing fast, and they wrapped my ribs and gave me prescriptions and sent me on my way. When I stepped through the front door I noticed that Charly had cleaned the entire house and straightened up the clutter. I could just make out the slight fragrance of her perfume in small pockets of the house and half-expected to find a note from her, perhaps a sorrowful farewell, but none was found. I ambled about the house for most of the morning, reading the paper, calling the office, peeking here and there for something which Charly might have forgotten, but the silence was stifling, and by noon I had to leave. I climbed into my car which had been delivered sometime earlier in the week and slowly drove around the city trying to enjoy the dry cool October air and the turning leaves of blended reds. It had been nearly a year since I'd arrived in the city, yet I had nothing to show for it save for a weak lung, broken ribs, a shattered friendship and the memory of a lost love. I suppose that's why I drove to their home a final time and found Charly dressed in a painter's smock and jeans as she opened the door. Her hair was pulled back tightly, sharpening her fine features, and her eyes were clear and warm, surprisingly approachable.

"May I come in," I asked, leaning against the door frame.

"Yes, yes of course." She stood to the side to allow me in. "How are you feeling?"

"Better. Still sore, but better," I answered, trying to smile.

"Something to drink?"

"Just a soda, thanks," I replied. She walked to the kitchen and then returned with two glasses. She sat on a sofa and I took a chair opposite her.

"How much longer will you need to be away from the bank?" she asked, trying to be kind, the awkwardness still recognizable in her voice.

"Perhaps a week or two. I'll be leaving town soon thereafter."

"I'm sorry," she said, looking away. Sorry for what? Sorry that I'd be leaving, or sorry that it had ended in this manner? Had she ever thought that it might have worked? Did she still love Johnnie R.? Did she refuse to leave because of the gamble? Did it involve too much emotional work? I wanted to know.

"Will you come with me?" I asked, leaning forward a bit in the chair.

"Oh, Nick."

"I have to hear you say it, Charly."

"I can't go with you. It wouldn't work."

"Why?"

"We're too nearly the same, Nick. We're both too prone to react badly to the weaknesses of the other," she replied, looking down and away from me.

"The night we met you intimated that we were soul mates. Remember?"

"I was wrong. Our weaknesses -"

"My weakness is money, or the lack of it."

"You know that's not true. And it's not fair."

"I believe it is true, and I agree it isn't fair." I paused and then said, "You're afraid to see the truth."

"I don't know the truth anymore, Nick. I'm drained by all of the broken dreams. So naive in the beginning, now I've come to pay the price for losing it," she said, tears welling in her eyes.

"Do you love him?"

"No," she said, hesitating, "I don't know. I feel nothing any longer. Nothing."

"Do you love me?"

"I'm drained by the mere commitment to love!" she shouted, standing. She walked to a window looking out onto Meridian Street. From there I could see her lovely silhouette as the sun played with her as with a shadow. How much I wanted her, needed her.

"So it's easier to remain here, secure though compromised," I suggested. She said nothing, and I added, "Try to love again with me."

"I can't, Nick. And you need to leave now. Please leave," she said, abruptly turning away and walking out of the den. Moments later I heard the back door open and close. I stood and walked to the windows and looked out into the front yard, numb and confused, and then noticed smoke wafting from the backyard. Puzzled, I walked to the back door and looked out. At first I thought she was burning trash, but then I saw several canvases to the side of the flames. She was piling many of her paintings on top of the flames one by one. She had doused them with kerosene and they were burning on a concrete slab adjacent to the driveway.

Several of the paintings were placed face up beside her, ready for the fire. I opened the screen door and walked out onto the porch to get a better view. When I walked closer yet, standing just behind Charly, I looked down and found several portraits of Talbott Street. Oh yes, I found the original painting among the others in the heap, but she'd painted numerous portraits of the bar. The one I saw her pick up and throw on the fire differed from the earlier painting in that a figure of a very young man, almost a boy, appeared near the foreground. I recognized him as Charly's brother. Confused, I turned to get a closer look at the others lying on the ground. Again, as I inched closer I found yet another portrait of Charly's brother, this time his face appearing at a slightly different angle. I walked close enough to pick up the canvases, and as I sifted through them I found that each one was a separate painting of the bar. Each one revealed a slightly different version of her brother. Sometimes he was walking toward the bar, sometimes walking away. Some contained simple portraits. Others contained images of ambiguous intent: a short grimace on the boy's face, laughter, sorrow, fear. There were perhaps ten of them, and as I put the last of them down Charly picked it up and threw it on the flames.

"How awful," I muttered as I looked down. "I'm sorry."

We stood in silence beside the pile of paintings and from there I observed the ever-changing expressions on her brother's face. From every angle you could see the sweet face of the boy and his dark ambiguous eyes. It was then that I began to understand her pain, her unassimilated grief, her need to work with it, to make it go away. For a short moment I realized that I knew very little about pain. I knew very little at all, really. Nothing at all. I only knew that she'd returned to the bar even after the kid's death as her longtime project had continued. Such a curious blend - Charly's brother, Johnnie R.'s lover and Talbott Street. She'd wanted to deliver herself from the pain and anguish; she'd wanted to paint the misery away. The pain she'd found with Johnnie R. The pain of being one of a multitude of lovers. The pain she'd felt when she'd lost her own innocence. It was the pain she'd experienced as her marriage had crumbled. Just a huge heap of burning pain. And since she hadn't succeeded in painting the pain away she'd burn the memories instead.

As the flames climbed higher, some nearly to the limbs of an old oak nearby, they engulfed everything in a red, stinking, snarling fire. Charly stood only a few feet from the blaze, arms to her side, as I glanced at the fire and then at her and back at the fire, she watched the cool breeze spread the ashes throughout the yard. The flames became smaller as the fuel burned out, and the bushes and trees and grass caught the small fragile silver pieces of her former paintings, early clothing for winter. Afterward, she turned to me, her face calm, her features worn.

"You must go now, Nick. It's all over. Everything is over," she said very calmly.

Those were her last words to me, and I was too confused, too hurt, too tired, much too enervated emotionally, to fight it. I gazed into her eyes a final time, found the emptiness again, and then returned to my car. Moments later, she stood by the edge of her drive on Meridian Street, the wealthy house of Thayer, and watched my car back down the drive toward the street, and as I pulled away I felt a remnant of the last sliding hope from my first days in Indianapolis drop away as the cool autumn breezes fall away.

*   *   *

231

I remained in Indianapolis for less than a month. I made phone calls back East following my discharge from the hospital and was fortunate to have hooked up with an old professor for whom I'd done some work in Princeton. He lined me up with a Princeton firm, and the job offer was firmed up within three days of my return to the bank. When I dropped by Johnnie R.'s office to give him the news, he said, "You don't have to, you know. We can still make it work if you want, Nick."

I opted out and spent days packing and running endless errands in the cool autumn weather. Up to that very last day I thought I might see Charly once more, but thought better of it. In fact, after the movers had packed and gone I stood alone in the empty house on an early Monday morning looking out of the window while thinking of her. Through the mist, a subtle allusive hunter capturing the light and all sense of depth and proportion, I could see the church steeple lying far in the distance. Hovering above the shingled housetops and chimneys and antennas, mingled in with the tree line, it was a large, indifferent spire made nearly invisible by the climbing fog. And only when the fog rose to hide the steeple completely did I leave the window, lock the door and drive away.

The flight out was delayed by the fog, a sign, I believed, that I was getting out just in time. "Hell, the fog might stay for months," I grumbled to myself. A thick endless London fog transported to Indy. I paced for a long stretch of time, only to end my anxious treading before a large tinted window looking out upon the tarmac. I stood there impatiently trying to make out the outline of the plane I'd be boarding, but the looming darkness of the fog blocked all vision as the glass transformed into a mirror.

I watched as the crowd stirred behind me, a simple, arbitrary blur. Perhaps fifteen minutes passed as I peered into the makeshift mirror before a familiar image came into view. I'd noticed moments before someone stepping rather close to me, slightly hidden by my own mirrored image. Rather than turn I slightly moved to the side for a better view of the incomplete reflection, and I saw Johnnie R.

"I asked you here, picked you up nearly a year ago. I thought I'd see you off too, Nick," he said very quietly but with a slight ironic smile, his hands behind his back. I didn't bother to ask him how he'd discovered my flight plans. He always found a way. Instead, I took a good look at him, comparing his attire to the blue jeans he'd worn on the day of my arrival. In his suit and tie and freshly starched shirt he was immaculate. Handsome. Sophisticated. Intelligent. On the surface he seemed to have it all. There would be bumps along the way, most assuredly, but it appeared that he'd make it. I sensed he simply couldn't fail.

"I appreciate your gesture, Johnnie R.," I said, reaching over to shake his hand, still hoping for some emotional distance. The occasion was almost unseemly in its formality, much too starch for old friends. We both felt the awkwardness, and to compound the discomfort I noticed that he'd brought along a gift. With one hand he took my own, and with the other he offered the wrapped present.

"Oh, I can't, Johnnie R. I just can't. I'm sorry," I begged him off, releasing his hand quickly as I held my hands up as if to surrender.

"Please, Nick, I want you to take it. I searched for it a long time ago. Bought it for you years ago. Please take it," he insisted, his voice still quiet and soft.

"Really, I can't-"

"Please," he insisted, his hand still outstretched with the gift. I shook my head slowly, but his eyes conveyed a harder insistence than his airy voice. He was pleading for one more moment together. For old time's sake. The last hurrah.

"Okay," I said flatly, taking the gift and turning quickly to lay it beside my coat. "Thank you, Johnnie R."

"I want you to open it," he pursued, a very slight nervous smile upon his face.

"Now?" I asked.

"Yes, please."

I said nothing and turned to grab the gift. A small card was attached, and I purposely set it aside. I dared not open it just then.

"The card? Aren't you going to open the card first?" he asked.

"I think not. I'd rather wait."

"Come on."

"No, Johnnie R. Now it's my turn to ask for indulgence. Let me read it later," I said sternly.

He shrugged and then stood back to give me light as I pulled the wrapping paper off the box holding the gift. I was surprised to find a watch inside.

"It's a *Movado*," he said.

"It's very nice. Thank you," I answered, moved by his display of kindness.

"There's one in the Museum of Modern Art. Very unique," he offered, moving closer to me as I took the watch from the box.

"The dot is gold," he said, pointing at the face of the watch. Obviously it had been an expensive purchase.

"I see," I said, looking at it closely. "Again, thanks."

It was quite nice looking. Black and gold with a black leather band. I touched the crystal with an index finger as he spoke.

"Come on and put it on. Let's see how it looks."

I played with the watch, trying to get the strap around my wrist. I nearly dropped it and Johnnie R. rushed his hand forward and grabbed it quickly. Eventually I held out my wrist and he clasped the watch band tight.

"Beautiful!" he announced, smiling widely, happy I'd accepted it.

"It really is. Much too nice. Thank you."

Tilting his head ever so slightly, he said, "You've never worn a watch, and I could never understand it. Not once in all of these years have I seen one on your arm."

"It's true."

"Why?" he asked, the puzzled expression on his face puzzling me in return.

"I don't know, really. I don't like jewelry, I suppose. I'm not sure."

"I know why," he came back quickly, the smile fading to seriousness, his eyes narrowed for effect. "I know exactly why. I mean it took me years, but now I know. Of course, I had no idea when I bought it, but recently it came to me. Maybe two weeks ago. That's why I had to get it to you."

"What?" I asked, not following him.

"Look, Nick. I bought it during the last semester at Princeton. A farewell gift. I'd always been puzzled that an adult in the late twentieth century didn't wear a watch. I mean, Christ, you've got schedules to meet, meetings to attend, and at the time I bought it, classes to attend. I mean, look, you have a plane to catch. How can you manage. I mean really?"

"It's not as if I don't look at a clock, Johnnie R."

"Well, anyway, I always noticed it, and I badly wanted to give you something in commemoration of our friendship. So I bought it just as spring came," he said with some embarrassment, looking beyond my shoulder at the window.

"I appreciate it after all these years, Johnnie R."

"You know, I couldn't bring myself to give it to you. I thought you might take it the wrong way. Which of course was the right way," he snickered, his face a bit red. He looked back at me, and I shrugged, smiling, as he continued.

"Anyway, I couldn't do it, so I took it home and kept it in a drawer all these years. Not once did I wear it, though I replaced the batteries. So I was thinking about all that's happened, the entire mess of the last few weeks -"

"Let's not," I suggested.

"No, I won't," he said, quietly. "I mean I was thinking about you, remembered the gift and wanted to give it to you. That's when I discovered why you never wear one."

"And?"

"And," he continued, "I had to research it a little. Frankly, you would've been proud. I went to the public library a week or so ago and did some reading. Nothing deep, really. I read up on some of your old favorites from school, and on the nature of time."

"Pretty boring stuff, Johnnie R. You should get a medal," I said, smiling. He laughed and touched me lightly on the shoulder.

"Admittedly, this *time-turf* stuff is dry. But it was also interesting in the way it shed some light on you."

"Sounds dangerous," I commented dryly.

"Oh sure, I got all wrapped up in the arcane vocabulary, all the definitions. Got lost here and there. I even touched upon some Greek. Enough to distinguish between *chronos* and *aion,* the Greek conceptions of time and that bit. Hey, Nick, I got pretty good at it. Plato's *moving image of eternity*; Aristotle's *before and after*; Plotinus' *restless energy*; the paradoxes of St. Augustine; Hobbes' *present, past and future*; Newton's *absolute time*"

"I'm impressed, Johnnie R.," I said, smiling.

"I even got to know your old buddy, Bergson. Strange fellow. I read all about his view of duration, time as a qualitative change, an irreversible becoming. I understood immediately where you'd come from. Reason spatializes time, wrongly I'm supposing, and intuition is therefore a more adequate means of coming to terms with it. Understanding it. Well, hell, there you were suddenly. For years you'd been playing with all of these conceptions, all your life, way way out. Philosophical time. Besides Bergson you used to talk of Leibniz and his *order of successive existence,* and more than once you ended with Einstein and his *world-lines.* You kept going for the big picture, not time, but Time. The absolute, final, infinite thing. Always way up there, somewhere, far out of reach, with some plan to capture it all and name it. I understood that we lived in the same world but understood two different conceptions of time. Just as the Greeks did. Clock time, time on the make if you will, and the abstract image of time, the philosophical side. And I realized immediately that you did have a watch, wore it all the time, always kept it wound, and it was right in your head. But," Johnnie R. paused, took a short step toward me, looked straight at me, a cool little smile on his face, "but you know what Nick?"

"What, Johnnie R.?" I asked, taking his gaze, and smiling.

"You need a new watch!" he said, snickering, and I couldn't help but laugh. I looked down at the new watch on my arm, back at Johnnie R. and shrugged my shoulders. I waited a moment and laughed out loud again.

"I suppose I do," I eventually answered, still smiling, amused that he would've gone through the entire charade to make his point.

"Look, your initials are engraved on the back," he said, trying to get the watch off my arm. He wrestled it from me, pointed out the letters and looked for a comment.

"It's so nice, really," was all I could muster. He took a small step back and I fiddled with the band, trying to get the watch back on my wrist. He helped me again, and when it was done another great wave of awkwardness overcame us. He put his hands in his pockets; I played nervously with the gift box in my hands.

"Coffee?" he suggested, looking at his own watch.

I hesitated, looked around, looked for the right words if nothing else, and then weakly offered, "God, Johnnie R., I don't think I could. I really don't think I could. It would be too hard." I said it softly, my voice nearly, surprisingly, breaking. I felt the spasm in the throat which comes with choking back the tears.

"I understand," he said, looking away. His eyes watered a bit, and then it passed.

He joined me by the window, and we both stared vacantly out into the vast gray picture before us. The fog was lifting rapidly. As he looked out I couldn't help but catch a peek at him through the mirroring windows. He remained to that day secretive and cautious, a cocoon of ambiguous emotion, a man with a bag full of dreams complemented by his ball-busting realism. For all of his problems - bisexuality, broken marriage, the changing of his world - he was a man of undying hope. It occurred to me then that this was the particular feature of his personality which had kept Charly close by. It had been for years the one trait I hadn't nourished. Simple hope usually had lost out to unending despair. That's why he was a winner.

We both shuffled our feet over the carpet, nervously, and I thought of how we had walked to the edge of time together. Johnnie R.'s philosophical category of time. There I stood, the man who had made love to his wife, indeed, who would've taken her away, the man who had cursed and fought him, inflicted pain, stolen from him, and yet Johnnie R. remained the closest friend of my life. We'd each bared his soul to the other; perhaps that's why I could continue to love him so deeply and why our friendship didn't simply fall away. Unfathomable, this. I thought of time undone on the smallest of human scales and in turn was curious as to what he was thinking then. If the nuances of his gestures could but find a voice, I wondered, what would the voice say? Perhaps nothing more than that he, like me, had found the haunting voice of his own tortured limits, and he was humbled by it. And did he know, as I did, that my walking through the doors of the plane would never really deliver me from those secrets we'd found unfolded before us in Indianapolis? Would he ever try to escape them himself? Neither of us could ask for total deliverance, a divine deliverance which takes one through the many emotional levels between tribulation and rapture. We didn't believe; we couldn't be delivered. No, all that was given to us on that day was the door to the plane and the deep diving space of the tunnel leading to it. It wasn't enough, but we had to go on.

Moments passed by without a word. The airport noise was now audible to me. I tried to dwell on the miscellaneous voices surrounding us as if I might become lost myself within one of those voices of crying mothers. Crippled by another loss, another goodbye, we both shuffled a bit as the announcement was made to begin boarding the plane. Johnnie R. faintly smiled, his fine teeth showing through his parted lips. At that distance, some two or three feet, I looked him straight in the eye and gripped myself for the emotional release about to come. Ah, so much time gone by, I thought. Time seemingly gone wrong. Suddenly, he put his face in his hands and shook slightly. It was then that I took him to me, hugging him hard as we wept. So close, yet so far. For several minutes we held each other - a moment of grief, a shudder and then it was over.

We dried our eyes and then it was done. It was all we had left to give, both of us already having taken so much from the other. The passengers had begun boarding; time was running out. I hugged him again and said, "I'm sorry, very sorry. I love you buddy."

"Thank you," he said. How odd. A thank you. To the thief who was also his best friend. I picked up my bag and walked toward the gate.

"Nick!" he yelled after me.

"Goodbye, Johnnie R.," I shouted back, unable to face him.

"The twenty year reunion!" he shouted after me, trying for laughter.

I was wretched as I entered the plane, my eyes still blurred from the tears, and I had trouble finding my seat as I tried to cast off the paralysis of loss, the deep ache of futility. Back at the terminal I could see Johnnie R. standing against the glass. He waved, as every one was waving, though they couldn't see us, and continued waving as I watched his image become smaller as we taxied away. Moments later we were airborne, a mere spot in the sky, and somewhere below Johnnie R. was watching us ascend and then vanish altogether.

25

Indianapolis, 1991

Johnnie R.'s Journal

from **Requiem for a Virus**

you're still part of this creation,
this givenness called our world,
each of us lingering on a dying planet,
dependent on a reticent, if not silent, god,
frightened of mortality
as we push the envelope of unwordedness,
and that's the key, maybe,
to whatever meaning we might muster -
embrasure of that which confuses us,
thwarts us, obstructs our every ambition.
We must kiss the tendered kiss which kills us.

And the key is empathy:
recognition that beyond the moment of death
all points of view remain forever equal.

*   *   *

As the memory faded I returned to the present and found Johnnie R. asleep. His head lay on my chest, and I maneuvered my arm from beneath him to check the time on the very watch he'd given me eight years earlier. Two p.m. Charly had walked in more than once, only to leave as she saw him in my arms, but when she entered the third time I signaled for her help, and together we maneuvered his body so that I might slip away without waking him. We carefully centered him on the bed, and I climbed away from the wires and tubes and monitors. We stood there for a long while silently watching him breathe, and then Charly leaned forward and hugged me. She saw tears in my eyes - were those nineteen eighty-three tears or nineteen ninety-one tears? - and she rocked with me for a short while, without uttering a word. And then she looked at me and said, "Nick, you need to get away. Take a breather." She gave me her car keys. "Go for ride. I'll stay here with John."

238

Moments later I was driving north on Meridian, a street I hadn't driven since returning to the city. My days had been spent at the hospital, my nights at Johnnie R.'s apartment, so it was with some surprise that I found the Corridor, like the Indy skyline, had transformed dramatically during my absence, sporting a cleaner look. Many of the dilapidated buildings had been renovated, and some of the old boarded homes had been leveled and replaced by modern commercial buildings. I turned east on Twenty-second Street and drove slowly to Talbott Avenue where I stopped the car at the corner and peered ahead.

The bar was gone. The building still stood, but it had been renovated - repainted and refurbished and renamed - and it sported nice black awnings in lieu of the old garish marquee. I sat there for several minutes taking in the view, trying to picture the bar as it had appeared years before, and with the help of Charly's many portraits of the bar the old image returned. I saw the old broken street, the bad curbs, the debris, the old door, the gaudy marquee. I remembered where I'd stood the evening Johnnie R. had taken Charly by the arm and had pulled her away from the bar. I looked over and noticed the freshly paved parking lot where Charly had painted the building, and further east I saw the alley where her brother had been killed. Just a little jog of the imagination and it was there to see, just as I'd been forced to jog my memory in order to reconstruct London's Talbott Street a couple of years back when I'd revisited the city and had decided to take a stroll down lonely Talbott Street only to find it gone. No more. Kaput. In its place I found the English equivalent of a strip mall and its companion parking lot. A few kiosks. A bench or two. Some walks. But there was no brownstone building I once called home.

Before returning to the hospital I took a jaunt through Holliday Park. I left the car and walked around the fountain and then sat on a bench for half an hour as I watched the winter light play with the trees. It was quite nice, really, sitting there watching the passersby. A few people were out walking their dogs. Here and there a few men were cruising. And when I stood to stretch I heard for the first time in over eight years that peculiar yet always recognizable voice.

"I knew you was gay, man," the kid surprised me.

I quickly turned to find him only a few feet behind me, smiling broadly. I too smiled as I gazed into his mischievous eyes. He'd changed. With the passage of eight years he was no longer a kid. His hair was much shorter following the trend, and as I looked closely I noticed that the jaw Johnnie R. had snapped with his powerful punch was aslant, not quite right. It hadn't healed well, and there seemed to be a lump near the joint as if a bone chip had become lodged outwardly. He was no longer handsome. Creases, little crow's feet at the corners of his eyes, had appeared, and small soft lines ran around the corners of his lips which remained after he stopped smiling. His face was leaner with age, a bit taut, but he still sported a youthful body. Perhaps the most prominent change was in his clothing. Somewhere along the line he'd discarded his blue jeans and tennis shoes for slick looking Italian slacks and shoes as well as an Armani shirt. He also wore a nice leather bomber jacket. He was dressed to kill, probably literally. The kid was still hustling, it was easy to tell, and statistically it was quite reasonable to believe that he was a carrier of HIV.

"Cat got your tongue, man?" He stepped closer.

"No. No, I simply didn't expect to hear your voice."

"Thought I'd still be in prison, huh?"

"No, I knew you were out," I said. I remembered that he'd been sent to a reformatory since he sported a petty criminal's record for solicitation and other such illegal goings-on. Johnnie R. remained untouched - the the word of a prominent Ivy League banker against a foul-mouthed hustler. Not an ounce of scandal surfaced to touch the bank or Johnnie R.

"That's right, man. I beat the system. I got out in a year for good behavior. They wasn't goin' to keep me for long," he said, sauntering back and forth as he talked.

"Somehow that doesn't surprise me."

"That asshole, John, thought he had me, but I slipped away."

"That's a long way in the past," I said.

"Well he finally got what he deserved. He's goin' down with the BIG A! I know all about it. Everybody does," he offered, circling me.

"It's nearly over. Like the past. It's best to forget," I said, turning to follow his moves.

"Easy for ya to say, man. Ya didn't get your fuckin' jaw broke. Shit, I coulda been a big time model or somethin'. Now I gotta hustle," he spit the words out, touching his jaw. For the first time I saw the old tic as his eyes performed that odd two-step dance of opening widely and then narrowing, all the while gazing straight ahead. "Fortunately, it may be broke but it didn't take the trade away." I didn't respond, looking away, and he said, "So, where d'ya move to?"

"East."

"I tried to find ya," he said, tilting his head curiously.

"Why?"

"To see if I was right about your bein' sweet. I still got that hunch. I ain't usually wrong," he said, smiling again.

"Well, I'm not."

"Don't worry, man. I ain't mad at ya for what John done to me. I know that ya didn't set me up. He did, that bastard!"

"Forget it," I said. "He's nearly dead."

"Sure ya don't wanna have some fun?" he asked, his usual desultory conversation remaining true to form.

"No thanks, Kid."

"I hate that kid stuff, man."

"Danny."

"Yeah, and like I was sayin', ya can tell me now. Was ya his lover?"

"No, Danny. A friend. A very good friend. The closest friend I've ever had."

He looked down and away, realizing he'd struck a nerve. Then he turned toward me again and asked, his eyes tic-wide, "Ya around long?"

"No. I'm leaving tonight," I lied.

"Well, shit, I'm just wastin' time then, right?" he said "I ain't got time to shoot the shit. I gotta earn a livin', ya know."

"Sure."

"So, goodbye then," he said, running his hands over his pants to smooth the creases as he turned to walk off. He took a few steps away from me and then turned around to add, "Sorry about John, but he was an asshole."

He turned again and walked toward the road, laughing. He swaggered and flaunted his stuff up and down the horseshoe for perhaps ten minutes before a big Cadillac stopped and picked him up. An old pro by then, he made it look easy. As he opened the door he looked back at me and waved, laughing. Then he disappeared inside, and the car sped off. And now I'd come full circle. To Indianapolis from Indianapolis to Indianapolis. To and from, to and from, to and from Johnnie R. The circle game. I could only sit longer and watch the empty trees cast their vacant shadows amid the cool December breeze and reflect that the kid, like the various Talbott Streets, were merely simple signs of invariable change. The days come and go. We grow old; we die. And Johnnie R. was nearly gone as well.

*　　*　　*

I later returned to the hospital and sat with Charly and watched Johnnie R. slowly slip away. A day went by, and then two, each successive day finding him weaker, closer to death, and then two days before Christmas my buddy Johnnie R., Jonathan Randolph Thayer, died from complications associated with AIDS. Oh sure, the death certificate would talk in terms of pulmonary failure and pneumonia, kidney failure and cytomegalovirus, dementia and toxoplasmosis. But behind each of these so called causes there lay a silent predator dubbed HIV, and it is what killed Johnnie R.

And so I temporarily remain in a city which isn't my home while mourning a man whose absence tears at me deeply. Time apart from Charly and her son has been spent in Johnnie R.'s apartment, usually out here on the balcony high above the city where the silence is calming. I need the silence just now, the cool thin December air, the cloudless sky, the hope of the moon, the surprise of the stars. It's better that the tinny sounds of the city are left hundreds of feet below while the wind and I share this tiny cool soft space. And while passing time out here, wrapped in gloves and coat and hat, I've been seeking a core of meaning which might unravel the significance of Johnnie R.'s death as one does when pondering the fragile wisp of life hovering above the abyss before it disappears altogether. Each time, however, my thoughts obsessively return to that black meaningless space transposed onto the very fabric of this vital, animated world. That is what Johnnie R. feared most - the lurid accoutrements of death: the uncertainty, the dark aspects of extinction, nothingness. But his life, for me, was always a simple contract with the the the wild, daring, rancorous world of daylight where he created pockets of meaning from the vast spaces of light. And now that he is gone, how shall I sweep away the barren mentalscape of tangled and bitter bits of the past, short and stormy soliloquies, thoughts after the heartache?

Rilke, perhaps, provides a tentative answer in a fragment from *The Ninth Elegy:*

> ....*Maybe we're here only to say: house,*
> *bridge, well, gate, jug, olive tree, window -*
> *at most, pillar, tower....but to say them, remember,*
> *oh, to say them in a way that the things themselves*
> *never dreamed of existing so intensely....*

Yes, maybe we're here simply to utter words, and to experience them with nearly unbearable intensity. Words like: Johnnie R. Yes, the words of my life now come back to one name - his - as his memory probes easily at the surface of my mind. Sitting eighteen floors up while listening to the cold wind brush against my jacket, I try to misplace the loneliness among the stars. With my feet propped up and legs crossed, I want to recall his voice, his gestures and his moods as I throw despair away with the heart of the southern child I once was.

But there's little time, really. I'm due at Charly's in an hour. Ah, Charly. True, I continue to feel deeply for her, but it is a changed love. With the insurmountable distances created by those magnificent companions, time and space, my love long ago began to labor under the weight of simple abstraction, no matter how powerful its passion, and sometime before my return its tenuous hold became more a nuisance than a strangle hold. My love for Charly slowly buried itself, and hidden away, deeply embedded within the lower layers of inconvenient memory, it surfaced only during a particularly bad moment. So it is a love of adjustments, transformed by age.

So I'll say goodbye to Charly and return next week to Princeton. There are bills to pay. Friends to see. An altogether different life to live. But when I say goodbye to her, will she remember, as I embrace her, those embraces of the past? Or will she, like me, remember instead the hug I gave her the day Johnnie R. died? You see, just after he died she wept, and as I held her I seemed to focus on the silliest of details as they prepared to take his body away. As the staff began loosening the wires and tubes and monitors and IVs from him, I walked to the window with Charly and held her as I looked about, melding into the landscape. I noted the simplest and most unimportant sights and sounds. Looking out the window I saw the strange meandering curve of a tree trunk nearby. I noticed the small brown leaves not quite escaping all the trees. I was struck by patches of green pigment among the shades of brown and gray. I glanced up at the somber gray sky and noted the even consistency of the solid cloud cover. Looking back into the room I followed the multiple chaotic patterns of the little veins in the tile beneath our feet which stretched from us to Johnnie R. These were the details at the edge of death. These were what I saw, and Charly's crying is what I heard.

I also remember peering over at Johnnie R.'s body one last time and wondering to myself whether this end was a matter of chemical reactions only, another lost footnote to the pulse of the mechanical world. Did Johnnie R. find, as he went under, some strange informative medium, some concoction of ethereal tissues connecting the very nerve to the totally blind beyond? I couldn't know. But oddly, with Charly still in my arms, something surfaced I'd not thought of in years. What came to mind wasn't one of Johnnie R.'s death ditties or journal entries or poems, but rather a few simple words contained in the note which came with the watch he'd given me some eight years earlier. Yes, I could see the words from the note as I turned my head away from Johnnie R.'s now-limp body while trying to make the pain go away. Funny, I hadn't been able to read the note while facing him that day, so many years ago now, when I left him crying at the terminal in Indianapolis. No, and I couldn't read it as I sat and tried to make out his face through the blur of the window and the blur of my tears as the plane taxied away. Instead, I'd waited until the plane was high in the air before opening it. It was short and simple, and it read:

> *Nick, you ole son-of-a-bitch, keep your eye on the watch!*
> *And listen, Nick. The only gift in words I have for you is this:*
> *As our failures and their lessons transform from forced burdens*
> *to lightened reprieves the shield to the past falls away.*
> *I love you. J.R.*

END

243

The Poems of Johnnie R.

Hutton Hayes

Ode to my Son

They don't make it anymore, or if they do I've not seen it in years,
but as a kid of five or six, or six or seven, it was my favorite toy -
beanie cap they called it, from a cartoon dubbed *Beanie and Cecil,*
a much-watched show by kids my age when your age I once was.

Two buddies, these. Cecil was a sea serpent and Beanie ...
well, son, Beanie was just a boy who wore a funny cap,
a beanie with magical powers and small propellers off the top
and an invitation to fly. Ah, son, to fly! Like Icarus and Daedalus.

True, an unhappy myth, as some myths are, now best left alone,
but nonetheless I desired to fly with propeller atop my beanie head;
yet in the end I made due with more nearly mortal forms of pleasure,
like polished tokens of muted love and little ditties from the heart.

But listen: beanie caps were made of plastic - a tiny red cap,
a yellow chin strap and a propeller like sprouting goldenrod!
And at the center a tiny compartment, a storehouse for secrets
and childlike wares, bugs and paper and wishes and prayers.

With a pull of the strap the blades crashed into the air,
sending little-boy secrets through the midday glare,
though for the longest time I had no one to send them to,
an only child, like you, awaiting his turn as heir to a bank.

I was cared for by a governess who taught me to pee and poop
in a pot and to read and to eat, and best of all, to make imaginary
friends my own age! This was a real wonder to me, friends that don't
talk back! They think what you think, pee when you pee, you see.

But in order to provide some mortal forms for these fleshless creatures
I demanded certain human qualities from them. That's why, for a year,
duplicate sandwiches were made at lunch so that they might eat too,
just like your buddy, Armony, who I trust is doing quite well, thank you.

Of course, I always ate the sandwiches myself, making excuses for them:
Not hungry better go to the doctor okay here we go I'll drive come on.
(Ah, the excuses we're always able to make on behalf of those we love,
singing the heart with a profligate flame as unconditional love tends to do).

By the way, my buddies came in handy should I get into a bit of a scrape,
blame-sponges I think of them now, softening the blows of my hapless fate,
though your grandfather, a strong-willed man who holds his world in a solid
fist rather than palms-up hand for motives remaining unclear to me, was
unamused.

Didn't matter though. I was never alone when with my invisible friends,
sharing beanie messages, stale sandwiches, spankings, cartoons, ice cream, naps;
but as I said, they don't make them anymore, though some weekend flea market
just might scare one up in this seemingly endless, rag-tag Age of Nostalgia.

How wonderfully shocking such a find would be, like an ancient soda add
preserved on the side of a rural brick building, perky as a postage stamp.
Imagine, if you will, this: a little girl with golden curls and rosy cheeks and
eager smile holding a soda, and these words beside her in white bold letters:

Tastes real good, oh so good! and scribbles, scratches and curlicues
resembling art and then, in bold: **5 cents.** Whoever could have painted it?
I sometimes think God or some underling in charge of pastoral advertising
licked the back side of that add and thumbed it in place while we were asleep.

Anyway, their day has come and gone; they don't make them anymore,
but your mother and I saw that very add when antique-hunting in rural Indiana.
We turned a corner and there it was on the side of a building housing antiques.
We threw a blanket and ate a picnic lunch as the little girl watched us, and
smiled.

Swear to God! It was like going to the drive-in movies without a car!
And she said, as we lay there after lunch while trying to keep the crows at bay,
John, I've never been happier in all my life. She said that. And you know why?
Because you were there too, right there with us. Six months worth of you.

She was pregnant and such a sheen shone from her fine soft lardy flesh,
dimples all over her body, plump as a pin cushion, and all just for you, son!
Yes, you were there the day we saw God's postage stamp pasted to a building
in southern Indiana as your mother said, smiling, *John, I've never been happier.*

My God! The happiest day of her life and I held you both in my arms
in the summer heat and fell to sleep and didn't wake 'til the crows gained
the courage to plan stealth raids on our bread crumbs: *Caw, caw, caw!*
Yet, I was thinking this: *I'm more like my father than my son will ever know.*

And I suppose I meant this: bankers both of us, your grandfather and I,
and better with numbers than feelings; we suffered from a modern disease,
feeling wordlessly worthless in the face of the likes of your mother's challenge.
Yes, a challenge, a challenge it was to feel life as deeply as she then did.

You must understand that I was at a disadvantage in that there exists
no mortal power greater than maternal energies - a species apart, these,
like a spiritual IV connecting straight to God. But I thought a lot
about what she'd said and it scared me, and it scared me because I was mute,

utterly so in the face of her challenge, and so I remembered my father's
muteness as well. I remembered that he never told me, not once during
this far-too-short life, *I love you.* He didn't know how, and I was him.
Rolling up the blanket I said to your mother, *My God, it's like the beanie cap!*

Now your mother by then had to pee so bad, the extra pressure of pregnancy
being what it is, that I had to walk her to a secluded spot behind the vacant store
and allow her to prop against me while she squatted and I shewed flies away.
And I said again to your mother, *My God, honey! It's like the beanie cap!*

And she said, *What, John?* And I said, *The antique soda add. It's like a beanie cap.*
They don't make them anymore. And that's when she said, *Oh, John, just let me pee,*
honey. And I answered, *He's already making himself known to us. Kicking earlier,*
making you pee now. And both of you more articulate than I have it within me to be.

I thought about that at the three gas stations we vanquished during the ride home.
(God made bladders to enforce a minimum amount of daily rumination.)
I thought, *What can I say to my son that won't be taken as a lecture,*
or pandering? What can I offer my son that my father couldn't offer me?

Tell me, what? And that's when I remembered the beanie cap again
and understood that I could send along to you secrets of the muted heart,
secrets nourished for a lifetime, hidden from everyone until now,
everyone, that is, save for my beanie-induced imaginary friends.

By the way, they all suddenly disappeared as I entered kindergarten,
and I often wonder whatever happened to them. There were three in all,
nameless to me now. Did they become bankers too, or perhaps poets?
Do they still tread somewhere in an internal circuit, an imaginary path within?

Or have they been released for others to use, boys just like you, son?
Who can say what becomes of imaginary worlds once we've let them go?
But as I was saying, for years I sent messages to imaginary friends,
and then they joined me in sending messages to anyone else who might listen,

find my message, respond in kind with one of his own. And now I've found him,
following all these many years of silence. Yes, now I know I was waiting for you,
just beyond the generational fence, a lifetime between us, and a good thing I've kept
the secret message stowed away and polished and shorn of all unnecessary words.

In this way you might pick up the beanie propeller that is this poem
flying over you now, like a miracle, and open it, like the secret compartment,
and find in it a short message scratched in six-year old script,
a message I've held for a lifetime. It's very simple and reads: *I love you.*

the nap

in a sleep without dream
in a life without sum
in a room without time
in a world without hope

i'm sheathed in shrouds
of plastic tubing
swaddled in clothes
of altered meaning
of what it is to be human

or rather
of what it was
to have once been
human, though dying
inhumanely, like the winding
down of a century's metabolic clock

so enter me here
a prurient desire
and find in trenches
of deepest despair
a viral ditty

a giddy dig
a membrane cruise
to tissues bruised
congealed textures
of discontent

capillary pops
of rotting flesh
pierced by invaders
ranging my body
like heated entries
of forcible rape

filling me here
with bodily fluids
as if not yet sated

by fluids created
soon enough to kill me

draining me there
of my own pale ale
yellow detritus
too weak to leave
of its own accord

puny powers
these

all the result of
a virus visitation
coursing my veins
magenta-in-heat

filling my lungs
with hardened
detritus
a texture
the likes of a wasp nest

life retreats
in wisps of regret
too shallow to muster
lesser energies
formed by the hands of guilt

too proud to muster
greater energies
speaking the tongue
of human redemption

and not by the grace of god
do bruises straddle walls
of ever-seeping veins

and not by the grace of god
do metallic trajectories
fuck me of innocence
or whatever lingers

in the wake of blood
not yet tainted
by the devouring beast

and not by the grace of god
do prayers skiff lightly
from time-chapped lips

see here
prayers are fears finding words
words are tools in lieu of love
love is now forgotten grammar
grammar breeds accommodation

orthodoxy of white-flagged guilt

but guilt I have no time for
only time for a breath
maybe two

yes

like those stuffed
in the lungs
of the boy
who was me

a boy in
a sandbox
forgetful of time

clothed in soft cotton
to swaddle the sewers
of fecal despair

shit
and a shovel
for measuring it

like the sand
grain by grain
oozing into the rusting pail

death ain't no fashion-plate

until the call comes
to leave it
leave it now
in favor of
certain postures
of a little boy's
midafternoon

where hands lay me down
and eyes observe
as sleep rolls in
particles playing
on waves of light
through slatted blinds

and muted stirrings
lead to the long
the very very long
the infinitely long
afternoon nap

Elegy for Charly

Ah, Charly. How funny the fates,
providing the irony of a bisexual
man marrying a woman named
Charly, or nicknamed so.

And yes, dear, it does hurt
to know that you continue,
against all odds, to love me.
I'd prefer that you remarry.

Yes, guilt is the culprit here.
That you might find love again
releases the fetters of guilt, helps
me to prepare for the long sleep.

But I'd not exchange any of it,
not even the bad moments
following your discovery
of my once-tightly-held secret.

Because love is unworded mystery
and fate is the word now lost to us
we must embrace what is given
rather than pine for what is not.

I rather enjoyed my dual role,
a lover of woman and men,
since it made clear to me
a dual vision of reality.

Any vision of some clarity
I welcome to this opaque planet,
something to amend the view
formed by tendered ambiguous gifts.

Yes, dear, yes, I've already written to
our son, a rather elegiac poem
relating our experience of the antique
soda add to the era of beanie caps.

And I told him it was on that day
that you offered to me, with such
sweetness, *John, I've never been
happier.* He'll like that, Charly.

And Charly, try to let go of me
as soon as you can. No, not before
I die, I confess in weakness,
but as soon thereafter as is possible.

I ask this with the knowledge
that you're the strongest person
I've ever known. Stronger than the
old man, oh, far stronger than the

old man. His strength, to be sure,
is brutal and incisive, very secure
in its knowledge of human weakness,
but your love is greater nonetheless,

greater because it contains a treasure
unavailable to him, unavailable to so many,
and I speak not of faith nor hope nor justice
nor prudence nor temperance nor fortitude

but rather of charity. Yes, you are merciful,
and this provides such great strength as to
allow the other virtues to blossom
far beyond the capacity of the old man

and somewhere near to the strength
of time, certainly stronger than Nick,
the man I hope you'll love, who needs,
with all of his poetical sensibility,

a practical strength to carry him through.
The only man, as you know, I ever loved,
and who, in turn, could only love you.
But such, again, are the mysteries of fate.

Sweetie, I spoke of time being merciful,
merciful in that it kills us soon enough,
though often not before we've had a bit
of fun, and never before we've released

a river of tears, an ocean of tiny tears,
which, I believe, some Greek myth
suggests is responsible for making
flowers grow. *You* makes flowers grow.

And I can tell you now, a little secret,
of no great import to others, though
meaningful to you. You taught me
something not easily taught to a man,

any man, wrapped in testosterone
duplicities and other hormonal energies
not easily domesticated. Yes, you taught
me the love of a home, the warmth of it,

the kindred sensibilities of the hearth,
the beauty of a glass of wine on the patio
on a Friday evening, following a long week,
and the simplicity of a Wednesday meal,

the lovely melancholy of a Sunday drive,
the exhilaration of a Saturday barbeque,
and all of the other mysteries of the nondescript days leading on to old age.

You taught me that, helped me to love it,
and I thank you for it, from shopping to
planning a vacation, even the sickness,
colds and flus, that stomach thing

from Mexico we shared, and now this.
Yes, and most of all that greatest of
miracles, the fruit of love, the selfless sharing
that led to the birth of our little son.

A lady killer, he, with his wild good looks
and cocky manner, though I pray he finds
happiness in books and children and the
other fine things less related to appetite.

He is the finest thing we accomplished
together as man and wife, and to think I
wanted no children at one time. The few
years I've had with him is a form of redemption.

Let him fly, Charly, an exotically wild free-flying
bird. Let him scrape his knees and get a bit bloodied
up. Allow him to see the terror of true freedom.
And kiss him for me too 'till he says he's had enough.

And when he kisses you back with those wet little kid
lips, smeared with chocolate and a score of other
unidentifiable little kid things, sour breathed and
snotty-nosed, hair askew, eyes alive in utter astonishment,

yes, find in the small parting of his lips, in just that
way of his, so like his old man, that excitable mouth,
an opening through which might skiff a breezy
afterthought of love held in reserve for you, from me.

hiv

hiv
can't you see
it means all the world to me

enter here
oh my dear
do you think they'll say I'm queer

in the ass
like a lass
this all seems so very crass

tick tock tick
tick tock tick
what's that coming from your dick

biding time
such a crime
then to kill me in my prime

got no drug
for this bug
don'tcha hate a viral thug

retro-high
say goodbye
viral load so high I cry

T-cell rape
foot to nape
slimming down at quite a rate

viral flux
clogging ducts
caused by one too many fucks

soar throat here
large node there
what's that in my underwear

Hutton Hayes

lose an eye
bruise a thigh
why do doctors always lie

first I sneeze
then I wheeze
now I suffer Kaposi's

swollen leg
spit up egg
simple symptoms of the plague

I can't eat
quite a feat
just to stand on my two feet

slapped a nurse
with her purse
now I got dementia curse

can't much breathe
only seethe
still alive, can you believe

rash on rump
stomach pump
still I had a solid dump

up so late
balding pate
T-cells down to thirty-eight

I won't lie
wanna die
tried and tried but couldn't cry

dad's a prick
make's me sick
still in love with lovely Nick.

perky dick
quite a trick
quite a trooper when he's sick

still it's time
such a crime
bought a casket, so sublime

by and by
soon I'll die
it's okay now, don'tcha cry

lest you know
what I know
ain't no god beyond this show

in which case
stone and lace
quite a thing, the human race

Hutton Hayes

Elegy for Nick

Such a lovely man, unduplicable, to use a favorite word, so very graceful
in your ethereal way, a rarity of some dimension in this era of gracelessness,
of inhumanity, of the grossest form of snow-pallored heartlessness.

Ah, Nick. What if the book could be rewritten? Would you rewrite it with me?
Would you help me to red-line it, chapter by chapter, and then begin again?
Agree to edit this life as the consummation of your philosophical endeavors?

That's a tough one, I know; all questions in the shadow of death are tough.
Believe you me, death's preparatory procedures require tenacity of soul,
fierceness of resolve in the face of fear dressed by the simple emollient of love.

Speaking of love, I must tell you again, and then be done with it - *I love you.*
There, now the rest shall be easier, no more heart-fluttering moments between
words, no more emotional enjambments or forced rhythms in lieu of simple rhyme.

As you might guess, if I could write the book over I'd remain unchanged,
but not you. You'd be forced to change - gay, and happily so, of course,
and you'd love me unendingly, vaporizing jealousy into the ever-thinning air.

Loving you only, that was my problem. Since you couldn't love me *that way*
I was forced to find pieces of you in a variety of lovers, like shopping for clothes
at Good Will - eyes here, torso there, legs here, cock there. But never your mind.

Unduplicable, as I said, and that's what I loved most. Still do, that wacky vision,
so consistently romantic, so delicate a temperament, like a white orchid growing
only in a certain clime and in a certain place and for a certain time. A human orchid.

I fear your species' struggle shall not survive Darwin's scheme of the fittest, so oddly
absent are your natural defenses, a tiny albino chameleon in a very hungry forest;
that you've survived this long must be chronicled by science as a freak of nature.

They eat people like you, swallowing you whole like a plate of raw oysters -
a real pity, since your talent lies in the slow introverted task of forming pearls.
Soon, there will be no more pearls, and diamonds are fucked too, since anything

of value must be tended by a slow-moving-mother-of-love sensibility and such sensibilities this world abhors, having lost the taste for mystery long before; mystery requires nearly infinite patience, but this is the era of the three-minute

attention span, not enough time to take a pee during the breaks between the nightly lineup of sitcoms, our newest form of literature. The postmodernists wanted a new canon, and they got it. Digital, paperless, soulless, weightless, meaningless. It's us.

Ah, Nick, remember the long evenings at the Firestone? Princeton pups, we were, daring the world to throw at us all the power she could muster. We *believed* then in something unstained by the reality of human greed; you believed in poetry,

I believed in you. Still do. You taught me how to dream, unwittingly, since dreams project unrequited desire. Before I met you I dreamed but remember nothing; since I've known you I remember every dream as a reminder of what can't be mine.

Beer bottles, peanut husks, pizza boxes, girlie mags, dirty laundry and *Duino Elegies.* That's my memory of your dormitory room. My memory of your face anchors on your eyes: green and large, seeking and lonely, all in a long-lashed blinking sort of way.

How many gay men have fallen for straight men during the sad history of human love? Answer: How many gay men have their been during the long history of human love? And I fell for the melancholy boy from Mobile, from the heart of friggin' Dixie!

If Shakespeare were alive today, in the Age of AIDS, would Hamlet have spoken thus: *HIV or no HIV, that is the question*? And speaking of Shakespeare, may I share with you my favorite Shakespearean work? No, not mighty *Hamlet*, dear friend, but *The Tempest.*

Yes, I've come to appreciate the farewell works of all great writers at this late stage, and there's something soothing about Ariel's quixotic comings and goings and Prospero's ancient need and the lusty energies of Caliban and the slow fading of the imagination.

As with Wordsworth's *Ode to Mortality* or Eliot's *Little Gidding* or, for that matter, Bergman's *Fanny and Alexander,* it's quite wonderful to witness human transformation from mortal to immortal - a process of molting (a shucking of the husk of imagination

as the old skin crumbles into the forgiving earth) and a shrill echo of ancient yearning muffled into oblivion, subdued in the sublimely silent embrasure of spiritual surrender. Maybe transcendence is memory culled from the deep, or maybe its the smell of the rose,

I don't know, Nick. The smallest of things, the greatest of things - such considerations are now beyond me, dependent on a linear mind still seeking the future. I'm still stuck on the past, buddy. My mind's a maven of remorse. I'm seeking simple redemption.

That's why I seek memory, our finest metaphor for redemption - a slow dredging of the lake beds of the past, the muck and slime of millennia, for the treasure-trove of immortality. And the only image I have is the image of your eyes on the first night I met you, that first

drunken night when I learned to love, and how it is you loved me back with the sharing of your secrets and the telling of your lies, and how in bedding you, once only, slender-bodied sweet-smelling Nick, murmuring so needily as I took you into me, you shared for

a moment a gift of love, remembered always as a centrifugal pressure thrusting me out of the world of childhood, casting me deep-spaceward like a quanta of lonely light, pushing through the darkest ether before crashing through an aperture of utter brilliance,

where, looking back, I find your eyes blinking in utter astonishment. Perhaps that's redemption.

moments

a soft dream-state
of textured bliss
comes hard as slate
a wincing kiss
recoiling, this,
from death's cracked lips
slurps and slips
beneath the crates
of memories amiss

to the moment

but what's a moment
when you're lying
in wait, dying
to the world, crying
to yourself that it be done
soon, this death, done

a moment is anything
but now, anything
earlier, not here,
not near
not clear
not dear

not abrupt

like the ending
of a rhyme
you once got hold of
now lost to powers
greater than yourself
because more alive
than you can ever
again be

what's in a moment
but an excuse
to seek it out
like a memory
once it's gone

a moment is hell
because concrete
and touched by borders
of what is not
borders unseen
these

and what's a life
but a string of knots
in a whirligig
of quantum physics

smaller than quarks
or monads or flavors
or whatever it is
that's smallest these days
which shall in turn
give way to fragments
tinier than Heidegger's Nothing

till the inner sash
to that centripetal world
flings open for God
to peek through

and scare shit out of us

or maybe the devil
which is still okay
since God's not far behind

or nothing at all
absolutely nothing at all
to peek back at us
nothing but reflections
of bloodshot eyes

and palsied hands
and bands of hope
come undone
in the withering
which is the end
of immortality

so what is a moment
or what is it not
same thing
what is and what is not
what can't be known
like a knock in the night
not really there
and not in a dream
as the dream fades away
slipping away to
hypnogogic hell

yes, hell, this
bleary-eyed
bleary-brained
bleary-hearted
hell

as are all recognitions
of meaninglessness
of deciphered despair
of tangential fears
of naught

though, you ask,
how is it I speak
as if I knew that
hell is not what I am now
and dream is just
another word for impatience
that it all be done with
sooner than later
later than never

and I say this
when the rhyme's
done with
so am I
lack of meter
lack of rhyme
are enjambments
of the soul

as frightful
as an intersection
in Mexico
near where
once, years ago,
I laid with a man
who killed me

pushing his dagger in
sweetly at first
then harder
but with a sweet word
then not so sweet at all
just lunging forward
like a poet seeking
the word he cannot find

forward
into me
taking from me
as he gave me death
the memory of
what God used to be
before even that
disappeared
in the bleak light
of a midnight cigarette

Requiem for a Virus

I

You invaded my body as if settling a planet,
crossing six time zones on your inter-galactic way
(six time zones to humans, though galaxies to you).
And how many enlisted in that rag-tag regiment,
bidding adieu before spinning away?
Who are your forefathers? Why did you leave?
These questions I ask, asserting my rights,
settling as you did without grant of permission.
You staked your land grant without fear of eviction,
suburban aliens seeking trendier homes.
And such a mobile bunch, never happy in one place -
move, move, move, move, move, move, move.
And that little thing you do, so amusing to your children,
mutating so quickly as to thwart all defenses,
the dwindling defenders of my mythically-plagued land.

II

Why am I now condescending to speak?
No, I'm not calling a truce - much too late for that.
Forgive my formality, my lack of smile,
my reticence - for my mission is grim,
not so unlike, in fact, that of a well-dressed officer
tapping the hollow creaking shuddering door
beyond which await a slain soldier's kin.

So here's the hitch: You all must soon die.

Please! Please! Climb from your knees!
You haven't a prayer that a prayer might save your lives,
anymore than these briny tears might save mine.
Understand, if it helps, it is I who first must die,
only then followed by each of you.
There is absolutely nothing you might do,
no escaping the kiss of the moment of death,
and when the thumping white noise of human life
ceases, then you too shall fade away. And no,
I'm not God, though funny you should ask.

I've been mistaken for many things,
a burglar once, sneaking home drunk
late one winter night, and once, that blue-eyed actor,
ole what's-his-name; still others call me the devil.
And those who find my particular death too difficult
to absorb prefer to refer to me as a monster.
So call me monster if you wish, but not the devil.

I am not God.

A miracle? you ask.
Though anything's possible, I really think not.
Unsafe sex? you suggest. I'm frankly offended
that you'd drag that up, and I'd not count on it.
Erections are priceless trophies not easily obtained.
My former good looks have faded to a rag-doll man.
A pin prick of some unsuspecting nurse?
Most wear layers and layers of gloves, so the only chance
is the draining process as they pump me clean of tainted blood.
I've still no idea into what great reservoir I'll be emptied.

Best just to bow to fate.

III

Why? you ask.
Ah, the great question, one I've often asked myself,
and my answer relies on pure conjecture. So allow me
to pilfer the metaphor of the planet. When you found me,
a young planet as planets go, you thought I was good, say,
for half a billion years, give or take, since I was in my prime,
my atmosphere perfectly suited to your biological needs.
Nearly paradise if you ponder it. All those nodes, glands,
pliable tissues. All that blood! Have you ever seen sexier T-cells?
Most likely not since most were born here - such a fertile bunch -
and it remains an issue with me that you weren't more moderate,
suggesting to me that not one among you is a modern Catholic.

And speaking of eco-sensibilities and planetary responsibilities,
if I had to answer the *why* question I'd simply offer this:
You were environmentally irresponsible. That's it in a nutshell.
This planet you're on, the planet of me, is dying, oh-so-slowly so,

not unlike the planet upon which I live but for a short time longer.
Frankly, you weren't environmentally progressive, destroying much,
far too fast, a glutton in paradise. Party animals! Drinking and driving,
brush fires, polluting the rivers of blood, excessive logging of delicate
rain forests, in particular the national shrine at T-Cell National Park.

Still, it's possible to view this misfortune metaphorically
and hope there's a Noah among you, but hear this:
the ark ain't in sight and I absolutely refuse to provide transport.
Absolutely. So none of this one-by-one, two-by-two stuff.
Yes, you shall die, but try if you might to view it this way:
though you shall die, literally, you're memory remains,
(a fine metaphor, memory - a mark in the present with the quill of the past)
and metaphor remains as the greatest transport of all.
It is, perchance, our only available vehicle to immortality.

+IV

And speaking of metaphor, what an entry!
Quite a scare, huh? Not quite the brave new world,
entering the dark rectal cave of me where so many were killed,
far too many to bury, on the battlefield of anal stench,
of biological debris. Hear tell, there was nearly a mutiny,
but where to go once within the gravitational grasp of me?
Not that all hope was lost. Some of you, veterans of many
a sphincter entry, having invaded four, maybe five planets
since joining the force, never gave up, knew to look for certain
qualities in the landscape, and there, just maybe,
find the magenta-splash of the fountain of youth.
That group of smartalecky vets found a less inhospitable milieu,
eventually discovering a fluid less viscous than the mucousy cave;
a few snuck forward for a closer look, and *presto*!
You found the life source, a small broken capillary,
microscopic to me but the friggin' Grand Canyon to you.
And did you just stand there, admiring it for a long while,
tourists on vacation, bowing to give thanks to the god of all viruses?
Finally, you must have thought, the promised land!
Not exactly forty years in the desert, the anal cave,
but it lacks a view; it's nothing to write home about,
seized as it is by the scent of human despair.
And how lucky those fortunate few who escaped the dying planet,
wandering from the river red, drilling deeper into the soil,

271

finding against all odds that creamy viscous fluid,
like an oil strike, then ejaculating into immediate transport.
Yes, transported through the window to another world,
a lively planet where seeking life's source begins all over again.
I mean, some of your autobiographies will read like a novel,
all those close calls as you wandered through foreign terrain.
But it was all for naught, and I'm afraid your art, too,
shall come to a hapless end - your equivalent of The Bard
shall find your language hardened into indecipherable moon rock;
your music shall find no ears, a cold wind in a dead world.

V

But I can't, in the end, remain angry with you.
Not that I will ever *like* you, frankly -
I'm not that kind-hearted,
though I respect your perseverance,
your desire, like mine, to beat the fates.
You're not a villain, just a puny virus
(with a talent for mutation)
though you'll have to admit
the whole lot of you are blood-suckers,
yes, blood-suckers of no meager talent.

Never mind, though;
it all comes down to point of view;
you're still part of this creation,
this givenness called our world,
each of us lingering on a dying planet,
dependent on a reticent, if not silent, god,
frightened of mortality
as we push the envelope of unwordedness,
and that's the key, maybe,
to whatever meaning we might muster -
embrasure of that which confuses us,
thwarts us, obstructs our every ambition.
We must kiss the tendered kiss which kills us.

And the key is empathy:
recognition that beyond the moment of death
all points of view remain forever equal.

Ode to Three Queens

I

Stalking the halls in sweet satins and lace,
so very hard in this difficult place.
Death lingers on only soon to give chase,
pull up your bloomers and quicken the pace.

(A fine fragile thing, our slow-dying race.)

I've always admired the singular stamp
the trio provides for the letters of camp.
Applying your make-up with mirror and lamp,
a touch of high drama, and presto, a vamp!

(Your eyeliner wide as an interstate ramp.)

I admire the ease with which you can tease
with a bow of the head and a curtsy of knees,
still I object, though I hate to displease,
someone's perfume makes me endlessly wheeze.

(Oh do tell who is it who's making me sneeze?)

I'd prefer a nice party, much sooner than later;
someone call someone who might like to cater.
Ratchet will give us a good imprimatur,
if only we find a dumb doc who will date her.

(Why, tell me why, must we so deeply hate her?)

Hospital clubs call for names with some sheen,
tincture of class with a load of hot spleen,
something to make our sweet Ratchet turn green,
how 'bout the nice name, *Herr Ratchet's Four Queens?*

(No? Then, *Four Princesses Who Would Be Queen?*)

Soon I'll be going; it is quite a shame,
for this I most humbly accept all the blame.
Nightly are echoes; they're calling my name,

the virus is winning this tiresome game.

(Someone go pop us expensive champagne!)

Four queens to three, and soon three to two,
vanishing royalty, what shall we do?
Out goes the old, soon in comes the new,
a fine farewell party in lieu of the blues.

(Have I shared with you, I do love those shoes?)

Now leave me sweet queens, scatter and run,
we've so much to do, prepare to have fun.
Grab a fine priest if you dress as a nun,
Join me soon after, my day in the sun.

(Hear me, please, no scatological puns.)

II

You bear your gifts like three wise kings,
cross-dressing,
though kings nonetheless,
and transmute the chorus of strident voices,
voices tone deaf to the dissonances
of God's ineluctable creation,
into a simple refrain of muted forgiveness,
somehow deflecting the hardened hatred
only zealots manage to nourish.

I suggest muted as the flavor of your mercy,
rather than as a portrait of your voices.
Yours is not exactly a soft chanting,
but no matter, those who will never understand
shall not be deterred by slight variations of manner,
and those who understand but disagree
shall simply employ subtler means of coercion.
Same result - coercion by force, coercion by words -
so might had as well transmute gender as well,
make 'em think twice about the sanctity of norms,
artificial constructions born to blot out *difference.*

Think about it.
Society handicaps you, instantly,
by virtue of your being, simply,
human, though differently so,
and your argument must not be,
gender itself is an artificial construction
(silly argument, that)
but rather, gender differences should not,
in turn, engender difference.

III

Homosexuality:
a directedness of self toward a natural
center of sexual repose,
though those not in the know
conflate the natural with the familiar,
damning same-sex embrasure
as somehow against a nature
they are too blind to see
in all its neutral diversity.

So why the self-loathing?

For the longest time I held it against you,
interpreting as weakness
your Norma Desmond get-ups
and Bette Davis airs,
your Judy Garland pin-ups
and Barbara Streisand flairs.
But I was wrong.
You were simply dividing
that you might then conquer,
a two-birds-with-one-stone
approach to victory, so to speak.

By placing into question
our preconceptions
of manliness, of masculine expectation,
you take the first step toward freedom,
and from there, the transformation

275

that is redemption.
Freedom from the tethers binding
biology to culture's whims,
and redemption,
well, redemption is simply embrasure
of nature without the tragic Greek chorus
or the commentary of the common lot.
In so doing
you protect yourself from physical assault
should violence come your way;
though anyone is apt to be beaten,
it's still harder to
beat those in women's clothes.
Still, do be aware
of the wife-beaters out there
and all those for whom
the pallor of flesh
is a simple canvas for magenta paintings.

Blood is not your fear, though,
nor words tainted with hatred,
but rather the slow absorption
of loathing into self-loathing.
That is the key to the success
of all prejudice, of all arguments
condemning difference.
There is no greater power
in the arsenal of evil
than the unsweetened power
of personal judgment,
than the critical moment
when love of self
mistakenly embraces evil's reflection
in the mirror of your soul.

IV

A bit of Windex and a rag might do the trick,
scraping away toothpaste stains, notions of discontent,
just as my bias against the *femme*
in certain articulate sweet young men
was rubbed away on the very day

I held my son as if I were his mother.
And now I know, even if I simply imagine it,
what it is to wear a prissy robe and heels and hose
and all the other accouterments of femininity,
whether seriously or as a game,
because I have held in my arms a boy
who cared not a wit about the nature of my gender
as long as I held him tightly, kissed him just so
and cradled and rocked him with the arms and legs
which lack, for the moment, all sexual definition,
only hold him because I am human, and he is vulnerable,
in need of love.

So camp it up,
if you must,
triumvirate sojourners
on life's royal path,
sometimes kings,
sometimes queens,
and don't be afraid to say,
like Norma,
I'm ready for my closeup, Mr. DeMille!
Just don't shoot
the lovely young man
who can never quite understand
your ambiguous needs,
and raise your chin,
if you must,
and click your heels
like Dorothy in Oz,
and force the world
to follow you back to Kansas.
That's where the real work must yet be done.

death at dawn

sunsets are second worst
red splayed to magenta
like old blood finding lung

a spattered dusk canvas
with splotches of angst
specks of black
like frenzied birds
sequestered in time
by abstract feedings
a supper of worms
to succor the young
awake to the darkness
of heartless isolation

dawns are the worst
magenta to pink
like blood from the lung

misty morning
pastel canvas
of splayed intensity
marking the mark
of colorless desolation
forsaken of feeling
a stupor of drowsiness
dappling down to sleep
sifting through spaces
left empty by regret

a dawn ditty:
lips offer kisses
red-tipped coals
beneficent blisses
near-to-dry souls

yes
I think I died at dawn
as he plopped onto me
still groggy

and entered
me gingerly enough
coaxing me with kisses
inching into me
hard and steady and harder yet
then not so hard
then too hard
then not so hard
then so nice
I couldn't push him off
rubberless
following an all-nighter
of safe sex
and so he took
his (sic) advantage
hiv advantage
twice
it turns out
and in the damp
mellow afterglow
I swear it's true
I knew he'd killed me

the kiss was lethal
his flicking tongue
gauging my heat
like a serpent

a wet kiss
a pink-fleshed cleansing
a wet pirouette
a lingual dance

bilingual actually
a tango of wet desire
since I fought back
tongue for tongue
but couldn't match
his oral aplomb

such mastery as this
is reserved for the gods

so it was
as they say
all down hill from there

funny
that magical tongue
that purified flesh
not so unlike
metaphysical acrobatics
of a soul's arabesque

what I remember best
what I still feel
isn't the heft of him
on me
nor in me
but the heart
the heart of a god
providing bass
thumping out time
to the jazzy duet
of our love-making

not so unlike
this
not so unlike
ethereal thrumming
of angels' wings
bass being bass
beat for beat
god and man
share the need
for proper timing

but those weren't
the great god's lips
I accepted
rather
fantasy lips

a taste of other lips
lips not present
lips not yet tasted
Nick's lips

out of bounds
those
taboo
but such yearning
as this
rawer than meat
in a butcher's bag

smell the blood-dipped scent
of it
touch the raw-grained weave
of it
and such color
magenta back to pink
or was it pink to magenta
I don't know
so dark it was
though not dark enough
to hide the desolation
glowering from the god's lips
crimson to anemone
blood-red lips
that weren't Nick's
who'd left me
years ago
to be devoured by this beast

Ode to the Kid

You've never read it, and never will
but it's a play,
the finest penned by man
by a poet of the Renaissance
(a rebirth as wondrous as your first Indy hustle)
and the play is portrayed, as many might our battle,
as a story of *revenge:*
they are wrong, though
for *Hamlet* is, in truth,
a restless meditation on our hapless mortal ways.

There's a tragic scene:
Hamlet, a prince, duels with Laertes,
the son of the man Hamlet unwittingly slew
and by some trickery they each kill the other
with a dab of poison from a single sword
they both manage to use
(mechanical manipulation of the plot, you know)
and I was thinking, kid
that's us - envenomed foils, minor wounds,
desire to destroy, dueling warriors,
a single fate of death in lieu of love.

But hear this:
ours isn't a story of revenge
neither a pound of flesh nor time in prison
might sate my metaphysical hunger
revenge was but a decoy deflecting deeper needs
true, you took much,
but only as much as a kid will take
and intended no one's death
you're just marked, that's all
not so much evil as by evil's hand formed
buffeted by powers beyond your control
you were merely a stand-in,
a *doppelganger* of the soul
and so absorbed my violence
(passion without a cause, a pause in search of hope)
since the boy had died and Nick, my love,
orbited alternate galaxies optioned to a higher bidder:

the Companion, or perfect lover -
a ghostly concoction of Rilkean rag and wounded heart.

Victims of circumstance, we
and I ask your pardon
though you wish me to die
and soon enough I shall
and then you'll be avenged
if vengeance remains your cause
but nonetheless I'll suggest
well, not exactly mercy
(not in the genetic cards)
but rather, empathy
since we have dueled each with the other
and each with immortal Fate
both pricked by a swordsman
piercing our flesh with a tragic foil,
envenomed tip and all
drawing our wounds like Zorro's *Z*
with the double helix of HIV
and casting our fates with tainted blood
before casting away into silence.

And this is a stretch
but in the play Hamlet's buddy, Horatio
(curiously close, those two)
says to dying Hamlet,
Here's yet some liquor left
an elevated manner of speaking thus
I'll drink the poison as an equal
I'm ducking out of Shakespeare's sequel
that he might follow Hamlet
into the sweet silence of death
to which Hamlet responds, wondrously
Absent thee from felicity for a while
yet another elevation of language meaning
Stay behind for a bit, won't you
and though the bitter winds of life
pummel you, tell my story, please?
Well, kid, we're not buddies
you'd not die for me, nor I for you
though we do fight a common enemy

and by God there is a story to tell:

We are bitter nerve and brittle bone
a puny petty palsied thing
a palimpsest of bloodied flesh
a crusting on magenta hide
a mark in hues of fading ink
a viral script by Nature's hand
a feeble form of weakened will
a ditty scored in muted notes
an echo in a soundless land
a yearning in a spaceless space
grieving yet another death
of yet another layering
upon another layering
upon a listless canvas
of ever-rotting flesh.

All those lost stories, so silent now
crushed beneath a centripetal weight
a casual trajectory, the gyre of mortality
spiraling down to the grave:
a splatter of crimson on a spatter of white
wide-arced drippings of historical fate
a lethal palette of palimpsests splaying a canvas of flesh
with yet another script from yet another land
Nature's quirky trickery forging flesh by sleight of hand.

So don't go yet, kid
talk us up a bit
and tell the world before you're silenced
the story of the broken jaw
(a case of mistaken identity)
as I lashed at you with raging fists
shattering bones and delicate dreams
and how the parchments of weakened flesh
form palimpsests of humanity
and only then free-float away
into a choreography of silence
where fallible scribes shall scribble no more
and meaning shall sign in wordless form
with a flourish of peripatetic hands.

love fever

a fever
a finely timbered fever
is a wonderful thing
cleaving to you like a second skin
heated energies eagerly seeking
remoter tissues
like a tuber digging through
the heated source of you

or am I wrong
is a fever less a digger
than an embracer of things
running deep wild free
tendrils seeking more
than you can possibly give

and so
so very much
the mirror image of love
of love's ways
heated beyond what's natural
or healthy

reflect on the fevers man has known
malaria influenza cholera tuberculosis
pneumocystis carinii pneumonia

stand-ins these
for all illnesses everywhere
though not for less obvious fevers
gold rush fevers sexual fevers
warrior fevers angst fevers
god fevers ambition fevers
greed fevers guilt fevers

oh
and love fevers
oh
and hiv fevers too
a marriage of fevers

these two
walking the aisle hand in hand
the price we sometimes pay for love
is the moistened hand of viral fevers

and see the arc of ages
and see the arc of aids
and see the arc of love
squeezing within an elliptical frame
the orbits of desire

around what star do we revolve
in arced arc love

through what
uncharted galaxy
do we venture
eyes closed
hearts open
arced as we are
in the great ellipse
of love

and what mammoth force
shall pull us to
stretching the arc
straightening the line
the plangent rush of crushing us
to a single point
and graphing us on the axis of no return

a vacuum in lieu of love

yet stars die
then explode
hurtling our energies outward again
in search of finer forms
lasting perhaps a billion years

true
not long enough for a great love
a billion years

to find again the natural arc of lovers' lives
a mere picnic blip on time's scale
but enough perhaps
for the finger exercises leading to love
or time enough to conquer time
outwitting her necessity
with tales of higher purpose

a quanta of love
wave and particle both
neither here nor there
though present always in the arc
of the possible

then plop
we're back again winding down
through gyred time
into a present we once knew
to live it all again
no longer than before
but somehow longer than before
nonetheless

since memory contains
within it the possibility of always
and memory we have always in abundance
memory is love's source
love always looks back
sheepish of the future
and so we dig like a fever
sending tendrils deep
to find the source that shall sustain us
always

digging
and digging more feverishly
seeking a host to love
for love requires a host
like a virus
something able to mutate as it burrows in
and so immune to fate's indifference

Hutton Hayes

yes
love is a virus

hiv is someone's form of love
somewhere
though not here
but somewhere
as the arc curves
in the time it takes to mutate
or hurtle out again into an orbit
in an ellipse of nearly no return
a turning gyre of astral fevers
where love is safe for another billion years

Indy Eclogues

I

True,
ever-hopeful Monument Circle,
you're modestly heated pubescent heart
of metal and glass and mortar and brick,
shall not be conflated with *Ringstrasse*,
lacking, as it does, Vienna patina,
medieval encrustings on pock-marked masks,
time-gouged eyes of siege and invasion,
historical blemishes of random pain.

Vienna,
two and a half millennia ago
erupted like magic to form a crossroads
(to some also known as the great Amber Road
where traders conflated profit and rape)
sieged by Turks in centenary fashion,
seized by invaders for coffee and art,
while you were a simple bend in a river,
occasional home to native canoes.

Born,
a mere moment ago as such things go,
in the beckoning year of 1820,
a breech-birth bend on a beachless river,
a capillary near a newborn heart,
unlike the Danube, uniquely remote;
and it won't do to belittle *Ringstrasse*
(uttering its cry well after your birth)
as a tethered matron's ancient dream.

Sure,
the natives died upon your birth,
and there were random sins to pay
as trails of tears flowed westward ho,
with bloody creeks, foot-furrowed soil;
footings of bones anchored your homes,
no foreign knuckles rapped your door
suspending dreamscapes seeking more than

289

glacier-made mountainless oceanless homes.

Look,
you've not known backyard war, fear of siege,
homelessness, hunger or disembowelment.
You've really not yet known history;
consider: even the hapless Hapsburgs
ruled a roulette world for six hundred years
'til death by war eventually tore asunder
the ancient soul; a weak-willed comparison -
you're simply the home of Republican mores.

Yes,
a pale parallel, duly acknowledged,
drawn by a fateful historical hand
(Viennese operas, Hapsburg *hauteur*,
coffee house squabbling, Freudian feuds -
corn-storing silos and barnyard *hog-teur*,
Tuesday night bowling with fat corncrib crews)
distinctions of soul rather than taste,
illiberal thumpings, heart-rending waste.

II

So,
you say, *if Vienna gave us high culture,*
we, in turn, gladly feed vats of vultures.
A good comeback, methinks, timely and quaint,
though still not quite to the historical point.
As the ravaging centuries passed you by
with unsoiled mask and ungouged eye
you suffered the ironical impediment -
a surface in search of a sediment.

Ah!
Raised on Christ and corn and basketball
I lacked an inkling of the secular Fall,
no Mahler on music, no Freud on the pot,
no hint of fresh breezes removing the rot
from a culture too young to yet cut its teeth
on the liberal impulse still buried beneath
that dark-loamed and near-virgin deep prairie floor

where Protestant digs buried Indian lore.

Indy,
no one, ever, will define you in terms
of *Gesamtkunstwerk*, a funny term
best rendered as *total work of art*,
like the *Ringstrasse* of Vienna's aged heart,
yet, you harbor pretensions of some import,
existential longings transformed to bloodsport,
nourished by ambivalent midwestern flairs:
moral innocence seeking historical airs.

And,
that center of centers, your stone-hearted heat,
that vast limestone belly fashioned replete
with obelisk resting on pads of concrete,
Victorian details in Gothic mystique,
was financed by barons who cared not a stitch
for anything save for emotional kitsch
despising sweet men with sweet-shallow breaths
kids of the fifties with harsh nineties' deaths.

Okay,
this is the axis where opposites merge,
Vienna and Indy clasped to a foul scourge,
stones in the arc of a rococo necklace
(surface details for the silly and feckless)
hiding an ancient babe's deep aged crease,
the wrinkles of time suggesting surcease,
suggesting we're formed by powers of fate
translated by some as the duty to hate.

III

How odd,
the distillations of history,
the overcoming of historical obstacles,
the young whippersnapper, Indy,
finding a home next to Vienna
two baubles on a crowded chain,
a necklace on an ancient neck,
the viral chain of HIV

291

arcs the neck of soiled worlds,
staining flesh with tainted beads
first strung in distant Africa
and adding to the lethal chain
urban stones along the way.

(HIV
meets QVC
and recent forms of history.)

Ah,
Vienna - *total work of art* -
defended her own, siege after siege,
fending off various catastrophes,
in unity fought the infidels
or whatever name it is you give
a given enemy on a given day,
giving honor to a soul by giving
a name to something hauntingly nameless.

Hear, hear:
to be historical you must fight as one,
each soul but a portion of the Oversoul,
for there is no partial soul in a city
when the common enemy raps the door,
but rather, a clumsily conflicted single soul
seeking historical unity.

And,
you do not choose your invaders,
you may not choose not to have them,
and when the knock comes,
a hardened knuckle on a virgin door,
it's all or nothing;
don't crack the door that some might be taken,
either bolt it, or open it
and fight with all your might as one.

Also,
it's no longer advisable to mimic
the ancient Greek habit of sacrifice;
magic for Agamemnon

is superstition for us,
and the myth translated:
not a daughter for a city,
but the selling of a city-soiled soul,
tossing out, in this case, the sons,
one by sickened one;
the myth transposed
from the good of the many
to ignorance keeping knowledge at bay.

Yes,
we're all tainted,
painted by the palsied hand
of our common humanity,
and none are virgin to the lusts
which seek, in lieu of flesh,
enticements of immortality,
and such farcical gods
who played that game,
if gods they were, are now long dead,
and what's left is this:
the tainted aged cheese of regret,
tinny tones of meager hearts,
salty tears topping the brim
of the rusty ocean of humanity.

We,
history-makers together, we,
alone within a lonely world,
save for barbarians climbing the walls
as mutant forms shake our city,
picking clean a rusting lock,
forcing open a weakened gate;
shall you cut your losses,
throw me out, sacrifice me
on the altar of your fear?

Perhaps,
though tomorrow they return,
seeking your son, brother, spouse,
because a siege is a test of wills
and they never stop at just one,

but return again and again
for another and then another,
to sate their astonishing appetite,
since they eat until they die;
whether sent by a sultan
or nature's cunning crafting hand,
they are fateful warriors both;
they'll return at dawn for all of us
to pick our bones clean.

Look,
humanity is not a thing,
nor an abstraction,
but a response,
a knowing,
an instinctive rebuttal
to death's wayward ways,
an anxious quivering of the heart,
and, Indy, surely yours still beats;
true, already I'm undone,
like Agamemnon's daughter,
but others shall soon follow.

Quick,
before it's too late,
shuck off the puritanical zeal
conflating *difference* with the enemy,
and cast your fate with the liberal pulse,
the lone murmur of a lonely heart
buried now so long ago
beneath the prairie soil,
murmuring,
soft as a dirge,
an elegy whispered by the dead,
beating out time with Indian bones
which feed the earth
which find the seeds
which nourish the roots
that make your corn grow.

Elegy for My Father

I

You observed him from a distance,
calculating coldly
the contingent trajectory
of a son's life,
molding him, impartially,
with the restrained flourish of deified hands,
or the hands of a man lacking human touch:

a touchlessness so remote
a constraint so tightly twined
a restriction so brutally enforced
as to bridle all emotion

suggesting to him a ghostly scrim
behind which a god plays
once silence becomes the language of choice.

Behind this screen of determined detachment
you weaved the plot of a son's life
(so very Bard-like in your regal repose,
here and there and nowhere at all:
detached, objective, remote, obscure)
and the boy trekked through that thickening plot
in search of hidden paternal devotion
only to be cast spaceward ho:

a revolving pattern in a dependent ellipse,
a filial rotation through heatless space,
the hauntingly empty cool cosmos of you.

How mystifying our modern physics:
a vacated stretch of absolute silence,
an eerie retreat of deified breath,
shoals of stars a backdrop to nothing,
nothing a backdrop to echoes of death,

from big bang to black hole
from live stars to dead,

from limitless teeth-gnashing ghastly explosions
to measureless tombs that go bump in the night;

the cosmic tunes of cosmic tombs, how cruel:
dead stars we know form only dead planets,
dead planets in turn form only dead sons,
each awhirl, endlessly,

exotic rotations in search of stillness,
wanton memories seeking virgin minds.

II

It is only right that I should die now, Dad;
your star offers no heat for this dying planet
which buckles under its own dead weight,
black-hole densities sucking me dry;
and that you continue, as might a good engineer,
to maneuver the compass of your swollen desire
upon the orbitless tissues of me,
splaying my paper with intricate jottings
(frigid, remote, sequestered, deceived)
would be remembered as a marvel of science,
if science indeed could survive a dead world.

But, Pop, it's meaningless:
as our planet dies so does our physics -
our math, our science, our history, our art -
since quantum mechanics teaches quite clearly
without an observer all is for naught,
all human invention reduces to fable;
quantum crumbs are the terms of our fate.

So bye, bye to science; and bye, bye to art,
and bye, bye tyrannical old puppeteer
whose puppetless stage must soon disappear.

Still, you're so immaculate in banker's garb
(no fine English tweeds for this pinstripe suit:
so impartial, so neutral, so distant, aloof,
so very much above the human fray).

Never allow emotions to enter
into human transactions,
you once said with glee
as you coldly parsed me from afar,
from the secluded distance of your silent galaxy.

Now, I understand your need for distance,
at least in matters of commerce and art,
but in matters of filial devotion, Dad?

All matters must remain
arms-length transactions,

particularly encounters between man and man.

III

Ah, Pop, such power you have.
From the cool distance you control me,
effortlessly,
forming my orbit as a god forms fate
which is why I must ask, rhetorically,
why must fathers exert such power,
such awful power over their mortal sons?

I haven't an answer for that one, Dad.
I can only say,
almost hideously,

I love you.

Yes, I love you nonetheless.
Why, I haven't a clue, unless
biologically we are wired from birth
to accomplish what most would
agree is an impossible task.
But I love you, Dad.

Hate you too, of course.
God, I hate you.

Tough thing, juggling both love and hate
in the same one-act play,
smiling with devotion and a slap on the back
while dreaming of cutting your nuts off.

Yet, what good will my hate do me now?
I mean, *honestly,* Dad?

If I am to learn the grammar of silence,
if I am to grasp patterns smaller than dust,
if I am to find the forms of forgetting
if I am to wisp away on a vaporless gust,
I'd best release more than a body's weight.

If I am to drain into the cool ineffable expanse
of nothing, I must nurture nothingness.

Sure, I've been shedding all these pounds
in preparation for what is to come,
but that's not enough.
Even thoughts, weightless,
substanceless thoughts,
are too large, far too large
to take with you into nothing;
emotions won't fit either,
must be dispensed with lest
they plug the drain to nowhere,
leaving part of me in endless purgatory,
an ugly, unwanted topside mold.

So, I must let go of everything.
Everything, Dad, everything.
Everything, that is, except for love.

Sure, it too is too big to slip into nothing,
as large and cumbrous as a mammoth star,
but I've still a hunch that, drains being drains,
plugged holes are as common
during the physics of dying
as hairballs found in a bathroom sink.

So I'll hold onto love until the very end,
treat it as a balm, a dying salve,
as fine a lubricant as a mother's placenta
to push me along the tender walls
leading on to the world of no return:

while, topside, a residue forms
from love's ineffable patina,
hinting to some that all wasn't for naught.

ABOUT THE AUTHOR

Hutton Hayes was born in Indianapolis and later raised in Monroeville, Alabama (home of Harper Lee and the setting for *To Kill a Mockingbird*) where the literary bug bit him at an early age. He received degrees in English and History from the University of Alabama and Indiana University, respectively, and attended the Indiana University School of Law, graduating with Honors. He practiced law in a corporate setting in Indianapolis until 1997, when he left the company and the practice of law to devote his energies to full-time writing. He has completed four novels, a book of poetry and a short work of nonfiction exploring spiritual forms of psychotherapy. He is currently working on a novel of the South and a sequel to *Keegan's Folly*.